The Birdwatchers of Childen Under Blean

The Sexual Exploits of a Sleepy Village

James Apps

Copyright, James Apps, 2018

ISBN: 9781791536091

All characters contained in this book are fictional. Otherwise all rights reserved. No part of this publication may be reproduced or transmitted in any form or by any means electronic or mechanical, including photocopy, or recording on any information retrieval system, without the permission in writing from the copyright holder/publisher, except in the case of brief quotations embodied in critical articles or reviews.

TaupUK
enquiries@taup.uk
Sheerness. UK

Cover design by James Apps

Disclaimer.
The opinions of characters in this book do not reflect the opinions of the author. Or they may, it depends upon your point of view.

Table of Contents

In the Beginning -..1
The Birdwatchers..3
An Unwise Decision..101
Under Siege..217
Aftermath...233
In Memoriam...249
- And in Conclusion..253

*There are times when even a worm will turn and
things are not always what they seem.*

In the Beginning -

The quiet and quaint village of Childen Under Blean is the gateway to a Woodland Trust park situated on some of the highest hills of the North Downs. Below this park, Childen under Blean sits either side of a stream masquerading as the river Eden that eventually wanders down to the Medway valley. Visitors to the village can take lunch and a pint at the Dog and Duck hotel and public house, or enjoy the experience of homemade cakes and pastries in the tea rooms attached to the local store.

The centre of the village is the cricket green and duck pond surrounded by a mixture of modern and period houses spanning five centuries of history. A loop of lanes, suitably traffic calmed, edges the green to join the main road, named The Street, which passes through the village in front of the Dog and Duck en-route from the town to the hills beyond.

St Seraph's Anglican Church overlooks the village at the end of Church Lane that wanders up from a small square where a horse trough remains as a monument to its rural past. Church Lane with its rows of terraced houses and olde world cottages, 19th century C of E primary school and 18th century vicarage, is considered one of the prettiest sights in Childen Under Blean.

To the south, cut into the hill lies the abandoned Lindeman quarry that supplied stone for local buildings. Abandoned in the 1990's the quarry has long been on the council agenda for purchase but, in line with national government procedure procrastination prevails, nobody has the courage to spend the money. As a result the quarry is overgrown, the old huts and sheds the operators left behind are rotting away, but it is a boon to the local birdwatchers and wildlife spotters, and couples who cannot find a convenient spot in a cornfield.

It was birdwatching of a kind that began the "troubles" and changed the history of Childen Under Blean; a history that is remembered now more than the two world conflicts that took the young of the village.

To walk Church Lane is to see the history of Childen, and if the hiker was to take the footpath leading up into the hills from there, the rewards of good views and pleasant gardens are to be had.

And yet one may pause on the way and gaze with curiosity at another, smaller monument that each year in early September bears a wreath and a spread of tributes, of which one always calls for an explanation.

The Birdwatchers of Childen Under Blean

The legend cut into stone simply says: The Battle of Childen Under Blean and underneath is inscribed the date and the line: "Erected by the grateful residents of Childen Under Blean in honour of one of their own"

The names of the sponsors include the local self styled Squire, Lord Massingham, and Ebenezer Scroggins on behalf of his family.

This is the story of that battle.

The Birdwatchers

Horace Oswald, the landlord of the Dog and Duck public house and hotel, was sure that something was dreadfully wrong in the village of Childen Under Blean. Hidden in the hills, the village is a backwater dependent on the hikers who frequent his establishment and those who could afford to buy the cottages that once housed farm workers. These last were his regular customers who drank in his house and who occasionally worshipped in Saint Seraph's church, doing both with equal fervour.

This enthusiasm was disturbing.

The Reverend Jones who based his ministry at St Seraph's lived in the Vicarage and was often to be seen quaffing ale in the Dog and Duck bar. Reverend Jones was once a Rugby prop who at one time played semi-professionally. He was a big man and knew how to put it away.

It wasn't the reverend.

The word Charismatic came to mind.

'Charismatic, Charismas; the Gifts; Speaking in Tongues and all that,' he said.

Beside him his wife Molly and chief barmaid looked up from stacking the glasses.

'What you on about Horace?'

'I was thinking of the vicar and his Christian Community. You know, the lot who go on about being touched by the gifts, tongues of holy fire and all that gabbling they do. You've seen them, waving their arms above their heads like so many human Triffids,' he said.

'What about them?'

'They seem to be more active lately. Singing and talking about God and Jesus and the Acts of the Apostles and all that stuff, you know, preaching in little groups. But that's not it,' he said.

'What's not it?'

'I'm feeling disturbed.'

'Well if you feel like that you had better go and lie down,' she said.

'Not that, what I mean is there's a sort of feeling that something's rotten in the village of Childen,' he said.

'Silly bugger. It's your imagination. Other than the normal illicit fornication, bickering, petty thieving, teenagers necking, secret drinkers and the general suspicion of local authority creaming off the profits, there's not much going on,' she said.

Nevertheless he was puzzled. More and more of his locals complained about the activity in church recently. That they bought more beer was welcome but he realised that was part of the disturbance.

'It might be the church,' he said.

'Explain please,' she said, stacking glasses.

'There are some from the church who talk of strange goings on within St Seraph's. It seems the older, more established parishioners are not happy.'

'What do you mean?'

'You know, all that gabbling and falling over, the alleluia's and yelling out "Praise the Lord" and all that. They sing songs the older folks don't know and they are even talking of bringing guitars in to the church. It's that Morris Davis and his crowd, the leaping christians, as my old mum would call them. She calls 'em that because they sort of leap on you in groups and pray for you whether you want them to or not. Mad buggers they are. Our equivalent of the Hare Krishna people, you know the chanting mob in orange robes,' he said.

'Well that's all right as long as they are happy and we get more customers,' she said. 'What's wrong with that?'

He would have replied, but it was time to open up and with his keys jangling he marched to the main doors and made a show of unlocking them. The vague shadows on the etched glass resolved into three regulars who shuffled in and argued about whose turn it was to buy. It didn't matter anyway because they always had three pints each and lunch.

Not long after their arrival a small group of cyclists arrived followed by a trickle of hikers all demanding drinks and lunch. Not bad for a Wednesday, he thought.

On that Wednesday Mathew Grace sat at a table in the coffee bar a few doors down from the store where he worked stacking shelves, and sighed. His coffee cooled down too quickly and tasted foul. The toastie he paid too much for was barely edible unless he doused it with sauce, and in a few minutes he was due back at work. He finished the toastie and gulped the nearly cold coffee. In his hurry he knocked the chair over.

'Oh fuck it,' he said kicking the thing across the floor where it crashed into the next table.

'Oy, watch it mate.'

The man at the table glowered at him and with bad grace Mathew righted the chair and put it back. The girl behind the counter gave him a disgusted look.

'Some people...' she said, shaking her head.

'I didn't fancy you anyway,' he said as he passed her, but he did. She was the reason he had chosen the café. But his remark fell on deaf ears as she was already busy with another customer.

Oh well, he thought, it was back to the Birdwatching Boys.

Set on the hill overlooking the village, Saint Seraph's Anglican Church dominated the village of Childen Under Blean. Adjacent to the church stood the vicarage, and between it and the C of E Primary School was glebe land and playing fields much desired by greedy developers. This land was owned by the village whose councillors were not prepared to give it up.

The village valued its community spirit.

Childen Under Blean was a farming community and that was reflected in the number of market gardeners offering their wares, and the local store that sold just about everything. On the lower slopes of the nearby downs there was an abandoned quarry, which once supplied stone for local buildings. It was left to fall in to ruin and was now overgrown with sheds left to rot, and fences left to rust.

In the great scheme of things Childen Under Blean sat in the North Downs remote from almost anywhere of importance. If it was not for the Woodland Trust lands the village would have died a natural death some years before this tale evolved. The modern villagers were aware of the world around them through the telly and the myriad computerised devices available, augmented by the blaring headlines of the national papers. They knew of Europe, of America and were familiar with much of the United Kingdom, especially infinitely minute details of their favourite football teams. Arguments of a political nature often reflected the opinions of the newspapers they purchased and, if queried, very few of them knew who was their member of parliament.

Childen Under Blean residents voted by party, if they "could be arsed", as the common phraseology would have it.

The Birdwatchers of Childen Under Blean

As far as the rest of the world was concerned the village was just another place to pass through. In general the villagers, although inclined to favour anything British, were interested in the rest of the world, especially the bits where you lay down on the beach and got tanned. Spain was popular with many holiday makers although there were some who liked to head for Cornwall or the Isle of White. Some, so it was said, visited Scotland or Ireland and even Wales where most of the people living there didn't speak foreign. In Europe you had to speak slowly or shout and you couldn't get a decent cup of tea, and they only drank lager or strong smelling spirits; and what's more you had to look for a place that sold decent fish and chips.

And even if you did try to speak the local language they only spoke back at you in English with accents you couldn't understand.

The local landowners kept their footpaths clear and looked after the gates and stiles in order to keep the riff-raff off their crops. The more affluent residents were suspicious of the visitors and liked the fact that signposts directed hikers and casual walkers away from the village. Sir Ronald Massingham, the largest private landowner, patron of the Childen Pony Club with its Riding for the Disabled group, kept his lands in excellent order and set the standard for the village. He was well respected in the district by most, despised by a few and as far as local councils were concerned was a good man to have on your side.

He didn't approve of visitors but put up with them because it was good business for the village. Besides, the proximity of a Woodland Trust meant good land management, a thing he was passionate about. The locals tolerated the gawking hikers and the sight of lycra clad cyclists because they were extra customers for roadside stalls selling seasonal fruit and vegetables. The bonus being that they too could buy fresh, organically grown produce, which they bought from the local shop.

As Sylvester Simon, leading light of the Dog and Duck drinkers, remarked: 'It was amazing what a load of horse shit will do on a garden, and with a few chickens waddling around crapping on the deck and laying eggs in huts, they think we are all organic, rustic idiots. As long as it brings in the money I'm happy.' Sylvester Simon was a shareholder of the local store.

The local store, and post office served the community well and in the cosy tea rooms on Wednesday afternoons some of the local women gathered to gossip. Over tea and toasted sandwiches they discussed the problems of the village.

'I don't know about this so-called bird watching club. My Stanley wanders around the village late in the afternoon and evening with his binoculars. He says he is watching for owls.' Said Jenny.

'And my Terry is thick with that Mathew Grace and they go mooning around the village with binoculars and cameras.'

'Sneaking around. I've seen them suddenly appearing from all sorts of odd places and no birds in sight.'

'What are they up to is what I want to know?'

'I know what they're up to,' Maggie said and leaned forward allowing the others to do the same before continuing. 'I think they're up to no good.'

'We know that but what?'

'I think they are, you know…'

'Perving on the girls?'

There was a collective in-drawing of breath and a moment of stunned silence before Maggie spoke again.

'Exactly. The dirty little buggers are spying on them when they undress or,' and here she lowered her voice even further, 'when they are sunbathing in the back gardens. I seen some of them up on the slopes looking down.'

Just who it was she had seen and how she knew, the others did not question; the revelation deliciously stunned them.

'What will we do about it?'

'I think we should discuss the situation with our husbands or partners,' Amanda said.

She was always a little more correct with her language than the others. She was the leader of their little group and could always be relied upon to lead a campaign. Like them, she devoted her time to her household and was concerned with the matters arising in the village. The little group described themselves as the conscience of Childen.

They were known locally as the Coven.

Martin Crook, the Real Ale drinker and member of the Childen Cricket Eleven, raised his glass and sighed with pleasure. He looked extremely smug and took another drink before lowering the glass to the table around which the men were seated.

'That's a good drop of light. Horace should be praised for

choosing this one,' he said and beamed.

'I might try some meself,' said Swanson Mackenzie the Best Bitter man, and fine leg fielder.

Forest Maloney, who had called them there sipped in silence.

The other two looked at each other. As far as they were concerned a drink was a drink and Lager did the trick.

But that wasn't why they were there.

'Rightho Forest why have you dragged me away from my house and home and the telly on a Wednesday evening?'

'Amanda asked me to talk to you all about a problem,' he said.

The men looked worried.

Amanda Maloney, leader of the Coven was on the warpath and that did not bode well with the husbands of Childen Under Blean, and certainly not the elite drinkers of the Dog and Duck. Forest himself was described by some as an active member of village society and by others as a nosy shit stirrer whose ever nagging wife was the self styled conscience of the village. As Sylvester Simon, Sly to his friends and well known ex-lager lout, stated in his summing up of the woman; was that the only antidote to her was Saint George with an army of Holy Lancers. He also had the greatest respect for Forest who was brave enough to live with her.

Sly marvelled that at some time during the marriage Forest had become so intimately familiar with the formidable Madam Maloney to father a daughter. This intimacy, however, was below the national average of 1.9 children thus fitting in with the steady gentrification of Childen Under Blean.

Sly himself was busy in the locale attempting to raise the average to a more even figure. He considered that 0.9 of a chid was messy and impractical. He had succeeded at least three times but unfortunately for his efforts the recipients of his seed had moved elsewhere and he was left to comfort the local widows and the lonely. It was a task he thoroughly enjoyed.

However, despite his comfortable and happy disposition, Sly was as worried as the rest of the group.

'The problem is the activities of the so-called Birdwatchers in our village. Not the genuine ornithologists but the young lads and boys sneaking around the village spying on our daughters,' Forest explained.

'I've seen them, the dirty minded little buggers,' said Sly.

'What, when you were also sneaking around?' Martin observed.

'I like walking out in the evenings. Anyway, I caught one of the spotty herberts hiding in my hedge spying on my girl. He ran off before I could kick his arse. I gave our Cheryl a right bollocking about leaving her curtains open in her bedroom. Provocative that is,' Sly, the indignant father, said.

'Flaunting herself was she?'

'Probably.'

'But that is beside the point. Amanda and her little group have asked me to make the village fathers aware that their daughters are being spied on by a group of peeping toms. You know Amanda and her group; they don't like it and want something done,' Forest said looking anxious.

'And you want us to lead the way?' Asked Swanson Mackenzie.

'Yes I do and bear in mind that if my home life is to maintain its harmony it depends on you lot co-operating, and need I remind you that it is your home life that will also suffer if we do not work together on this mission,' Forest said, his voice revealing his panic.

The men fell silent glancing guiltily at one another until at last one decided to speak.

'Put like that, Forest, we have no choice but we need a plan.' Davey Tomms, lager drinker and reliable lower order batsman, said.

'Thank you Davey. If everybody agrees let me explain.' Forest was about to hold forth with his pearls of wisdom when Sly grunted and growled.

'We need more beer before that happens. You can buy it Forest.'

'Thank you very much, I am honoured to spend my hard earned salary on my friends in their need,' Forest said. It took him three trips, and slightly niggled that his friends moved not a limb to help, he explained Amanda's concerns.

'You can all help out by making sure your daughters close their curtains, not sunbathe in their gardens and those of you with teenage boys make sure you know where they are. Spread the word to your neighbours. My wife has a plan but as yet she has simply asked me to help. I will tell you about it later.' Forest looked apologetic.

'In other words she hasn't told you anything?' Said Miles, beer drinker and a mainstay of the bowling.

The Birdwatchers of Childen Under Blean

'Amanda knows what she's doing,' Martin pointed out grinning when Forest blushed. It was obvious that Forest could never think of a plan by himself or be trusted to tell it all at once and get it right.

Melissa Jones sat on the tack box explaining to her friends what was going on in the village. Salina nodded agreement as she spoke and when she had finished she added her news.

'Since we last met up my dear mother has persuaded my dear father to deal with the lads and their Birdwatcher's Club. I heard them talking about it. Actually it was my dear father reporting progress to my dear mother. He said that the plan was going to be carried out. She put him through the third degree. It was quite messy. We have to talk to that Cheryl Simon at some time.'

'What of your situation Sara?'

'I'm fine and will get a chance to hack into my brother's computer again soon. I could do it whilst he's masturbating over his latest images,' she said brightly.

'You're so crude Sara but what is he doing lately. How many new members has he ...' Marion said, stuttering to a halt when the others started giggling. She blushed red when she realised what she had said.

'They're all called Willy!' Sara cried out unable to control her giggling and for a few hysterical moments the girls were rolling around laughing helplessly. Even Marion was caught up with the merriment.

Eventually Melissa calmed them down and proposed that "something should be done" but what to do she did not explain. She was aware that Salina would sort something out. She was right. Salina raised her hand for silence.

'If the village fathers are ganging up on the lads, God bless their moronic little hearts, the boys I mean, then we have to do something about the situation. I know that the lads are not the choicest of the male population but they are all we have unless we want to venture beyond the borders of our domain. We know that the sight of our nubile bodies drives the little sweeties mad with lust, but their crude approaches and chauvinistic attitudes are unacceptable. I think what we need to do is persuade the girls to stop provoking the boys for a few weeks. It will mean reviving the choir but at least we know now what to do,' Salina said, and waited for comments.

'Daddy will be pleased. He likes male voices in the choir,' Melissa said.

'That is a bonus for him but we will have to persuade your daddy to keep us separate. The fumbling hands of a leering labourer is not my idea of recreation,' said Salina.

'My sister and I will do our best on that.'

'What shall we do about the girls who like the idea of being straddled by the local yokels?' Asked Sara.

Marion bit her lip.

Sara being crude again.

'Simple, just let them get on with it and we will attend the Christenings,' said Salina.

Marion gasped.

How could she!

'We could give them condoms?' Suggested Sara.

Melissa made a note in her book and grinned.

'A most sensible idea, Sister,' she said.

'Right, now that's settled let's pack in and go home. We all know what to do,' Salina said. 'I will keep you informed about my dear mother's plans and rantings.'

The others grinned.

They all knew what Salina meant and were always amused by her sarcastic depiction of her parents. Her mother was a pillar of the church and it was a joke amongst them that her father was the prop.

The reverend Jones climbed gratefully into his car. He sighed as he belted up, locked both doors, started the engine, switched on the lights and drove off quickly before anybody could call him back. Getting away from the Wednesday meeting was, he thought, marginally more successful than the retreat from Dunkirk.

'Harpies, harridans and horrors,' he said as he attacked the lane leading out of the small village of Hamden, and away from St Giles church hall. The committee were made up mostly of rich, middle aged women whose largesse was expected to be paid for by his subservience. He had wanted to introduce "messy church" to St Giles but the women on the committee had rejected the proposal. He had argued that the Good Lord had called on his followers to welcome the poor and needy but their vociferous arguments against their beautiful church being messed up by gangs of unruly, scruffy little hooligans prevailed, and he was forced to back down.

And to top it all, earlier that afternoon, he had had to listen to Amanda Forest explaining the "disgusting behaviour of the unwashed" in his own village. He served too many churches.

He reflected that at Easter time he was too knackered after the Holy Week to work in his garden when it needed it most. Christmas, when all he wanted to do was sleep, eat, drink and watch the telly, was even worse. Dark nights and sermons in a freezing church, bloody awful road conditions and sneezing parishioners spelled misery. And just when he was getting over the colds and flu along comes Lent and the calendar starts all over again. No rest for the wicked, he thought, and corrected himself.

'No rest for the Holy, no, representative of the Holy. Oh sod it, bloody vicar comfort thyself,' he said and when he found he was wandering across the road he concentrated on his driving.

As he drove he reflected on the way his church had changed. When the small, local Christian community had approached him with the request to run their church from St. Seraph's he had resisted. But when Elder Morris Davis had explained that his community wanted to work with the local Church and offered a portion of the tithes, he had relented. He had talked to his bishop who pursed his ecclesiastical lips and warned him.

'It's not C of E. That sort of thing belongs to the fringes of the papal church. It is more like an America gospel church, if you know what I mean. Sort of Southern States revivalists, if you understand,' the bishop said, disdainfully.

'He quotes the teaching of Peter from Acts 2, most of it anyway, and has pledged tithes to the church,' the reverend Jones explained.

The bishop looked startled.

'And what specifically?'

'Verses two to four; cloven tongues of fire and speaking in tongues, the charismas of the Lord,' Jones said, and smiled broadly. 'He is very devout.'

The bishop reluctantly agreed.

The church, so Jones assumed, needed the money. Which attitude he thought was a corruption of the gifts of Pentecost. The proviso on his part was that Davis and his lay preachers be part of the congregation in deference to the stolid locals.

'As long as we are free to worship as we please.'

'I also have an excellent choir master I would like to keep.'

'We can help with musicians,' Davis said.

And that was a bonus because the ancient organ was beginning to wheeze itself to an asthmatic demise.

'You're on, and to blazes with the bishop,' Jones said.

It took a while to ease the newcomers into the church community but when the congregation found themselves being treated like friends and respected for their own ways the mixture seemed to work. At least he had somebody to conduct the services when he was visiting other churches.

The memories kept him amused as he drove the lanes and arriving home he was pleased to see that supper was ready laid out for him but mildly annoyed when his wife said that Melissa wanted to speak to him.

'Oh dear what on Earth does she want now?'

'I'm afraid it is to do with that Amanda Forest,' she said. 'Sorry dear. Mel said she will wait until you have had your supper.' The announcement didn't help his mood but eventually he wandered into his office where both Melissa and his younger daughter Terri were waiting for him. Both girls were dressed to kill in skimpy, revealing clothing that would drive any boy of their age mad with desire. Melissa poured a measure of sherry into a cut glass and handed it to him. He sipped at it and laid it on the desk taking the seat beside it.

'Mum told you?'

He nodded.

'We think you should start the choir again,' Melissa said.

'Please explain,' he said.

Melissa explained in more practical and proper terms what the girls had decided.

'Firstly it will satisfy Church Warden Forest's wife that something is being done; it will mean that we will know where and what the boys are doing and, of course, it will likely attract some male voices to join with us,' Melissa said.

'And will keep that interfering baggage occupied,' interjected Terri who fluttered her eyelids at her father before gazing at him wide-eyed and anxious. It was her "cute puppy" look that her father found exceeding difficult to resist.

The vicar saw the virtue of the plan and saw no reason to refuse. 'Very well, we will bring back the choir,' he said.

'Only one more request Daddy,' said Terri.

'And that is?'

'We think it would be a good idea if the boys and girls sang from opposite sides of the choir. We think the acoustics suit such a sensible arrangement. It will also help us all to concentrate on the singing,' Melissa said.

He had no choice but to agree and as he finished his glass of sherry it was with a shock the reverend Jones realised that his daughters had effectively seduced him. And, he wondered, when did they learn that dressing well and showing a cleavage was the right way to persuade him?

He also realised that the village boys and their Birdwatching Club were possibly spying on his daughters, and that made him angry. To assuage that anger he poured another sherry and sat behind his desk letting his imagination run riot.

'The lad behind all this is that Mathew Grace. It was he who started the club.' He said to the half empty glass. Somebody had to put a stop to this and realised that Forest Maloney's dragon of a wife was on the case.

'In a way I should pity these lads,' he said, 'After all they are following their natural instincts.' And that remark reminded him of his own natural instincts when he was a younger man. He and Elizabeth knew a lot about natural instincts. He smiled at memories of excursions into cornfields during their beloved country walks.

'Gosh, they were great times,' he said and sipped at the sherry fondly recalling the fondling and foreplay that took place amid that agricultural idyll. And with that in mind he realised why he was so worried about the Birdwatcher's Club.

Mathew Grace sat in front of his computer knowing that he would not be disturbed for an hour at least. It was late and he had some stuff to do. Donny's message was dire. Somebody had quacked. It wasn't one of the guys, he was sure of that. Somebody had found out and quacked to the bill. Somebody had made a complaint, dobbed him in to that horrible Forest cow. Mathew was proud of his crude code. Anybody in charge and like, lawful or even the ones the village called the Coven, were the Bill, named after the telly program his grandad was always going on about. Quacking was talking to the Bill. His mates thought it was quite witty and fitted in with the Bird Watchers code.

None of the group would think about quacking to anybody.

Yet somebody had.

Donny's message was short but to the point and it was up to him to find out who. Stanley was unlikely to say anything because Mathew could easily quack on him and get him right in the shit. Terry was hardly likely to say anything for the same reason. That meant somebody outside had done it.

'I dunno, I got things to do,' he said and tapped keys, clicked icons until at last he was in to his special place. He had a few to load up and went through the procedure. Load, edit, save, encrypt and clear his camera. Next it was back to his pictures, check carefully finding some to eliminate and replace them with pictures of sparrows farting or whatever they did.

'Noisy little shits,' he said.

Still, with sparrows at least you could tell which ones were male and which were female. Some of the other birds were a pain in the arse to identify but the Club had to do it to cover their own arses. Mathew chuckled.

'Some of the newer recruits actually went bird watching. Awningology or something that little prick Graham called it,' he said and glanced at the time. 'Shit, the old man will be up here moaning about the noise.' He turned the music down, pissed off because his earphones were buggered. He would buy some new ones.

A few minutes later, after a visit to the bathroom he lay in bed thinking about Marion Mackenzie sunbathing naked in her back yard. Unable to concentrate on the leak of information and feeling the sexual heat of his puerile imagination he lay naked in his bed and relieved his frustration finishing with a groan of ecstasy.

He thought he heard something scrape against the bedroom wall but in his post seminal euphoria he could not be sure.

Sara Grace replaced the long tumbler on her bedside table and with a smile on her face she switched off her light and rolled over in bed. She wondered which one of her friends her brother was wanking over. She expected it might be Marion.

On Thursday the news that the choir was looking for male voices reached the regular customers of the Dog and Duck. The Drinkers, as they were known, demanded Forest Maloney explain.

'It's your old lady what's running the show so you have the news straight from the dragon's mouth so to speak,' said Miles.

Taking time to settle his dog, Mutley, before answering, Forest began. 'Excuse me, my dear wife Amanda, persuaded the vicar to set up the choir again with the emphasis on recruiting the young men and boys of the village. As you may be aware there has been complaints both to the parish and to the church committee of the activity of some of the lads,' Forest said. Mutley wriggled at his feet giving a great doggy sigh.

'Get on with it Forest you old windbag,' called another.

Forest glared at him.

'In short, we thought that letting the lads meet up with the girls where we can see them, will stop them creeping around the village spying on our daughters,' he said.

'Playing on their sense of lust,' observed Miles.

Amid the burst of laughter Forest feebly tried to explain the logic of allowing good, wholesome interaction between the youngsters but failed completely. The rude comments, and suggestions that the local pharmacy in town was about to do a roaring trade in contraceptives, and others suggesting that in a few months they should alert the maternity ward; and interjections suggesting "thrashing the randy little buggers", swamped his rational arguments.

Eventually when the comments died down Forest managed to explain. 'However, the young people will be controlled during rehearsals and separated with boys and men on one side of the choir and girls and women on the opposite side during church services.

'Christ! The poor little spotty faced herberts will explode with frustration,' Miles said. 'Some of them girls is bloody dynamite!' This remark caused much laughter and ribald remarks that Forest, or even Miles for that matter, could not repeat to his wife.

'The problem will be getting the boys to join the choir,' said Sylvester.

'We have thought of that Sly my friend,' Forest said, and paused to stop Mutley chewing a table leg. 'We will be asking the parents to help persuade them but before I tell you anymore you will have to wait. My lips are sealed. We have an exceedingly cunning plan.'

He gave them his best mysterious look and swallowed the rest of his pint. He had to take Mutley for his walk. He felt in his pocket for the plastic doggy doo-da bags and with a wink at the others he left the bar.

'Remember, the cunning plan.'

As he walked out of the bar with Mutley the dog dragging him out to his favourite pathway, Miles nodded, and turning, said to his pals: 'Bloody pompous dickhead.'

In general the rest of the drinkers agreed with him.

Friday morning opened with a shower of rain and as usual Forest Maloney walked Mutley around the village. The residents who observed him saw the dog squat on the verge near the bus stop, turn around twice before evacuating his bowels and watched Forest with a plastic bag on his hand pick up the wet excrement and tie it into the bag. They saw him walk back to his house with Mutley trotting happily behind him. What they didn't see was Forest handing the poo bag to his wife who nodded and placed it in the kitchen trash can.

'Good boy,' she said.

Forest was long past asking which one of them she meant. He hated picking up dog poo but it was his duty to take Mutley for his daily walks. He liked Mutley but was disappointed that his wife treated the dog with more respect than she did him. Forest had to return from the walks with a poo-bag full of dog shit or go out again regardless of the weather. Amanda did not like doggy doo-doos on her immaculate Forest mowed lawn. Thinking of this as he walked back home he muttered quietly.

'I love her, she loves me not, she loves me I love her not,' he chanted as he walked and groaned when Mutley pissed up against Amanda's Rosemary bush.

The handing over of the evidence completed Forest got ready for work dodging around Salina and Amanda as they carried out their independent arrangements. The one ready for College and the other fussing around ready to start on her daily round of good works and volunteering.

'Christ, how did this happen?' he said unaware that he was thinking aloud.

'Forest Maloney! How dare you take the Lord's name in vain.'

'Sorry my love. I was thinking aloud. You know, about "the problem",' he said.

And before Amanda could berate him further Salina interrupted. 'Dad, don't forget we have to pick up Marion as well.'

'Must be off then,' he said and collected his briefcase, jingled his keys and with his daughter in tow hurried out. He had managed to avoid the dry peck of parting and soon with the two

The Birdwatchers of Childen Under Blean

girls chatting happily on the back seats he drove into town.

He looked forward to going to work and was dreading the thought of retirement. The prospect of spending more time at home with Amanda Mary Forest née Carter was daunting and somewhat terrifying. He shuddered.

An even worse prospect was when Salina left home.

Neither the dog or his wife treated him with much respect but at least Salina was mostly pleasant to him. He dropped the girls off and carried on to travel another twelve miles to the Council Offices. He parked in his allocated space, walked to the section entrance, swiped his card and before taking his place at his desk signed in. On the way he greeted his colleagues with a cheerful 'good morning' and settled down to his day.

It was on the third assignment of the morning that he suddenly received enlightenment. The content was dull; the arguments for and against were both poor and he realised that neither party had made any attempt to compromise. Normally he would have taken elements of both sides and made a recommendation that both the approving officer and the appellant had to follow, favouring the approving officer.

Enlightenment came when he sat musing on the case and realised that he was merely following established, common, office procedure. There was more to life than that.

'The trouble with me is that I let everybody tell me what to do. My wife tells me what to do, my dog does as he likes, my bosses take no notice of me and even my friends seem to treat me like a joke.'

He remembered the last departmental meeting. He was too afraid to say anything, virtually rubber stamped the decisions and, although he should have had a say, nobody asked him. He had overheard Atkinson, the head of department, describe him as "that worm Maloney" and laughingly made comments about how he could be relied on to follow the party line.

'Break the mould Forest old chap, break the mould. Even a worm will turn,' he said and reached for the "book", the manual from which he worked. Setting it on his desk he carefully searched for references relating to the current task. Next he did an archive search and began to build a case. He arrived at a solution just before lunch and took a stroll to the canteen for his daily coffee and a roll.

'Your usual Mister Maloney?'

'No, I think I will have the quiche today, and side salad. I will also have a pot of Turkish with sugar,' he said.

He watched, amused, as the girl looked startled and hesitant.

'But you...'

'Today I have the quiche. It has much to do with worms turning, if you get my drift,' he said and smiled.

She served him with his order and he carried the tray to a table chosen at random instead of his usual place in a corner. He sat by a window with a view of the gardens which were enjoying a general dousing of good old English rain.

As he ate and drank he felt a little more at peace with himself and the little spark inside him did indeed begin to turn. He began to imagine retirement without Amanda and with insight into the nature of his friends he knew just who it was to consult on the matter. The one man who could keep a secret to himself despite rumours of his bad behaviour.

'I will talk to him this evening if I get the chance,' he said, and selecting a newspaper from the rack nearby he spread it out on the table to read whilst he ate his lunch.

Lunch over he cobbled up a creative solution to his assignment and sent it off for perusal. He was certain that the approving officer would have no choice but to pass the proposal and the appellant would be suitably pleased with his solution.

As he left for home that afternoon he had images of earthworms wriggling in fertile soil and that gave him another hint of enlightenment. The richness within him was under the surface and it was time for him to show his mettle. For the first Friday night in many years he was looking forward to the weekend. And as he drove home the rain eased off and the late afternoon sun promised a pleasant sunny evening.

Like his vicar, Coren Evans was a rugby enthusiast. He was an average size man, strong for his size and agile. On Winter Saturdays he played for the local Rugby Union team known as "the Bulls" and on Sundays he was to be seen dressed in robes as a choir master in St Seraph's for at least one of the services. Often the services in St. Seraph's were conducted without the vicar. That was when Morris Davis was let loose on the regulars with his hollering and swaying praying.

'Bloody madman,' Evans muttered when he first saw him perform 'And his followers ought to be locked up.'

The Birdwatchers of Childen Under Blean

But they always put part of their tithe's in the collection bags so he did not openly complain.

Most Sundays the reverend Jones managed evensong at St Seraph's and communion at least once in each month. During the good weather it was common for the members of the other churches to visit St Seraph's for services. Two of the less well attended churches, St Peter's and St Mathew's had joined forces but even with that reduction there were precious few attending church. Coren Evans sighed when he thought of the situation.

It meant fewer people to make up a choir.

But now that the committee and that awful Maloney woman had decided to invite the men and boys he was feeling much better.

Being Welsh he was expected to sing and being a rugby player, in the eyes of the young lads, he was the epitome of masculinity. He was an excellent village choir master and took his calling seriously. He called practice twice each week if possible and more if there was a Feast Day coming up. He was not religious but he liked religious music. He was attracted to choral work as much for hearing trained voices singing as for the robes he wore doing his duty. It was the nearest thing to dressing up like a woman he could get in public.

Evans the Choir liked playing rugby and during the Summer season although he played cricket for the Childen Under Blean eleven he looked forward to the rough and tumble of rugby. During practice and training, and the eighty minutes spent on the field, he got to grapple closely with his fellow men.

Being an openly gay rugby player was a non-starter but as long as nobody cottoned on he could indulge in his sexual preferences undetected. Even in this enlightened age there were some places where a gay man was not exactly welcome. Sadly, he reflected, he would one day have to give up the rugby.

But right now he was happy to rehearse the small choir of mostly women and a few dedicated men including Thomas and Melanie Grace, a couple whose singing needed careful nurturing. Their daughter Sara had a sweet voice and with her friends created the core of the sopranos. He was happy on this Friday evening to listen to their music. It was a most welcome relief from his normal employment.

'Once more boys and girls. The last one was very good so remember how you did it and sing like you mean it.'

He raised his hand and began to conduct their efforts. The organist, Barry Smythe, a creaking old man whose normal mode of progression was little more than a snail's pace played the ancient and wheezing instrument with a passion limited by his arthritis. The result was an asthmatic rendering of the old favourite *How Great thou art* which the choir did their best to match. The last great notes faded away and with a flourish Evans brought the choir to a halt.

'Very good but is a pity we have no strong male voices to add more depth to the lovely song,' he said. 'That last chorus needs a swelling sound.'

Some of the young girls giggled and sniggered drawing dark looks from the adults. He ignored it and said: 'Let us break for refreshment.'

Refreshment was supplied by that dreadful Amanda Maloney who made a pot of tea and hot water for coffee. Coren Evans would have preferred a tall pink gin, a large one, or maybe two.

'You teach our people to sing beautiful music,' Amanda Maloney said.

'I am thinking it is a pleasure to work with such wonderful people, such good voices,' Coren replied, taking a cup of indifferent tea knowing the coffee would be worse.

'We have a plan to help boost the choir numbers. I am sure you will like that mister Evans?'

Inwardly he groaned but managed to maintain his affable demeanour pretending to show interest.

'We will be asking the boys and younger men to come along. We have devised a plan to persuade them which includes suggesting that our girls are looking forward to singing with them. The only proviso is that the male and female members of the choir be set on opposite sides of the choir and we will require you to train them in like manner. We need the boys and girls to concentrate on the musical abilities with little distraction, if you get my meaning,' she said, smiling archly.

Prevent fornication but dangle the possibility, he thought, but said: 'Ah yes, getting the best from their voices. I understand that well.'

She looked puzzled and he waited whilst she wrestled with the real explanation eventually giving him a bland answer.

'We wish to prevent any impropriety.'

'A fine sentiment,' he said and finished the tea and, refusing a refill, hurried away. This, he thought was a situation he did not want to deal with. The potential for a sexual explosion was extremely high. It was one he could, with a bit of manipulation, exploit to enhance the performance of the choir. The alternative was that the whole thing could fall apart ending in someone throwing a tantrum.

He speculated that the tantrum thrower would be one Coren Evens Choir Master of this parish. That was not something to look forward to.

The second half of the choir practice was predictably a shambles. He lost his concentration and at one point drifted off into speculation of what to do with the boys if he got them. At the end of the session, the goodnights said and the washing up done he hurried home to tell his troubles to Tiddlington his bossy little cat. She didn't mind if he poured a pink gin and cared little if, once home and inside for the night, he changed into his panties, stockings and bra and wore a favourite dress. As long as she had a lap to sit on and was fed and fussed she cared little for anything else. That Friday evening he wore his black matching underwear, the red dress and, realising he hadn't shaved his legs, did not wear the stockings.

'The hair looks awful, just not me,' he said to Tiddlington who purred and waved her tail rubbing against his hairy calves. He should get his legs waxed.

He tuned into the classic FM station and relaxed in his easy chair with the cat on his lap and a tall, cool pink gin close to hand. Lost in the music, the gin and comfort of Tiddlington's purr he did not see Mathew Grace watching him from his position behind a high hedgerow. The lace curtains that covered three quarters of his window height allowing the evening sun to light his lounge also allowed Mathew to make yet another note of his transformation from man to woman. It was information that Mathew kept to himself until it was time to make use of it, but Coren was not aware of that.

Earlier that Friday Mathew and his mates met in the tea rooms drinking Coke and Red Bull to discuss the latest situation.

'Somebody quacked and if I find out who it is I'll kick the fucking shit out of him,' Mathew said, looking over his shoulder guiltily at Maddy Green. She didn't like them swearing.

'It ain't me.' Donald.

The Birdwatchers of Childen Under Blean

'Nor is me.' Stanley.

'And I don't done it,' added Terry.

The boys fell silent trying to think of who might have told whoever what but, as their minds churned over the facts, what they had to work with made very little sense. Even the mildly expansive intellect of Mathew Grace failed to find a solution.

'I suppose we ought to try and find out who by watching some of the others,' offered Stanley. 'Some of them others might of done it.'

Mathew's face brightened up at that suggestion and, with a sigh of relief, he drew out a list of names and using a pencil he marked the boys and added an initial beside each name.

'What's that what you are doing Matt?'

'Sorting out who watches who. In a minute I'll give you each a list and you gotta watch them blokes on your list and report back what you see or hear. Got it?'

His three companions nodded and with much muttered swearing, careful writing, pencil sharpening and more coke and red bull Mathew finally managed to hand each boy a list. The task took a frenetic fifteen minutes and by the time it was finished Terry had forgotten what he was to do.

'What I gotta do then?' Terry asked.

'It's written down on your list,' Mathew replied patiently. He was always patient with Terry. 'All you have to do is watch and listen and let us know. Whoever quacked might of done it accidentally. We don't need to do any kickin' until we know, right?'

'You don't want me to punch him?'

'We haven't found him yet.'

'Oh, right, yeah, gotta find him first. Then I punch him?'

'Not until we say so.'

Terry looked blankly at Mathew for a time and then he nodded.

'All right.'

Mathew sighed. Dealing with Terry was hard work.

If it wasn't for his old man Mathew wouldn't have started the club. His parents and Sara liked to go walking just to look at the hills and trees and wildlife. He had tried it but found it boring. His old man insisted he have a hobby and gave him some options, none of which he liked the sound of until his father had suggested he do birdwatching and gave him a good pair of binoculars.

'The RSPB recommend these, Mathew, and you should get

The Birdwatchers of Childen Under Blean

some pleasure out of watching birds close up. You can observe the kingfishers by the lake and the stream.' His Father said. He also gave him a book of birds from the RSPB and a guide to good bird watching. When he told Donald what his old man had said his friend was sympathetic.

'So you'll get in the shit if you don't get on with it?'

'That's right. I mean bird watching. I don't wanna know nothin' about birds; noisy little shits,' Mathew said.

'The sort of birds my grandad talked about wasn't with the RS whatsit. He calls girls, birds and told me what he and his mates got to up before he was married, doing just that,' Donald said.

'Doing what?'

'Bird watching, you know, chasing girls, rumpo and all that,' Donald said making a rude gesture with his arm and a fist.

Mathew grinned. He understood.

'You get a pair of these and we will do some bird watching. Feathered ones and the less feathered variety. And if we get a camera we can take some pictures.

And so the Birdwatcher's Club was formed and with Donald guiding him Mathew managed to convince his parents that he had taken up an interesting and fascinating hobby.

Since that start he had learned much about birds and their habits and could identify a few species. He still didn't like the little horrors. He and his mates were reluctant experts and although they had to show results; show a growing interest in the hobby with cameras, and actually visiting bird watcher's places that their parents insisted on carting them to, it was an excellent cover. The hassle with the old folks lasted until they left school and for the convenience of the deceit they more or less carried on.

It was Donald's idea to make a regular counts of garden birds and join in the RSPB's Great Bird Watch. Up until recently the ploy had worked. The problem was that more boys wanted to join in and once they found out what was going on the newcomers had resorted to a form of blackmail to be admitted to the club.

It had got out of hand.

Or in it if you thought about the frustration of watching the girls when what they really wanted to do was fondle them and all that follows. It was a most frustrating situation because no matter how hard he and his mates tried to satisfy their natural urges the girls of their village were determined to prevent them.

It had a lot to do with the church and being pure before

marriage and all that rot. Luckily not all the girls were part of the group but they were too few, or too snobby preferring boys who liked poetry and music and all that posh shit.

His sister Sara was one of the snobby girls.

Her with her A levels and college computer courses.

Snobby bitch.

Terry fancied her.

'You don't stand a chance mate. She's got other things in mind.'

'I can look can't I?' Terry said and grinned.

And although Mathew knew that was what the club was about he felt a twinge of defensive anger. That was his sister Terry was having wet dreams over. The dirty minded bastard.

Anyway, it was dark now and he had things to do. He sat at his computer and started on the evening's work. In the morning some of the lads had planned an actual bird watching trip just to make sure that their folks were happy with their progress. Oddly enough it was Vernon Green, the shop owner and organiser of village events, who had offered to take them to the marshes close to the estuary for the day. The Friends of St Seraph's had clubbed together to pay for a mini-bus and a picnic. It was time they got something from the rich gits, he thought.

Saturday began as usual, quietly. Forest Maloney and Mutley did their usual circuit and fortunately Mutley dropped his poo on the paving opposite the village shop where Vernon Green was busy cleaning the minibus and packing the picnic in for the boys.

'Mornin' Forest, mornin' Mutley. Good doggie, dropped your daily doo-dah for the nice man to pick up,' Vernon said and laughed. He looked surprised when the normally docile Forest, finishing his task crossed the road to stand facing him.

'Excuse me, mister Green, I'll bother you to stop taking the piss. This worm is for turning,' Forest Maloney said and waited for a few moments for Vernon Green to recover from his mild surprise. 'Understand?'

'I suppose so,' Green said, and watched, perplexed as Forest Maloney walked off.

He noticed that Mutley suddenly seemed to be well behaved and he wondered what had happened to the most nagged husband in the village.

The Birdwatchers of Childen Under Blean

'Bloody hell,' he muttered and absentmindedly dropped a picnic box on his foot, gasping as it scraped down his bare shin. 'Oh fuck, that hurt.'

Hopping and swearing he made his way to a bench seat outside the shop and examined his naked shin wishing he had worn trousers instead of shorts.

An hour later when the lads arrived for their trip he was wearing trousers that covered a long, taped up dressing under which despite the salve applied to the wound stung painfully. He was surprised when he realised that most of the lads had reasonably good equipment; nothing expensive but it all seemed businesslike. Having dabbled in ornithology himself he was impressed by their obvious enthusiasm.

'Right lads, we start off soon,' he said when they were all gathered. 'You must wear your seat belts. The picnics are in the coolers and everything except stuff in the gift shops is paid for. Let's make this a good day and send a positive message back to the nosy, bossy buggers of Childen Under Blean.'

That last elicited a ragged cheer and with a little hope in his heart he started the motor, and smoothly drove off. It was a sunny day with clouds threatening rain but the weather forecast suggested showers and good conditions. Just right for a good day out bird watching.

Vernon Green, hopeful as he was, knew nothing of the forces building up behind him in the Village, and was totally unaware that the outing had an ulterior motive. Vernon Green did not know that his good deed was all part of a cunning plan that if it followed its course would solve a problem in such a way as to baffle the participants. He smiled. Vernon had volunteered when his wife had suggested they hire the minibus to the Friends for the trip.

'You will be doing the lads a service and if we let the minibus for this trip at a discount we will get more hires later on,' she said.

And that, he thought, was all to the good.

'Right, I will take them out on the trip then,' he said and wallowed in her smiles and hugs.

'Good boy,' she said.

With the lads out of the way for the day the Coven and their supporters swung into action. The telephones were busy, people met up briefly for a chat as they spread the word. Daughters were aware of the activity and those boys who were not part of the birdwatchers' group noted the people walking around and gathering in small, animated groups but dismissed it as "old farts' stuff". Melissa and Terri, aware of the plan but pretending not to know of it, acted as the hub of information for their group, and like any good CCTV camera crew, followed the movements of conspiring adults.

Salina Maloney's plan was working and although it was Amanda and the Coven who put it into practice with a few tweaks from their group congratulations to their leader were in order. The flutter of < well dun hun > messages was well received.

With the boys out of the way things might change; hopefully for the better. It was time, so said Salina, for the girls of the village to reconsider the vow of chastity.

'Not with these lads,' Salina said thinking more about meeting somebody outside the village than in.

On the green that Saturday the Childen Eleven was taking on the visiting Stoat Malbury team who boasted a fast bowler with a reputation for shattering stumps and the occasional bat. Thomas Grace, a medium pace bowler himself and captain of the team gave the lads a pep-talk before the match. He wanted to speak to them in the small pavilion but he was delayed by the arrangements he had to make for the church service on Sunday and the lads were already imbibing in the Dog and Duck.

Thomas Grace was not a teetotaller but he did not approve of drinking before the match. He had played cricket in the Army and was keen on sports which meant that as he wanted to do well he drank very little liquor.

When he finished his army service he and Melanie already had Mathew and Sara. Being a man who controlled his drinking and liked to save his money, plus what Melanie had earned part time, he had suggested they buy a house of their own.

When the house came up for sale in Childen Under Blean he and Melanie were lucky. They managed to sell their house in town for a good price that left them on the plus side although, Thomas insisted on taking a mortgage.

'We need the money to start off our savings again,' he said, and shoved some of it in Premium Bonds. They forgot about them until one day a cheque arrived in the post. The money was invested in fixed term bonds.

Village life suited them.

The church was his refuge and cricket was his passion. He

The Birdwatchers of Childen Under Blean

preferred hockey for the winter but settled instead for running and walking. Melanie joined him for that. Sara took up horse riding and liked to go walking with her parents. Unfortunately Mathew didn't like anything the family did. Perhaps it was his early life in army quarters that had affected him. Or maybe the boy was just stupid. Thomas suggested that Mathew took after his grandfather who had learning difficulties, as understood in today's jargon.

In other words Mathew Grace was the Childen Under Blean Village Idiot.

However, to the matter in hand.

'This Peter, whatever his name is, has a reputation as a fast bowler. I suggest we take a defensive approach when he bowls and allow our batsmen to belt a few from the others. Singles are as good as fours when you score a lot of them and lose few wickets. And no, I will not have a beer but I will have a nice glass of orange,' he said. The tall glass of orange was duly delivered and he carried on chatting.

Thomas was a good cricketer and a popular captain and most of the lads respected his ability. They also respected his attempts to make them feel comfortable about facing this Peter Mann who may or may not be a terror.

The visitors arrived, parked their vehicles and as they were early Horace suggested the teams get together and have a drink.

'Get to know each other a bit,' Horace said, his face a picture of innocence.

Sylvester Simon gave him the thumbs up.

It was a convivial meeting as both teams knew each other except for a few newcomers who were introduced and welcomed. Peter Mann turned out to be a tall man with long arms and a moustache that wobbled when he spoke. It turned out he was an Oxford Blue. That attribute intrigued Sylvester who engaged him in conversation. Sylvester knew Oxford. Not the University but as a young man he had worked the area for his company for many years, and could talk convincingly of the ancient halls, giving the impression that he too was an Oxford Alumnus.

'Oh, played for years have you?'

'Yes, moved to Stoat Malbury and just sort of drifted into the club. Oh, thank you, I don't mind if I do,' Peter Mann said as Sylvester paid for two more pints. 'Lovely villages around here.'

'Yes, its the hills and the trees with the farmlands of course. That and we are remote from a major city,' Sylvester said. He was

The Birdwatchers of Childen Under Blean

pleased when Peter Mann drank deeply. It was a good thing that the pub was close to the green because the lads could sneak a quick one. Not only that but at half time Horace always put on a spread. Visitors were fed free but they paid for their drinks. The exception today was that Peter Mann was treated twice and insisted on buying Sylvester another one before the game got under way.

Sylvester was pleased that when the visitors won the toss they chose to bat.

The score at the end of the forty overs was 161 for 8 with Thomas taking four wickets. Peter Mann batting at number six scored 27 and lost his wicket when he missed his partner's call.

Evans the Choir threw from cover directly at the stumps and Mann was dismissed. The visitors added a few more runs after that dismissal and went to the break looking smug. It was a good score and Thomas was worried.

The break went well with sandwiches all round and some of the lads having soft drinks instead of beer. Peter Mann was no exception but Sylvester noted he seemed more animated than when he had first arrived. Sylvester sidled up to his captain who was devouring a tuna and mayonnaise sandwich washed down with a glass of orange.

'Be of good cheer my captain. I think our lads will make a good score,' he said.

Thomas and Evans the Choir opened for the Childen eleven. Thomas waited anxiously for the Stoat Malbury fast bowler's first ball. The run up was long and the tall man angled to the crease bowling a full toss racing half way down the wicket from the momentum of his release. True the ball was fast but the bowler's action was so easy to read that Thomas hit it neatly sending the ball into a long arc well out of the reach of the fielders over the boundary for six.

That first over surprised Thomas. It seemed to him that Peter Mann was more or less giving him practice balls and apart from one defensive stroke he scored on each of the others. He made twelve runs and faced the bowler on the next over.

The second over was more conventional gaining the batting side only three runs with four dot balls. Evans the Choir faced the fast bowler and treated the wonderful Peter Mann to a devastating destruction scoring three boundaries from the first three balls. The fast bowler seemed unable to bowl anything but full length that

The Birdwatchers of Childen Under Blean

the batsman could easily hit or redirect to the boundary. His run up and delivery was a study in human anatomy. The arms and legs seemed to lack coordination and appeared to act independently of each other. The bowler's gaze seemed to be fixed on a point somewhat remote from the wicket and the ball was projected in the right direction through habit of long practice. Otherwise it lacked the speed potential of its delivery which, for the two opening batsman, was a gift.

Thomas and Evans the Choir added another string of fours and singles bringing their partnership to 46 before the Stoat Malbury captain rested Peter Mann.

Three more overs and Evans the Choir clipped an edge and was caught behind.

'Howzat! went up the shout from several voices.

The umpire's finger was elevated and Evans the Choir walked off passing Sly who waddled to the crease giving him a high five.

'Good one Coren, watch the wonder boy,' he said indicating Mann who was standing at square leg looking on.

Sylvester took his stance and with Thomas at the other end batted steadily scoring twos and singles. Sylvester, owing to his girth and propensity for sinking ales, sweated profusely with the effort of running between the wickets. The ones and twos were wearing him down and as the score rose slowly it was obvious they were going to need some big hitting. Thomas made runs and scored a couple of fours when one of the opposition bowlers got enthusiastic and bowled a couple of easy balls.

Thomas was sitting on a solid 48 when he got cocky and tried to sweep a swinger and missed. He looked at the shattered wicket and simply tucked his bat under his arm and walked. The umpire's finger was up but it didn't matter.

The new batsman was Miles who took up his stance to face the last ball of the over. He defended and dropped the ball at his feet.

The Stoat Malbury captain called on Peter Mann to bowl again at Sly who was beginning to dig in.

The Childen score stood at 89 for 2.

The demon bowler ran in and Sly waited for the tell tale movement smacked it low to mid field for four. At the end of that over Sly had added eight runs to the total and ducked for the last ball of the over which was collected by the keeper. Miles managed to get off the mark and at the end of the over was left to face Peter Mann.

He managed a single against a poor ball from Mann and Sly whacked another four but noted that somehow Mann had recovered his coordination and the next ball was so well bowled he could only take a single. Miles' face was a picture of amazement when with hardly a chance to act the ball bounced and appeared to go through a hole in his bat knocking the middle stump out with a clack.

The new batsman took his stance to face the demon bowler who took his run up and bowled another steamer. The poor man walked back to the pavilion to the sound of quacking from the Stoat Malbury fielders.

The next man in lasted long enough to get Sly on strike.

'Bugger this,' Sly said and watched as the bowler took his run up, swung the ball back and bowled. It left his hand at speed but Sly had it in sight and forgetting all else he struck hard and hoped. The ball rocketed back along the pitch and as Peter Mann moved to his right on the overrun he met the returning ball. Instinctively he clutched it with both hands but it was travelling so fast it powered through his fingers and punched his stomach.

The effect was interesting.

The fast bowler fell sideways still clutching the ball but groaned and writhed on the grass.

The umpire raised his finger and with a grin Sylvester walked. 'Both of us out,' he said.

The first aid person, a spotty St John's Ambulance lad hurried across and retrieving the ball from Peter Mann's clutching fingers began his work.

Play was stopped to allow the stricken man to be taken to the Dog and Duck for further attention. It was obvious that Peter Mann, ace fast bowler and Oxford Blue was no longer a threat.

The score stood at 112 for 5.

The rest of the match followed its inevitable course and with new enthusiasm his replacement, Swanson Mackenzie found his pace and added another 37 to make it 149 for 6 before lobbing an easy catch to second slip.

Martin Crook waddled in and settled down to play defensively, building runs in singles. He watched impassively as number eight, a new lad who was a bowler and fielder was clean bowled. The last man in was Davey who was dubbed as King of the Ducks but although he rarely scored any runs could be relied upon to bat his end.

At this stage the Childen eleven needed eleven to win with two overs left and one wicket in hand.

Martin was aware of this.

The score whittled down to eight and Martin was sure they would make it when a ball snicked off his bat straight into the hands of second slip.

'Howzat! for Christ sake?'

'Oh shit,' he said and walked passing the pale faced lad on the way and smiled at him. 'Do your best lad.' The last man in was the lad Oliver from the junior team who was brought in for experience. He had taken a catch earlier and was good in the field but he was unknown as a batsman.

'I'll try,' squeaked the boy.

It seemed to Martin that the Stoat Malbury team was going to win. He took his place alongside the rest of the team and watched the play.

The two lads touched gloves and took up their places.

'Holy shit!' exclaimed Martin when the new lad whacked a four on the first ball. Two dot balls followed and he began to get nervous. But whether it was the bowler making a wrong call or desperate to get a wicket the next ball was just right and the lad punted it over the bowler's head to the short boundary where it bounced over the line and hit the roadway where a boy picked it up and hurled it back.

'Good Lord, we've won!' said Thomas looking pleased.

In the Dog and Duck after the match it was discovered that poor Peter Mann had suffered from stomach cramps and worse.

'He shat hisself,' said Horace. 'Poor bugger. Too many drinks before the match, so the medic said.

But Brian Gossop, the Stoat Malbury captain glowered at the Landlord and with his pint still in his hand made a statement.

'He was nobbled. Somethink you put in his beer, pal,' he said and jutted his chin out.

Horace looked shocked.

He faced the irate captain and calmly and quietly he said: 'Nobody accuses me of putting anything in anybody's beer.

'I do,' said Brian Gossop.

In the hush that followed all that could be heard was the rapid downing of drinks, the shuffling of feet and the undefined indignation of the Childen eleven and their supporters. It hit the

Stoat Malbury team and their supporters like a wall of disapproval, a feeling that somebody had said something wrong. This was accentuated by the collective sigh that swished through the pub as the accusation was whispered from patron to patron.

Horace glowered at Gossop.

'I repeat, nobody accuses me of nobbling.'

Brian Gossop was aware now of the menacing group of locals that had swiftly but quietly surrounded his men and the size of the fists on the end of Horace Oswald's arms.

'He was all right before he got here.'

'Maybe it was something he ate for breakfast and all that running about on the field with too much beer in his skinny Oxford Blue belly,' Horace said rolling up his sleeves to reveal thick tattooed arms as he stepped out from behind the bar.

'I'll handle this Horace,' said Sylvester coming between the two men. 'It was my fault, we were chatting friendly like and drank too many ales. I can take me beer but I can't run too much with a skinful. I didn't drink that much meself but your mate got all enthusiastic and had a couple of chasers to, "settle himself down" he said, and I think it was all that running about when he was batting, and the staying in like he did. I mean he made a good innings,' Sylvester explained and gave Gossop a hard look.

'You're a liar moosh.'

Sylvester sighed.

'Oh well, I tried,' he said and with a movement that started from his hips and legs he floored Gossop with an uppercut that lifted the irate captain off his feet.

The two patient police officers investigating the brawl that followed Sylvester's mighty blow came to the conclusion that they would not lay any charges. They were busy officers and had criminals to catch. The paper work for such a trivial matter as a stand off between rival cricket teams was not worth the bother.

'Look, shall we just put it down to the Stoat Malbury side being poor losers?' suggested Horace.

The senior constable grinned.

'Why not, after all it's only a game,' he said and the two officers left the village to continue their patrol.

On the whole, for the Childen eleven, it was a satisfactory solution.

However for some of the Stoat Malbury players it was not so good. Two of them, driving their mates back after their contested defeat, were stopped on the road by the same two officers and breath tested. Both drivers were over the limit. As none of their passengers were entirely sober they were forced to abandon their vehicles.

As luck would have it Vernon Green and his minibus was returning from the birdwatching trip and he cheerfully promised to return with the bus to take them home. He added that in the circumstances he would charge them a reasonable fee. What irked them was that he insisted on being paid in advance and that payment be made at the shop in Childen Under Blean.

At least they all returned home safely driven to their doors in turn with Vernon's words of encouragement ringing in their ears.

'Better luck next time, eh lads?'

St. Seraph's was fortunate enough to have room in its building for a chapel, a vestry and space adapted to make room for a kitchen and toilets. By removing some of the rear pews the elders and Friends had created a raised platform above the cold stone flags with part of it partitioned off to allow meetings to be held. On the Saturday morning before the plan was to be put in operation the Coven were inside this partitioned area drinking tea and nibbling biscuits. All five were present and from an observer's point of view all that was needed to convey an atmosphere close to the Shakespearean ideal was a steaming pot and a surfeit of cackling. Instead, although the conversation was animated, it was quiet to prevent too much being overheard should a visitor venture into the nave.

Amanda Maloney was summing up. The biscuits were almost devoured and the tea was at that point of staleness where it was almost drinkable but not quite palatable.

'So my friends, you all know what to do. You have your immediate families to guide and will of course do your best to enlighten those on your individual lists,' she said.

To a chorus of "yes Amanda's" she smiled and bowed her head. The plan was going well so far, if all do their part.

'Of course there are some girls who deliberately flaunt themselves. We must guard against that and watch out for loose morals. We all know who these gels are,' she said and gave Sylvia Simon a meaningful gaze.

'My Cheryl is a good girl,' Sylvia said bristling with indignation.

'Perhaps she is, but be aware that I live opposite and have

seen her open her curtains,' Amanda said giving Sylvia a penetrating stare as if to defy the woman to disagree with her.

'My Cheryl is a good girl,' Sylvia insisted.

'Be that as it may but I implore you to take care of her,' Amanda said, even more insistent.

The strained silence that followed seemed to last an eternity but in fact it was no longer than a mere thirty seconds such was the tension between the two women. It was broken by a nervous tinkle of a spoon dropping into a saucer and with a suddenness that reactivated the group, clearing of the tea things began, and soon all was clean and tidy. The women left the church precincts, and if a building could sigh with relief, it did.

In his office on that Saturday morning the reverend Jones finished writing his Sunday sermon and with lunch in his belly at noon he strolled down to the green to watch the cricket. it was his chance to mix with his parishioners and sneak in a pint or two before the meeting with the organist.

He watched the local eleven struggle to bowl the Stoat Mulbury eleven before the forty overs and knowing that Peter Mann was on their team he gave in to the inevitable defeat of his home team. Peter was a demon bowler and at times when he had faced him in a match the result was a duck. The man was insufferable but Michael Jones had to agree that he was a good bowler. Fortunately the teams were already on the field when he arrived and it was a simple matter of slipping into the quiet bar during their break to avoid any contact with him. From his observation point the reverend Jones saw Sylvester Simon and Horace Oswald wink at each other when the latter pulled the two pints Sylvester purchased for him and his companion. Peter Mann, so the vicar thought, was about to be Mickey Finned.

When the game resumed he moved to the tables outside to watch and saw Peter working his usual attack but seemingly unable to select the length he normally found that made the ball rise up and send the batsman backwards in panic. Something was definitely wrong. He was convinced when Thomas Grace hammered a four off one of Peter's fast balls.

Much later in the game when Sylvester hammered a ball directly at Peter Mann causing him to fall yet sacrificing his wicket the reverend was convinced. Something naughty had been done.

'May the good Lord forgive them,' he said and looked at his watch. Time to go and meet Barry.

The Birdwatchers of Childen Under Blean

The reverend Jones heard about the brawl on Sunday morning and tutted sympathetically but unconvincingly as his wife told the story.

'It happens my dear,' he said.

'I thought it was supposed to be a gentlemen's game,' she said.

'Oh no anybody can play, even women play cricket now,' he said and looked at her with some concern. 'Do you realise even the Americans have a team?'

'No dear I did not know that.'

'The game is no longer gentlemanly. God forbid, the French might even take it up,' he said sounding shocked at his own suggestion.

'Do you really think so?' she said looking shocked.

'They took up rugby,' he said sadly.

Elizabeth shook her head; she did not understand.

Sunday morning was a lazy day for most in the village and except for those things that were considered normal little out of the ordinary happened. Normal was that Forest Maloney and Mutley took their extended walk around the village and up into the hills above the abandoned quarry. On this Sunday morning he let Mutley off the lead once he was out of the village. Instead of the dog racing for home after a good sniffing run around the common land and the quarry looking for rabbits, he followed his master.

Forest Maloney's new confidence had rubbed off on the dog who decided that Forest was a little closer to alpha than he was accustomed to. Mutley felt comfortable in the new regime. Mutley, you could say, had experienced enlightenment.

The revelation took both creatures by surprise. It was a novel experience. Forest tried throwing sticks for the dog and for the first time since his wife had owned Mutley the animal actually returned to him with one in his mouth. Normally he would leave it for Forest to collect and throw again and perhaps race after it.

In Mutley's opinion Forest was responding better to training.

As a reward for Forest's efforts Mutley dropped his morning poo on the smooth footpath making it easier for his developing master to gather up. The ritual puzzled the dog. You dropped your poo and left it. Why pick it up and carry it back to the den? What did they use it for? When he did his poo back at the den they shouted at him unless he dropped it neatly on the hard surface.

The other thing that always puzzled him was why the master didn't mark his territory whenever they went out.

Strange creatures, people.

Didn't do a lot of sniffing either.

Evans the Choir, dressed in a track suit that hid silk panties and matching top, with a pair of trainers on his feet and a baseball cap with the peak facing forwards, ran the footpaths and the bridle ways around the village. He saw Forest and Mutley out for their walk and noted that Forest was apparently enjoying himself. As they crossed paths Evans the Choir jogged to a halt and greeted his near neighbour.

'Enjoy the match yesterday?'

'Yes, I bowled three,' Forest replied.

'What do you mean by bowled out three?'

'I flattened three Stoat Malbury players in the post match punch-up,' Forest said looking pleased with himself. 'The worm has turned.'

Alarmed that Forest Maloney was pleased to count himself as a brawler, Evans the Choir was taken aback. 'You were part of the brawl last night?'

'Oh yes, I had to stand by the lads; my place as chief critic calls for loyalty to them as well as loyalty from them to me. The worm has turned and I could not let them down by running away.'

Evans the Choir was impressed but puzzled.

To help understand he resorted to referring to Christian values. Sensing that something was different about Forest this morning he thought about the gospels and stretched his agnostic memory for some good words. Something Forest said was nagging at him, worms, or rather the worm, which bothered him.

'Did not Christ say "love thy neighbour as thyself" yet here you are brawling with ours.'

'He wasn't accused of nobbling,' Forest said.

'Ah yes, nobbling, the noble art of cheating.'

'You were there.'

'Yes, yes of course, Evans said, realising that Forest meant at the match and not with Christ and his Disciples. He was a little distracted when Forest reached down and tickled Mutley behind the ears as the animal sat on his haunches beside him looking up floppy tongued and tail waggingly excited. That was something

The Birdwatchers of Childen Under Blean

that had never happened before when he had met Forest. By this time the dog had usually gotten fed up and scooted off home.

'So anyway, if our neighbours are going to accuse us of nobbling whenever they lose a match they can get..."

'Stuffed?' ventured Evans the Choir.

'More or less.'

Forest's smile was disturbing and Evans the Choir who was not easily disturbed decided it was time to move on.

'Must get going, see you in church?'

'Of course. Look forward to it.'

And as Evans the Choir trotted off to finish his circuit he thought he heard Forest Maloney say to the dog.

'Mutley my friend this worm is made for turning.'

But he couldn't be sure.

Sylvester Simon was looking forward to church as well. Sylvia and Cheryl were in the choir and between the hours of ten and twelve they would be warbling away like a couple of sopranos vying for the honour of being the first to shatter a drinking glass. It was a ghastly sound even when heard from a safe distance but close up it was too much to bear. However, Evans the Choir seemed to manage and even succeeded in controlling their volume.

Sly had a breakfast of boiled eggs and buttered soldiers, coffee and toast and afterwards perused the newspaper whilst the women got ready for church. They left to walk up the hill to church and with no hesitation he was off in the opposite direction via the back alleys to a house some two hundred metres from his own and within easy walking distance of the Dog and Duck.

He used a latch key hidden under a flowerpot and let himself in, and ignoring the front rooms made his way to the stairs and the master bedroom.

'Hullo Sly, coffee's ready and so am I,' said a soft voice from the bed.

'Ah Lily my love you know how to make a man feel good,' he said and undressed quickly to join her naked form under the bedclothes. One brief cuddle and a kiss or two and they drank the coffee which was at the right temperature to drink, placed their empty mugs on the floor and got on with the business of mutually agreed copulation.

Sly was a good lover having had plenty of practice. For these two stolen hours the widow Lily Williams embraced the pleasure she had been waiting for. She liked Sunday church almost as much as Evans the Choir did but for obviously differing reasons. For him it was wearing the robe like a dress and pretending he was a woman; for her it was taking the dress off and acting like one. It was a thing she missed since her husband had died, and when Sly had made crude suggestions to her during the Friends of Saint Seraph's Irish night she had solved her problem.

She lay gasping and when he suggested they do it again talking dirty to her like Lady Chatterley's gardener, she thought of Moll Flanders and grasped him tightly.

Sylvia Simon is one lucky woman, she thought, and lost herself in the ecstasy that was happening between her legs.

Horace Oswald watched Sylvester Simon walk casually from the widow Williams house and pulled a pint and a chaser placing it on the bar as his customer walked in. Sly handed over the money and drank the spirit.

'Ah nectar. Mornin' Horace.'

'Afternoon Sly, good service this morning?'

'Excellent, a communion of spirits that was most satisfying.'

'Your missus at church was she?'

'Singing more or less sweetly in the choir along with the other girls and my Cheryl,' Sly said and raised his glass. 'God bless 'em.'

'Indeed, and all who sail in her.'

'What was the damage yesterday Horace?'

'A dozen or so glasses, a cruet, and one of the outside tables but otherwise apart from a few sore heads and a clean up, all is well. You walloped Gossop proper. He was out of it for most of the time. The coppers couldn't be bothered and in spite of all that I made a profit,' Horace said.

'Good, here's to the gentleman's game, and the smack of willow on leather,' Sly said raising his glass and drinking.

'And a toast to a good clean uppercut,' Horace said.

'That too, now let me have another pint will you and one for yourself,' Sly said.

And until the bar began to fill up with Sunday lunchtime customers the two men chatted happily about the match.

Sly's extra-marital excursion was not discussed.

Sly was rather sensitive about his private life.

The Birdwatchers of Childen Under Blean

The reverend Jones was pleased with his sermon. The congregation had listened and seemed to absorb the message he was trying to convey. He concentrated on morality and doing right things by overcoming carnal desires. Judging by the attentive faces peering up at him he assumed he might be getting through.

'Some hopes,' he muttered, and called on Amanda Grace to read the notices. He sat in his chair and tried to appear attentive but as she rattled on all he heard was the last one.

'There will be the usual coffee morning on Thursday, and now I call on Coren Evans to announce the new arrangements regarding the choir,' she said, and sat down.

Evans, using a prompt in the form of a sheaf of cards made a short speech: 'We wish to open the choir to young men, boys and, of course, some of the older men and women to enhance the singing in time for Christmas and Easter next year. We have some funds allocated from the Friends and individuals to encourage recruitment. We will have some outings planned. It was suggested that we take trips to local attractions rather than more traditional "churchy" things. We also want to organise holidays throughout the year for choir members and their families,' Evans announced, and aware of the murmuring he held up his hand for silence. 'And so that others are not left out we can also organise holiday trips and day trips for members of the congregation.'

Evans the Choir waited for the inevitable flurry of questions and when everybody seemed to be talking at once he again held up his hand for silence.

'Simply this. You register as a member of the congregation and pay into a fund which Thomas here has kindly volunteered to administer. This will be set against your account so when, and if, you choose to take advantage of one of the trips a large portion of your contributions will be used to offset your final costs. We will take a small admin fee to help boost church funds and everybody gains.'

And before the noise began again Amanda Maloney interjected: 'The ushers will be amongst you with leaflets and forms which you can take home and return to us when you have filled them in.'

The girls in the choir sat quietly chatting in the boxes on the north side of the Choir and for the time being they were ignored. The scheme had already been explained to them and Reverend

Jones assumed they were talking about the new initiatives. In fact, led by Melissa Jones, they were planning strategy.

'Right, you know what is to be done. The Bird Watchers are not on although some of the village lads are all right. We can do better than this crowd of morons. Is that agreed?'

There was a series of nods, some enthusiastic and others not so excited. Cheryl Simon and Mandy Crook being the exceptions. Neither of them were keen on the horsey set. In fact Cheryl Simon was keen on Donald Tomms and hoped he would want to join the choir. Of course the discussion excluded the very young girls but they too would later be involved.

In spite of her desire, Cheryl Simon was aware that losing her virginity was her choice and in spite of her father's suspicion that she was likely to follow in the female equivalent of her father's footsteps she had no intention of doing so. Unfortunately, like the others, when the movement for purity in the church had arrived she had publicly signed the pledge. But that was before the hormones kicked in. Still, it was fun driving the lads mad with desire undressing with the curtains open and the lights on, or sunbathing naked in her back yard. She had a good figure and could wiggle with the best of them.

'I suppose so,' she said.

'Oh dear we have a rebel,' said Sara.

'Can't we just lead them on and watch them squirm in public but privately make our own choice,' she said. 'I really don't like the boffins.'

Sara smiled. The word boffin was as archaic as Evans the Choir's choice of language but it explained much about how Cheryl felt.

'I think, sister, you should take care,' Sara said.

'But what are we supposed to do?'

'My brother is a thicko but he managed to start the club to "perve" on all of us and all we are doing is teaching them a lesson,' Sara said.

'And all you have to do Cheryl is go along with the idea until the idiots grow up,' explained Salina. 'I mean, look at my father. Even the dog treats him like a kid.'

Cheryl wanted to say that it was because Salina's mother was a nagging cow with no sense of humour who treated her father like he was a naughty boy but refrained. Salina could be as harsh as her mother at times. Instead she said quietly: 'All right but...'

'We might be close to the end now,' Sara said, and touched her hand gently.

Their little conference had to end there because now Evans the Choir was approaching ready to conduct them in singing the last hymn.

As the last notes died away Cheryl blushed pink when she thought about where her father might be at that moment. She imagined his large naked body banging away on top of the widow Williams and felt urges in her belly that any good Christian girl should abhor.

But then, she was not a very good Christian girl.

And if that was not enough conflict on this Sunday, a mixture of change, and plans designed to destabilise the church community, and give new life there was another relationship in contention. The reverend Jones had noted that Forest Maloney was not in church this morning and that his wife, the ever dominating Amanda, was looking as dark as a hilltop thunderstorm.

Amanda Maloney angry was not a pleasant sight; nor even easy to deal with and Michael Jones was aware that he had to talk to his church warden after the service. The subject was recruiting Forest to the post in support of her.

The reverend Jones ended the service with a blessing and stood by the exit to speak with his flock. It was a pleasant part of the day and afterwards, if the meeting went well he would go home for lunch. Elizabeth had sloped off quickly to attend to the meal and make sure that Terri was managing. The girl liked cooking and had produced some excellent meals as practice for her course at the local Comprehensive. Sorry, Academy, he corrected himself.

At last the congregation was gone including the choir who had slipped out of their robes and dashed off. One service Evans the Choir insisted on was proper laundry. He charged the choir members for laundering their gowns stating that it was better to have them done professionally than rely on the vagaries of home washing.

'They sometimes come out all sorts of colours, light blue, green and pink, not that I mind pink, but let's have them white and black, ironed properly and looking pristine,' Evans said and pursed his lips.

'It's a gay thing isn't it?' Jones had said.

'I like to be neat and tidy.'

Jones smiled: 'Bless you Coren.'

He saw that Evans was putting the smocks in the laundry box assisted by Bonny Mason the organist for the day. Poor Barry was feeling poorly and had elected to turn the music for her. He had taught her to play properly and was happy to let her take his place. Waiting for him in the vestry was Amanda Maloney and whatever he wanted to do else he had to face her. She sat in her chair upright and rigid, her face grim. As he sat opposite she immediately spoke.

'My husband has declined to take office. I will therefore recommend Thomas Grace. Why my husband has declined and indeed defied me I have no idea but this morning he declared he was going for a walk and then was to have lunch at the Dog and Duck. He invited us to join him but I said we had a nice salad for lunch and he laughed. I would rather go for a walk, he said, and told me to enjoy church,' she said.

What she didn't tell him was that Forest had declared he was going to take Mutley with him and if and when he shat he would ignore it and let it steam in the sunshine. If she wanted to have it placed in their rubbish bin she could go out and find it and pick it up for herself. As far as he was concerned the dog could piss and shit wherever he bloody well liked and in addition, instead of eating her bloody awful salad he was going to have lunch at the Dog and Duck.

'And if you and Salina want to join me I will buy you a good lunch and a few drinks and you can stuff the church where the sun doesn't shine. Here-by the worm has definitely turned,' he said and grinned.

'You're not coming to church then?' she said firmly, expecting him to wilt.

'Certainly not,' he said resisting the urge to say "absolutely".

'You will be neglecting your duties Forest,' she said.

'Salina can hand out the books. I am going for a walk with the dog. God can go find another servant,' he said.

And that statement had taken the wind out of her sails and the efficacy she was used to went out of the metaphorical window. Her power was reduced by confusion.

Amanda stayed at home on that Sunday and ate her salad disappointed that Salina opted for the lure of a steak and ale pie and a measure of Merlot. It was a lonely, empty lunch for Amanda

Maloney and as the afternoon wore on with no relief for her misery and indignation, she grew even more determined to take back control.

In the Dog and Duck Forest Maloney and his daughter, with Mutley lying contentedly and well fed on the floor beneath his table, was enjoying the meal.

'Your mother was unhappy?'

'Spitting tacks but I couldn't turn down the chance of a good dinner,' Salina said.

'Enjoy the food and the merlot,' he said.

'Why, what's happened with you Dad?'

'The worm has turned Salina, and your father is no longer the nagged narrow man you are accustomed to. I am breaking out. I am a man, and I will no longer be the cowed halfwit who bows down to the rule of your despotic mother. I am taking control of my wife and family including you and the dog. In the meantime enjoy your dinner,' he said.

'Thanks daddy,' she said and tucked into the food.

And with great pleasure he too ate his lunch.

Mutley sighed with contentment and settled down onto his paws. Master had given him scraps and master had also given him orders in a firm fashion that screamed Alpha Male. For the first time in his life Mutley felt the positive influence of a leader. He was in doggy heaven.

It was not until Wednesday following the church choir announcement that the news of the changes sunk in to the minds of the Birdwatchers. Mathew and his friends and a few of the other lads were sitting in the tea rooms drinking soft drinks and red bull. The boys were puzzled, a normal situation for most of them when faced with tricky questions. The one they were wrestling with was why their parents had forbidden them to apply for the choir.

'My dad said I was to keep away from the girls. He told me he would be really pissed off if I joined their fucking choir. I don't get it. The vicar bloke and that bloody queer what waves his bloody arms about during the singing says we should join up. I don't get it,' said Donny.

'Fuck 'em, let's join anyway. They can't stop us,' said Mathew.

'Yeah, we can give 'em a grope or two and there ain't nothink they can do about it,' Terry said and grinned. 'I reckon if we join

The Birdwatchers of Childen Under Blean

up then some of them others will too. Get some willing birds in as well as them snooty bitches like your bloodyminded sister.'

'Most of them signed the pledge,' Stanley pointed out.

There was a contemplative silence.

'I think some of them wished they hadn't,' suggested one of the others.

His statement cheered them up and before they were asked to leave Mathew called on the group to agree that the boys could join the choir.

'I liked that fucking bird watching what we did in Saturday. Fucking interesting that was. Especially when that fucking falcon hooked that bleedin' seabird out of the water and ate the fucking thing. That was fucking ace,' Terry said.

'Oy, you boys watch your language,' called out Mrs Green.

'Fuck me its the Green Dragon,' remarked Terry and regretted his comment when Vernon was called upon to escort them out.

They had their binoculars with them so they spread out in the village to "do a bit of perving" in the dusk taking up their favourite positions. Mathew Grace had fancied looking in on a girl around the corner from his house. Molly her name was and she was a new recruit to the gang his sister and that stuck up cow Salina ran. As it was he took a wrong turn and barely missed being stomped on by Sylvester Simon who was sneaking along the lane. Hidden in some bushes Mathew watched Sly slip through a gate and hurry quietly up to a porch. Using his skills of sneaking around Mathew managed to get close when the man was admitted by the front door. Moments later an upstairs light went on and with practised skill he dashed across the road to a vantage spot where he could train his binoculars on the window.

In the few moments before the curtains were drawn Mathew saw the full frontal naked figure of the widow Sally Wise and behind her already groping her adequate breasts stood Sylvester Simon. Surprised as he was by their exposure he still managed to take a picture. This will be worth loading up Mathew thought and chuckled. Ten minutes later he was "perving" at the new girl and snapping some excellent pictures as she undressed, and slipped her nightdress on before closing the curtains.

He walked slowly home happy that he had at least got some useful pictures. Out of habit he sneaked from cover to cover and so intent was he doing so he failed to see the dark clad figure that flitted past him in the shadows with even more night skills than his own.

Late that evening he loaded the images on to his computer and licked his lips thinking about what he could do with the images.

'A lot if I play me cards right,' he said and with that thought in his mind he went to bed. He thought of the new girl before he went to sleep, especially the swell of her breasts under her nightie.

And thinking of similar swelling protuberances the reverend Jones lay in his bed beside Elizabeth enjoying images of Bonny Mason's bosom floating before his eyes. Bonny had left her spectacles behind in the church and when they were discovered Elizabeth had volunteered him to return them to her. On the way he thought he saw Sylvester Simon sneaking back home.

'Widow comforting I suppose,' he said softly. 'The man is a philanderer.' He didn't approve of married men cheating on their wives. That was why he was a man of the cloth; to disapprove of adultery and nefarious practices. He had almost resisted temptation many times and was glad of it. He knew he was taking the moral high road but he said a quiet prayer for Sylvester to mend his ways.

Full of good intentions he had walked to the woman's house, knocked on her door and apologised for disturbing her.

'My wife asked me to return your spectacles in case you need them,' he explained disturbed because already Bonny Mason could be described, as casually dressed. His eyes followed the shapely form, fascinated by the heaving bosom, unable to drag his gaze away from her nipples that made little volcanoes under her diaphanous top. The top left a large gap above her tight shorts exposing her belly button pierced with a tiny silver ornament.

'Oh Michael so kind of you. Tea or something stronger?' she asked as she more or less guided him inside and shut the door.

Fascinated by her undulating figure he murmured: 'Oh something stronger please. I've had enough tea for the day.'

'Sherry all right?'

'Sherry's fine.'

And with a glass each they sat side by side on her settee, the spectacles resting on the coffee table and the two sherry glasses settling neatly beside them. The reverend Michael Jones was discovering how easy it was to expose that magnificent bosom by simply undoing the knot securing the top. As he took off his jacket all thoughts of philandering and morality disappeared in a mist of rampant lust. He was about to undo his dog collar when she reached up and tickled his neck with her long, sensuous fingers.

'Leave it on. It's the trousers and pants should go,' she said.

He had to agree. He wanted to feel those large, bouncing nipples on his chest but lust was calling. As he manipulated his own rampant organ to pleasure her and himself, in his mind he heard the swelling tones of the church organ manipulated by the same animated fingers she was applying to his erogenous areas.

'Holy Christ!' He cried out as he reached a climax.

And as he lay in his own bed thinking of her pliant body and that cleavage he rolled over to press against Elizabeth, rampant once again. She stirred and suddenly awake gasped.

'What? Now?'

'As good a time as any,' he said, and as he rolled on top of her and pumped into her he had to curb his desire to call out Bonny's name. Afterwards he lay listening to his wife's gentle snores and quietly eased his unsatisfied desire groaning softly and shaking with passion when he reached the third climax of the night. He slept fitfully dreaming of bosoms to wake in the morning feeling exhausted.

Thursday breakfast in the Maloney household was a tense affair. Amanda fussed around her daughter snapping angrily when the girl assured her she was capable of getting her own stuff ready.

'Hurry up or you will be late.'

'Oh stop fussing woman. I will take her in the car. Mutley's had his morning shit in the garden and for once I have had a good breakfast. Your turn to clear up the dog muck,' Forest said and slurped his coffee. Mutley rubbed against his leg and wagged his tail. Forest reached down with a sliver of bacon and gave it to the dog who took it gently and gratefully from his fingers.

'I have no intention of picking it up.'

'Oh well suit yourself.'

'What's got into you these last few days?'

'It has a lot to do with worms,' he answered. 'Now if you are ready Salina, it is time to go. I will take Mutley out this evening. In the meantime please make sure he is cared for.'

Amanda stood open mouthed as Forest picked up his briefcase and inclining his head toward Salina headed for the door. That he gave her no other attention than a brief wave and a cheery "See Ya" was even more puzzling. She stood staring at the closed door until at last Mutley came and nuzzled her. She put her hand on his head and tickled his ears.

Neither Forest or Salina had cleared their things from the table.

What puzzled her most once she had cleared up and sat in the lounge watching the telly with a tot of sherry beside her was Forest's reference to worms.

'What on Earth does he mean?'

But she had lost control and was astute enough to know it. What she needed to do now was get that control back. She would start with the dog.

'Mutley! Come here!'

To her chagrin the dog remained where she had left him; in the utility room snoozing happily in his bed.

'Bugger the animal!'

She stood up and walked angrily to where Mutley lay sleeping and called again. Mutley wagged his tail a little and rolled into a different position.

'Come on out of there pooch.'

One ear flopped up and one eye opened but that was all except for a snort as the dog dug himself deeper into his bed. She stood tapping one foot angrily and with determination to make the dog behave she reached down and grabbed his collar lifting him bodily from the bed. It was like dragging a large bag of cement. Mutley was not going to move unless he wanted to and it was obvious he didn't want to. She let him go and watched forlornly as he nipped neatly back into his basket bed and with his head on his paws gazed at her with sad eyes.

Mutley was not about to give in.

The Alpha male was away and unless there was a threat to deal with he decided that sleeping and dreaming was what he wanted to do. Traipsing around the house all day pretending to be alert and interested when the bitch did nothing to make him happy was not his bowl of smelly water.

An hour after her unsuccessful encounter with Mutley, Amanda Maloney was sitting with the Coven tight lipped and angry. Maggie had just made a remark that was out of line.

'All I said was "about time"; what's wrong with that?'

'Are you implying that I am to blame for his disgusting behaviour?'

'Well, he always comes across as rather under the thumb. I

know we have to keep men in their place but I do think poor Forest is more under the thumb than the rest. We do know how to modify our control,' Maggie said. She was going for broke. Amanda had insulted her by calling her a sentimental cow when she had stated that she and her husband liked to cuddle and hold hands.

Amanda had explained that Forest was becoming a rebel and defying her of late.

'Even the dog is ignoring me!' Amanda wailed.

And that was when Maggie made her comment.

The argument after that was fierce and vicious. Maddy Green and her staff watched the proceedings with interest, glad that the ladies had had their morning tea and scones. When the women were gone the news that Amanda Maloney was losing her grip rushed around the village like a wildfire.

Although Donald Tomms was not a fast worker he was wise enough to do the tasks given to him and make as few mistakes as he could. His job was mundane but as far as he was concerned as long as he was paid every fortnight and didn't get too many bollockings he was happy. His folks were pleased with him. He paid his keep, saved up enough to buy his clothes and had enough left over to put in a savings account. Donald had very little imagination and couldn't be bothered to expand his horizons as his workmates put it.

'Like what?' he asked when they taxed him with his dullness.

'Holidays. France, Spain, Italy, Russia, America, you know overseas, see the world like.' Said with enthusiasm and a little anxiety as he showed blank indifference.

'What, foreign?'

'Yes, new places, new horizons, find out about how other people live.'

'They lives the same as us but talk foreign.'

'They all speak English mate. They have to, don't they?'

'I've heard foreigners jabbering away in their own language. Iggorant buggers won't even answer when you talk to 'em,' Donald said. 'They come over here to take our jobs. I seen 'em picking fruit near where I live.'

'Would you pick fruit?'

'Nah, fuck that. Bloody hard work that. Besides its not like a proper job is it?'

The Birdwatchers of Childen Under Blean

'And lumping crates of fruit and veggies around in here picked by immygrunts is all right, eh?'

'We got pallet lifts and fork trucks; machinery, technical stuff, more better ain't it, besides...' Donald said leaving the unsayable unsaid.

'Yeah, know what you mean, but just because they is foreigners it don't mean you can't go to their country and show them what civilisation can do.'

'But them Greeks and Romans was civilised. We gets a lot from the Greeks and Romans,' said Tommy the ganger. 'My grandad was in Greece. He said they was a rotten lot of thieves but they hated the Germans. Used to blow them up and spy on them but they got no bleedin' morals, said my grandad and he ought to know.'

What Tommy's grandparent had to do with Donald's horizons the rest of the crew did not understand but because Tommy was the ganger they let him ramble on. It was when he got to the point where he described the battles around Rome and the Italian collapse during 1943 that Donald interrupted.

'If the Romans had sorted out them Ities then they might of beaten the Germans,' Donald said thus proving the dire need for his educational expansion. 'Anyway we did all right last Saturday bird watching. I'm getting to like having a hobby, although when we do go out like that Terry gets on my wick.'

'Talking about wicks, you got any more of those pictures?'

The crew looked at each other and at Donald expectantly.

'I might have,' he said.

'Have a look and you know...'

Donald knew what the ganger meant and knew also that he would have some contact prints to show them on Friday. He could take orders and have full sized prints ready for sale on Monday as long as they didn't want too many.

'All right, I'll see what I can do.'

The bell went and the crew went back to their work.

At his place of work Mathew Grace checked the numbers coming in against the orders made and dutifully ticked them off. His sheets would be passed on to the data processors to be analysed and checked again. Sometimes goods that were supposed to arrive were held up. Most of the time it was small batches or boxes rather than whole crates. Checking the crates was a pain in the arse. Each one had to be unpacked, checked and the items consigned to their proper departments and sections.

When the trucks came in he and the rest of the team descended on the loads like ants and tore them apart. Each worker had a section of manifest to work with. It was mind boggling boring work but Mathew was content. He had a job and that was enough to stop his old man nagging him.

The warehouse was an archaic set up but if the rumours were true in about six months a new semi-automated monster of a building on the industrial estate was to open. There were no plans for compulsory redundancies but some of the employees had plans to leave on change over, some were to move to another site up north and the rest were to operate the new place. Mathew was one of those chosen to stay. That was a bonus, he got to stay with his mates.

The other bonus, one only possible in a rambling building like this one, was that he had managed to lose his virginity. It took him by surprise.

It took him by surprise because he hadn't expected to be "hit on" by one of the women. At the Christmas party where it happened he was vainly trying to seduce one of the young office girls and getting nowhere when a mature voice close by chuckled and called him by name.

'Mathew Grace what do you think you are doing?'

He tried to explain but the words wouldn't come. If it was one of the blokes he could have said but here was one of the senior checkers, a woman of about forty, shapely and attractive who had somehow moved him to a quiet spot without actually dragging him.

'I'll tell you shall I?' she said.

He gave a grin and remembered her name. Milly Soames, who was in charge down the line. She was smiling and he noted she had a bottle and two glasses in one hand held there as deftly and firmly as any barmaid could manage.

'Go on, what am I doing?'

'You are trying to get into her pants and I tell you what lad, you haven't a bleedin' chance nor a bleedin' clue,' she said and poked him with her free forefinger in the middle of his chest. 'I bet you haven't lost your cherry yet.'

He blushed deeply and tried to answer her.

'I get my share,' he said.

'Bollocks. All you know is Mrs Palmer and her five daughters,' she said.

He looked at her blankly.

'I don't know anybody named Palmer.'

She didn't laugh but simply came closer and lifted his chin with her finger underneath the point and smiled.

'Come on sonny, come with me. we can change all that,' she said, and it was at this point he understood what was about to happen. That it took place in a quiet office for which she had the key, and what was in the bottle was good red wine which they drank arms wrapped around at the elbows, was a new experience for him.

He was amused by her insistence that their clothes be laid out neatly. He was frustrated at first when she told him to slow down.

'Take your time boy, it will happen,' she said.

She guided him expertly whispering that as a married woman she had done this hundreds of times.

'Come on kiss and put your hands where you like, explore and when I am all nice and wet down there shove it in and I will give you a good fucking,' she said.

He did his best but it was she who made the moves. Eventually he got it right and lost himself in the action gasping as she squeezed him until at last he reached a climax. He cried out: 'Fucking arseholes! This is much better than wanking!'

'Doggy fashion you little arsehole!' she cried out and turned over.

With his hands grasping both her breasts feeling her nipples as hard as rocks between his fingers he did it again and this time she managed a climax although he thought she put in much of the effort.

It was good fun being an ex-virgin.

Dressed, with the warning that her husband was due to collect her soon, they sneaked back to the party and separated. He tried again with the office girl but there was no deal. Since then he and Milly had managed to do it twice more but rumours started to buzz and the pleasure had to stop.

What was bothering him now was what his father said at the breakfast table.

'I know that the church has asked for more boys to join the choir, and I am glad of that, but that does not mean you should join. You need to attend church regularly and I think that all you want is to get at the girls,' his father said.

'But dad I like singing and it did say they is looking for more male members.'

He was annoyed when from the breakfast bar Sara sniggered.

'Voices they said. I know what you are after. I forbid you to apply,' Thomas said his face stern with that look of "I am serious" that worried Mathew.

Mathew's sullen look meant that he was about to give in.

'Understand?'

'Yes dad,' Mathew said.

'Right, let that be an end to it.'

And he had to accept his father's ruling. His early life when his father was in the army had taught him to obey. He knew what his father did and it frightened him although he had never been punished with a beating. It was that voice of command that was effective.

He would follow the rules.

That was until the evening when he spoke with the lads. The flutter of texts that buzzed around that day was encouraging and by the time he was on the bus home he was looking forward to a lively meeting. They met in the tea rooms because Stanley was still under age for the pub by two weeks, and as Mathew had said: 'Noses clean and we can get away with anything.'

That afternoon in the tea rooms the seven member Birdwatcher's Club voted unanimously to sign up as members of the St Seraph's choir. The decision flew in the face of their male parents' exhortations but as it was obviously a concerted effort on the part of their parents to discourage them they had no choice but to sign up.

They didn't question the appearance of application forms in their midst smuggled in, so he said, by Stanley White who also supplied the cheap pens with which to inscribe their details above their signatures. He had found a pile of forms at home and sneaked a box of pens from his mother's untidy writing desk and, with them hidden under his coat, sneaked off to the meeting.

Maddy Green watched them filling in the forms and noted which one was charged with delivering them in the marked envelopes. She waited until they were gone and called Jenny White.

'The lads have done the deed. Do you want your pens back?'

Jenny laughed and told her to keep them in case a customer needed one.

The drinkers in the Dog and Duck were surprised when Forest Maloney arrived looking fresh and cheerful. Mutley walked in with him off the lead and settled down at his feet. Forest flashed some notes on the bar and ordered a round of drinks. He called his mates to the bar to collect their drinks and with Mutley in tow joined them at their window table.

'I chucked the doggy doos in the doggy doo waste bin tonight. Salina cooked the meal this evening as Amanda has had one of her turns. Well I say cooked, she took it out of the freezer and heated it in the microwave. Not the best food to eat but nourishing at least. Salina is meeting up with her mates and what with the missus having a grump poor old Mutley needs some company.' Forest grinned and waited for comments.

'You know what you are doing I hope?' Sly said, concerned for Forest, a man he had always tagged as a wimp.

'Sure do. I've spent the last nineteen years nagged narrow by a woman I thought I loved to distraction who also felt the same about me and at last I have turned,' he said and drank deeply.

The men stared at their friend in awe and wondered how long it would be before the lightning bolt of reality would thunder down and hit him. Blokes just didn't do that sort of thing, did they?

That nothing happened immediately encouraged them to ask questions. The first came from Miles.

'What do you mean by turned? You're not coming out gay are you?'

'No, no, nothing like that. I've released my mind from the trammels of subservience. I am enlightened. I no longer believe in the divine right and have taken myself in hand,' Forest said.

'You mean..." said Davey making a rude gesture with his hand.

'Don't be daft. I will no longer be in awe of authority especially will I not be cowed by the church or my wife who thinks she can rule me with an iron glance or a word of command. I am creative in my own right,' Forest said and banged his fist down on the table startling the dog. 'Ouch!'

Nursing his hand he grinned lopsidedly at his friends.

'Now to business.'

'I have it on authority from Smithy that the idiots have filled in their application forms and these will be duly delivered to Evans the Choir this very evening.' Martin said.

'And Evans will take the buggers on when some of the older men volunteer,' Sylvester said rubbing his hands.

'My missus wants me to volunteer but I managed to convince her I couldn't sing unless I was pissed, and that badly,' Swanson said.

'And now we got to keep a look out for the little buggers perving on the girls,' Miles offered, and showed them a list of complainants. 'We can do our own quiet patrol and make a chart of who is perving on who. Just mark down the name and the time and the house number with the initial and we will get a pattern. Let the little sods carry on for the time being and in the meantime I will call on some help finding out what they is doing otherwise. Vernon learned a lot last Saturday.'

'What's he got?'

'He's working on it,' Miles said.

And whilst all the activity was going on, Sara Grace was working on her assignments in her room, cocoa steaming in a mug on the desk beside her. Certain that her brother was out on his evening prowl she tapped into the trace that led to his computer. The idiot never switched it off. She drifted into his files and dug down where he had hidden his secret files and browsed the latest. She giggled when she saw them and downloaded them to her remote drive, deactivated the computer and closed the link. She retrieved the downloaded files and popped them into an encrypted folder, attached them to an email and sent them off.

A few minutes later she was once more working on her assignment and had drunk the cocoa. She worked until the words tumbled over each other and answered the messages on her mobile before wandering downstairs to where her parents were watching the telly.

The front door opened quietly and Mathew grunted greetings as he passed up the stairs to his room.

'Good evening son,' said Thomas to his retreating back.

'Who was that man,' said Sara.

'Sara, don't be so sarcastic,' Melanie said.

'Well he's so aloof. He never comes anywhere with us. He scoffs his dinner with hardly a word and rushes out to meet his mates. We don't see him at all.' She said and gazed up the stairs. 'We used to do things together when we were little.'

The Birdwatchers of Childen Under Blean

'He has his bird watching club and that must be good for him,' Melanie said brightly.

Thomas kept a straight face but Sara burst into a fit of giggles unable to explain to her mother actually what the bird watchers did.

'Why are you laughing Sara. Mathew has a hobby at least,' Melanie said.

It was at that point Sara rushed upstairs to her room shaking with merriment leaving her father to explain. As she dashed to her room she saw her brother's door was ajar and with a smooth movement she pushed it open. He looked up in alarm from his computer and glowered at her.

'What you doing?'

'You're an idiot Mathew,' she said, 'a right bloody dummy; a proper tosser.'

'Eh? What me?'

'Yes you. You should try being normal for once, you might like it and we might like you,' she said.

'Like how?'

'Doing normal things instead of creeping about like a weirdo bird watching, if that's what you are doing. You earn enough to take driving lessons but you can't be bothered. What's wrong with you?'

'Nothing. I'm not interested in driving. I might get a bike. We done bird watching at the reserve with the club and me and my mates is going to join the choir even if the bloke in charge is gay. Anyway, what's it got to do with you?' Mathew said, glad that the screen had gone blank.

She was about to say he had no ambition but with the news he and the boys were joining the choir she was taken aback.

'What all of you?'

'Yeah 'cos they want blokes and we is blokes and you know I like singing.'

'You will do the practice, sing at church and all that?'

'That's what you do when you join a bleedin' choir ennit?'

'Well then good for you,' she said and abruptly turned to go to her room.

'Up yours you snobby bitch,' Mathew said to the empty doorway. He angled himself from his chair quickly zipping his jeans and closed the door. He must remember not to play with himself when his sister was on the prowl.

'I don't see no point in having a car when I can go by bus.' His parents had one each and most of his mates couldn't afford it anyway so why bother when the folks would give him a lift. He shuddered when he thought of Sara and her snobby mates driving around the village to look after their horses.

His sister annoyed him.

She was good at school and now she was doing all right at college. What she was doing there, so she said, would get her into uni where she wanted to study philosophy. What was all that about? Ancient blokes rabbiting on about the meaning of life and so-called modern thinkers asking dumb questions. And what for? Like his mate Terry said, all that was no good once she had some kids and had to look after a family. You can't use philosophy to cook bleedin' sausages.

He'd done all right. Three GCSE passes at G and he got a job almost right away. He wasn't an idiot. He knew what he was doing and he was doing all right.

He reactivated the screen and closed the files and checked his messages. Donny had asked for some pictures and he had passed them on but now he wanted Donny to do some for him.

He texted Donny and waited for the reply and when it came he and Donny chatted until they had made their arrangements. They would meet up Friday night. He took a last look at his latest picture wishing that she was fully naked. However, with the towel wrapped around her legs at least her top half was exposed. That would do, he could imagine the rest.

He went to bed with that image on his mind. She had taken her togs off to change and in the brief few minutes when she had walked from the pool under the shelter he had snapped her.

Friday. A gloomy day threatening rain in the morning that fell a few minutes after eleven thirty when the Coven gathered in the café. Maggie Smith, Angela Tomms and Jenny White were already in their places when Amanda arrived looking as dark as the rain clouds outside. She removed her gloves and her coat hanging the coat on a hook and took her place at the table.

Maddy Green placed the tea things on the table sorting cups and milk from the tray and adding a pot of steaming hot water before asking the question.

'The usual, ladies?'

Maggie looked up after first giving Amanda a glance and said:

The Birdwatchers of Childen Under Blean

'Yes please with apple pie to follow.'

'I will have the tea only,' Amanda said from beneath her dripping hat. 'I cannot eat a thing.'

Maddy Green pursed her lips in mid jotting and the other three looked astonished. On Fridays Amanda always had the toasted sandwiches and the dessert of the day but here was a woman looking depressed and angry and very very tense. It was an explosive situation. Maddy Green was wise enough not to question the order.

'Be along soon,' she said having prepared the toasties earlier.

She gave the group a few minutes to pour the tea, drink some and start chatting before arriving with three plates of toasties on a tray and busied herself laying the table. Amanda Maloney was silently sipping tea, her face grim. She wondered what was the matter. She was too busy with other customers to find out but it was obvious that Amanda Maloney was furious and that was not good for anybody.

'So why the long face Amanda?' Maggie ventured.

'It is that useless husband of mine. He is defying me and no matter what I say or do I cannot get him to behave. That awful dog seems to have taken a liking to him and Salina is no help at all. For the first time in my married existence I am at a loss. The only consolation is that the plan for sorting out the boys seems to be working. Other than that I cannot understand what has happened to Forest. You noticed he was not at church on Sunday and last week he ate at the Dog and Duck taking Salina and the dog with him.

'Didn't he invite you to go with him?'

'I refuse to frequent such a den of iniquity. I do not approve of strong drink,' Amanda declared.

No you may not but you pop into our store for your regular bottle of sherry and gin, thought Maddy, who had overheard the remark. She realised what was wrong. Forest Maloney had finally gotten fed up with being downtrodden. She cleared the table and served the dessert. She was surprised when she heard Amanda Maloney insist on paying her quarter share and for the last few minutes of the witches meet dominate proceedings.

Maddy offered to loan Amanda an umbrella but the woman stopped briefly midway donning her coat and said with her old disdainful tone.

'I am quite capable of walking home in the rain without one.'

Maddy watched her striding angrily away from the green with her friends; they with brollies raised and her simply allowing her large hat to cope with the downpour.

She ate the toastie prepared for Amanda.

She had closed the tea rooms before the bird watchers arrived but served them with their cans of drinks and let them sit under the awning. They huddled close to the wall looking pathetic so she relented and opened the tea room.

'You can stay in there for a while but we are closed really so make the best of it now,' she said.

The boys seemed grateful. Mathew thanked her and soon they were in a huddle discussing their affairs. If she had known what they were talking about she would have had no hesitation but to throw them out. The plan they made was simple once they had realised what they could do with it.

'And if we do some digging and watching we might find some more. I'm sure that some of the other so-called upright citizens are doing the dirty,' Mathew said, and grinned broadly. 'The gay bloke dresses up in women's clothing when he's at home. I got a picture of him. Maybe the church or his rugby club wouldn't want to have nothin' to do with him if they knew. We should nose around and see whats goin' on but do it sort of quiet like and take your time. If people finds out before we are ready we could be in the shit.'

'Men and women?'

'Yeah - they all got secrets.'

Sworn to secrecy the boys of the bird watcher's club agreed to begin the big task that very weekend and split up feeling happier, if a little damp. When he got home Mathew found his sister being quizzed on the Highway Code by his mother.

'Hello mum, hello Sara, alright are you?' And instead of burying himself in his room for the evening he went upstairs, showered, changed into clean clothes and although he didn't help with the dinner he ate with the family and didn't complain when they had to wait for his father to arrive. They were even more surprised when he sat with them and watched the television in the lounge and didn't complain when they chose the programmes.

Later in her room before she flopped into bed Sara texted Salina. Her message explained that Mathew was acting strange.

<Wht u mean >

<Normal nt weird weird >

<OMG>
She sent more information eventually signing off to go to sleep. Her brother's behaviour needed watching. He was up to something, she was sure of it.

That Friday afternoon Evans the Choir returned from town and stopped at Green's to buy his groceries. In town during lunch, he had purchased some new books, collected a new suit and a pair of shoes. He waltzed into the store and placed his selections in a trolley. He bought a bottle of gin and a half dozen bottles of Rosé, paid for it and waltzed out to load it into his car. He drove off slowly passing Sara in her mother's car going for a practice drive with her nervous parent.

Evans noted that the most anxious of the pair was the mother.

He gave them a little toot on his horn and soon he was home putting the things away amused by the little pile of mail collected from his doormat.

He opened the envelopes with an ornate paper knife putting the applications for the choir to one side and the bills and other letters on another. The bills and letters he dealt with first and afterwards he made a list of applicants for the choir checking names against the list the vicar had given him. What surprised him was that Graham Cook was on the bird watcher's list. He would accept them all of course but he was glad that Graham was keen; the boy had a good voice. It was disturbing that he had joined the bird watcher's club and made a mental note to talk to him adding an asterisk against his name as a reminder.

He hoped the plan would work.

He needed more voices for his choir but he cared little for the aims of the vicar and the committee. Their holier than thou attitude made him sick and he questioned their motives. Boys will be what they are and the girls, in his experience, would do what they could to encourage them. Sex was the driving force and all creatures on this world and the many millions of other worlds in this universe practiced some version of it. It was only natural. Putting a God in the way of one's desires made sex a sinful act unless of course it was condoned for procreation. Therein lies the rub. People like sex for the sensual pleasure it gives and that is only natural.

He giggled.

The sexual stimulation he liked was considered by the church most unnatural. And yet he was more honest than some in the church whose predilection was for fondling young boys genitals, or even worse, all in the name of the God they professed to worship. Some, like him were gay, and therefore closet deviants according to their peers. Others were followers of Genesis chapter 1 v 28 with the intention to go forth and multiply, if a little more enthusiastic than their marital state would allow.

Rumour had it that the reverend Jones was one such man.

'Disgusting, and him with a wife and two children,' he said, and busied himself with the task of pouring a large pink gin. He sipped at it and having finished the task he relaxed in an armchair. He patted his belly and realised he had put on some weight. It was time to start training, and steadily downing the gin he rose from his seat and went to find his track suit and trainers. Ten minutes later with his keys wrapped in a small purse with some change in his pocket he left the house and began a gentle regime of warm up before beginning the jogging and walking he adopted for the pre-season runs. One of the letters had informed him that training was due to start and was he interested? After this run he would call the secretary and if he felt fine then he would put his name down. He was a good player, an occasional try scorer and had made many a move across the line with timely passes. Everybody agreed that he was good in the rucks and mauls; it was only a pity he was not powerful enough for the scrum.

Still, one can only thank the God he didn't believe in for small mercies.

On his run he noted the vicar on his rounds, smiled as he saw the walkers trooping back to their cars and the cyclists getting ready outside the cafe to ride off into the sunset. He returned home as dusk was beginning to banish the sunshine feeling weary but happy that he could still run.

It was with great pleasure he called the Rugby Club secretary and confirmed that he would be "absolutely delighted to take part" and hoped he would be selected.

'Come to training and we will find out,' the secretary said.

He noted that training was on Tuesdays and Thursdays which would fit in nicely with Choir practice. A dress in public on Monday and Wednesday and on Tuesdays and Thursdays gripped enthusiastically by other blokes.

Evans the Choir was a happy man.

For the drinkers, Friday night in the Dog and Duck was a chance to wind down after a week of work. It was also a sports night in the main bar and fish supper night in the restaurant. This Friday night the pub was alive with avid sports fans and the fish and chips were flying on to plates to be devoured by hungry mouths. Horace and Molly and the rest of the staff were busy. The early shift was over and those who had brought the kids were already home watching the telly. It was now the domain of the younger people and the older set.

The drinkers had brought their families for the meal, and although he had invited Amanda to partake, Forest turned up with his daughter and Mutley the dog. Mutley revelled in his surroundings and guzzled stray chips and bits of batter and fish as they descended like manna from heaven to his haven under the table. Above him under cover of the noisy feasting Salina questioned her father.

'This worm thing. Are you serious?'

'Couldn't be more determined my dear.'

'Mum's really upset.'

'I know, but she will get used to it.'

'Do you love me?'

'Most of the time but when you are like your mother I have my doubts. I don't like that bit of you but I still love you.'

'Do you love mum?'

'Sometimes, especially because she is your mother. Sometimes when she remembers to be a person, but really I should say right now I don't. I don't hate her. I just dislike what she has become.' He said and looked at her intently. 'Can you understand that?'

'It's not easy.'

'Question is, do you love her?'

'I suppose I do but she is difficult.'

'You can be difficult too.'

She smiled and looked at him directly.

'We've not done this before have we. Talked like this, you know, honest.'

'That's because I have barely spoken to you since you were small. I missed that and now before it is too late I had better start over again,' he said. He decided at that moment that his daughter was the friend he needed and relaxed.

'But this worm thing. Am I right in saying that you have decided to rebel. Are you doing it in your stuffy office too?'

'Yes, in a small way I am. The worm is weak and small and when it turns, so to speak, its effect is slow and steady. The immediate changes are close by and easy to see but from then on the worm has to get stronger before it can take proper control. I am learning that,' he said.

'Revolution starts at home?'

'It sure does and regime change is on its way my dear.'

'And if mum fights back?'

'No if about it. She will fight back but she will lose and if she does things right she will find she will like what happens next. For a start I will no longer attend church unless I want to. Yes I will contribute to the Friends and help out but I will no longer be your mother's dogsbody. I am revolting!'

She grinned.

'No father, rebelling, you are quite nice really,' she said.

'Thank you, I appreciate the compliment.'

'And Dad, I love you too,' she said.

And on the way home with Mutley bouncing around them he held her hand. When they arrived Amanda was in her work room and declined to come down. He took a mug of cocoa up to her and placed it on the desk beside her. She thanked him in a flat voice and quietly he told her of the evening.

'Salina and I had a nice chat. Have you eaten?'

'I had a sandwich.'

'Good,' he said, and when there was nothing more to say he went downstairs to watch the telly with his daughter. He was in bed and snoring when Amanda came to bed. She didn't disturb him, for long ago they had decided on separate beds. She stood beside her bed dressed in her nightshirt and listened to her husband's gentle nasal refrain.

The shock change in his demeanour and very manner had upset her and now that it seemed Salina had joined the dog in the general revolt she was unsure of herself. She gazed down at the shadowy form in the bed and whispered quietly.

'You won't get away with this.'

The rustling of her garments and the bedclothes as she climbed in between the sheets hid her husband's quiet reply.

'I bloody well will,' he muttered.

In his bed in the utility room Mutley fidgeted in the old blankets and towelling that made him feel so comfortable. With a doggy sigh that still held memories of potato chips and bits of battered fish gently nipped from lowered fingers he farted. Startled by the sharp sound and the sudden revolting smell that attacked his nostrils he got up and padded around the room looking for the author.

Translated into English his remark would have sounded like this: 'Jesus H Christ! Who the bloody hell did that?'

The event bothered him until he realised that it must have been him and he relaxed although he had a niggling feeling that there was another creature sharing his personal space. It took sometime for the air to clear of the delicious smell but eventually he settled back down into his bed, wriggled it into a comfortable mess and re-started his doggy dreams. He fell asleep before the next fart and dreamed of being gassed but thought of fingers offering chips and fish and managed to enjoy the experience without moving.

In the morning he had a vague feeling he wasn't alone in the room. He was wrong. Dogs have no concept of the intrusion of metaphorical elephants.

Which is not to say that in effect he might be right.

Colin Lawrence sat on the edge of the hotel bed and picked up the phone. Reception answered and he asked for an outside line.

'Charge or cash?'

'Charge please,' he said and moments later he dialled the number. He waited for the connection and gripped the instrument tightly as the rings buzzed in his ear. When she answered he was almost too startled to speak.

'Sally? Is that really you?'

There was a silence and then a gasp.

'Colin?'

'Yes, me, I'm in town.'

'What are you doing there?'

'Finding out how to get to your place.'

'Childen Under Blean, it's signposted off the main road heading west. Where are you staying?'

'Premier.'

'Easy, you're on the right road.'

'I'll see you tonight?'

'Please do. I will be waiting,' she said.

Colin put the phone down and began to pack his bags. Colin always travelled light; it was a habit that ensured his survival. Be ready to move out quickly, to take on a new contract, but that was all behind him now. He packed and called reception to ask for the bill and, with his bags over his shoulder, he headed down to the lobby. Three quarters of an hour later he was approaching Childen Under Blean with the sat-nav telling him the turns until at last he was stopped in her drive. Sally opened the door for him and carrying his bags he followed her inside the house.

Saturday began with the rain clearing and the regular sight of Forest and Mutley out on their morning walk. Vernon and Maddy opened up the shop and the tea rooms in readiness for the expected invasion of cyclists and walkers. The staff in the Dog and Duck were also getting ready for those who preferred a drink or two with their lunch and a flush of customers planning to watch the pre-season matches on the large screen in the sports bar. Breakfasts were cooked and eaten. The Childen Eleven crowded into Vernon's minibus late in the morning to be driven off to their match in town.

The bird watcher's club staggered out of their beds, grunted greetings to their respective families, ate breakfast and one by one wandered out to meet the day.

Until they had their first coke or red bull they were not exactly impressed with it. There was nothing much to do except "hang about" and so they were forced to indulge in their hobby. The quarry was a good site and it was there they headed, binoculars and cameras at the ready.

'We might suss out our areas,' Mathew said. 'You can see most of the village from up there. I got some good pictures so far this Summer.'

'Yeah, I got some good ones too,' said Terry looking eager.

'I took some good pictures of birds up there,' said one of the new lads.

Mathew laughed.

'Gotta have some genuine dicky birds on your list. What sorts?'

'Sparrows, thrushes, a pair of gold finches and there was a lot of blue tits. I even saw a Kestrel but I didn't get a good picture. Maybe we could see one today,' the lad said brightly.

'You get blue tits in the winter,' observed Donny.

His remark cheered them all up and a half hour of clambering

The Birdwatchers of Childen Under Blean

and climbing having reached the quarry saw them sitting in the warming sun on the rocks overlooking Childen Under Blean.

Mathew had a school exercise book and a crude map of the village with their normal spying spots marked out. The hides they called them, sniggering whenever they were mentioned. In effect this was the nearest the group came to planning a campaign and, although Mathew had to repeatedly spell out instruction to Terry and one of the new lads, the group seemed to grasp the idea. By twelve noon they had exhausted the subject leaving them the long afternoon to fill. Going home was out in case they were expected to do something useful and sitting on the tea rooms with sweaty cyclists and walkers had no appeal. If they mooched around the village people ganged up on them to move them on.

'Let's go for a walk,' suggested Mathew.

Sitting in the sun looking out over the scene below and seeing boredom looming the group could find no alternative. The trip out with Vernon had shown them that bird watching could actually be interesting and when the lad who had spoken up earlier suggested they might enjoy it, they agreed.

'I got my pocket bird book,' the boy said waving the tattered copy for them all to see. 'And I know about butterflies too.'

Bloody weirdo, thought Mathew, the fuckin' kid actually takes it seriously. And to confirm his enthusiasm the kid looked eagerly at them.

'We might even see some red kites or even a woodpecker,' he said.

Mathew felt sick when the rest of the boys agreed that the walk was a good idea. It was the new kid that led the way and as the afternoon wore on so Mathew realised the boy was serious about bird watching. The idiot made them walk quietly and look for birds pointing out species they had never heard of and quickly identifying bird calls. As far as Mathew was concerned the birds flying high and hovering could have been anything but this kid pointed out four Kestrels, a pair of Buzzards some Red Kites and many smaller birds they had all previously described as sparrows. At a welcome break the group sat on the old straw bales in an open barn and Mathew glared at the new kid.

'What's your name?'

'Graham Cook.'

'Well Graham fucking Cook why are you so geeky? What's with all this knowing what bird is what, eh? You some kind of weirdo?'

'I like watching birds. That's what the club is all about isn't it?'

The rest of the boys looked at Graham with their mouths open in surprise, or shock, it was difficult to tell. He looked from one to the other grinning broadly.

'Right, that's what we do isn't it?'

'Somebody tell him,' Mathew said.

Stanley took Graham aside and explained quietly whilst some of the others took a chance to have a smoke. More by accident than any attempt to take care the smokers indulged their habit away from the building; a reaction to being shoved out of their houses to smoke and the no-smoking laws they had to obey.

It was fortunate they did so because with general laziness none of them stood on their butts to put them out. It was the wet ground and the sudden afternoon shower that put out the would be straw fire.

Stanley stood facing the gang looking puzzled.

'I dunno which world he lives on but he seems to be happy. He ain't normal. I asked why he wanted to join the choir,' Stanley said and prodded Graham with his finger. 'Tell 'em.'

'Quite simple really, I like singing,' he said.

'I told him we only joined up to have a go at the girls. I explained that to him clear, like but like, he didn't sort of get it. Tell 'em.'

'I signed the pledge,' Graham said. 'My mother and father said I should.'

'Why'd he do a thing like that?' Mathew asked ignoring Graham as if he was a non-person.'

'We are Christians,' Graham said. 'My mum and Dad, my brother and sister and I all go to church on Sunday.'

'And you joined up with us. You're a right tosser.' Mathew said shrugging his shoulders.

'Well you seemed like such a nice bunch and when we went out with mister Green you were all very friendly. I had only joined that week and it was fun,' Graham said looking concerned. 'It's all right isn't it, me being part of the club. I can get other people to join.'

'Not fucking little prats like you,' sneered Terry.

'Maybe some of the girls might like to join,' Graham said brightly.

That statement hit the bird watchers with such enlightened force that it stunned them and again they stared at Graham open mouthed.

'That's all right isn't it?'

'Bollocks, why didn't we think of that?' said Donny.

None of them except Graham had an answer to Donny's question. Graham answering the question silently for himself refrained from telling them. It had a lot to do with them being extremely stupid. Sadly, he thought, it appears that I will have to follow my hobby alone unless I can get some friends to come with me.

He walked back to the quarry with them less enthusiastic about their bird watching enterprise and declined to join them when they clambered on the high points.

'Come on I'll show you what sort of birds we is after,' said Stanley and winked at the others.

Graham by now had some idea of what they were on about and with a pleasant smile; the one he used for idiots when he didn't want to obviously be seen patronising them, he said: 'I think that I would prefer at this moment in time to continue on home and decline your offer of company however compatible.'

'What?' Asked Stanley looking extremely puzzled. He hadn't understood a word.

'I will go home now if you please,' Graham said, and anticipating Stanley's anger tucked his bag tight on his back and in one smooth movement turned and disappeared quickly along the narrow pathway at a run.

'Come back you little fuckwit!' Stanley yelled and gave chase but gave up gasping and coughing after no more than fifty metres. Red-faced, catching his breath and feeling dizzy he stopped until the moment had passed and eventually returned to join the others.

'The fucking weirdo has run off,' he said.

The others were already searching for vantage spots and began to scan the village with their binoculars. They searched for some time but it seemed as if the only people who were out in the open were dressed. For a time the activity in the village held their wandering attention but there was nothing interesting to see.

'Nothing, we can't see nothing,' Mathew said.

They missed the sight of Old Man Scroggins and his lads sorting out and preparing game birds for sale in his back yard. They may have identified pheasant and wood-pigeon if they had bothered to look. In his own way you could say that Old Man Scroggins was a keen Ornithologist.

Some few doors down from the Scroggins house Graham Cook was making plans. He had seen many birds from the flock of sparrows to the little gathering of ring collared doves close to his own home and the starlings beginning their murmuration. It was at the point when he heard the lads mention girl's names he realised what Stanley was trying to say and blushed deep red.

The club was a cover for perverts.

And that was something he definitely did not want to be associated with. He decided nothing would be gained by telling anyone what he had discovered and before tea he managed to enter the observations and times in his bird diary. There was no time to add them to his files so with his face and hands scrubbed clean he presented himself for the meal.

If the rest of the Bird Watchers had seen him bowing his head at table whilst his mother said grace they would have laughed. As it was they wrote him off as a little geek and forgot about him.

Old Man Scroggins, who liked Graham, would have approved of his prayerful actions because he and his wife had seen the light and ran the Scroggins Clan on the premise that others of the family would follow suit. He was wrong but many of them respected his conversion and as a result their activities, whilst not actually ceasing, were curtailed and confined to outside the village. That they supplied the villagers through the Green's store with game and clean conies, herbs and jams as well as a source good kindling and firewood at reasonable prices was a bonus. Christmas fare was added in the form of pre-ordered turkeys and geese, and genuine Christmas trees.

Old man Scroggins was rich but so too was the clan and the reverend Jones was happy to have him as part of the congregation even if his language was over colourful.

Old Man Scroggins was pleased when he learned later that evening the Childen Eleven had won their match raising them within a few points of winning the championship. Some of the lads were in training and Young Scroggins was one with promise.

The brawl after the Stoat Malbury game was an eye opener. His clan, normally willing to join in, had hurried away leaving it to the rest of the locals. It was a mixture of avoiding the police and his own exhortation to use non violent methods to maintain the peace.

The Birdwatchers of Childen Under Blean

'Keep yer fucking' noses clean around here and we will do all right,' he said.

Graham Cook was aware that he too needed to do something similar and although a Christian he was not sanctimonious. He and his parents attended the church but did not take part in the enthusiasm of the charismatic holy rollers the vicar allowed to yell and holler as they worshipped. In that he was much like Old man Scroggins who didn't approve of all that nonsense.

Sunday morning and Forest and Mutley walked as usual, the latter dodging around sniffing and piddling encouraging master to mark his territory in like fashion by looking up at him pleadingly with each spray. Tired of getting no response the dog carried on anyway and dropped a steaming dollop of poo underneath the dog bin. Master picked it up and placed it inside and the walk could continue. Mutley was beginning to enjoy his outings and found that by following a routine of staying close to master, running when he was allowed to and the new game of chasing the ball, as long as he shat in the right place, he got his treats. And back in the den nobody shouted at him anymore.

Forest took Mutley for a longer walk on Saturdays and Sundays and although Mutley was on the lead where farm animals were grazing the dog was otherwise free to run. Forest himself was free all day having declared that morning he was no longer interested in any more God Walloping.

'But we are on the church committee,' Amanda said.

'I will remind you that it is you who are on the committee and I who is generally expected to follow orders. You are quite welcome to carry on but do not expect me to waste any more time in the face of overwhelming evidence against the existence of a divine presence. I do not wish to waste any more breath speaking words that have no meaning when I could be better occupied walking the dog. If such practice gives you comfort then please do so but do not expect me to follow suit. I will willingly help out at seasonal functions and may keep membership of the Friends of St Seraph's.' He spoke quietly and intently as if the explanation was a once only event, gazing at her shocked face feeling sorry for her.

Eventually she answered and it was obvious she was gathering her considerable personal forces to counteract his rebellion. But he was not to be so cowed and casually buttered toast, spread it with marmalade and chewed contentedly.

'So, this is it is it? You won't do as you are told. You won't go to church but you will condescend to help out. You let the dog run amok in the house and the garden; you take our daughter to that den of iniquity to indulge in the demon drink and you expect me to put up with it?'

'You could try loosening up and becoming a human being for a change. Be nice to people instead of wanting to dominate them. I'm sorry my dear if you are upset but...,' and here he paused briefly and smiled, 'quite frankly I don't give a damn.'[1]

He gave full marks for her white faced recovery liking the effort she put in and agreed in part with what she said next.

'And how am I supposed to live now? My husband's gone mad, my daughter no longer obeys me and even the dog ignores me. I suppose you expect me to be a dutiful mousy housewife content to work my fingers to the bone as a servant. Well, I will not do that. I ran this household extremely well until you suddenly rebelled against me. You expect me to come to terms with that?'

'Yep.'

She glowered at him and he noted that Salina sat quietly at the table eating her breakfast listening but saying nothing.

'You will come to terms with it. We will do our normal chores to help out. I will look after the dog as usual and from now on the garden will be my domain. I will grow the things I like and do what I always wanted to do and that is to go to work, pay the bills as we do and in my spare time work in the garden and go to the pub. I suggest you find a part time job and put some money aside for yourself in case you get fed up with me and want to leave.'

Salina dropped her spoon with a clatter and gasped.

Forest raised his hand and shushed Amanda.

'It may not come to that if you behave yourself. I am quite happy to live with you if you are willing to be nicer to me and other people. In other words practice some of the Christian love you profess to enjoy.'

Amanda had no answer to that, or at least she couldn't think of a suitable sensible retort and wisely kept her own counsel. When Forest was gone having loaded the dishwasher before he and Mutley went out she began to get ready for church.

Salina wasn't ready when it was time to go. In fact she was packing her gear to attach it to her bicycle in preparation for

---

1   *Forest was a fan of classic movies.*

riding.

'Not coming to church?'

'No mother, I am riding instead.'

'But you saw to your horse this morning?'

'I know but he needs an outing. I am going with a couple of the girls in the woodlands. Church can do without me today,' she said.

'I forbid you to do this.'

'No mother, I am old enough to make up my own mind and I agree with dad. I too have studied the worms.' She said and smiled gently. 'Give it a go mum. I still love you.'

And with that she left her mother standing in the kitchen as she went out of the back door to collect her bike and ride off.

Amanda Maloney collected her bag with its notices, bible and the usual things a woman carries with her, put her hat on and, taking her brolly, set off for church. She was seething inside, her mind a turmoil of emotions trying to sort out recent domestic events. Above all the emotion that grew in strength as she marched purposely up the hill to St Seraph's was anger.

Woe betide any who crossed her today.

Church followed its usual pattern. The alleluias punctuated the sermon and in between the singing cries of "Praise the Lord", "Save me Jesus" and some babbling from those who thought it was time for speaking in tongues peppered the once sedate and conventional Church of England establishment.

Evans the Choir was pleased with the crying out. His part in the worship was the music and, with Barry waxing lyrical on the organ the whole sounded like a mix of operetta and a concerto. It was always a brave performance.

'That organ is like me, Coren, falling apart. Its flatulence is almost as voluble as my own. I am afraid it is not long for this world.'

'But you manage to coax good music from it,' Coren replied. He marvelled at Barry's ability and smiled in return to the old man's wry smile.

'The singing makes up for the lack,' Barry said.

All they needed now was to bring in the new applicants and his choir could be one of the best in the region. Thanks to the local musicians who could fill in for the inadequacies of the organ, he would not be short of music. He imagined a line up of drums, tambourines and guitars and maybe a banjo and a couple of fiddles with maybe a touch of brass. Jazz the whole thing up. The organ was an ancient wheezing instrument that will soon need a lot of money spent on it and Barry himself had suggested they go electronic keyboard.

Bonny Mason, the stand-in organist, agreed with him.

For now the pair were content to use what they had.

He took a look around the church at the worshippers during prayers. The older people knelt against the back of the pew in front on the hassock or simply sat with hands together in the traditional pious pose. The rest of the congregation were making their own expressions felt. Some stood up and swayed to and fro arms high in the air, faces glowing with enthusiasm up to the dusty heavens, represented by the dirty church ceiling. Others prostrated themselves in the aisles; more knelt on the floor out back emulating Martin Luther, and others rocked to and fro in an ecstasy of emotion. The babbling and the calling began again and at a signal from him the choir began to sing softly with the organ wheezing along quietly, and out of tune underneath them.

It was time for the penitents to make their way to the front where the first two rows of pews were long ago removed creating what Evans the Choir called "the hard shoulder". A steady stream of parishioners migrated to the front and stood crying and hollering their readiness to "come to the Lord".

The Vicar descended from the pulpit and with his cross of office in his hand he touched each one in turn. Behind them men and women waited in anticipation. With one touch and a blessing the penitent crumpled gracefully to the floor or fell backwards into the arms of the catchers to be lowered gently to rest in the arms of Jesus.

The one exception to this gravitational attraction was Amanda Maloney whose thunderous glare seemed to melt the power of the vicar's cross and with her feet planted firmly she refused to fall down.

Wisely the reverend Jones blessed her and moved on but stopped in his tracks when Amanda spoke sharply.

'Are my alleluia's not good enough for Jesus this Holy Day?' She demanded.

The Vicar turned back to her and smiled benevolently.

'Sister Amanda, the Lord treasures all such praise and for this

The Birdwatchers of Childen Under Blean

Holy Day must needs find you penitent enough,' he said.

'Bullshit, he's turned against me just like everyone else,' she said omitting the capital letter, and turning on her heel she stalked, straight backed and stiff necked out of the church. All eyes followed her progress but nobody was brave enough to call her back.

One older parishioner turned to another and asked: 'Did she really say "bullshit"?

'I believe so.'

'Well I never did,' came the reply.

Evans the Choir raised his hand and urged the choir to sing a little louder and with that the last of the fallers lay supine on the carpeted floor experiencing their little slice of Heaven. The service rolled on to its inevitable conclusion including at the end the refreshments and biscuits served by the young people. Those of the children's ministry, relieved at returning their charges to their parents, took a few moments to unwind in the chapel.

In the vestry Evans the Choir thanked the singers and collected their vestments stacking them in the laundry basket.

'Before you all go I have to tell you that we have eleven candidates for the choir that I know and five I do not. We will call on them to come to practice during the next two weeks and see where they will fit in. After that we will reform the choir. I am pleased to say we do have some of the young men and boys applying. Let us hope they will stay with us,' he said and was pleased when he saw the amusement on some of the faces.

He smiled too but not because of the candidates but that he was anticipating the lunch he had ordered at the Dog and Duck. Horace had said that he would put him with Forest Maloney.

'If you don't mind his smelly dog?'

'Smelly dog is fine and Forest is an intelligent man. I will be happy with that.'

This would be his first roast of the season and he looked forward to that.

He walked from the church enjoying the early afternoon which was cool but pleasant. Ideal walking weather and as he expected the pub was full but Horace showed him to a small table where Forest was sitting with a pint. Flopped out under the table as if he was a regular was Mutley. As if by magic a large pink gin arrived and was set down at his place as he took his seat.

'I took the trouble to order your favourite tipple Coren.

Welcome to my table, or should I say your table?'

'Ours actually Forest. How are you?'

'Fine, fine, sorted a few things out and not missing church. I had a good long walk with Mutley and the poor creature is knackered. Amanda refuses to cook a dinner on Sundays and my daughter is off riding her horse with friends. I had an idea you were likely to want a meal and suggested to Horace he save a table for two. Salina will eat lunch at her stables, she made sandwiches, so here we are. Everything going all right?'

The meal was a carvery and with their tickets in hand the two men collected their portions and carried them back to the table. Forest had begged some meat for the dog and as they ate he fed tidbits to the animal under the table.

Coren told Forest about the choir and then with a grin he related the story of Amanda's dramatic exit.

'And she said bullshit to the vicar?'

'Yes, clear enough for even the deaf to hear.'

'Now that's a turn up for the books.'

'I thought so but tell me why.'

Forest told him and Coren became extremely thoughtful although like Forest he did not neglect his food.

'So what happens now?'

'She sorts herself out and either becomes the wife I once knew or we part; or alternatively we strike up a new relationship with each other and cope with it. Or not. I care little. But you say she looked determined?'

'Definitely and quite regal if I might say so.'

'Good, dessert?'

'In a moment or two.'

'Are you religious Coren or do you just like the music?'

'Its the music really. The lyrics are silly in the new songs, easy to sing but in the old hymns there's a sense of doom. There's an awareness of nature in some and the desire to tell a story that the writer believes in. Today's hymns are pop songs for the people to sing without thinking. I mean, you have to learn to sing hymns like How Great Thou Art and when you have done so it sounds glorious. No, I'm not religious.' Coren said.

Forest ordered two portions of fruit and ice cream for them and two more drinks.

'Like dressing up in the cassock do you?'

Coren grinned.

'I'd prefer a dress.'

Forest laughed and shook his head.

'I like the ones that are supposed to be inside them,' he said. 'But I like you anyway so I can assure you I am not religious either. The whole thing is silly. A waste of time except at Christmas when you get to sing some nice easy songs with great tunes, and get pissed without anybody moaning at you. I shall get pissed at Christmas this year. Do you approve of that?'

'My friend, I approve most heartedly, and for your company let me treat you to the meal.'

Forest looked at him smiling and shook his head.

'Ah now that's where you have me. I have already arranged to pay for the meal including the drinks but I will allow you to buy me a pint in the bar before we go home.'

And later as the afternoon drifted to a close the new found friends sat in the bar and chatted happily. Their conservation was entirely private and personal and as the pub doors closed behind them ending the afternoon's entertainment they walked home together. Evans the Choir to relax as he usually did dressed in women's clothing whilst watching the telly and Forest to enter his house and settle Mutley alongside him. He felt better after talking to Evans.

Amanda was in the kitchen making tea and with pursed lips and in silence handed him a cup and immediately disappeared to her work room. He drank the tea and spent the afternoon and early evening pottering in the garden with Mutley following him around.

Salina came out to find him and stood looking embarrassed.

'Mother is furious but I don't know why.'

'I think she is having a crisis with the church,' he said.

'Oh dear, I had better go and talk to her.'

'Yes please. Tell her about the worms,' he said.

'A good idea,' she said and wandered off. Mutley watched her go and padded a distance along the path and sat staring at the back door. Something was about to happen and maybe it had something to do with him. He sat for a while gazing at the door and slowly forgot why. With no reason to sit Mutley returned to where master was preparing to bury his bones and with the enthusiasm of renewed purpose he decided to help master and began to dig a hole in a flower bed.

Forest let him get on with it. He wanted to change the layout anyway. Man and dog were happy gardening; one digging with no real purpose; the other under the illusion that what he was doing was useful.

Which one was which is indeterminate.

On Sunday evening the drinkers convened to talk about the match. All but Thomas Grace were looking and feeling seedy. They had won their match fair and square with a margin of seven runs and two wickets having bowled the opposing side out within the forty overs allowed before they reached the target of 128 to win. It was a useful victory but they made the mistake of celebrating too much afterwards.

'I reckon we ought to forget about Vernon and his minibus,' said Sly, as a sufferer.

'We could try not drinking so much beer,' said Thomas as the opening batsman and Captain.

'That's all right for you being a tee - bloody - totaler and a Holy Roller. We was just being friendly. At least we didn't start a fight,' said Sly, trying to hit a six.

'Right, it's a home game on Saturday and I think we need to do some work in the nets before the game. If its fine on Thursday we will have a couple of hours. We have the return match with Stoat Malbury away next month and this time we will not nobble the players or get nobbled ourselves. Is that understood?'

The little group nodded.

'Pass that on to the others,' Thomas said wishing they could meet in the quiet atmosphere of the church. The problem with that was on Sunday evenings most of the cricket team would rather meet in the Dog and Duck. This evening apart from himself, Martin, Sly, Swanson and Miles and three others whose heads could manage the excesses of the demon drink only half the team had turned up.

'We pick the team on Thursday; that will get the rest on side,' said Miles.

'I agree on that and let people know they will have to come up to standard,' Thomas said. His business done Thomas left the others to their drinking and went home.

The boys of the bird watcher's club were too tired to sneak around the village that evening, except that was for Donald who had seen the Vicar slip into the back garden of his neighbour the Widow Mason. It was a matter of him hurriedly slipping out onto his father's garden shed which was shaded by a tree and under its boughs he aimed his binoculars and his camera on the Widow Mason's bedroom window. The house was just a few metres below his and from the shed he could look down into the room from the top of the window.

He grinned.

The hilly nature of Childen Under Blean was one of the reasons why the club was formed. He and his mates could perve on the girls from all sorts of angles and especially in many places down into the windows. He saw lights go on, small wall lamps giving the room a nice glow even with the fading light of sunset. He set up the small telescope and clipped the camera on watching the display on the small screen.

'Ace, they're at it!'

Using the remote button he clicked away as the Vicar and Widow Mason stripped naked and was amused when the vicar himself, bollock naked, closed the curtains. That finished his picture taking but he had enough to stitch the holy roller up.

'Good man Mathew,' he said and packed up his gear and sneaked back into his room. In the house below his mother and his brother were getting on with the Sunday telly totally unaware of his exit and re-entry. He downloaded the pictures and printed a selection out. He put them in a separate envelope marking them M G and slid them into his box file. The ones for the lads at work were already packed in his bag. He would pack his lunch as usual in the morning and add change if the lads wanted any spares.

Before he went to bed he sent the photos of the vicar and widow Mason to Mathew.

The drift into August wandered by with nothing much happening as far as the Birdwatchers were concerned. School was out for the Summer and colleges having already finished the girls were free to get on with their horse riding, tennis and cycling. The boys played cricket on the primary school grounds and there was the general activity of young people in the village. St Seraph's opened its precincts out for Summer activities using local women as volunteers and the vicar and his wife overseeing events. Vernon Green's bus was hired for a series of outings to places of interest and the choir was now up and singing.

Mathew and his friends arrived expecting to meet at close

hand the girls of the village. They were there of course but so also were some of their parents. If that was a shock the announcement that male singers including the young boys, and female singers were to sing from opposite sides of the choir was devastating for Mathew and his mates. However, the fact that there were some potentially friendly girls just joined up was a definite attraction.

The announcement at the first session when the whole choir was assembled that choir members would get discounts on trips and holidays, and that some of the trips were, as Mathew put it, "bloody worth it", convinced them to stay.

The drawback as far as the boys was concerned apart from the enforced division was the holy rollers acting like a bunch of frantic fanatics.

The shock news within the church community was that Amanda Maloney had taken a part time job in town and although for the time being she continued her duties as a Church Warden she declared that she would resign.

'Let some other dumb cluck take over,' she said and would not be persuaded otherwise.

When asked by Thomas Grace why she was so set on leaving the post she looked at him steadily and gave him a blunt reply.

'I no longer wish to be part of this church community. I want to belong to a church that worships a God I understand,' she said. 'I would rather go to chapel.'

Thomas gasped and shook his head but before he could reply she spoke again.

'Failing that I would rather not belong to any church. It has a lot to do with turning over worms according to my cranky husband,' she said and left him standing to gaze after her puzzled by her observation.

What has gardening got to do with her attitude, he thought.

That second Sunday of August was a success. The church was filled with worshippers. The choir more or less sang together. Vernon Green and his wife were busy. Sara Grace was earning a wage in the tea-rooms waiting on tables and the Dog and Duck was doing a roaring trade.

The day before was a good one too as the Childen Eleven had played a lively match in which Thomas Grace had scored a 100 with an amazing flurry of fours and sixes. The celebration afterwards was more or less orderly.

When Sally Wise entered the Dog and Duck on the arm of a

stranger all eyes turned to watch. Sylvester Simon followed her progress across the bar room to the bar where her escort bought them both drinks and spoke with the barman who gave them menus.

'Who's that?' Sly said.

'Sally Wise,' Miles replied.

'No, not her, the bloke with her.'

'I have no idea. He's not local is he?'

'No and that's what I don't like,' Sly said glaring at them over the top of his pint.

'Nothing to do with you what she does or who she goes with; you being a married man and all that,' said Miles stepping back a little.

'But...,' Sly began and sighed. 'You're right, nothing to do with me what she does.'

Miles grinned and gripped his friend by the elbow.

'Better not make a scene mate, it could have repercussions.'

Sly smiled and said: 'I get my share I suppose.'

But later, when Sly went to the gents to relieve himself the stranger was in there washing his hands and the green eyed god of jealousy raised itself above the parapet. Sly faced the man as he turned to dry his hands.

'There's some in this village that thinks interlopers taking our women is not on pal,' he said looking large and menacing expecting the stranger to be bothered. Instead the man smiled at him.

'I take it you object to me taking Sally for a dinner?'

'Taking her anywhere mister.'

'Oh dear, emphatic are we?'

'Pardon?'

'Mean it do you?'

Sly was a little confused. This sort of thing was not supposed to happen. It was time for the uppercut and despite his screaming bladder he made a lunge. To his surprise the vertical changed to horizontal and, with a gasp of agony, he crashed to the floor to thump against the tiled wall. He came to a sudden stop and as his bladder gave way soaking his trousers he heard the stranger drying his hands on the blower.

'I suggest, fatso, you be a little more polite in future,' he said and banged out of the door leaving Sly groaning on the floor damp and in pain.

Inside the restaurant Sally and her escort rose from their table and stood at the bar.

'My sister and I wish to settle the bill,' he said and paid with his card.

Just before they left Sally said to the barman, giving him a wide grin: 'You had better get Horace to check the gents, it might need cleaning.'

A half hour later Sylvia Simon arrived at the rear entrance of the Dog and Duck with a clean pair of trousers, underpants and a shirt for her husband into which he changed. Carrying the soiled clothes in a dry-cleaning bag Sly followed his wife home trying to explain what had happened.

He wasn't very convincing.

It is said that like attracts like and in Childen Under Blean this was quite true. The Friends of St Seraph's were Atheists or Agnostics although some of them liked to be passive members of the church. The core members of the Bird Watchers were all sex starved morons. The Coven were frustrated housewives and those villagers who wandered around the village trying to remain unseen were merely fornicators. Their raison de etre was plain to understand. That the young people, the girls and boys of the choir and of the village proper were attracted to each other had a lot to do with natural hormonal urges but here we must make distinctions. There were those girls who were attracted to lads whose minds could grasp ideas above the waistline as well as below and, in contrast, there were those whose intellectual ability stayed firmly in the gutter.

Some of the girls did not mind sex starved morons and were willing to feed the fires of passion. A few of the girls thought that holding on to their virginity was a crime, or at least a waste and the sooner they relinquished it the better for all concerned.

Across the aisle between the two sections of the choir it was possible, so it seemed, to feel the tangible presence of a force that held one in thrall should he or she be brave enough to pass between the rows

One such force crossed the gulf between the unlikely pair of Cheryl Simon and Mathew Grace. She wanted it to act on Donald Tomms but when she saw Mathew gazing at her in between notes she felt the longing and knew what she wanted.

Because her father was grounded she had walked to the

church with her friends and promised to walk back home with them. The two girls she arrived with and one of the boys were asked to join in with the special group afterwards for some extra training. She bumped into Mathew and apologised.

'Sorry, I er, didn't realise you were so close,' she said.

His gaze was locked on her ample bosom and when he looked up to answer she gave him a coy smile.

'Cor you got a nice pair of knockers,' he said.

That wasn't quite the reaction she expected but she let it pass and dropped her head modestly and gave a little giggle. The effect on him was predictable. He licked his lips, looked eager and began to speak, hesitant at first but, warming to his task, he asked the question.

'You wanna walk home with me?'

'All right,' she said.

As soon as they were on their own he led her to the footpath to the old quarry and, grinning broadly, he said: 'You gonna show me your tits?'

'I might.'

'I'll let you play with my dick.'

'You don't do small talk do you?' she said.

He looked puzzled. He thought he was doing all right.

'Come on, let's go, shall we?'

She followed him along the path and in a secluded sunny spot on rocks surrounded by buddleias she opened her top and undid her bra.

'I seen 'em but it ain't the same as close up like this,' he said as she took his hand and pressed it to her bosom.

'What do you mean Mathew?'

'Oh shit, I fucked that up didn't I,' he said.

'Tell me,' she said.

He told her about the Bird Watchers Club and, taking out his phone, he showed her some pictures surprised that instead of getting angry she seemed interested.

'You got some of me?'

'Yeah, I got some.'

He showed her the pictures and lamely added.

'Them's my favourites. You spread out like that starkers,' he said and thought about the times he had sat on the bed with her picture on his screen. Now she was here.

'How long you been doing this?'

'Nearly three years. You always leave your curtains open. Bloody sexy.'

'You want to find out how sexy I am?' she asked and with a wriggle she removed her panties and giggled.

It wasn't quite like the time in the store room but what she lacked in experience she made up for in enthusiasm. He liked her bouncy form and when he had finished he held her close nibbling at a nipple wanting to do it again.

'At last, I been waiting since I was thirteen for this,' she said. 'Three years and two weeks and at last I'm an ex-virgin!'

And just to make a point she demanded he do it to her again.

Afterwards having exchanged mobile numbers they hurriedly dressed and quickly using the pathways behind the houses made for home.

'My Dad better not see you,' she said, and disappeared into her garden. 'Give me a text when you want another one.'

That evening after the meal Mathew took to his room and kept a watch on Cheryl's window. When it was fully dark she stood in the lighted room and undressed to stand with her phone in her hands tapping at the screen.

She told him her father had gone ballistic, her mother had stood up for her and she was now banished to her room. 'Watch.'

What she did next reduced him to a lust filled frustrated jelly. When at last she drew her curtains and switched out the light he was shaking with desire and dropped into his bed eventually to indulge in an onanistic orgy that left him utterly exhausted.

Cheryl lay in her bed thinking of what had happened that day with Mathew. The words he had used and the feel of him inside her. Her father's anger at her being late was the least of her worries. What bothered her was if her father found out what she had done and who she had done it with.

She said she had stayed behind with the other girls which argument her father had reluctantly accepted but glowered at her when he made his final pronouncement.

'If I thought you had been with that bloody no-hoper from across the road I would give you a thrashing and beat the living shit out of the stupid bugger,' he said.

'I'm not likely to do that dad, he's a moron,' she said.

However, her father banished her to her room for the rest of the evening; a so-called punishment which gave her the freedom to talk to her friends. Her father had no idea.

Sara Grace was sad. This was the last year her friends would be together. Salina, Melissa and Marion were off to uni. She had another year to go which left Jemima and Terri next year. Cheryl Simon had her own friends, none of whom fitted in with her set, although she and the other village girls were always friendly.

She thought about the driving lessons and the hassle of finding the money to pay for them. She worked at the Greens, and during her break, she did some calculations. She wrote down the estimated costs of keeping the horse and the expenses relating to a car and came to a conclusion.

'Sod it, Figaro is more important,' she exclaimed.

That afternoon after work she surprised her mother with her decision.

'So you are going to put off the driving license for now?'

'Yes, Figaro is more important,' she said.

She wasn't the only young person to make a wise decision that morning. Graham Cook considered that the two wisest people in the village other than his parents were Vernon and Maddy Green. He could not share what he had seen with his parents for shame of revealing what he knew and for not immediately telling them. It took him a long time to pluck up the courage to broach the subject with Maddy. It cost him a glass of her excellent cordial and a sandwich he didn't really want but at last he was sitting in the Green's back room trying to explain.

'Like I said. I joined the club to do bird watching and thanks to mister Green we did some as a group but then I found out they were not doing that,' he said and described the day out in the hills. 'So I determined to carry on and do it by myself. Yesterday I was up in the quarry trying to spot some of the small birds when I saw Mathew Grace and Cheryl Simon walk up the path. They went into the quarry and stayed just below me where I was hidden up.'

'Go on, what happened,' Maddy asked and gave him another glass of cordial.

'I saw them copulating,' he said. using the word naturally. 'Twice, and then they dressed and hurried off home.'

'And what's wrong with that?'

'Er, well, if her father knew he would get violent with her and Mathew. I mean, don't get me wrong, I think Mathew is a bit thick and Cheryl is not the brightest and I think neither of them thought about using condoms like we are taught to do at school by the sex teacher.'

'You mean the teacher tells you what to do?'

He nodded.

'If I said that you are a nosy boy what would you think?'

For a moment or two he was quiet and saw what she was getting at.

'I could have moved away but where I was perched it was hard to move without being seen. I was bothered by what I saw and I suppose it is more how I feel than what was going on,' Graham said.

'So in reality it is you who are disturbed and want some help.'

'Yes but Mrs Green, I wasn't the only one watching them. And I didn't take any pictures but somebody did,' he said. He managed the lie without flinching knowing that in part it was true. He hadn't intended to take any pictures but he had. They were nice clear ones showing details and although he was tempted to delete them he didn't.

'Right, so you think there might be some shenanigans over this and you are worried about it enough to talk about it. You think somebody might be wanting to stir things up a bit?'

'Most emphatically and all I want to do is watch birds.'

'All right Graham, leave it with me for the time being and I will listen out for any news,' she said, and when he was gone she had an idea why somebody would want to take pictures. She watched the lad walk off and shook her head.

She was amused when that same day Sara Grace confided in her that she was going to give up driving lessons and save her money for the horse.

'I think Figaro deserves looking after and when I come home I can ride him. One of the girls at the stables will look after him and keep him happy when I'm away. That Sally can take him for riding for the disabled school.' Sara looked anxious. 'That will be all right won't it?'

Maddy Green smiled warmly and said: 'I should imagine so, as long as you arrange it properly.' She would have a word with Daphne and make sure that Figaro was cared for. She liked Sara and she liked her horse, a sprightly Chestnut who loved to be fussed, and Sara was good with him. She deserved a break.

'You have another year yet Sara.'

'I know but I am planning ahead. I should go to Uni with the

The Birdwatchers of Childen Under Blean

others but I have decided to continue at the college into year three. I believe I can choose my papers with more discretion,' Sara said.

'In the meantime we welcome your efforts here,' Maddy said.

Life in Childen Under Blean during August pottered on. The children's programmes at the church steadily fizzled out. The lads too old for the church and not yet ready for work mooched around the village eying up the girls who not altogether ignored them but were frustrated by the censorious monitoring by the local housewives and retirees.

As a result of this chivvying, prior to the harvest, small, thrashed depressions appeared in the crop fields surrounding the village. The quarry itself was far too busy with, dog walkers, birdwatchers, casual walkers and clambering youngsters for any but the most brazen fornicators.

Aware of this activity, and determined to prevent it, Morris Davis called for a prayer meeting of his faithful followers.

'Let us pray for purity,' he intoned and bent his head. 'Oh Lord, let our young folk see the error of their ways, and with your grace, let them not wander on the path of lust and carnal desire. Help keep them pure and free from carnal knowledge, and send your blessings on their pure and innocent hearts. Amen'

There was a chorus of amens and in the pious silence that followed a follower spoke up.

'Brother Morris, would it not be better if we went out in the fields ourselves and prised them apart?'

Morris Davis looked up from his prayerful position and glared at the speaker.

'Brother Robin, much as I agree with your suggestion, I would prefer you to couch it in more genteel terms,' he said.

Brother Robin looked puzzled.

'Well, I'm picking if we don't get out there now and stop the randy little buggers shagging themselves silly, we will be attending a few Christenings,' he said.

There was a murmur of agreement and within a few minutes the meeting broke up and men and women in pairs moved off to carry out Robin's suggestion.

Morris Davis stood alone and forlorn.

His followers were getting out of hand lately.

'I need some more fire and brimstone sermons,' he said.

However, although he did not take part in the scourge of the crop fields, he was glad when he saw penitent youngsters being herded back where they could be seen.

'Maybe the fete will give them something more wholesome to do,' he said, and sighed.

The week of the Summer Fete arrived and soon the cricket pitch was blossoming with marks for stalls and the usual entertainments. The village came alive with a carnival atmosphere, which, in part satisfied Morris Davis's desire for purity, but in reality had no effect at all on the sexual activities of the village youth.

A few days before the event the village was buzzing with excitement. Perversely the weather was hot and sultry and on the Friday before the event the heavens opened swamping the village with water. The stream overflowed its banks creating a panic as water washed The Street and burbled around the drains. It was an effort of heroic proportions when Old Man Scroggins ordered his young men out with drain clearing equipment to battle the flooding. By mid morning, in the sunshine that followed the downpour the drains were clear and the water was drained away.

In the afternoon sunshine the streets glowed brightly, the green gleamed, flowers in the gardens looked eager and the village looked gay and cheerful.

The Fete organisers were happy and as a bonus the avian occupants of the picturesque water feature at the Southern end of the green received an excess of fresh water. In their own way they all agreed that it was most quackingly good.

Thomas Grace had led his team to an ignominious defeat against the Stoat Malbury team the week prior to the fete and as a result his heart was not in the festivities. The demon bowler had cleaned up and bowled them all out for 61 in 25 overs. In reply the Stoat Malbury eleven reached that total in twenty overs and finished with a four on the last ball to win by six wickets.

Sylvester's remark afterwards was unhelpful.

'If we had nobbled the bugger we might have stood a chance,' and Thomas, in spite of his Christian ethics had to agree with him. The good news apart from the rain that watered his garden was that Peter Mann had fallen over in his driveway and broken his wrist. Uncharitably Thomas was pleased about that.

The Birdwatchers of Childen Under Blean

Released from his domestic purgatory Sylvester gave some of his time to organising the fete joining the team of enthusiastic revellers determined to make Childen Under Blean's annual event a success.

On the day, the attractions included the WI stalls, pony rides, flower and vegetable competitions, Morris dancing, folk music, demonstrations by local clubs and the local art society. The popular Punch and Judy show that included a policeman knocking the daylights out of people, displays of brutality to a baby and a lot of noise was ready to go. The audience, mostly children plonked in front of the booth for a 50p performance roared with laughter, booed at the right time and called out excited warnings to come away from the performance feeling happy.

There were food stalls, tombola, hoopla, a few mechanical children's rides, a steam powered organ, a display of classic, vintage and veteran motor vehicles, silly enactments, fancy dress competitions and sports.

Children screamed happily racing with eggs in spoons, just running, three legged races, sack races, Dad's and Mum's races, throwing the wellie, the bell and hammer, a coconut shy, darts and a shooting range.

The Vicar had selected a patch in which to place a little wooden cross that could be purchased at £1 a time to mark out the exact spot where treasure might be buried. The prize was hamper donated by the Greens.

But one of the most interesting stalls amongst the hobby and local interest section was that of Graham Cook. He had arranged a display of excellent bird photographs on standing boards, and was willing to explain how to use the simple equipment on display to indulge in bird watching.

He was busy taking names and contacts for his newly formed club grandly titled "The Junior Amateur Ornithological Society of Childen Village" complete with a plan to hire the Green's minibus via sponsors to visit local reserves.

He was explaining his idea to a lad when Mathew mooched in under the canopy and glared at him. Mathew waited for the boy to wander off and looked at Graham disdainfully.

'What's all this then, geeky kid?'

'Proper bird watching sir.'

'You mean real birds with feathers?'

'Yes sir, proper bird watching,' Graham said.

'You taking the piss?'

'No sir, merely stating the facts.'

'Well it won't last long. Me and my mates will see to that,' Mathew said.

'Oh dear, sir, I don't think you should be so hasty,' Graham said and waited for Mathew to react. He was ready for this.

'What you talking about you little nerd?'

Graham reached into his jacket pocket and handed Mathew an envelope.

'Perhaps you would like to see what is inside before you go any further.'

Scowling, Mathew opened the envelope and slowly drew from it a postcard size picture wrapped in soft tissue and gazed at it horrified.

'Of course I have the original,' Graham said with a smile. 'You can understand what sort of position that places you in should it go public. it might be awkward for you.'

'You nasty little shit.'

'Yes, I suppose you could say that but you are not exactly an angel are you?'

'What you gonna do with this?'

'Nothing unless you want me to. Just leave me alone to get on with what I want to do and behave yourself or I will send copies of this to mister Simon, your parents and perhaps even twitter it. You never know it might get some followers,' Graham said.

'You don't want money.'

'It's not that sort of blackmail, my friend.'

Mathew left the tent feeling as if the bottom had just fallen out of his world. He could imagine Sylvester Simon bearing down on him with his sleeves rolled up over his massive arms and he trembled. As he walked away he tried to imagine murdering Graham Cook and wondered what the kid really wanted from him.

He managed to gather the lads during the Morris dancing, the stuff the old farts liked, and explained that Graham Cook was throwing his weight about.

'I'm gonna get in first right? We use that picture I took of old Sylvester and his widow, right?''

'We send it to his old lady?'

'Yeah, Stanley can do that, he knows how. Now I reckon we should get some cider down us,' Mathew said. He wanted to meet up with Cheryl but she was with her parents and some cousins. They moved to the cider tent and strangely enough they were allowed to buy tumblers and drink as much as they wanted. It was during the session his mobile vibrated and quickly he read the message.

'Gotta go lads,' he said and hurried off.

She emerged from the shadows of the small cricket pavilion and soon they were sneaking into the shadows between the extended wall of the pavilion toilets and the tool shed, a dark secluded space.

'I'm not wearing any,' she said as he straddled her in the upright position.

A passing fox looking for castaway scraps was the only witness to Mathew's oscillating derrière that reflected what little light filtered into the space and, unless in a perverse turn of fate the fox wanted to bite a naked bum, the animal instead passed on by. For different reasons Mathew and the fox had to hurry their respective liaisons.

The fox never satisfied his curiosity.

The lovers however, satisfied theirs.

Mathew rejoined his friends under the cider tent and feeling happy he drank his fill and when it was time to go he staggered home. He was too tipsy to do much on his computer and fell asleep dreaming of Cheryl's bosom. His friends in their turn staggered home and all except Stanley dropped into bed and fell asleep.

Stanley dozed off but woke in the early hours to empty his bladder and found it difficult to get back to sleep.

'I may as well get on with it,' he muttered and fired up his laptop. Not sure what he was supposed to do, bemused by the effects of the cider and unable to sleep he made up a little packet of pictures from those he had taken and those sent to him. He printed out those to be sent to the subjects of the prints and put sets in envelopes. He printed the names on the fronts, sealed them ready for posting. He was going to sneak out and post them but the drink took over and he fell asleep leaving the envelopes on his table. Like most people on that Sunday morning after the fete he slept in.

The Village Green was cleared during the morning and the two establishments prepared for lunch, tea and in the evening, dinner in the Dog and Duck.

Vernon Green treated his Maddy to a meal at the local pub and like many who had organised the fete the previous day congratulated themselves on a successful fund raising exercise.

'It appears that according to Thomas the amounts made after expenses, plus donations from traders, with the money made out of the games, we have cleared something like three and a half thousand pounds. We have made enough to donate a few hundred to the fund and most amazing of all young Graham Cook has recruited a crowd of interested bird watchers at two pounds each, and promises to donate fifty pence per person and thanks us for supplying his stall for free. It seems he is talking to Thomas here about opening a club account and talks of negotiating for a supply of bird watching binoculars,' Vernon explained to the fete committee at an impromptu meeting held in the Green's tea rooms.

'And he asked us if we could handle the supply of bird food for the local children,' added Maddy.

'The boy is a treasure,' Miriam Small remarked.

'The amount is higher actually and will go even higher once all the amounts are in. We collected a lot of money for the choir and the scheme during the singing. I noticed that even my boy was singing his heart out. The pony club made some money from the rides and they have yet to make a donation. I understand that Sir Ronald is willing to match any amount they give.'

There was a chorus of well done's and hear hear's.

'The treasure hunt was a roaring success. It seems that so many people wanted to win the hamper, so kindly filled by Vernon and Maddy with donations from you all, that I could have extended the space by nearly double. The winner was one of the estate children who, so my dear Elizabeth informs me, paid for his attempt with five pence coins. His family will be pleased.' Said the reverend Jones.

'Snotty little bugger tried to nick a bag of toffee from the sweet stall. If it wasn't for that the little sod would have run off with the hamper and scoffed the lot. His father gave the little bugger a clip around the ear and made him stay with the family after that,' said Miriam Small, WI organiser and a no-nonsense housewife who served the dinners at the local primary school. She was the happy dragon of St Seraph's C of E infants and primary school that served Childen and the surrounding area. 'I know that little sod.

His parents will be thankful for the hamper but he's turning into a wayward child.'

The reverend Jones looked somewhat annoyed by her description but brightened up when he realised the hamper was going to a worthy cause.

'God works in mysterious ways,' he said piously.

Miriam Small sniggered.

Eventually the meeting wound to its conclusion and the Sunday afternoon wound toward evening.

Maddy felt like a girlfriend when Vernon escorted her across the green to the Dog and Duck and laughed happily as they walked up the steps into the restaurant hand in hand.

'We can get pissed if we want to,' she said.

It was his turn to laugh.

Maddy had never been drunk all the time he had known her but maybe this night she would likely get a Little tiddly. He certainly would.

The village settled down to rest for Sunday evening. The drinkers met briefly in the bar and made excuses to return home. Thomas Grace spent his evening with Melanie and Sara watching the telly after a morning helping to clear up the fete and part of the afternoon with the committee. Melanie spent the afternoon in the garden pottering around. Sara had spent some of the day at the stables with her horse and some of it working at Green's. Mathew had finally emerged from his room at noon demanding food and was given a ham sandwich with a salad which he ate slowly and steadily complaining of a hangover.

'Too much cider,' his father said. 'Serves you right.'

'You don't care about me.'

'I do care Mathew but when you do something silly I think you need to suffer without sympathy. On your own head be it,' Thomas said.

Mathew groaned. He hated being preached at.

Reverend Jones attended services at two other churches in the parish that morning returning to take part in the wind up meeting. Throughout that afternoon he was disturbed by images of the attractive parishioner in St Margaret's who wore a figure hugging dress with a low cut top. The view from the pulpit was overwhelming for a part time lecher like him and as he drove back home along the country lanes all he could think of was the perfect creamy curve of the woman's breasts that heaved as she breathed and swelled as she sang creating havoc with his responses. He struggled to keep his place in the service as much as trying to control his physical response.

She was Colleen Wyvern, he discovered, and was new to the area. Using his status as the religious incumbent he found out her address, her marital status and much about her domestic life that he filed away as useful.

'You should call on me sometime,' she said. 'Tell me what is happening in the parish. I am sure I can fit in some time to help.'

I hope so, he thought, and smiled warmly.

'You will be most welcome and yes, I will call on you if you would like to arrange it,' he said.'I do rounds on Wednesdays and Thursdays.'

'Oh good, next Thursday. I will give you morning tea,' she said and all too soon she was gone and it was time to greet the rest of his flock before driving back to Childen.

It was a steamy, disturbing journey.

Sylvester Simon passed by Sally Wise's house and saw that her visitor, lover, creepy git, and his rival was still there. He fumed. He had thought that Sally was his special girl but it seemed that she was no better than any of the others. Anyway, he had given Lily a call and good old dependable Lily had replied.

'Get on with it then before I find somebody else.'

He had left Sylvia and Cheryl to their clearing up, muttered about going to the pub for a jar and set off. He would have to get something from town for Lily during the week and sneak it to her.

'For services rendered,' he said and chuckled.

As usual he reached her door and was immediately let in, grabbed and eaten as he put it. He liked that and when he had disengaged he laughed.

'I could hang up my jacket?'

'Like a drink or do you want to get straight on with it?'

That's what he liked about her, no messing around. Her favourite position was naked on her back. It was a start anyway.

'We could try the drink,' he said.

She poured him a scotch and half filled a glass with sherry for herself. They placed the drinks on the low table in front of her large settee and with their bodies tangled sipped at the drinks in between expertly undressing each other. Naked, with her sitting on him sipping her sherry and he trying to sip his scotch they eventually gave in and placed the glasses on the table.

'Oh for Christ's sake let me...' she said and slid herself onto him gasping as he thrust back. Not for the first time since he had known her Sly did not actually make it upstairs to her bed. The pair satisfied their lust on and around the settee and afterwards when she reminded him he was supposed to be at the pub he reluctantly dressed and hurried off. She took a shower and wearing just a dressing gown went downstairs to the kitchen to make a supper. It was getting dark and through the window she could see shadows of plants and trees out in the garden. She was startled by a sudden tapping on her kitchen window but smiled when she realised it was a familiar code. A sort of morse password.

She let him in, put the supper in the microwave and sighed.

'All right, you had better come up.'

Much later she zapped the food in the microwave and sat at the kitchen table eating it, washing it down with a glass of beer.

'Men, they all want the same thing but that's no matter because I don't mind giving it to them. In fact Lily old girl you like giving it to them because you like what they have to give,' she said, and looked at the empty space between the kitchen cupboards, and further into the utility space beside the back door.

She missed having a cat and decided to get a kitten.

She would deal with that tomorrow.

She climbed the stairs to her bedroom and tidied the bedclothes that had been rumpled by the recent activity and stumbled when her bare feet came down on something with an edge that crackled under her foot.

'Oh fuck, my bloody foot,' she said and hopped around before plumping on the bed to lift it up and look at it. The edge had made a livid mark but had not broken the skin and soon with a bit of rubbing and massage the pain subsided. She looked down to find the culprit. On the carpet crushed and bent where she had trodden on it was an ecclesiastical dog collar.

She laughed and picking it up dropped it in her waste bin.

'I think I would cause a riot if I gave that back to him,' she said, and donning her nightdress she got in to bed. In the morning she would change the sheets and the duvet cover, and call Sylvester to order a kitten.

Sunday slumbered like a dormant volcano with nobody knowing if or when it was due to explode. Eruptions, they say, often follow a period of peaceful complacency.

On Monday morning Forest took Mutley for his normal walk and returned to find Salina cooking breakfast.

'Mum's gone to work on the early bus. I need a lift into town if you will. I have an interview and I would like to be fresh for it,' she said.

'A job interview?'

'Yes. I have decided to earn my living if I can.'

'Right, serve me breakfast when I have sorted the dog and I will take you in. Let him out when you get back.'

In fact the exodus for the workers at all levels proceeded as normal. The reduced Coven in the absence of Amanda Maloney met but had nothing to say. The dribble of tourists seemed to prefer the tea rooms to the pub and of those children who were off school only a few were attracted to the summer activities.

Colin Lawrence took Sally Wise into town and there they purchased two medium sized suitcases, and some new clothes. Sally had business in town that she and Colin had agreed upon. The arrangements she wanted to make required a visit to a real estate agent and her solicitor.

Graham Cook was, to a point, one of those who enjoyed the small events but on this morning he was, like Salina, embarking on a new venture. He sat with Maddy Green for an hour negotiating the financing and purchase of birdseed, and asked her to create a line of trade with a camera shop in town to supply his group with discounted equipment.

'I am of the opinion that in the future, considering that some of the current interest will drop due to factors such as age and location of current members, the ability to sustain interest, coupled with my ability to maintain their enthusiasm, and of course costs, will no doubt reduce membership. I am prepared for such eventualities and will set up a network that is designed to expand in to adult life and maybe stimulate a life long interest in amateur ornithology,' he said smiling owlishly at her.

'Er yes, I suppose so,' she said and wondered what he was like at home. How on Earth did his parents cope with him?

'I have my member's interests at heart and their concerns and ideas are central to the success of the club,' he said.

'Yes, of course, now, I have examined your proposal and I think we should be able to help you. If mister Grace can set up the account for you and monitor it then we have a deal,' she said and found herself shaking hands like true business partners. This intense thirteen year old with his round spectacles and sticky out ears was destined to do well, she thought. He was good at negotiating and however you looked at it the deal he wanted was sound and she and Vernon would make a profit.

The boy looked at her and grinned.

'Did you get a little bit tiddly last night Mrs Green?'

'Just a little,' she answered realising she had confided in the boy without thinking and grinned. 'A little but Vern said I would and it was a nice dinner.'

'I am glad you enjoyed your evening,' he said and meant it.

In town Sylvester used his lunch break to speak to the owner of a pet shop with the intention of purchasing a kitten.

'We don't actually sell kittens from the shop but we do source them for you if you want breeds.'

'How much?'

'Oh anything from sixty to six-hundred, depending on the breed,' she said.

'Bugger that, All I want is a moggie for a friend not a bloody pedigree zoo,' he said glaring at her.

'In that case you should call the RSPCA or Cats Protection.'

'Or call a friend,' he said, and grinned remembering Dotty Dorothy who seemed to have cats and kittens filling her whole house.

He left the shop and later that afternoon he called Dotty's number.

'I don't do that anymore. Me bits are buggered,' Dotty said a few moments after he reminded her who he was.

'I'm after a kitten for a friend. A little pussy-cat. If you can help.'

'Come round this afternoon and no funny business.'

He hadn't planned any funny business.

And that afternoon she let him in to her living room which although it smelled of cats it was neat and tidy in that fussy way he remembered. She was dressed in slacks and a top that seemed to be festooned with cat hairs. The top turned out to be a badly worn out angora jersey.

She shoved some cats off the settee and he sat waiting for her to finish rabbiting on about cats and memories of their encounters before she served him some weak looking tea. She added biscuits and he sat munching them with a cat on his lap feeling vulnerable. The tea was down to her usual standard and the biscuits were slightly soggy but he was there for a purpose and put up with the discomfort.

'Now, would she like a little black one or a tabby?'

'I like black cats so I suppose we could have one of those,' he said and moments later she came in with a box in which were four lively kittens.

He picked up a black one holding it gently and examined its rear end. It was female. He handed that one to her to hold and lifted another one from the box. This one had a white patch and two white front paws. It too was a female and when he tickled it's chin it patted at him and purred.

He made a decision.

'I would like to have them both. One for me and one for my friend,' he said.

She grinned and then her face changed and she looked at him with hard eyes.

'They are both healthy cats and ready for homes. You can have them for thirty quid each plus I will book them in for spaying and inoculations, plus I will supply you with dishes, a cat carrying cage, dirt box and arrange for them both to be chipped. In return you will have two healthy pussy-cats at a price you can afford,' she explained.

'And no bit on the side.'

'No. When I lost me bits I lost all desire for that sort of thing. You are out of luck mister. Oh, and no cheques, cash please. I'm not illegal but I don't want to pay no unnecessary taxes,' She said.

Sylvester nodded and agreed.

'Two weeks but I will need your names and addresses for the chipping,' she said.

He gave her the details and saw her smile when she looked at Lily's name.

'Services rendered is it?' she said.

Not trusting himself to speak he nodded.

'Don't worry I'll keep me gob shut, You knows me,' she said.

That was why he had come to her although if he had known how complex the process would be and how much it would cost him to satisfy Lily's request he would have tried to persuade Lily to ask for something less demanding.

Anyhow, he liked cats.

Dotty Dorothy didn't run a kitten farm. She took in strays, looked after them and, if there were any kittens she made sure they were healthy and cared for. The council had tried to close her down but she could prove that her operation was doing a good job. The neighbours couldn't complain because her house stood in its own grounds, was properly fenced, and was always neat and tidy. She was well off but practical and in her time had worked for the same company as Sylvester until she got fed up with misogynistic superiors whose intention was to grope her against the filing cabinet.

The only man she couldn't resist was Sylvester who had the raw animal magnetism of a Tom Cat. He was irresistible until; as she explained, she had had her bits removed.

But she gazed after him as he drove off feeling wistful and wishing that things were different. Sylvester hadn't even tried and that was most unusual. What was even more unusual in her present state was that she felt aroused and, as she put it to Sammy, her favourite Tom, 'I come over all peculiar.' Sammy stretched and yawned.

Salina was annoyed. She didn't get the job. She would have to start again and perhaps lower her sights a little and go for whatever she could get. She scoured the vacancy columns, looked on the job centre notice board and did a tour of the town on Tuesday making notes of the offers. The library was a good place to start and soon she was busy working on a new CV. She sat in a coffee bar at lunch time with a cup and a cake working through the local free paper.

She was surprised to see Mathew Grace come in and was amused when he leered at the girl serving and tried to chat her up. She was polite but other than to serve him with his coffee and a toasted sandwich she ignored him. Luckily he didn't see her and found a table across the room. A few minutes after he arrived Stanley arrived, ordered a coffee and sat down with Mathew. The two boys seemed to be arguing. She finished her cake and left.

'Bloody hell that was that bleedin' stuck up Maloney cow wasn't it?' said Mathew.

'Yeah, what's she doing in here?'

'Dunno,' said Mathew, completely missing the point that like them she was having a quick lunch.

'Anyway, stuff her, I done what you said but when do I send them off?'

'When you sorted them out and we got some more to back 'em up. Then we does the tossers,' Mathew said. 'Listen mate, we waits until they gets heavy then we hits 'em. You sort 'em, stamp 'em and send 'em when they gets nasty. I got a feelin' people are beginnin' to get wise to us because of who quacked. We find the quacker and we put his fuckin' lights out, button his beak, right?'

'We gotta find him first,' Stanley said.

And with that thought they sat at the table, brows knitted, in deep thought. Well, deepish anyway.

In Old Man Scroggins house that lunch time a meeting was held concerning the four bird watching friends. The old man was sitting in his winged chair with his feet resting on an ottoman and he had listened to the complaints, drew on his pipe, coughed, blowing smoke rings out as he did so and taking the smelly briar from his mouth and using it to emphasise his points he spoke.

'I fucking reckons that what them lads need is a fucking good hiding, but seeing as what me and the missus is proper fucking churchgoers and Christians, despite all the 'ollering them silly buggers do of a Sunday, we got to do it peaceful like. I reckon we ought to get Josh to have a word with 'em, sort of quiet like. If we tells him not to rough 'em up too much then we ought to of done enough.' The Old Man said, and waited for the nodding to stop before addressing Josh directly. 'It ain't an order, but if you volunteers like, then we knows you will be acting like a Christian and givin' the little fuckers a fucking good spiritual bollocking. All right?'

The big man with the dark complexion and curly hair so typical of his great uncle's family grinned and bowed his head.

'I will volunteer, as you asks, and have a nice friendly word or two in their shell likes. If they smitest me doth I smiteth them back?' Josh said and grinned broadly.

'Thou shalt turn the other cheek unless it hurteth thee too fucking much,' replied the Old Man and guffawed. The rest of the meeting joined in with the laughter. 'In the meantime let Joshua do his work.'

Maisie Scroggins, the Matriarch of the Scroggins Clan, approved of the action.

'We oughter pray for them in church on Sunday just in case

Josh has to duff 'em up,' she said and grinned.

'That would be a good thing to do. A good Christian thing to do. If the almighty can hear us over all that 'ollerin',' the Old Man said. It was odd being part of the church but It helped keep the lads in line and showed the rest of the village that the family was trying to fit in. Old Man Scroggins smiled to himself as Maisie cleared the tables.

'If only the villagers knew how much of their village we owned,' he said. Lord Massingham did but he was the local Toff and a magistrate and ought to know. Massingham didn't like the charismatics much either, and in that they were both in full accord. One day soon the reverend Jones would find out just how much the Triffid-like worship was disliked and go back to normal. Sorting out the bird watchers was the first task. After that we can sort out the church, he thought, and smiled again.

Being a "Christian" made him respectable.

An Unwise Decision.

Saturday arrived hot and steaming as only August can do. The Childen Eleven and some of the villagers were away on the other side of town having fun with a match that they knew they could win.

Mutley enjoyed a day of walks and farting. He was allowed to help with the garden and Forest himself suggested that Salina try for a job at the Dog and Duck. Amanda was grumpy but that, as Forest confided to Mutley, was to be expected. Nothing to be done. He was simply part of village life following a predictable pattern. He felt better now that he was taking control of his life and especially breaking away from the church. He knew he was one of the regulars at the Dog and Duck, a middle aged drinker set in his ways, but one who was willing to change.

'I am a man who is taking control of his life and finding it suits him very well,' he said to Mutley who pricked up his ears and with his eyes closed farted.

'God almighty! Bloody mutt! You stink!'

Mutley wagged his tail enthusiastically.

Master was pleased.

Others in the village were taking part in local sports or preparing to go off on holiday, taking trips out to visit family or just spending time at home. It was late in the morning when the birdwatchers crawled from their beds and eventually wandered down to their meeting place in the tea rooms. They were not aware of Joshua Scroggins watching them from his vantage point of the Dog and Duck garden bar and even if they had been they would have thought nothing of it. Only when they split up did Joshua move and then it was to finish his pint and wander off as if he was going home.

He caught up with Donny first.

'Hello Donald. A little chat, in the alley, right?'

Donny tried to run but Joshua held him by the wrist and guided him to the alleyway.

'All right, what you want then?'

'Simple. You stop perving on the girls or I will punch your fucking lights out, right?' He grinned at Donny.

'I ain't done nothing.'

'Piss off, we know you have. I sees you doing anything and I'll smash yer teeth in,' Joshua said and added: 'And if I hears you done anything you get it, right?'

'That's a bit unfair... yerk,' Donny gasped. He was lifted up against the wooden fence that edged the alley. A ham sized fist hovered close by ready to apply some crude dentistry.

'What was that, moosh?'

'I'll behave meself,' Donny said wondering why he didn't stutter as he normally did when threatened with extreme violence. The de-elevation was a relief although he felt the tremble in Joshua's grabbing fist as he lowered him slowly to the ground.

'Christ, you nearly squeezed me nuts out,' Donny said.

'Good. Now listen to me you shithead, you go tell them others what I just said. Understand?'

Donny nodded his head vigorously.

'Right, now fuck off before I change me mind.'

Donny, carried by watery legs, did as he was bid.

Joshua, his task partly done strolled back to Old Man Scroggins' house.

'I did as you asked. I told that Donny to tell his mates but if you wants me to visit them all then I will,' Joshua said.

'I suggest you show yourself in the following days and sort of glare at them. They will be kacking themselves but, like I said, we is Christians and we must turn the other cheek. You was polite to him I hope?'

'Oh yes Uncle of course I was,' Joshua said. 'As polite as he deserved.'

The old man looked askance at him, questioningly but Joshua was made of stern stuff and remained calm. He hadn't hit the little shit, just frightened him, so all was well.

'I hope so. Well done.'

Donny on his part reported his experience to the others with no embellishments. He knew that any false tales of bravado against Joshua would be the ultimate in bullshit. He told it straight including his feelings of utter terror at the time and with the telling the four friends sat around the table in silence.

'I think we ought to think about this,' said Mathew.

Donny muttered, 'yeah' and Terry and Stanley nodded. The thinking was the hard part. It was a long period of silence except for the slurp of drinking that was broken when Mathew spoke softly.

'We gotta get something on that Scroggins bloke.'

'Like what?'

'Well most of 'em are into nicking stuff and all that. Surely there's something?'

Terry snorted and suddenly brightened.

'I got it. Listen, I got an idea,' he said. 'Thing is we don't want nobody to know what we is doing so lets go and buy some cider and go to the quarry. As long as that little shithead Cook and his arsehole friends are not there we should be all right.'

And by pooling their cash the little gang bought bottles of cider from the shop and walked dejectedly to the quarry. Their usual hangout was empty and so, with bottles opened they listened to Terry's plan. 'At least,' he said, 'we can use our cameras.'

His plan was adopted, tasks allocated and with something approaching optimism the gang set out to protect themselves.

Mathew walked back home with Donny and on the way he spotted Sara riding her horse alongside that toff kid Robert.

'Look at that Donny, my bloody stuck-up sister with that smarmy prat. Her and her horses.'

'They look like they is getting on all right. You reckon he shags her?'

Mathew was stunned. The thought of his sister having it off with a bloke like Robert made him sick. Did they?

'I think she's too up herself for that,' he said.

'I'd shag her,' Donny said, and the blow that never fell from Joshua's massive fist landed on his jaw from Mathew's bony one. The fight that followed was a foregone conclusion.

'Sorry mate but you don't hit your mates for what they says before lettin' them apologise. She's an all right looker your sister and anybody could say the same as me. Now, stop your snivelling and let's go home for tea,' Donny said and brushed Mathew down with his hands removing the leaves and debris from his clothes.

'Yeah, well, she's my sister.'

'She wouldn't have me anyway,' Donny said.

Mathew cheered up at that and punched his mate lightly on the arm. 'Right, you is as ugly as sin.'

'That makes two of us,' Donny replied grinning.

Mathew said nothing.

The reverend Jones was pleased that Old Man Scroggins was among the congregation but was surprised that the man most likely to succeed in going to Hell was with him. Joshua Scroggins was dressed smartly, polished and scrubbed up, with his wife and children in tow looking out of place but ready, so it seemed, for worship.

The choir sang softly as the people filed in and apart from a sudden drop in the male section's output, rather tuneful. Perhaps Joshua's appearance in church was the cause. The reverend saw how Mathew and his friends reacted when Joshua cast his glowering gaze in their direction. The boys looked pale and nervous.

Old Man Scroggins came across the aisle smiling and with his usual strong grip shook his hand.

'Morning vicar, bought me nephew with me today to see how the church works. He's keeping an eye on them fucking idiots what's been going around perving, if you get my meaning. The little dickheads are being warned off. You know about their activities? Right?'

'Of course, that's why we wanted them in the choir,' replied the vicar glad that the old man had spoken quietly.

'Good, the little fuckwits might get the fucking message, eh your reverence?'

'I suppose so. Er, Ebenezer, er do you think you could control your language a little? This is God's house you know.' Jones said, hopefully.

'Sorry vicar I'll try but I'm so used to fucking swearing, the habit's hard to break,' the Old Man said.

'Give it a try, will you? For the Lord.'

'You must think I'm a foul old ... er bloke.'

'No, just wary of the children. Mustn't encourage them to use bad language must we,' the reverend said and was glad when the old man smiled and went off to find his pew.

Barry Smythe was unwell so Bonny Mason took over opting for the keyboard instead and Jones was glad of it. The old organ was getting beyond use and even Smythe was hard put to it to wheedle a tune from its ancient frame. You could hear the hiss of air escaping before it even entered the pipes but somehow Barry managed. Bonny found it hard going.

Evans the Choir preferred the pipe organ but even he was glad of the crisp sound of the keyboard. Right now he was bouncing up and down conducting the music. The reverend was surprised to see that under the robes he was wearing high heels and stockings. My God, Jones thought, the man really is queer and got tangled up trying to think politically correct. He saw his two girls warbling away and Elizabeth helping to greet the worshippers and he felt complete.

His thoughts wandered to Colleen Wyvern and with the realisation he was beginning to steam he pushed all thoughts of her away and concentrated on greeting others of the congregation. He was glad of the cassock. The voluminous garment with all the dangling outer vestments hid his embarrassing rampant member until at last it subsided.

Came time for the service to begin and so the circus began. The songs and chanting seemed to work for half the people whilst the rest got on with being conservative and traditional. He was amused by old Nobby Clarke and his lady who carried on as they had always done and ignored the ecstatic cries around them. They were indifferent to the speaking in tongues and the ecstasy of the Spirit; kneeling down to pray with their hands together, heads bowed and eyes closed. It was like conducting two different services at the same time. He wondered if he was becoming a split personality. A schizophrenic vicar.

Frightened by the appearance of Joshua Scroggins in church the core members of the Birdwatchers panicked and took to the Dog and Duck that evening. The Childen Eleven sat in their normal section with the regular drinkers and related tales of the match. Forest Maloney and Mutley were there and the landlord had laid on plates of leftovers from the Sunday roast.

'Look at that. The fuckin' dog gets more than what we do,' observed Mathew.

'Everybody does. We gets fuck-all.'

'Yeah, bastards,' said Terry.

'Shit heads,' added Stanley.

That evening the lads drank far too much cider. On the way home before parting to go their separate ways Mathew suggested they send the pictures.

'If they, you know, them,' Mathew said waving his arm in the general direction of the village, 'If they don't fucking well leave us a-fucking-lone we oughter shove it up 'em.'

'Right, let's fuckin' do it,' Stanley said gasping as the cider took over. He threw up and, disgusted by the sight and not wanting to emulate his actions, the others left him to get on with it.

Stanley eventually staggered home, groaned out an excuse to his folks and went up to bed. He lay on his back waiting for the world to stop spinning and when it did he tried to sleep. He rose shakily from the bed and scrabbled underneath it for the bottle he kept hidden and drew it out. There was plenty left and with shaking fingers he undid the top, put the neck to his mouth and sucked. The spirit was raw but welcome and soon he was pleasantly pissed. Stoppering the bottle he put it back.

'Right, now let's sort you out, he said, gathering the envelopes from the bottom drawer of his desk.

'Better check 'em first,' he said, and laid the pictures out on the desk. There was the new one from that little turd Willy to add but he couldn't find it. That was until he remembered it needed printing. He shifted the pile of pictures and envelopes and activated his laptop. He found the new picture and idly searched for others finding some good ones of Melissa and Terri Jones.

'I'll do some more,' he said and searched for others including some of the Scroggins' clan. He printed them out and started to sort them. His arm brushed the untidy pile knocking the lot on the floor and in the semi-dark – he had only switched on his desk lamp – he scrambled to pick them up. He heard a noise in the passage and, quickly shoving the lot in a pile, he switched off his lamp and dived into bed.

Moments later his father quietly opened his door and peered inside. There was enough light from the passage to light up the bed. His father saw him sleeping and quietly closed the door. Stanley gave him a half hour before getting out of bed to sort the problem out. By this time the spirit had taken its toll and he felt woozy. Quickly he re-filled the envelopes, addressed the new one and made sure they all had stamps.

'Post,'em, gotta post 'em,' he mumbled and had a vision of Joshua Scroggins glaring at them in the church. 'I gotta post 'em.' There was only one thing for it.

He struggled to slip his sneakers on managing eventually to thrust his feet in the correct shoe. With the craft of the drunk and from long habit he sneaked out of his room via the window, slid down onto the shed roof, and was off in the night carrying the post. Somehow he made it down to the village green and the shop. He shoved the letters in the post box and leaned against it gasping.

'Nice le-er box,' he giggled patting it affectionately.

Fazed by the effects of the drink he wandered aimlessly around the village; once slipping into a damp patch beside the river that sobered him long enough to admit he was lost.

'Shit, where am I?'

The question was addressed to a lamp post against which he was leaning. It failed to answer him.

The light was bright enough to illuminate clearly a familiar part of the village. He swayed, steadied himself and let the homing instinct take over. He staggered back to his home to eventually clamber over the windowsill feeling awful. He had sense enough to undress and stagger to the loo in his underwear, use the toilet and stagger back to his bed.

He fell into a drunken sleep filled with semi-erotic dreams, of letter boxes and naked women that turned into nightmares. On the edge of sleep and terror he was rudely awakened by his father bellowing at him to get up.

'Out of bed you! Come on! You have to go to work!'

It was a rude introduction to Monday morning.

That Monday morning with his father's anger spurring him on Stanley dressed and hurried downstairs, ignored the toast and tea and followed his father out to the car. The journey to work was silent except for the moment his father dropped him off.

'Drunken idiot. Tidy your room tonight.'

He worried all day about what his father was going to do to him and instead of dawdling home he took the normal bus.

He tidied his room as instructed.

Before tea he listened his father lecture him and trembled. The theme was unpleasant. Leaving home was mentioned and so was taking his turn at doing some of the housework. It was not a good start to the week but by keeping his head down, as he put it, the rest of the week rolled on uneventfully.

Thursday was the day Stanley's letters arrived. In the Simon household brown envelopes one to Sylvia and one to Sylvester lay on the mat. He was at work and Sylvia was in the village so Cheryl left the mail on the table along with other letters and walked off to the church.

The brown envelope delivered to the Vicarage was placed in the vicar's 'in' tray ready for his secretary to deal with.

Unfortunately for the reverend Jones his secretary was his wife Elizabeth.

The envelope destined for the Grace doormat was underpaid so instead the postie delivered a card informing the addressee of the charges due.

'Oh bother, why don't people put the proper stamps on?' Melanie said and placed the card on Thomas's desk.

The reverend Jones arrived at the Wyvern house and parked his car in the shade of a tree and walked to the impressive front door. He pressed the door bell and heard the tones ringing inside. She opened the door and led him into a lounge where soon he was sitting opposite her drinking tea.

'This is a lovely house,' he said.

'Yes, it is, come on let us go for a tour. You can tell me what I can do for the parish on the way,' she said and rose elegantly to lead him first through the lower rooms and finally upstairs.

He saw the master bedroom, the bathrooms and guest rooms, admired the views and told her about the organisations in the parish, suggesting ones she might like to join. They were viewing the last guest room when she turned and face him.

'Do you like my bosom, reverend?'

He licked his lips and, staring at the creamy, exposed skin heaving in time to her breathing he couldn't draw his gaze from her cleavage.

'Dear God forgive me,' he said. 'It is a magnificent bosom.'

'Would you like to fondle my breasts?'

His one desire at that moment was to throw her onto the bed behind her and do much more than fondle her breasts but all he could say was. 'Yes.'

'If we take our clothes off we can do much more than that,' she said and almost before he knew it she was lying naked on the bed and he was frantically trying wriggle out of his underwear.

Afterwards he asked her if she was in the habit of seducing the clergy.

'A girl sometimes needs the comfort of the church,' she said.

And as he adjusted his new dog collar the reverend Jones realised that explained why, when they were at their most energetic heights, she called on the Lord in what could only be described as close to charismatic ecstasy.

Forest Maloney read the note and smiled. His in-tray was

clear except for the circulars and this was the last important message; a hand written note from his boss under the department's memoranda heading.

Make an appointment to see me – urgent. Mason

'He could have sent an e-mail.'

He buzzed the secretary and waited for her reply. She looked after all six people in his office and was often doing something else when he called. She answered almost immediately.

'I have to go see his nibs. Delia, will you call him and make a note of the time please.'

As a precaution he took with him a small recorder he used for interviews with clients, he rarely made any but always kept the battery charged, just in case.

'Yes sir,' she said and was pleased that at last she was also beginning to understand that he had changed. The new dynamic me. Moments later she called him back.

'Mister Mason will see you immediately, sir,' she said.

He walked to the lift, changed his mind and used the stairs to march directly to his bosses's office. Mason's minder, the ever efficient and frosty Ms Lawrence, looked over the top of her spectacles and buzzed her boss.

'Go in directly, you are late and he is not happy,' she said.

'That's his problem,' Forest said.

She looked suitably shocked.

He tapped the door with his knuckles more to announce that he had arrived than out of politeness and walked confidently inside the plush office.

'Take a seat Maloney.'

The boss, the almost honourable Richard Mason MA, glowered at him. Forest switched the recorder on and placed it on the desk in front of him. Forest mentioned the date and the time and Mason, irritated by the reference, scowled.

'I am hearing reports of your activities of late. It has been brought to my notice that you are fast tracking applications; making it easier for applications to go through and creating a heavier workload for our inspectors. What is the meaning of this activity?'

'Quite simple sir; I simply cut out the unnecessary processing with simple and logical solutions. That way the applicants are told why they were turned down and how to correct the situation without all this silly referring to rules and regulations, for which they have to pay fees. We simply tell them what to do.' He explained, and was about to explain the benefits when Mason snorted angrily like some angry bovine and demanded he listen.

'It's not on Maloney. There is a procedure which must be followed. I insist it will be followed as a policy of our department. Do you understand?'

'Quite clearly sir. I do follow procedure but I cut out the bullshit. We collect more fees because we enable applicants to complete their projects instead of abandoning them which leads...' he paused to raise his hand and one finger wagging it as his boss and continued. 'Please, don't interrupt. I suggest that so called fast tracking, I prefer to say making it easier for residents to comply with the bylaws, has enormous benefits. The first is that we gain more revenue from new tax payers, plus the steady flow of trade is good for council and there are more local people employed. Internally we will likely save on administration costs including materials and resources. We have efficiency.' Forest said, gazing at Mason who appeared to be swelling like a red ballon.

He smiled at his boss and waited for the inevitable explosion. It came at last and with the smile still on his face Forest waited for the man to finish.

'We cannot have junior officers making unilateral decisions with the intention of changing set procedures. We will have to do something about this situation. Do you understand what I mean Maloney?'

'You have a choice. To promote me or to fire me. Either way you get a result. I know which one I would make but it is up to you,' Forest said giving Mason a friendly smile.

Mason leaned forward. With spittle running down from the left side of his mouth he spoke quietly in a tone filled with menace.

'And what would you do, mister bloody clever dick?'

'I would promote me and give me a chance to shine,' Forest said as equally quiet but with extreme confidence.

'You are fucking well fired!' Mason said.

Forest got up from his seat and grinned.

'I'll fuck off then shall I? I will have that in writing in order to better contest unfair dismissal.'

Mason looked shocked.

'You will not do that!'

'Of course I will. I have no other choice, sir.'

'Nevertheless as of this moment you are fired.'

'Thank you sir, I understand,' Forest said and stood up gathering his recorder. 'Oh and you might want to wipe the spittle from your chin. See you in court, sir,' Forest said and walked out of the office. The Ms Lawrence glared at him and to cheer her up he gave her a grin.

'Your boss might need some comfort; he's had a tantrum and is spitting his dummy,' he said in passing, amused at her open-mouthed response.

He went back to his office and soon, as expected, his supervisor, the man they called Smiley because he didn't, came in with a security officer and stated he was to clear his desk.

'Already done, sir.'

He gathered his personal belongings, chucked the regulation mug in the waste bin, carefully picked up the plastic bag with his pot plants inside and allowed the supervisor to check his briefcase and, saying goodbye to Delia on the way out, deliberately paced the corridors to the car park at a rapid rate amused that neither the supervisor or the security officer could keep up. They watched him get into his car; the security officer used his radio to alert the gate.

He smiled at the supervisor.

'Oh, Smiley, tell old Mason that I would like him to know that the worm has turned.'

'Pardon?'

'Just tell him you miserable bugger.' He said as he drove slowly off. On his way through the gate he gave the man on duty a wave.

There was no response.

He arrived home just after lunch and went inside, released Mutley who bounced around excitedly and whilst the dog roared around the garden he made some cheese sandwiches and with a cup of coffee at his side he sat at his laptop and sent messages to two destinations.

Within a few minutes replies came back and he in turn replied, as the Americans would say, "in the affirmative". With that done he changed his clothes and took Mutley for a walk. And, just to celebrate, he and Mutley called in at the Dog and Duck for a pint. On the whole it was a good Thursday and one he would remember for years.

When Salina came home she was surprised to see the car in

the driveway and when her mother came home she remarked on the absence of the dog.

'What's happened to Dad?'

'I have no idea, my God I'm tired,' Amanda said. 'Darling, be a sweetie and make me a cuppa will you?'

Salina's look of surprise was genuine. Her mother had not called her darling since she was a little girl. However she made the tea and added biscuits and sat with her mother at the kitchen table. Amanda slumped in her chair.

'I am buggered. And I have seen the light,' Amanda said.

'Yes mother,' said Salina cautiously.

'Oh no, not that sort of light. Until the reverend Jones stops his silly upbeat worship I can't be arsed with church. No, I have seen the light of reason. Your cranky father talking about worms turning and all that sort of rot about not giving a stuff, or a damn whatever it was, he said and ignoring me has made me think. I realised what a bloody awful nagging old bag I was becoming and how bloody miserable I was making everybody,' she said staring at the now empty cup. 'You're eighteen now are you not?'

'Yes mum, you gave me a birthday card.'

'Right, come with me. We are going to the pub. I will buy you a drink.' she said and looked at Salina sitting gazing at her open mouthed.

''Well child, don't just sit their like a wide mouthed frog, get your shoes on and let's go.'

When Horace Oswald saw Amanda Maloney and her daughter walking up the steps into his bar he was moved to warn Forest that trouble was approaching. However he was too late because as soon as the pair entered the bar Amanda saw her husband and the dog relaxing with his pint beside the window and addressed him.

'Forest Maloney what are you doing home so early?'

Forest looked startled and even Mutley looked up.

'Ah madam, I have been fortunately fired from my post at the council offices. I should ask what you are doing here?'

'I am buying my daughter a drink and if you would like another allow me to order one,' she said. 'Come on cloth ears whatever my daughter would like, a glass of red wine for me and beer for my husband.' This last addressed to Horace.

Horace poured the beer, made up the drink for Salina, poured the red wine and handed Amanda the change. He watched as the family sat drinking and talking and from the snippets of conversation he gathered that Forest was now working from home, his wife was after a job and now that Salina was of age she was thinking of working for him. He grinned. If Amanda Maloney got her power back but redirected it she could be an asset. Her daughter was by all accounts a good worker and he needed replacement staff.

His cue was when Forest called him over.

'Horace, book us a table in the side bar for dinner will you. My wife and I are celebrating a ceasefire. She is disillusioned with the church, I am likely to be home most of the time and my daughter thinks things might get better. Optimism, old chap, is good thing for all of us. Amanda is optimistic about finding a new job, Salina is looking for one and I have secured some useful work and will be negotiating a redundancy package. All this information is so that you can scotch any rumours should they begin,' Forest said. 'Seven thirty or thereabouts?'

Horace looked somewhat abashed and muttered to himself. Looking up he grinned broadly.

'I can offer both of the ladies jobs. Part time on a roster. That helps most people stay happy and customers see new faces. Besides, you get time to yourselves. I give good training and a uniform,' Horace said. He didn't add that he charged for laundry but that would come later. Between him and Vernon they did all right with the laundry and soon intended to create a service attached to the tea rooms.

But whatever was happening to the Maloney family the news that spread through the village that evening took everybody by surprise.

The reverend Michael Jones parked his car late that afternoon having finished his rounds and stood for a moment or two looking out over the view. The summer was at its best despite the rain earlier in the year and the sudden heat that lingered on through June and July the harvest was going ahead. The fete was over, the Childen Eleven was doing well in the tables and the new choir was expanding with the young lads adding their voices. True it was difficult to keep the girls and boys apart and chaste but that was youth and although the church did not approve he was never worried. His own carnal urges were in need of satisfaction and although he would not be tempted to approach any of the young girls he was not above temptation otherwise. He had to admit that when they were wearing their skimpy clothing and showing their breasts barely covered by cloth he was distracted. How the young boys managed without exploding in sexual frustration he did not know.

But here was a thing he liked most above casual sexual encounters and ogling women, and that was the countryside. He liked the trees and fields, the blackberries and the damson fruit, the fruit and vegetables sold from the roadside stalls and the movement locally to follow the Woodland Trust's land management directives.

Childen Under Blean was a lovely village and a pleasant community in which to live. It had its troubles and its bad eggs but that was normal for anywhere. The living suited him.

He took a deep breath smelling the scents given up by the sun on the land. He walked from the car around the back of the house and lifting the latch slipped into the kitchen. The house was quiet and he assumed that Elizabeth and the girls were out.

'Elizabeth? Are you there?'

He was answered by profound silence punctuated only by the hum of the fridge from the kitchen and the birdsong penetrating the silence from outside.

'Elizabeth,' he called again as he moved though the house. Perhaps she had left a note in the office.

Entering the room he was even more aware of the silence. On his desk he saw the mail sorted as usual; important mail in one pile and social in the other, each stack piled up neatly. Elizabeth had been busy, the mail opened and with envelopes slit and the contents displayed. Nothing unusual there except for the small pile on top of which, attached by a paper clip, was a hand written note. He stared at the note not even bothering to sit down. It read:

"To the Reverend M Jones. - I have taken Melissa and Terri to my brother's where we will be staying. You will be hearing from me when I calm down. The envelope to which this is attached explain's why. Elizabeth."

He lifted the note away and opened the envelope.

The pictures shocked him and he understood why Elizabeth had left. He reached for the whiskey bottle and poured a generous measure.

When, later that evening the vicar and his daughters failed to turn up for the choir practice Evans the Choir, still in his robe, having dismissed the singers, went to look for him. Bonny Mason and David, a choir member, came with him.

The vicar's car was parked in the driveway but there was no sign of Elizabeth's VW. There was no sign of life in the house and at first they knocked on the door but eventually David went around the back to return beckoning them to come.

'The back door's wide open.'

They entered the rear of the house one by one. Evans called out but his voice echoed in the empty rooms.

'Michael! Elizabeth! Yoo hoo!'

The silence remained.

Cautiously they made their way to the front of the house and finally arrived at the vicar's office. From within there came the sound of snoring and a smell that meant only one thing.

'Christ, the bugger's pissed!' exclaimed Evans the Choir.

The very drunken reverend Jones lay on the floor snoring and bubbling, emitting noises and with feeble efforts appeared to be trying to move.

Bonny dropped to her knees beside him and examined him closely trying to get him to speak but with no result. She looked up at Evans.

'I think we should call an ambulance. He's drunk far too much. Look on the floor,' she said pointing to the carpet where partially covered by mail was an empty whiskey bottle and clutched in one hand the vicar had another.

David acted quickly using the desk phone calling emergency services whilst Evans searched the room. He was about to say that somebody should look for Elizabeth and the girls when he saw the note and read it. Alongside it in full view was a little fan of pictures.

One was of the very active reverend stark naked on top of Sally Wise in her bedroom. One was of the vicar standing stark naked about to close a pair of curtains of a woman Evans did not know, but realised was offering a service whilst her husband was away. He had seen her with him often enough in church. The other was of the Vicar and Bonny Mason standing, again stark naked, behind her bedroom window. It was obvious what they were doing and Evans gazed at the picture not knowing what to do with it.

He was startled when beside him he heard a gasp and turned to find Bonny Mason staring at the photo.

''You got a nice pair of knockers,' he said trying to placate her but thinking that what the reverend Jones was offering her was more to his liking.

'Ambulance is on its way ... fucking arseholes! Who took that?' said David.

'I have no idea but I believe it is likely to have an effect on this village we did not expect,' Evans said, and turned to speak to Bonny.

She was sitting in an arm chair flopped, staring at the wall and muttering.

'A nice pair of knockers, oh dear, oh dear, oh dear...' she trailed off into a sob.

Evans the Choir stared at the envelope and realised that he had one similar sitting on his desk at home as yet unopened. He liked to deal with his mail late in the day. His comfort after work was more important than mail on choir practice days.

In the Simon household there was a virtual siege. Cheryl Simon had forced a chair against the door knob and beside her she laid a large kitchen knife. Downstairs her mother was in the kitchen and every time Sylvester tried to talk to her she threw something at him. So far he had collected three cans of baked beans, a jar of marmite that had bruised his shoulder, half the crockery, and had deftly dodged some flying cutlery.

'Come on talk to me at least. Let's talk about Cheryl and that little bastard Grace,' he called out to her dodging a cut glass milk jug.

'No! Go away! You disgusting man!' Sylvia yelled.

'Come on we can't go on like this.'

'Leave the house and leave us alone. Go to one of your tarts,' she screamed at him and hurled the breadboard which bounced off the door jamb and caught him across the nose. He had forgotten she was once a local champion discus thrower. The thing knocked him down temporarily blinding him. Instinct and agility cut in and he rolled to one side, dived out of the way as she sprang at him wielding a carving knife. Not exactly leaping to his feet he staggered to the front door and rushed out into the street. He always had his keys with him and his wallet and soon he was on his way to the Dog and Duck. He staggered into the bar and ordered a pint.

'Christ, the world's gone bloody mad,' he said and gazed

morosely into the amber fluid. 'Are there any real people here tonight?'

'Miles and Davey are in and I see Swanee and Martin on their way. What's up mate?'

'That little bastard Grace, that's what's up. I'll murder the little fucker when I find him.' Sylvester said and headed to where Miles and Davey were quietly chatting. He sat down and with one long draught sunk most of the pint before speaking.

'Life's a right bastard at times,' he said.

'You been in a fight Sly?'

'My missus got her knickers in a strangulated knot. My daughter's been having it off with that bloody spotty faced little shithead Mathew Grace and somebody's blown the gaffe on my natural pleasures,' he said and made mangling gestures with his big hands.

At that moment they were joined by Martin and Swanson who grinned and pointed to the quiet bar across the way. Sitting at a table apparently in convivial harmony was Forest, Amanda and Salina enjoying an evening meal with the smelly Mutley lying contentedly under the table accepting scraps.

'The world is turning to shit,' observed Sly.

'Tell us about it,' said Swanson. 'I'll fill that for you. You look like you need it.'

With the fresh pint in front of him Sly related the whole sordid incident. He explained that his wife had barricaded herself into the kitchen and more or less emptied it of all heavy throwable objects. His daughter was upstairs barricaded in her room with a kitchen knife threatening to stab him if he tried to get in.

'I was going to give her a thrashing but then my bloody missus opened her envelope and there was some pictures of me shagging the local widows and lonely women,' he said and looked wistful. 'I suppose going home tonight is not a good idea.'

'What will you do Sly?'

'I think I will have to call on a few favours.'

The drinkers nodded and settled down to talk about the match on Saturday although Sly found it difficult to concentrate.

The meeting of the Bird Watcher's Club took place in the shelter of the church porch. Nobody was there to disturb them. The girls had gone although some had promised to meet up at the weekend and all else was quiet. The ancient wooden benches in

The Birdwatchers of Childen Under Blean

the porch were pleasant to sit on and with the evening sunlight illuminating the inside the boys discussed the latest developments.

'That little prick Cook has started something with his bloody pornowhatsit group and he has the bloody cheek to ask us if we want to join. Eddicational he ses and as we already got the equipment we can fit right in. Cocky little bugger,' said Mathew.

'You told him to get fucked?'

'Yes, I did and I told him we was different. The little prick laughed and if it wasn't for his old man hanging around I would of punched his lights out,' Mathew said.

'Yeah, little shit.'

'You done them pictures yet Stan?'

Stanley looked up from where he was slumped against the wall and sounding surprised he replied: 'I give 'em to you didn't I?'

'I ain't got 'em,' Mathew said. 'What did you do with 'em?'

'I put 'em in envelopes with the names on and got 'em ready to…' he trailed off and there was a silence from his corner that needed to be filled.

'Ready to what?'

'I dunno.'

'Come on Stan what did you do with 'em. Come on man think.'

Terry and Donald blocked his exit; Stan had a tendency to run and hide when things went wrong and they knew that right now things were going very wrong.

'All right Stanley what you done this time?'

'I was pissed. I was drunk too much cider. You know whats like when I gets pissed. I gets confunked,' Stanley said, his voice tremulous and thick. In a few moments he would wet his pants. He was already beginning to babble.

As predicted there was a whimper, the smell of warm urine soaking his underwear, and the excess dribbling on the ancient flagstones. Stanley babbled. What emerged was a dreadful tale of a boy who, with the effects of cider completely taking over, had played a game of post office with the brown envelopes he was supposed to pack up into a secret folder and keep safe. They were addressed and with stamps stolen from his father he had posted them. He was trying to explain that they were safe in a box file.

'So you went out early in the morning and stuffed the envelopes in the postbox?'

'I think I wanted to catch the early morning collection,' Stanley said.

'The post is collected at 11:30 in the morning you stupid prick,' Terry said.

Stanley fell silent and sat on the bench unable to answer any more questions.

Mathew was quiet for a time and stood up eventually, fists clenched, glaring at Stanley's terrified form.

'You gonna kick his fuckin' head in?' asked Terry.

'We oughter.'

Stanley was saved by the blue light arrival of an ambulance that came to a halt outside the vicarage. Stanley's dreadful actions were forgotten for the time being as the boys watched the ambulance staff enter the house and eventually come out again with the recumbent figure of the vicar on a stretcher. The ambulance hurried off with the lights flashing. In the light from the open front door they saw the organist and the choir master fussing around.

'Let's go,' said Mathew.

Terry and Donald followed leaving Stanley to the dampened contemplation of his predicament including his status with the Bird Watchers. He was relieved when instead of being beaten up all he had to contend with was his urinary discomfort. That was something he could deal with.

Mathew arrived home, mumbled about being sorry he was late back from choir and looked anxiously around for the brown envelope. He went to his room and stayed there.

Evans the Choir walked Bonny Mason home and sat in her room for a while listening to her complaining about Sylvester and wondering who it was that took the pictures. Evans had a good idea but kept the knowledge to himself. The truth would out soon enough without his contribution. At a point during the proceedings she made a play for him and he smiled at her.

'Sorry love, no offence meant, but I don't fancy you,' he said, and when she looked affronted he added. 'Wrong gender luvvy.'

'Oh shit, a bloody pouf. I might have guessed something like that would happen,' she said. 'Our vicar is a randy sod. A lecher but I have a feeling his lechery will bite his bum.'

'Possibly, most likely. I had better go home,' he said.

Evans the Choir opened his mail leaving the fat envelope to last. He was amused that whoever had posted it had pasted enough stamps on it to send it to Australia. There was nothing much else of note although his club had accepted him for training again this year. Good news. And now for the brown envelope.

He slit the flap and spilled the contents onto his desk.

The pictures were obviously a complete set and he was amused to find pictures of himself dressed in his finest attire quietly drinking a pink gin. Nothing sexy there and nothing anybody could use against him. It was time for him to "come out" and he thought that there was no time like the present. He looked at his watch and saw that if he hurried he could make it down to the Dog and Duck in time.

The drinkers, including Sylvester watched as the man they knew as Evans the Choir strolled daintily up the steps dressed in his best red dress, with a black shawl draped tastefully over his shoulders, and his dark hair or wig sparkling with a diamond pin. His ears adorned with pendants set off the necklace sparkling on his exposed chest. With dark hose covering his legs and a modest pair of heels on his feet he walked gracefully up to the bar and politely asked for a pink gin.

That he was barely made up was a good thing because he had had no time to trim his eyebrows or shave off the light moustache and beard he always wore.

The drinkers and the customers that knew him gaped in surprise and, waiting until he had his drink in hand and taking a dainty sip first he raised the glass and smiled at them all.

'To trannies everywhere,' he said caring little if they joined him or not.

'Coo. I think Evans the Choir is coming out at last, 'Salina said and raised her wine glass to take a sip. 'To trannies.'

What bothered her father was that she already knew that Evans was gay.

From the drinkers' table Sylvester stopped gaping and looked at Evans and shook his head. This was unexpected.

'Bloody hell, our choir master's a bloody shirt lifter,' he said. He was extremely nervous when Evans came over to their table and, finding a spare seat, joined them.

'Let's get a few things straight shall we? I am not interested in fondling boys, nor am I interested in you nice strong heterosexuals. All I want to do is train the choir, wear dresses when I want to and clutch desperately at rugby players. In the light of certain impending revelations I thought it best I reveal my true self. I might suggest you try Lily Williams this evening Sylvester. Now chaps, we should sort out this problem, I think, before it gets out of hand. I have to tell you that our dear reverend Jones is at the moment having his stomach pumped or whatever they do to alcoholics to save them from being permanently pickled. We found the very reverend very drunk on his office floor and a note from his wife telling him she had gone away. The note was pinned to a brown envelope of naughty pictures. Nice one of you with Bonny,' he said addressing Sly with a smile.

Sly took a swipe at him but Evans easily evaded the blow and with hardly any effort held his wrist and forcing the arm down by applying a cripplingly painful lock. He tut-tutted.

'Oh dear, you shouldn't do that sort of thing to an ex-soldier,' Evans said.

When Horace called "time" the pub was buzzing with rumours and villagers lingered before eventually going home knowing that something exciting was afoot.

The chatter at their homes before bedtime was enough to start the rumours running amok even before breakfast on Friday.

In the Simon house Sylvia eventually persuaded her daughter to abandon her determination to slice bits off her father. With the girl watching she locked the front door, slid the bolts, and did the same with the back door. The ground floor windows had locks on them for insurance purposes which were all carefully shut, and despite how angry she felt about her daughter's actions she allowed the girl to sleep with her.

They both placed sharp knives beside the bed and slept fitfully to wake to the sound of Sylvester's car starting up. It was certain now that the Williams home was likely to have two kittens added to it and one rather penitent philanderer.

On the Friday following the fall of the reverend Jones, the dramatic "coming out" of Evans the Choir, or as he was unkindly labelled by the non PC men and women in the village as Evans the Queer, things became interesting. Amanda and Salina Maloney were now on the Dog and Duck staff, and it was said that Forest Maloney was now a freelance IT worker.

Of interest to many was the pile of clothes including his cricket whites stacked on the Simon household lawn along with Sylvester's trophies, his books and his electronic gadgets. Luckily the weather remained dry.

The Birdwatchers of Childen Under Blean

The news that the vicar was recovering in hospital was a comfort to many of the congregation and a worry to others. It was said that the Sunday service would be taken by a vicar from another parish.

The cricket match scheduled for Saturday was to go ahead as usual and as it was expected to be a pleasant day people looked forward to a fun weekend.

Vernon Green and Maddy appeared to know nothing of the recent events and opened the tea rooms as usual but wallowed in the results of the gossip. The village youngsters were still active but the events related to the church were severely curtailed owing to the absence of the vicar and his wife. Graham Cook was active with his Junior Bird Watchers and with their notes, binoculars and packs of sandwiches set off in little groups to look for birds to observe and note down. The Greens were happy to supply drinks and snacks in exchange for their pounds and pence and noted that the sales of bird seed increased steadily as parents bought more and more to supply their recently purchased bird feeders. Graham Cook was a valuable asset which they hoped would continue long past his pubescence.

In all, apart from those residents who had received packets of pictures on Thursday, everything in Childen Under Blean was moving along nicely. The rumours and counter rumours raced around the gossip channels no less rapidly amongst the older generations than with the young.

Sara Grace and her friends were busy slapping thumbs on keys sending notes and messages flying to friends and back as the situation developed. The main topic of the morning was Cheryl Simon's relationship with Mathew for which Sara had to defend or not as she felt fit. She hacked into her brother's laptop and soon she was confirming the rumours.

She listened to the gossip at the tea rooms and learned of Evans the Choir's action the night before and smiled. Why they hadn't seen it coming she didn't know but there it was. The gay rugby player was outed at last.

'Good on him,' she said and grinned.

'Good on who?' asked Miriam Small.

'Oh sorry I was talking to myself but if you must know I was thinking of Evans the Choir,' she said and smiled, placing the order on the table.

'Oh him, yes that cross dresser,' she said. 'About time he

showed his true colours.'

It was later that day when she hacked into her brother's laptop and found the frantic messages describing the cock-up with the pictures.

'Oh dear Mathew you have really done it this time.'

And that was what happened when Thomas Grace collected the undercharged package from the post office in town and grumpily paid the stamp price and the extra for a brown envelope addressed to Mister Grace. Curious as to its contents and assuming it was for him he opened it at the counter and gasped when he saw the contents. Being a bright lad he realised that the package should have been addressed to his son. The scrawled note from Stanley White confirmed it. The counter hand shook his head when Thomas Grace walked off with the package muttering about having somebody's guts for garters.

He was captain of the Childen Eleven and as such he was not going to let his son's perversions get in the way of the game on Saturday. The team were due in the nets on Friday evening. His son's problem can wait he told himself. Arriving home that afternoon he took the envelope to his den and put it in the safe. He changed into casual clothes and walked to the green where the lads were gathering. They spent the next two hours practising. Sylvester was there but instead of his usual caustic self he was more dedicated to doing as he was told. There must be something drastically wrong with him to prevent him taking the mickey, thought Thomas. It was not like him to miss out on a laugh at somebody else's expense.

Thomas Grace was the only one in the village who had not heard of Sylvester's sudden eviction.

He hurried home for a late meal which he ate whilst Sara and Melanie watched the telly and then it was time to talk to Mathew.

'Is Mathew home Melanie?'

''He's upstairs in his room,' she replied.

'He's not very happy,' said Sara.

'Neither am I as far as he is concerned.' Thomas dutifully put his crockery and cutlery in the dishwasher and went to his den. He took the envelope from the safe and with a heavy heart he climbed the stairs to his son's room. Giving a perfunctory knock he opened the door and went in to find his son sitting at his laptop looking guilty.

'Dad, do you have to?'

The Birdwatchers of Childen Under Blean

Thomas shut the door and held out the envelope.

Mathew stared at it wide eyed and panicky.

'I believe this was meant for you. I have perused the contents and quite frankly I am disgusted. I am disappointed in you and I want to know what you intended to do with them. Well?' Thomas asked.

Mathew stared at the brown envelope and the edges of the photos inside and knew that whatever he said next would be wrong. he could lie. He could deny. He could bluster. He could grovel. He could blame the others.

Instead he threw a tantrum.

Thomas watched as the boy started to smash his fists down on his desktop. He yelled out and cried and kicked out with his feet and began to bounce around in his chair.

'You don't love me! Nobody loves me! I do me best and all anybody does is have a go at me. All people do is put me down all the time. I'm human like anybody else, enni?' He continued for some minutes yelling and soon the door opened and framed in the open doorway looking worried was Sara and Melanie.

Mathew pointed at Melanie and yelled. 'You always treat Sara like your favourite. Why not me?' And with a lunge he rose from his chair and lunched himself at Sara.

'And as for you, you nasty bitch you're always sneering at me!'

He made it halfway across the room. Thomas felled him with a fist alongside his ear and lowered him on his bed.

'What's this all about husband?'

In answer he showed them the pictures.

'Oh dear what a mess,' said Melanie.

Sara remained silent and bit her lip.

She helped her parents take Mathew downstairs to the kitchen where they made him sit in a chair at the table and with the pictures spread out they began to interrogate him. Sara was amused at how her father played the role of bad cop and her mother the kindly good one. Amid sobs and much backtracking, lies and self justification, aided by hot sweet tea and the promise of painkillers for his headache the whole sordid story gradually unfolded. The three at the table did not notice that Sara had slipped out of the room.

She slipped into her own bedroom and within moments she had hacked into her brother's laptop and viewed what he had placed in what he thought was secure areas. She made a list of the people affected and downloaded some of the images to a USB memory stick.

'Old tech but useful.' She closed the contact and wandered back downstairs. Her brother was crying and snuffling like a booby and making tearful promises to behave himself in future. To add even more pathos to the scene her parents laid hands on his head and began to pray for him.

She went into the living room and turned on the telly.

Saturday dawned bright and clear with perhaps a hint of rain forecast for the evening and as the match was scheduled for an earlier start the village green was alive with locals anticipating the afternoon's entertainment. The Tea Room was doing well with visitors heading for the hills and cyclists making a stop before tackling the lanes, and a smattering of locals eager to share the gossip.

Sara worked her tables with smiles and cheerful chat, and with the other two girls "working their tits off" as Sally put it, the tips were mounting up. Maddy put the jar beside the till each shift with a little cash in it already, a mix of 50p and £1 and £2 coins which she deducted for use again. This morning the coins and a few notes were mounting up. The boob parade was working.

Sally's advice was to look good, smile a lot, be polite and friendly and show 'em yer tits. Sally was a practical girl who despite her atrocious language much modified for the situation, knew how to wait tables and taught Sara and the other girls what to do. One piece of advice Sara took to heart was simple.

'Forget about what you are doing after your shift or anything at home and concentrate on the punters; they are your extras if you work it right. Good skills girls,' she said. Her advice seemed to work. They always made good tips on the Saturday sessions.

Being attentive to the punters also meant learning much about village life that she would otherwise not know. The trick was to keep your mouth shut and your ears open. Acting dumb was no good but showing a little intelligence and acting a little cute worked well. You sort of blended in to the background.

Thomas Grace stood on the green and watched the umpire toss the coin. His opposite number called "heads", won the toss and elected to bat. They shook hands and soon he had his team sorted out with Sylvester at wicket looking furious and others in the team bristling with anticipation. Sylvester woke up with a hangover and overindulgence of sexual activity with the Widow Williams.

Thomas had noted with horror how he had dragged himself to the pitch, swore and grumbled when anybody shouted and lumbered around the practice nets during warm up.

'You're not fit,' Thomas said frowning at him.

'I'm as fit as I'm fucking going to be,' Sly said and downed a pill for his headache.

'Drink lots of water and have a good piddle before we take the field. You going to be all right on wicket?'

'Of course I am. I'm a fucking wicket keeper. You going to chuck me out today?'

'If you don't come up to scratch. Young Scroggins will take your place.'

'Fuck off. I'm on the committee and if I say I am fit then I will play. Scroggins can go fuck himself,' Sylvester said.

Thomas nodded his head and said: 'Right. I will play you but if you fail I will have you off and you can sit and watch.'

And now the opposing side were reaping the benefit. In five overs Sylvester had allowed twelve byes, missed two easy catches and was swearing like a trooper at all and sundry. At the change over for the sixth over Thomas had a word with Miles.

'Listen Miles. This is a very unchristian thing but do you think you can stop bowling at the stumps and knock our keeper over? He's useless.'

Miles looked at him and grinned.

'I'll do me best.'

The first ball of that over smashed the wicket of the terrified batsman much to Miles' surprise, and when the new batsman had sighted up Miles bowled one over the stumps that bounced up high. Unfortunately the batsman deflected it and scored a run. The next one bounced from leg side and whether it was aimed or just luck flew through Sylvester's hands hitting his chest with a resounding thud. Sylvester's backward flip was pretty to watch. He threw his hands up over his head and with his legs bent at the knees appeared to simulate a high jumper at the height of his leap. He landed on his back and settled like a deflated balloon.

'Got the bugger,' said Miles.

From the seating arranged outside the Dog and Duck there came a mixture of sympathetic cries, cheers, a few loud Alleluias and a chorus of Praise the Lords.

Sylvester was stretchered off minus his pads and gloves and young Scroggins who was twenty-one years younger, about half Sylvester's size and much less of a target, took up position. It has to be said that Miles, not wanting to destroy his own team concentrated on bowling out the opposition.

The innings finished with the opposition all out for 118. Miles was credited with four wickets and one wicket keeper. During the break Thomas stood facing Sylvester, who lay on a couch supplied by the landlord, and spoke his mind.

'Next time you turn up like that I will send you home for your own safety. Young Scroggins did all right and unless you come up to scratch I am thinking of putting him in your place and leaving you as twelfth man. You can start qualifying for the team like anybody else after this. It's time you straightened your life out, and you can start today. Watch the rest of the match and learn,' Thomas said and stamped his foot.

'Temper, temper,' Sylvester said adding all the sarcasm he could bear into the two words. He followed the remark with a string of oaths that ended with a gurgle.

Thomas Grace moved forward and despite his obvious unfair advantage walloped Sylvester with his bunched fists blacking both his eyes and turning to where Sly had rested his beer he picked up the nearly full jar and emptied the contents over the groaning face. He liked the gurgle as Sly tried to slurp beer down his throat. He was too surprised to fight back and even if he had attempted to, the pain in his bruised chest would have prevented him.

Thomas walked away and anybody close enough to hear him would have heard a strange recitation.

'At times even a worm may turn. He that striketh me, turn unto him the other cheek. Sod that, the bloke deserved it.'

The home team's innings started with Thomas and young Scroggins as openers and to his surprise Thomas discovered that with Sylvester no longer opposite as second bat the runs came faster. He lost his wicket to put on a comfortable 31 and young Scroggins remained at the crease to ease the team to a three wicket win posting 121 runs in total. Scroggins closed the game with a neat boundary to square leg.

When they went back to the Dog and Duck Sylvester had left.

The opposition was puzzled that in spite of young Scroggins'

The Birdwatchers of Childen Under Blean

debut 45 not out, the real hero of the Childen Eleven seemed to be Miles. The explanation was given simply as:

'He's never bowled so well,' and they had to accept that.

The hospitality was consistent with the Dog and Duck cuisine, the food was paid for by the Cricket Club but not the drinks. The surprise of the evening was that Thomas Grace for the first time since they had known him brought a pint for himself and ordered something a little stronger for Miles.

In all, the match that day was a success for all concerned.

It was noticeable that although they restricted themselves to one or two drinks many of the Davis Community watched the game. It was from them the earlier Alleluias emanated.

The other change that many of the team noticed was that Amanda Maloney and her daughter were being trained that afternoon as Dog and Duck staff members. What they didn't see was Sally Wise and her male companion slip in to the restaurant and take their places at a pre-booked table.

One person in the village who was aware of them more than idle curiosity was Sara Grace. She was riding her horse that afternoon and had seen the pair out walking and had puzzled over why a brother and sister would hold hands so lovingly.

Another was young Graham Cook who with his team of dedicated bird watchers met them on their way to the top of the hill above the quarry. The pair were not holding hands but were chatting happily together and being polite the little group bid them a good afternoon.

'Thank you, and good afternoon to you.'

Graham's little group of eager girls and boys smiled and trotted off eager to find at least some of the birds on their lists. Graham was puzzled. He knew that Mrs Wise was a widow, his mother had explained, and he was told that her brother had come to stay but when he looked back down the road he saw them kissing like lovers, and that, he thought, was odd. But like most youngsters intent on an interesting hobby he forgot about the encounter and busied himself with the rest of the day. When they returned, the bird watchers exchanged notes in a larger group having purchased sticky drinks and ice creams from the tea rooms.

Some of the birdwatchers remained to watch the match.

Graham was surprised to see his uncle Joe playing in the place of Mr Simon and wondered what had happened. Uncle Joe was scoring a lot of runs which would please Joe's dad who would like

The Birdwatchers of Childen Under Blean

to play but had no talent for cricket however much he tried. Joe's father made some dreadful jokes. One of the worst was when Graham announced his bird watching scheme.

'I can help you there because in my time I have scored enough ducks to cover a cricket pitch,' he said, and laughed uproariously.

Graham had politely chuckled finding that as much as he could manage. A chortle would be difficult and an outright laugh an impossibility. However despite his memory of Joe's father suddenly popping into his head Graham couldn't help thinking there was something seriously wrong in the village of Childen under Blean. Graham had an idea that it had a lot to do with Mathew Grace and his version of the bird watcher's club. He remembered the disturbing event in the quarry.

'Crikey, things are going wrong,' he said quietly.

He was distracted from his thoughts because now the group were casting the votes for best sighting and he was pleased to see that it was one of the girls. She was presented with the badge by the current best sighter and her name marked in the book. When they had enough money in the kitty they would buy replica badges so that each winner could wear them.

When it was time for tea the group split up and walked home in pairs and groups chatting happily and as he turned into the close that led to his own small street he saw Sylvester Simon walking with the widow Williams. Mr Simon looked upset and as he walked he complained of pain and as usual he was swearing profusely. The subjects of his invective seemed to be "the whole *@!*&** Grace family" and that skinny gutted ***** Joe *@!*&** Scroggins.

Elder Davis would not approve of such language.

Graham noted with amusement the two black eyes Sylvester sported reminding him of a somewhat angry panda.

Things were hotting up.

From Evans the Choir's point of view the Sunday service was fun. The borrowed clergyman who arrived to do the honours drove sedately up to the church in a grey Volvo saloon. He parked the car and climbed out to take a look around; standing with his hands on his hips looking first at the church, and then at the view from the space close to the lich gate. He took a few paces around the car as if to make sure everything was all right and leaned down to unlock the boot.

Evans thought the reverend Townsend looked much like an old time preacher in his black suit and the ecclesiastical shirt with the collar showing predominantly at his throat. The man's overgrown eyebrows gave him the appearance of a horned beetle and as he walked solemnly along the path the image of an older world cleric was even more powerful.

'A fire and brimstone preacher, I've no doubt,' said Evans as he watched the man approach.

'Welcome to our church, your reverence,' said Evans the Choir, reaching out a hand which was barely grasped.

'Indeed, I am John Townsend. Bishop Mathews directed me to conduct the worship here.'

'Oh, you are standing in until the reverend Jones returns?' Evans asked brightly.

'That may or may not be,' Townsend said, glaring at Evans and beyond the choir master to where the musicians were setting up their instruments.

That is the question, thought Evans, and followed the clergyman's disapproving stare.

'I hope you are not expecting me to deal with all this charismatic nonsense,' Townsend said pointing at the guitars and drums. 'You can dispense with that lot for a start. Reverend Jones may have approved of such fripperies but I will not tolerate this modern jangle. Go play in a popular music band if you want to, but such noises do not belong in a church. This is a house of God not of mammon.'

Morris Davis, the lay preacher, attempted to explain that he was prepared to conduct services.

'Whilst our revered pastor is indisposed, I am quite capable of leading the worship of our Lord and minister to the needs of our people,' Davis said.

'Not whilst I am given the care of the church under the direction of Bishop Mathews,' Townsend said and glowered at Davis.

'As you please, your reverence,' Davis replied and quietly instructed the band to do as they were asked. He watched them pack up. His dearly beloved wife and fellow preacher gripped his sleeve.

'Are you not going to put this fellow in his place?' she said.

'It is not my place to do that.'

'Tell him you can take the service,' she said.

The Birdwatchers of Childen Under Blean

Davis trembled.

Caught between duty to his followers and the fear of this irascible vicar, and the look on his dearly beloved's face, Davis quailed. Driving evil spirits from people who believed in him was easy compared to facing up to the real thing.

Davis quailed.

'I, er, will take the service,' he said and looked at the musicians. 'You may as well set up again.'

The reverend Townsend snorted like a bull and, bull like advanced on Davis angrily. Short of horns and cloven hooves Davis believed he was faced with the Devil in human form and backed away.

'I said, get rid of this rubbish. I will take the service and we will have none of this Gospel nonsense.' He boomed and faced Davis who withered.

'Yes, yes, your reverence,' he said and drifted away.

'Get on with it,' Townsend said to the musicians as Davis and dearly beloved moved off arguing.

The reverend Townsend waited until the young people had dismantled their equipment and stored the sound system in the small ante-room. He gave a list of hymns to Bonny Mason and with measured steps he returned to the vestry to don his robes.

The sacking of the band meant that Evans was once again fully in charge of the music and however badly Bonny Mason played the singing was always good. The people of Childen Under Blean were good singers. The bonus this Sunday morning was that after explaining how far the organ had deteriorated Bonny was allowed to play one of the keyboards and as a concession to the band the regular keyboard player was allowed to accompany her.

The congregation arrived and took their places. Some used the remaining pews and the rest claimed the chairs. The reverend Townsend raised his hand and blessed the congregation.

'In the absence of your regular pastor, I will be conducting services until it is decided by the diocese who will take over from Reverend Michael Jones,' Townsend said and gazed at the congregation. His glare was such that some of the more timid worshippers quailed in their seats. 'It seems that the reverend had a moral lapse...' And would have continued but for a timely interruption.

'The bloke was as pissed as a parrot and his wife and kids have buggered off. Some says the dirty bugger's been spreading it about a bit.' The speaker was Nobby Clarke, a supporter of conventional church.

'Alleluia to that!' cried another.

'Nevertheless I am here to minister the Lord's word to you in the manner to which the Church of England is accustomed. I suggest there is no call for the gabbling and yelling out the way they do in these Gospel Churches,' Townsend said. 'We are Anglicans not some American Gospel Group.' Nobody missed the emphasis of capital letters imagining the words underlined. They got the message.

It was obvious to Evans that Townsend and the Bishop related such worship with African Americans and didn't like it. Where Evans had lived as a child he was used to a diverse community and was shocked that such intolerance was expressed by a man of the cloth. He wondered about his attitude toward gays.

Evans saw the dark disapproval on the faces of those he had earlier dubbed the Triffids and the looks of relief from the rest. As they began the first hymn his choir started off a bit ragged but after the first few bars they were singing sweetly in harmony and with clear diction. He was proud of them. Even Mathew Grace and his friends seemed to be enjoying themselves.

Despite the new man's edict there were many who raised their hands and faces up to Heaven and cried out for salvation. As the service progressed so the reverend Townsend became more agitated and annoyed with the spurious interruptions. His prayers were punctuated by cries of "Praise the Lord!", 'Save me Jesus!" ecstatic groans and Alleluias that rose above a mild undertone of insane babbling.

Townsend tolerated all this, lived through another hymn although he fumed as the Triffids sang their own version. Finally it was time for his sermon. He stood in the pulpit looming over the wooden edge, his gown spreading as he leaned on the rim, his large hands gripping the edge like talons. The light from the stained glass windows cast a subdued sunlight on his gaunt features, and as he prepared to speak he reminded Evans, not of the carven Eagle of the lectern below, but a vulture, or the terrible bird-like creature from *The Wall*.

'It seems to me that what I am about to speak of is a lesson to be learned not only those sinners amongst you,' he said and swept a feathery wing with its accusing talon in an arc to include the whole congregation and paused a moment to listen to the low gasps and whimpers of the guilty, and continued. 'It is a pity that your spiritual leader was so tempted to indulge in this demon, the devil's liquor, the ruin of man's sensibilities, the despoiler of the minds and purity of women, the breaker of homes and families, and not act as a good example to his flock. We must abjure such evil practices, never letting such terrible substances pass our lips...'

Townsend swung into his theme with such fervour that Nobby, who loved a drop of ale himself, but rarely was ever in too drunken a state, thought was way over the top. When Townsend had reached the predictable description of the drooling, incomprehensible drunk imposing his excess on his fellow man Nobby could hold back no longer.

'And I say that this dreadful state of inebriation is the Devil's work ...' and in full fist thumping flight Townsend was interrupted by a mocking voice.

'Good on the hairy legged bugger, he does a fucking good job of getting me pissed on a Saturday. Gives me a reason for coming to church on Sunday to make up for it,' Nobby called out and with his hands held high he added. 'Bloody alleluia to that!'

The reverend Townsend stood in his pulpit dumbstruck as the congregation burst into noisy mirth. Except for a few stalwarts and those teetotallers who were enjoying the message, the conventional worshippers and the charismatic gospellers laughed uproariously sharing remarks and witty quips between them.

Evans tapped his stick on the lectern he used for his music and started the choir on an unaccompanied version of *Amazing Grace* sung Gospel style and a few bars into it Bonny and her companion was giving it their all. It was a good clapping and stomping beat.

It had little effect on the chaos in the aisles but he thought it was a nice ironic touch as Townsend tried to restore order.

'I command you all to be quiet!' Townsend shouted banging his hand on the pulpit to emphasise his demand, but to no effect.

Eventually the holy man stormed from the pulpit and with fire in his eyes he crossed to where Nobby was sitting rocking with laughter and grabbing his collar hauled him from his seat.

'Right, you heathen, out!'

Taken by surprise Nobby was dragged like an errant public schoolboy out of the church and pushed with some force on to the paving outside the door.

Nobby scrambled to his feet and with a roar of anger he charged at the vicar.

'Nobody chucks me out of church!'

Townsend was not one to turn the other cheek and parried the blows but Nobby was a strong man and a match for Townsend. The congregation surged from the church to see what was happening and formed a ring around the contestants.

The choir stopped singing and most of them joined the watching crowd,

The exceptions were Cheryl Simon and Mathew Grace who slipped out of the side door to a favourite spot. Terry Smith, grabbing Aggie Wilson before she could disappear with the crowd muttered in her ear.

'Come on, back end of the vestry for a quick shag.'

She giggled and they disappeared.

One thing choir practice had done for Terry was to give him a chance to practice his lechery and he had found that Aggie Wilson liked plenty of practice.

Bonny Mason quietly walked off using the same exit as Mathew and Cheryl taking her music with her. Evans the Choir sat down and waited.

Morris Davis stood in the gradually emptying church wringing his hands. He had no idea how to handle this situation. He could preach up a storm and call on the faithful to declare their faith but his personal house was built on sand and at the first signs of violence he had cringed behind his dearly beloved who had shrugged him off.

'This needs sorting out,' she said and hurried off.

Thomas and Melanie Grace followed the crowd and waited for the door to clear before emerging to see Nobby and Townsend facing each other. With Nobby swearing profusely and the vicar snarling and growling like an animal, the pair circled and closed, took wild swipes and backed off to circle again. It was an odd battle. Nobby, the brawler dived in boots and all, and the vicar managed to evade most of them and come at Nobby like a boxer.

'Oh dear Thomas, is this really the way we want our church leaders to behave?' Melanie said grasping him. 'Shall we call the police?'

'My dear, forgive me but I will have to step in and sort this out,' Thomas said.

'Be careful.'

In answer Thomas smiled and pushed his way through the crowd.

'Stop this disgusting brawling!' he cried out standing a little apart from the two antagonists.

The fighting men ignored him and lunged one at the other. He sighed and with precision of footwork and economy of movement he took Nobby by the right wrist and, watched by an astonished crowd, flipped him neatly on his back. Turning to Townsend who was looking for a body to hit, with another swift movement he dropped the man neatly on to his adversary and with a voice of command he ordered some of the men to grab them both and escort them back into the church.

Inside the church, sitting on a chair, Nobby groaned. Held down by two young Scroggins men he looked at Thomas and said.

'What the fuck did you do to me?'

'Kotegeishi, and please curb your language. Stay there Nobby or else I will hurt you again,' Thomas said. 'I have a vicar to return to the fold.'

The reverend Townsend glowered at Thomas and was about to speak when Thomas smiled at him benevolently and explained.

'You will take your holy books and go from this place to your car and drive away and never come back here again. Is that understood?'

'I have a mission to preach here and..."

'Fight members of the congregation? Turn the other cheek my friend. We will wait for our reverend Jones to return, for despite his flaws he is most respected, even if he likes to be a little bit more generous with his love,' Thomas said.

Men escorted the vicar to the vestry where he changed, fussily folded up his robes and carrying his books walked unsteadily back to his car. Thomas urged the congregation to watch him leave to give Terry and Aggie time to escape from their tryst. He was aware that Mathew and Cheryl were missing, Bonny had gone home and Coren Evans was sitting in the pulpit grinning like an ape.

'Shall we have a closing hymn Coren?'

Soon most of the choir was assembled, the lad who played second keyboard was ready and as Evans the Choir began to lead them into some of the popular christian songs Thomas noted with relief that his son and Cheryl had returned and somehow

Terry and Aggie had taken their places.

After the congregation had gone, and the choir had put their gowns in the basket Thomas and Melanie with Coren fussing around were surprised to see Nobby Clarke still sitting in his seat.

'Are you all right Nobby?'

'I am now. Sorry about all that. I got out of hand a bit there. I should of shut me gob but he was a pompous bas ... er man. What we goin' to do about Jonesey?'

'Let us wait for him to return and find out then. I am afraid the reverend Jones has more to worry him than how the services are conducted.'

'We can put up with the Triffids. Besides, I like the singing,' Nobby said and grinned. 'But where did you learn to scrap like that Thomas?'

'I used to teach unarmed combat in the Army. Next time you get stroppy remember that will you?'

'Ah, so it was you what give Sylvester his panda face.'

'So what do we do about Jones?' asked Coren.

'I think we wait for him to decide whether or not to come back and Morris can run the services.

'Nah, not him, he hid up when the punch up started. I seen him looking scared when that Vicar grabbed me. I might have bashed the bugger then if I wasn't so startled,' Nobby said.

Thomas looked around for Morris but he was gone.

'Who then Nobby?'

'Amanda Forest, she's knows what's what and is stroppy enough to control the Triffids as his reverence calls 'em.'

'Oh dear, who will ask her.'

'I'll talk to her. I ain't scared of her like you lot,' Nobby said.

That Sunday afternoon although the drinkers, the cricket team including Thomas and the Childen Eleven supporters celebrated the win there was trouble brewing.

Under the surface of pleasure at the win, the story of Nobby facing up to the new vicar and Thomas once again solving a problem there was a seething anger. Those who had received revealing envelopes had worked out who had sent them. What they did not yet know was that electronic copies were set free on the internet. In one particular media outlet they were about to go viral.

Evans the Choir was content to leave the rumour mill alone and sat in his room that evening watching the telly. He had completed his run that afternoon, sorted his diet for the coming season and had fed the cat. He had also spent some time in the garden making good the flower beds and cutting flowers for his vases.

The incident that morning at the church still amused him and with his pink gin beside him, wearing his favourite dress he was comfortable. Evans the Choir was pleased that things had turned out as they had.

Nobby Clarke found Amanda Maloney serving behind the bar and on his second trip he spoke to her.

'You heard about the church this morning Mandy?'

'I was there you idiot,' she said.

'Oh, I thought you walked out?'

'I did but I popped in to see what the new vicar was like.'

'I flattened him,' Nobby said.

'No you didn't. Thomas Grace flipped you both on the ground. I was there. What do you want?'

'I reckons you ought to look after the services until his nibs gets back. You got the voice and you know how to look after them what does the hollerin' and gabbling,' he said.

'You mean it?'

'Yeah.'

'Nope, not me. Melanie Grace can do that.'

'Oh gawd, I never thought of her but she won't talk to me,' he said.

She glared at him and seeing that he was not affected by it she said: 'I'll ask her shall I?'

'Good idea Mandy my lovely,' he said and grinned,

'You're an idiot,' she said slightly miffed that he had conned her into doing his work for him.

'This one will cost an extra quid. Tips.' She said and poured his pint. He paid up giving her a tenner and gave her five back.

'Thanks Nobby,' she said, surprised. But Nobby was gone.

Cheryl and her mother were busy sorting through the house having decided that if things got difficult they would make a decision on what to do with Sylvester. They both loved him and despite his faults they missed him. Facing each other across the dining table they both burst into tears. Sylvia because her anger had subsided and Cheryl because she had discovered she was pregnant. She knew there was something missing from her relationship with Mathew and now she had to tell her mother what it was.

'Condoms,' she sobbed, 'that's what we didn't remember.'

'What? What's that you said Cheryl?'

'Got a bun in the oven. We forgot condoms, Mathew and me,' she said and putting her head in her arms on the table she sobbed. In between the sobs she muttered about her dad killing her and what are they going to with a baby, what with Mathew being such a bloody idiot.

'Christ, you stupid little cow,' exclaimed her mother and then with the realisation that her daughter really was upset she placed a hand on hers and said softly. 'Don't worry love, we will help you.'

'I don't want to live with him. All I wanted was a good shagging and now look what's happened. Dad will murder me,' she wailed and looked up at her mother red-faced and confused. 'What am I going to do?'

'Get used to potty training,' her mother said and added quietly, 'for both of them.'

After that interlude, to keep the girl's mind off her predicament, she suggested they give the place a good tidy-up.

On that same Sunday afternoon Graham Cook was busy making a vlog for his group and when he had finally sorted it he posted it under the name Childen Under Blean Ornithologists. He was surprised when other vlogs popped up under the Childen name. One was about the cricket and the other was, well, rather shocking, and already it had over 500 000 hits.

'Oh dear that is awkward,' he said and wondered who the vlogger was. To find out he had to become the 500 123rd viewer. He skipped most of it and eventually found the name. He felt sorry for the lad and although he did so he could only leave a comment on the vlogger's address. Getting the vlog taken down was not that easy and when he tried he was denied.

'Oh dear oh dear,' he said and signed off.

Sylvester Simon called in sick on Monday and took the week off. He had to attend the local walk in clinic to gain an appointment with his GP who simply signed a sick note for five working days. During that week he remained with Lily Williams unaware that Sylvia and Cheryl planned to ask him to come home. He was surprised to see Bonny Mason driving her ancient

Peugot out of the village on Tuesday to return with the vicar who sat in the vehicle looking pale and shocked.

'She's collected him from the Central and we all know what she will be doing,' Lily said and grinned.

'You mean old Jonesy has been comforting the local widows?'

'Well yes, just like you really,' she said, and gazed after the slowly disappearing car. 'I suppose we will all miss him now she has got her claws into him.'

'She's a funny woman that one,' he said.

Lily was deep within her own thoughts and between them they missed the meanings of their comments. She was beginning to feel uncomfortable with him mooching around the place and he was steadily feeling more like a guest than a lover and itched, in spite of his hurts and the face full of blue and yellow bruises, to get back to work. However, on Wednesday, although the spicy rumour of an amorous liaison between the vicar and Bonny Mason was making the rounds, he was bored. What saved him was the call from Dotty Dolly telling him the kittens were ready. He told Lily who brightened up and looked interested when he suggested they go and collect them.

'Them? I thought you were getting one for me?'

'Of course but until Sylvia chucked me out I was getting one for the family as well,' he said. 'I paid for them and their gear so we may as well go and get them.'

'I only want one.'

'Then I will have the other,' he said realising that whatever he did he had to go back home. Life, he thought, was getting bloody messy.

Lily sniffed at the mess inside Dotty's house but said nothing to upset the woman whose obsession with cats seemed over the top. This was a cat lady and she wondered how Sylvester knew her. She assumed they were lovers at some time but could barely conceive how the relationship would go.

'You wants both them pussycats?'

'Yes, one each,' Lily said and smiled. They were nice healthy cats, lively and friendly and she knew she was going to get on with hers and hoped Sly would manage. She would rescue it if he bogged out.

They loaded the cats into his car, belted their cage into the rear seat and ignored the yelling as they drove off. She saw Dotty Dolly waving a handkerchief as they drove off and soon they were home with the outside doors and windows shut settling the cats into their new home. The animals explored the lower rooms first, became used to the new environment and little by little spread their domain to include the kitchen and dining room and eventually the stairs.

Lily gushed effusively over her gift and, when it was obvious Sylvester was not that interested in the creatures, with no sign of embarrassment she named hers Tiddles.

'Give your little one a name,' she said rolling the kitten over and tickling its belly.

'You give it a name,' he said grumpily seeing her attention focusing on the cats more than on him and not liking it. He was even more disgusted when she grinned and tickled its neck with one long graceful finger and declared solemnly.

'I name this cat Miss Grumps,' she said and laughed.

He groaned.

He knew that whatever his objections the kittens would be given the names that will show up on their chips. He reasoned that if he wanted his extra-marital nooky he had better not argue unless of course he could go home and take his kitten with him. By Thursday morning he was sick of her obsession with the kittens and declared that he would pop in to work and put up with the ribbing. The bruising across his chest was not so painful now and he could move more easily. When she agreed, he was happy to put up with the discomfort to drive to the office.

They didn't need him and his boss told him to say hello and bugger off home.

'See you on Monday.'

There was nothing he could do and putting off going home he wandered around the shopping centre and dropped into a coffee shop for a cup and a sandwich. He was surprised when as he was collecting his order he saw Mathew Grace suddenly get up from his seat near the window looking like a startled chicken and hurry out clutching the remains of a sandwich.

'That little sod,' he said but unable to do more than watch him go he found a seat and sat down to eat. He didn't enjoy his lunch. Seeing that little ratbag up close had rattled him. 'I'll punch the little bugger's lights out if I get the chance.'

He sat thinking about the mess he had made.

His daughter and that ratbag Grace. He getting found out and chucked out of home and his chosen mistress obviously happier with the kittens than with him. He felt very much alone.

'Christ, what a bloody mess,' he said.

Which was exactly what Sylvia Simon thought when she learned that Cheryl was pregnant. She knew where Sylvester had gone and with her mind made up she decided to call on them both and have a chat. She rang Lily's doorbell and almost turned back when the door remained closed. She was about to ring again when it opened to reveal Lily dressed casually looking at her with a welcoming smile.

'Ah, Sylvia, come in. I've been expecting you,' she said and closing the door behind them she led the way into the kitchen. Two lively kittens raced around playing with a fluffy ball. She shuddered. She didn't like cats.

'One's mine the other is supposed to be Sylvester's. I have the feeling that they will both be mine,' she said. 'Now, I suppose you want the stupid bugger back?'

She sighed and with huge sobs she put her head in her hands and managed to babble a garbled version of her plea.

'I love the idiot. He's all I got and now my Cheryl is pregnant. It's so unfair!'

Lily made some tea and gave her a cup which seemed to calm her down and softly told her that she had planned to chuck him out that very day but was planning to come and see her before that to take him back.'

'I don't want the kitten,' she said, sniffing but pleased.

'That's fine. I named her after him. He's paying for the treatment and the chipping plus their first inoculations so you won't have to worry. I will take both of them. Now, how shall we do this sister?'

Sylvia smiled and made a suggestion which amused Lily and between them they made a plan. Sylvia left Lily's home feeling much better and instead of slapping a meal together with indifference for her and Cheryl she took her time over the task to prepare the food properly. When Cheryl came home she would tell her what she had learned and how things would be if her father came back.

That Thursday evening the drinkers were surprised to see Sylvester's car parked outside the Dog and Duck. Even more surprising was that Sylvester was already in the bar sitting at their usual table supping on a jar. One by one they joined him and eventually after the usual banter they demanded Sylvester explain. Before he could start telling the tale Forest breezed in with Mutley, left the dog with Miles and went to the bar to order a round of drinks. The ales replenished Forest settled, with the dog under his seat, Sylvester began his story.

'We went and fetched the pussycats, spent Tuesday and Wednesday getting used to them. I expected to take one back home with me as a gift for the missus and me girl to say bloody sorry for being an arsehole but it all went tits up,' he said.

Forest was amazed that Sly had admitted to his failings and approved.

'So why are you here?'

'Well Miles my friend, it is simple. I found this under her bed. Well actually it was one of the kittens that found it and I did me nut.' He held up a twisted clerical dog collar. 'Evidence. That randy bloody vicar tromping on my patch.'

Forest roared with laughter and when the others realised what had happened and saw Sly sitting looking glum and hurt holding the battered collar they too started laughing.

'What's so bloody funny?'

'So what happened Sly?'

'I accused her of being unfaithful with a man of faith, and she told me I was total prat, said if I didn't like it I could pack my bags and bugger off.'

'So I guess you said she was an ungrateful bitch and a slag and before you knew it you was out the door and bundled in your car with the well known phrase or saying "Good Riddance" ringing in your glowing ears?' said Forest.

'Were you listening at the bloody door mate or are you a bloody smart arse?'

'A smart arse will do. So where to now my friend. If it wasn't for your predilection for homing in on other people's wives and the widows of our village I would invite you to stay with us.'

'I wouldn't want to. Your Amanda is a dragon and Salina sees right through me, and I bet the dog would take a bite out of my bum after a day or two. I'm staying here. Horace does a nice breakfast so they say.' He looked even more glum and said quietly and bitterly, 'I bought her the cat, for christ's sake.'

'Cat? You said two kittens.'

'That's right, one for her and one for me.'

'How sweet,' said Forest.

'Bollocks mate. She called hers Tiddles, for crying out loud, and give mine a name I didn't like, but them's the breaks,' Sly said and shrugged.

'Oh what did she call it?'

'Miss Grumps,' he said and snarled when they laughed. It was Martin who changed the subject when it was obvious Sly was working up a fury.

'Right mate, what about the Vicar and that Bonny Mason?' asked Martin. 'I saw them go in the vicarage when I passed. He looked bloody awful and she looked like she was keen on him. You know, arms around him and holding hands and all that. They was unloading groceries and it looked like she was moving in.'

'And you saw all that just passing?'

'Well I did sort of go by slow like,' he replied.

'Passing slowly on a no exit road,' said Davey with a broad grin.

'My missus says she was doing his washing,' said Swanson. 'And earlier today they went down to her house and collected a car load of her stuff.'

He would have said more but at that moment Sally Wise came in with the man they knew as her brother. The pair were met by Salina Maloney who saw them to their table and politely took their order. The drinkers watched the interaction between Salina and her customers until the girl had moved off to place the order. They did not see the arrival of a bottle of red house wine and Salina's new found skill in pouring it and the sparkle in their eyes as they toasted one another and thanked their hostess. Instead they were trying work out who the bloody hell the geezer was.

Sylvester remembered his encounter with the man with embarrassment. He had failed to stake his claim then and now he had to keep his gob shut and hope that nobody knew about his clandestine trysts with her.

'Didn't you used to have a thing with Sally?' asked Davey addressing Sly.

'Yeah I used to. Looks like I'm out of luck with all of them,' he said and gloomily mooched up to the bar and bought a round of drinks. He thought the Vicar was right. Get totally pissed and somebody will look after you when everything else turns to shit.

'My life's falling apart Horace,' he said as that worthy served him.

'You seem to be having it tough mate,' Horace said but did not tell him about what he had seen earlier on one of the kitchen hand's mobile phone. What would happen next he had no idea but he had a feeling that Sylvester was in for an even rougher time. That sort of thing belonged in those magazines you bought from the top shelf or sent for from seamy outlets in plain envelopes. Horace smiled warmly and added. 'Don't worry mate it will all come right in the end.'

'I bloody hope so.'

Horace watched him as he carried the drinks two by two to the table. 'I bloody hope so too,' he muttered and shook his head.

In the Vicarage that evening as the drinkers were speculating on the relationship between Bonny and himself the reverend Jones was explaining that if it came to the pinch he could move in to her place.

'Now that would cause a scandal,' she said, and giggled. 'That Martin Crook stopped outside in his van long enough for us to invite him in for a cup of tea and a bun with me baking the bun. Nosy sod.'

'Ah yes, I am sure the village will know about it. Bonny, I feel so ashamed. I've let the congregation down, upset the diocese, lost the ones I love and all because I have natural carnal desires. What is to become of me?'

She gazed at him saying nothing.

'I could be de-frocked,' he said.

'Oh stop whingeing you silly bugger and get on with it. You have work to do and a church to run. As for carnal desires you have me for that sort of thing. Concentrate on the vicaring until they undresses you. Brazen it out. We can do it together,' she said. 'Make yourself useful and peel some spuds whilst I put my clothes away. When Elizabeth and the girls come to collect their gear tomorrow you can bugger off if you want.'

'You think I will be de-frocked?'

'More than likely.'

'Oh my God what will I do?'

'Stop wearing ecclesiastical dresses. Carry on as you are and see what happens,' she said. 'Pull yourself together you silly bugger and take things day by day.'

'I don't wear dresses,' he said.

'The cassock is a dress.'

'It's a smock, or rather a Holy vestment designed to show my position in the community as a spiritual leader,' he said and was about to expand on the idea when she giggled.

'You certainly are a spiritual leader with the amount of scotch you put away. Your consumption is the talk of the village,' she said.

He looked at her and instead of an organist and church helper he saw a woman in control who was treating the situation pragmatically. A no nonsense person who in this mode was somewhat frightening.

'Trust in the Lord?' he asked hopefully.

'If you wish, but I would suggest you look at what else you can do other than preaching, and get on with it,' she said.

He stared at her and suddenly realised what he should have known all along.

'Bonny, are you a Christian. I don't mean because you put C of E on the census form but truly a believer?'

'Ha ha ha ha! I gave that up when my Gary popped his clogs. He was a part time lay preacher at the baptist chapel where we lived and I was expected to be part of it. Essentially he was a fire and brimstone fundamentalist who bashed the Old Testament. All that stuff you allowed to get started here is nothing compared to Gary's madness. The difference is that you are really a dyed in the wool Anglican and a part time lecher, whereas Gary couldn't keep his hands off any woman. You got caught out and got extremely pissed in response. Gary managed an accident before he was metaphorically tarred and feathered and run out of town. I had to leave and settled here hoping to while away my time with work and playing the organ. The trouble is I like a bit of nooky on the side and that gets awkward,' she said.

'What am I going to do?'

'Get a grip man. Make up with Elizabeth or change your life,' she said. 'You can start by sorting out your office and getting things sorted for church. I have to go to work. See you,' she said and hurried off.

He sat for a while staring at the wall and then with a shrug he began the task. As he worked he wondered what had happened to Gary. Eventually with a cup of instant and a soggy ginger nut he turned on his computer. He dealt with the messages, sorted out his mail and was about to shut down the net to get on with writing a sermon when he checked his junk mail.

The name seemed familiar and without thinking too much he

clicked on it. The link led to a YouTube video which started running immediately. He gasped when he saw the contents and gasped even louder when he saw the number of hits. Over one point four million had seen it already. He realised that one of the perpetrators was that snotty little ratbag Mathew Grace.

'If the Lord Jesus expects me to turn the other cheek over this then I will repudiate his teachings and follow the dictates of Exodus chapter twenty one verses, twenty three to er twenty five and to hell with it,' he said and banged his hand down hard on his desk. 'Ouch oh fuck!'

He looked out of the window and over the rooftops he could see the green and the Dog and Duck lit up by the afternoon sunshine. He wished he could join the drinkers and drown his sorrows in their church instead of sitting alone in his empty vicarage.

'Choir practice this evening, thank the Lord,' he said.

Bonny arrived after work and cooked a meal which they shared before going across to the church and he felt some comfort from that.

Whilst the drinkers were enjoying their ales, Sally Wise was enjoying her meal, and the village settled in to watch that evening's telly, or plod on with garden tasks and the never ending DIY projects, the Bird Watchers fingers and thumbs were busy stabbing phones trying to understand what had gone wrong.

< Mt at c prac.ok?>

Mathew called the club to order and, obeying his parents, he took off for the church. Evans the Choir was already getting them to warm up and with the others of the club in place he began singing. Perversely he enjoyed the singing although like the others he had joined up to have a crack at the girls. He was disturbed by Cheryl's intense gaze at him and although he desperately wanted to be with her he had to talk to the lads. During the break he managed to get close to her.

'We gotta talk,' they said almost together.

'All right, you better join us after,' he said and would have said more but for the arrival of the reverend Jones and Bonny Mason. It was obvious that the vicar was upset and that Bonny Mason was holding him back. He was a big man and Mathew knew he had played rugby in his time, and now that the pictures were already sent out it was a volatile combination.

'Shall we get started again boys and girls,' called out Evans.

The first to head for the stalls was Mathew who watched as Evans deftly interfered with the vicar's progress and muttered something to the angry cleric that Mathew couldn't catch. Bonny Mason started playing the keyboard and Evans announced the start of the accompanied practice. Although Jones joined in, as he often did, Mathew kept an eye on him in case he made a move.

'I don't trust that holy sod,' he muttered.

A few minutes before the session was due to end Mathew made his own panicky move and taking everybody by surprise he dashed from his stall and ran like a clumsy gazelle out the door to comparative freedom.

Behind him the reverend Jones turned from his watchful position and gave chase. Evans, with a look of ecstasy dropped his baton and unencumbered by his gown followed at a gallop and wrapped his arms around the vicar's waist, shoulder against a heaving buttock and dropped him to the floor.

Lying on the flagstones, the vicar, winded from the unexpected thump of a solid body tackling him so easily, he groaned. Feet seemed to thunder past him and for a moment he imagined he was on the rugby field. Evans, loving the contact and thinking of the coming season shushed him.

'We'll get the bugger. I too have need of words with him. Better not get carried away with vengeance my dear chap,' Evans said fondling bits the vicar did not really want fondled.

'Get your hands off me you raving poof,' Jones said and tried to disengage from the choirmaster's affectionate embrace.

'Sorry, I thought you cared the way you lay there not trying to fight me off,' Evans said, and reluctantly let go, he got his feet slowly and dusted himself down with this hands.

The vicar scrambled to his feet, furious and stood legs wide apart clenching and unclenching his fists. The little arc of singers watched breathlessly waiting in anticipation of more action. Bonny sat calmly at her keyboard playing a sotto voce version of *Jealousy* whilst Evans stood facing him with a smile.

The vicar saw the choir and noted that Mathew's mates were missing and Cheryl Simon was gone too. That explained the thundering feet.

'I would have got him...'

'Too much Exodus and Deuteronomy. Like my old man. Only in this case its a...' began Bonny Mason.

'Please madam, remember you are in a holy place,' said Evans the Choir with firm authority. 'I suggest we all go home and come back on Sunday when the reverend Jones will conduct a most empowering service.'

The people left, leaving Bonny Mason, Evans and the Vicar standing in the cold church each trying to think of something to say.

'Back to my place for a sherry,' Jones said, and soon they were sitting in his office sipping at the contents of his second best cut glasses. He had explained why he was so angry and showed them the video which was now up over two million hits and had humbly asked them for their help.

'Simple really, try and get the damn thing pulled before it goes any further and I suggest you make a complaint to the police,' Evans said.

'But what will happen to me and the church and my reputation in the village?'

'Oh, I think you will do all right. You could be a bit of a hero with some. Imagine the sermons on morality you can devise as the fornicating vicar. They'll get over it and you never know the church might get some more punters on board,' Evans said.

'But what about you Coren, surely the image of you is on there too. Do you want that?'

'Nah, but most people know I'm a gay Welshman already, and a man can wear what he likes at home.' he said and grinned.

'So when do we start?' Jones said.

'No time like the present,' Bonny said, and elbowing the vicar aside she took over his computer and began the process of complaint.

Unaware of the clouds of doom hanging over them Mathew and his friends including Cheryl sneaked home after deciding to trace the "little shitface vlogger and punch his fucking lights out" with Stanley in charge of the search.

'You dropped us in the shit; you get us out,' Mathew said.

And as he walked Cheryl home she told him of her predicament.

Sara, chatting with her friends learned of her brother's sudden exit from the church; it was now common knowledge with them that Cheryl was pregnant. She had passed on the vlog link and asked for advice.

'Try getting rid of the originals,' Salina said and the others agreed.

The problem was that by the time she had their reply her brother had come home and gone to his room. She sent back a simple message. <ok lol> and went downstairs to watch the telly with her parents.

Friday morning was wet and business at the tea rooms was slow. The new Coven met for elevenses and instead of the usual energy instilled in them by Amanda Maloney it was a subdued chat covering topics that although interesting failed to enthuse. Sara served them with tea and buns hoping for a tip but although they did put some coins in the jar it was small change and by the time her shift was over her share was disappointing. The walkers came in the afternoon and tips were plentiful but by that time she was at the stables. She had no chance that day to hack into her brother's computer and so with her wet gear on she rode Figaro out into the Woodlands accompanied by three of the younger girls and their ponies. On one of the more open stretches of the bridle way they could look down on to the village and saw something interesting happening at the vicarage.

'Look there's miss Melissa and miss Terri,' said one of the girls.

The track was close enough to see that it was Sara's two friends and their mother. They were loading belongings into a hired van helped by two men. Hovering around them was the reverend Jones who every now and then was threatened by one of the men if he got too near.

The little party dismounted letting their horses graze and watched the drama unfold below. It appeared that in spite of the vicar's protestations the exodus of his family continued. Sara was about to call on her friends to mount up when she saw a car drive up the lane and stop beside the vicarage. A woman alighted and flipped an umbrella up before walking elegantly toward the action.

The activity ceased and Sara watched the woman speak first to the vicar and then to the vicar's wife. Her two friends stopped to watch and the two men finished loading a bed into the rear of the van and stood close, listening.

There was much waving of arms and gesticulating. Elizabeth Jones stood with her hands on her hips and addressed both the vicar and the woman. The woman's gestures did not suggest what happened next but it seemed that both women were adamant. They stepped forward and with the newcomer still holding her umbrella and Elizabeth stepping forward beside her they acted as one.

'Coo, he didn't 'arf go down,' said one of the girls.

Sara laughed and agreed, but in a way she felt sorry for the reverend Jones. They mounted up and continued their trek. Behind them the loading continued. The vicar crawled into his office and the visitor, Mrs Colleen Wyvern, drove off.

The exodus continued with no more holy interference.

Sara and her party trotted on and eventually, wet and yet happy they arrived back at the stables.

'We walk back together?' Sara said and the other two agreed. She helped them finish up and made sure their horses were settled and comfortable.

'My mum said the vicar was drunk.'

'He was very drunk,' Sara said.

'I heard his wife and Miss Melissa and Miss Terri have gone to live in town.'

'Well you saw them moving their stuff out.'

'We like them.'

Sara realised that these two were part of the club that Melissa and Terri used to run and she felt sad. The girls were nice kids and deserved a break.

'You miss the club do you?'

'Yes, very much. It was fun, and we all used to do things.'

'I wish it would start up again.'

Sara looked at them and nodded.

'You know, I think you're right. We ought to do it again.'

'Oh, great! There's lots who would like that.'

'Better than the vicar's silly activities. We could run some too better than that. I mean some of the older boys and girls know what to do.'

'Graham Cook's got the right idea.'

'He's a nerd but we like him.'

'We've got the ponies but others cannot afford them.'

'So, if the club started again you would be happy?'

'Yep.'

'Yep.'

'I will see what I can do,' Sara said, and as they walked so they chatted about ideas. She learned a lot about Graham and his birdwatching and realised that the nerdy kid had everything well organised. She parted with the girls feeling enthusiastic and determined to put the idea to her friends.

The idea would more than make up for her brother's stupidity.

The envelope lay on Sally Wise's hall table. She had left it with the other junk mail ready to be re-cycled and forgot about it. When she and Colin collected the mail that Friday morning from the mat she picked it up and took it into the kitchen.

There was none for him and one or two for her and more junk. They read through it and was about to put the junk in the bin when Colin saw the envelope.

'What's this I wonder?' he said ripping it open. He tipped the contents out and stared at it. 'Pictures. Who would send you pictures?'

And when he saw what they were he spread them on the table top for her to see.

'Bloody hell! So this is what the row is all about,' Sally said. 'Nice one of us.'

'What do you mean Sally?'

'I have an idea where these come from. Listen up and I will explain,' she said. When she had finished he sat staring at the picture of them standing stark naked at her bedroom window taking in the early morning sun.

'You realise we don't need this,' he said.

She looked up at him and understood.

'I never thought about that. We need to stop it somehow,' she said.

'Before it's too late,' he said and reached out for her hand covering it with his and gently squeezing it.

'One thing we need to do is sort out the sender,' he said.

'What do you mean?'

'Well if it is the boy you say it is we need to shut him up.'

She stiffened and thought about what he was planning to do and realised that they were in trouble anyway. She knew what Colin meant and drew in a deep breath before answering.

'I think we could do ourselves a disservice if we did that. It would be better to leave as soon as possible,' she said.

'Be good to shut the boy up.'

'There are four of them. Best to let the police sort them out and whilst they are doing that we make a dash for it. Start packing,' she said.

He looked at her for a few minutes and then making up his

mind he nodded.

Friday night in the Dog and Duck during the summer and early autumn was when Horace and Molly put on a special. This Friday it was fish supper night and instead of tables and chairs set out people ate al fresco and watched the sport on the big screen. For those who wanted to remain discreet there were a few tables set aside a-la-carte. In general the fish supper was a hit with the locals.

The drinkers and their families joined the queues for service and Horace and Molly did a good trade. The two Maloney women served, taking turns at the bar and at the makeshift bar set up of two solid tables where customers ordered and collected their food.

In the Davis home the Christian Community were having a shared meal. It was at that meal Morris Davis was asked to step down as Lay Preacher.

'Do I not serve you?'

'You defied not the unbeliever.'

'Hang on that's not us,' he said.

'He who believes not in the Lord but in his own powers is an unbeliever. That Vicar was one such and ye failed to deny him.'

'I am a peaceful man.'

'A back slider and one who fails in his duty to defy the foe.'

'What was I supposed to do? Preach fire and brimstone at him and call on the Lord to strike him down?' Davis said.

The silence that followed was broken by one of the women.

'Ye have no faith in the power of the Lord to smite His enemies. Ye should have called upon Him.'

'Woman, thou have no call to speak thus,' Davis said.

'Then is it not such that when Jesus called upon us all to honour Him we were not included? Is not the Mother of Jesus, dear Mary, a woman blessed by God? Was not Mary Magdalene one also of our kind? Can I not be permitted to speak when the gifts of heaven were laid on all of us? Or is it all just a load of shit?'

The silence that followed was profound.

Lay preacher and Community Elder Morris Davis stood stunned, unable to speak. The silence was broken by the woman who laughed and snapped her fingers.

'Come on, anybody want to try the fish supper at the Dog and

Duck?'

Her husband slipped in beside her and said quietly: 'Come Delia, I will pay for thee.'

And as they left the house the worshippers still standing in shocked and thoughtful silence heard her say to here husband: 'My darling, you can stop all this theeing and thouing. Time we had a drink in the pub and afterwards come home to a good ...' and the last few words were lost as the pair left the room.

Poor Morris Davis tried to restore order but one by one and in pairs his followers sneaked out to their own homes.

Mathew and his friends sneaked into the pub early and persuaded Horace to give them take-aways; paid their bills and hurried off with their food and some bottles of cider. Their objective was to keep clear of Sylvester Simon and his friends.

Sylvester joined his friends and grumbling about being regulars claimed their usual table.

'You know Molly, old Sly looks almost human today,' remarked Horace.

'I'll go for the almost,' she said and looked up in surprise. 'Well looky, looky, see who's here.' The reverend Jones and Bonny Mason walked up the steps and joined the queue which Molly considered was a first this summer anyway. And right behind them carrying the drinks was Evans the Choir. The reverend Jones ordered three portions, doused them with salt and vinegar and carried them to where Evans had claimed some table space.

Molly noted they had two tall pink gins and one pint of bitter.

She also noted that Sylvester Simon was glowering at the vicar and his party and fingering his dinner knife.

'Horace, watch that bugger Sly will you. I got a feeling he wants a piece of our holy man. Might you have a word with him?'

Horace called one of the boys over and asked him to serve. He sloped over to the drinker's table and grinned at them wiping his hands on his apron.

'All right lads? Fish supper to your liking?'

'Bloody good ho. Mutley likes the extra chips. Nice one Horace. Do my two girls get a taste of this?' Forest said and waited for an answer.

'Of course. Oh and I see the parson has arrived with his friends. Now, as I see it, this is not his normal style. I suggest we make the silly bugger welcome and try not to get too hot under the collar if he says the wrong thing, shall we?'

Sylvester growled and looked at Horace and with his heavy face pushed forward he said: 'Or what?'

'Or somebody might be sleeping out in the rain this night,' Horace said.

'Bloody hell, a man can't eat his dinner without somebody having a poke at him,' Sylvester said quietly.

'That goes for our holy roller too Sly. I wouldn't want to see either of you upsetting the clients with a bout of fisticuffs in my bar,' Horace said.

Sylvester slumped in his chair and said: 'All right, let me finish me dinner then and I'll promise not to punch the bugger's lights out.'

'Good man.'

Despite his annoyance at being spoken to, Sylvester ate his meal and enjoyed it realising that if he did have a go at Jones he would be shitting in his own nest and, apart from the solidness of such structures when thus lined, it was a messy idea. He allowed Swanson to buy the next round and decided that even if he did help Horace make a profit he was going to bed that night partially pissed.

The other person to go to bed that night partially pissed was Mathew Grace who managed to slip up the stairs to his room without making any contact with the aliens in his living room. As he lay on his bed, the world spinning wildly underneath him, he slipped in and out of sleep. They had found out who the vlogger was and Stanley was trying desperately to contact the bastard and stop it running. The full implication of the news from Cheryl hit him. When he had panicked trying to say the kid wasn't his she had grabbed his hair and twisted it tightly until he begged for mercy.

'Listen you bloody moron. You are the only one what done it with me. My mum knows and she is not happy. My dad doesn't know yet but when he finds out you better do the right thing or he will tear you apart, starting with these,' she said, and grabbed his testicles and twisted. The pain made his eyes water and he knew that between his Bird Watching activities and her father's anger he was to put it mildly, bollixed.

'All right, all right, for Christ's sake,' he squeaked.

'I have your word?'

'Yes, yes, but let go of me balls will yer?' he gasped, eyes streaming and body wriggling.

'Promise?'

'Let me go first!'

She eased off and gripped his wrist instead.

'Right, now promise.'

It must have been at that moment, recovering during the post testicle squeezing period, he fell in love. If a woman could be as direct as she was and know what she wanted then he was hooked.

'Listen you evil bitch, I reckon I have to promise. I don't got no choice,' he said.

'You mean that?'

'Yeah, I reckon I sort of finds yer, sort of all right,' he said, struggling with the words.

'What do you mean, arsehole?'

'Listen Cheryl, I think I love you,' he said and slumped against the wall. She had let him go and, standing back a little way glowered at him.

'You only think so?'

'Oh fuck it, I know so. Listen you stupid cow, I love you, see?' he said giving her a lop-sided grin.

Bloody twat. Why didn't you say?' she said.

'I dunno,' he said. 'But I got trouble.'

She was silent for while and then, with a few sobs, she came close, put her arms around him and nuzzled into his body.

'Kiss me you stupid bugger,' she said.

And for the first time since they had met he held her and kissed her properly feeling like he imagined they do in the movies.

Fucking ace, he thought.

Which was a help when he thought about the thing that Terry had pointed out.

'All them pictures what we got is dodgy if the police see 'em. We could get done if they finds out,' Terry said and looked at the others his face showing his fear.

'What we gotta do then?'

'We gotta get rid of 'em,' Terry said and told them what to do.

The trouble was that by the time they got home they had drunk too much cider to remember what it was Terry told them and instead they fell asleep to wake up late the next morning with hangovers.

Sara went to bed late, saw that her brother's door was slightly ajar with the lights on and with barely a sound she crept toward it and peeped in. Mathew was lying on his belly with his head to one side snoring. She switched off his light and quietly shut his door.

She sat at her desk with her door closed and her lights down and soon she was hacking into his system. it took some time to find everything but at last she did and steadily during the next two and a half hours she gave his computer a deep clean that she hoped would sort out the problem. When she had finished she relaxed in her chair, and sighed.

'My brother may be a right moronic twat but he is my brother and I owe it to him to try at least,' she said to the line of teddies and soft toys that sat on the top shelf of her bookcase. She undressed, put on her night clothes and went to the toilet. She filled a glass with fresh water, put it down neatly on her desk and climbed into bed.

Unlike her brother whose sleep was disturbed by nightmares she drifted into slumber and lay like the innocent princess between the clean sheets and her horse motif duvet. She woke early on Saturday morning ready for duty at the stables in the morning and the tea rooms in the afternoon.

That Saturday the Eleven were playing away and outwardly the village rested quiet except for the flow of walkers and cyclists using the tea rooms and the pub. Vernon had taken the cricketers out to the venue in the minibus leaving Maddy and the part time staff to work the shop.

Sylvester Simon was dropped from the team; a bitter disappointment for him but when Thomas Grace informed him that young Scroggins would take his place he remembered the battering Thomas had given him.

'I could be twelfth man?'

'Nope, the team will work better without you in your present mood Sly. I'm sorry but we need to win this match and quite frankly you are so grumpy of late that some of the others are a bit frightened of you. Quite frankly I don't want to keep on bashing you to shut you up,' Thomas said.

'This is me out altogether then is it?'

'No, when you are in form you are a good player and always add fun to the matches but, like I said, you are being unpleasant of late. It might pay for you to spend the time trying to solve your family problems,' Thomas said kindly, and gripped Sly's arm warmly. 'Listen, we are mates and quite honestly I want you to be back to normal.'

Sylvester looked at Thomas and saw only friendliness.

'You mean back with Sylvia and all that?'

Thomas gave him an enormous grin.

'You got it and for a time try keeping your cock in your trousers around other women and the local widows for a while,' Thomas said.

Sylvester was shocked. Thomas had never said anything like that before. This movement against the straight and narrow that had affected Forest's dragon of a wife and the vicar himself, seemed to be spreading.

'I'll try,' he said but when the minibus pulled away from outside the tea rooms he wished he was with them.

Graham Cook and his band of devotees gathered on the village green dressed for walking carrying small back packs containing bird books, notepads, mobile phones and their lunch to which they added drinks bought from Maddy, like a little troop of scouts they set off for the woodlands. Sara watched them moving off and wished that her stupid brother had really taken up bird watching.

Terry Smith gazing out of his bedroom window saw the troop pass his house marching single file up the alleyway to the footpath and snarled. 'I'll get that smarmy little prick. Me and Donny can knock seven bales out of the little bugger if we get him on his own.'

He snatched his phone from his bedside table and called Donny.

'You alone mate?'

Donny grunted an answer and Terry told him about Graham.

'The little fuckwit is off up the woods with his group of twittering arseholes. I reckon where they might be going. We could go up there and get the little fucker on his own.'

'What walking?'

The remark stumped Terry, but ever resourceful he brightened up. 'We got bikes.'

'We did have bikes.'

Not to be deterred and wanting revenge Terry suggested they sort them out and then go after the kids. 'The little fuckers will be wandering around and we can use the roads once the bikes is up and running. Bring yours round to my place and we will fix them up.'

Mid morning the sight of Donny and Terry busy fettling their bikes and sorting out new inner tubes, oiling chains and cables surprised Terry's family. It was an improvement on his usual weekend inactivity so they left him to it. It was close to noon when the two boys set off to explore the hills.

'Well done Terry, I have a packed lunch for each of you,' Maggie Smith said handing them both a bag with straps to throw over their shoulders.

It was not until they were struggling along the road out of the village did Terry remark in his mother's generosity.

'Bloody pink. What she think I am giving me a pink bag,' he said.

'Mine's bleedin' Kermit green, with little piggies on it. We look like a couple of fucking schoolkids.' Donny said but did not suggest ditching them. Terry's mother had said she wanted the bags back and Terry's dad was a big bloke. Donny, the coward didn't fancy arguing with him.

The steady slope leading from the village saw them gasping and wheezing with the effort which was an indication of their lack of fitness.

'Why do they make these hills so fucking steep,' Terry gasped when they stopped for a rest. Donny was about to answer when four lycra clad cyclists, two men and two women rode easily past them calling out a cheery good afternoon.

They were too astonished to answer.

For them it was a long slog up the slopes and down again until at last they were on the ridge where the road was more or less even and with renewed energy they cycled slowly along the lanes until at last they came to where Terry thought the birdwatchers might be. There was a car park off the lane and locking the bikes to a fence post they started off.

'What if we want a quick getaway?'

'What if the fucking things were nicked?' replied Terry.

And with their bags over their shoulders they set off looking for Graham's followers.

'I reckon they are close to the chalk pit, so we should try there first,' said Terry.

'Oh yeah, that place we went when we started.'

'Right then, let's go.'

They stomped along the narrow pathway pushing through the scrub that loomed over the track in places, swearing when brambles hit them until at last they reached the clear area of grass and small bushes close to the pit.

As they neared the edge they kept a look out for Graham and his friends. They moved cautiously intending to creep up on them quietly and unseen.

'We creep up on the little shit and grab him.' He said and Terry grinned.

'Yeah, and give him a good duffing,' said Donny, licking his lips in anticipation. He agreed that grabbing was a good idea.

From his position in the bushes close to the edge of the pit Graham heard Terry and Donny coming. The birds fluttered up in front of the pair showing their progress, although he had heard and recognised their voices he slipped off to investigate.

'Donald and Terence, now what plan have they in mind,' he whispered and keeping out of sight he listened to their sporadic conversation. Quickly he moved quietly back to the group and told them what was happening.

Lyla came up with a cunning plan. Her parents were Blackadder fans and anything bizarre appealed to her. Graham giggled.

'Pass it along,' he whispered, and like the rest of the group merged into the shrubbery.

Terry and Donny moved as quietly as they could along the track above the pit arguing about where to look until at last ahead of them they saw Graham moving steadily away from them concentrating it seemed on stalking a bird.

'He don't know we're here,' whispered Terry.

'Right then, let's get after the little shit.'

But it wasn't that easy. Their quarry remained ahead of them flitting in and out of the bushes until at last they had him in the open. The bushes opened out on to a natural platform of cropped grass and wild flowers humped by ant hills and dotted with rabbit burrows with trails of rabbit droppings warming in the sunshine. Their victim was trapped on the edge of the chalk pit.

Their quarry – quarried.

'Hello Graham, we want to have a little chat with you about a mate of yours what done a vid we don't bleedin' well want splashed all over. You gonna tell us how to find him,' Donny said. Graham stepped back nervously and glanced down at the edge as the two larger boys approached.

'I am sorry but I am unaware of the situation to which you are referring,' Graham said, giving them an owlish smile.

'Speak fucking English will you. What you on about?' Terry demanded.

'Oh dear I thought I had made myself quite clear,' Graham said.

'Let's kick the shit out of the little git,' said Donny and with Terry beside him they made a grab for the younger boy.

He wasn't there.

And before they could gather their senses missiles rained on them from behind. They both turned around to see Graham's crowd of followers running at them carrying sticks and rocks in their hands. Whooping and hollering, some crying out movie style Kung fu calls, they fanned out in two lines, intent on protecting their leader.

Terry and Donny dodged to and fro looking for an escape route but wherever they looked there was a wall of angry youngsters armed to the teeth intent on having a go at them. Too late they realised they had backed away too far.

As he lay flat on a small grassy ledge Graham watched them tumble in to the pit. He winced as they hit the bottom and bounced.

'Oh dear, how unfortunate,' he said.

With help from his friends he clambered up from the ledge and gazed down into the shallow pit where Terry and Donny lay groaning and moaning.

'I am thinking we should call for assistance,' he said, and grinned.

One of them made made contact with the emergency services whilst others climbed down to the injured boys to administer first aid. The rest sat in the sunshine and ate their lunches. Eventually the emergency crews arrived to deal with the two young lads and accepted Graham's somewhat convoluted explanation of what had happened.

As Graham said afterwards.

'The police officer was very sympathetic but seemed a little sceptical of exactly how Terry and Donny toppled over the edge but I did emphasise that they were about to assault me. I told them they became frightened when my friends arrived. It seemed they panicked and possibly tripped each other up. My friends rescued me from the ledge where I had fallen,' he said feeling guilty that he had contrived to stretch the truth a little.

It was not a good day for Terry and Donny.

They both suffered concussion, multiple bruising, broken bones, cuts and abrasions and above all that they never got to eat their packed lunches. Contrary to Terry's caution in locking the bikes to a fence post somebody with a strong bolt cutter nicked them anyway.

Otherwise life in and around Childen Under Blean continued as on any other Saturday. Cheryl and Sylvia Simon were busy washing curtains that afternoon. Having cleaned the place thoroughly the curtains looked dowdy and grubby. The curtains needed hand washing which was hard work but with a good breeze that afternoon the curtains soon dried ready for a light ironing. They saw the police cars and the ambulance hurry through the village but passed it off as a car crash or some such on one of the lanes. They were unaware of Terry and Donny's trek to the woods. They were also unaware that the number of hits on what was known now as "The Childen Story" had risen to 3, 748 112 in the last twenty four hours and that people in town and around the county were beginning to take a lot of interest. The question was "where was this den of iniquity?" and other less complimentary remarks.

Bored out of his brain and unwilling to get drunk in the afternoon, Sylvester stood on the village green and, straightening his tie, walked with determination to his house. With fading determination he pressed the bell button hearing the familiar tones in the hallway. A pink something glowed through the glass panel of the front door and it was opened by Cheryl wearing her old pink onesie.

'Er, may I come in love?'

From within there came a cry demanding to know who was at the door. Cheryl called out over her shoulder. 'It's dad, I think he want's to talk.' More noise from within and Cheryl said: 'Mum says come in but excuse us as we are working and not to get in the way.'

Committed now, he entered the house to find his wife plunging curtains in the large utility room sink. He approached cautiously and looked at her working away moving aside when Cheryl took over.

'Well?' Sylvia asked meaning much more.

He slumped. All his arrogance and determination was gone. He was the truly penitent and knew that whatever he asked for he would not get unless he agreed to return on her terms. He loved this woman and regretted his actions. Mostly he was regretting the assumption that he could sow his seed wherever he wanted.

'I want to come back if you will have me,' he said.

She looked at him seeing embarrassment, genuine remorse and, knowing her husband she knew he was truly sorry. She knew he couldn't cope outside his home and that this week of inactivity had shown him how useless he was without some direction.

'On my terms Sylvester.'

'On your terms.'

'Right, for a start you can go and collect your stuff from the pub and when you get back you can help us with this, and this evening we will talk about us,' she said.

That evening with one of her dinners inside him and feeling apprehensive, he listened as she laid down the terms of return. The terms, mollified by her love for him, were as harsh, in his mind, as the reparations imposed on Germany post world war one. Under her terms he was not allowed to rant and rave when he found out that Cheryl was to have Mathew Grace's child.

His homecoming was a mixed blessing.

He had paid for two kittens as gifts for a woman who would now be his ex-lover and his wife's bosom friend; consented to be friendly to a kid he detested who had caused his downfall, and promised that when he had urges, to "roger" his wife instead of the village's loose females. On the plus side he missed the influx of curious visitors to the Dog and Duck that evening who were intent on identifying the Childen Lovers.

The drinkers, bereft of Sylvester's company, were distracted from noticing the nosy strangers comparing notes over drinks and snacks, and the increase in motor traffic, by the discussion of the day's cricket match. It appeared that young Scroggins had matched his previous performance and helped their captain to lead the team to a win.

When Thomas Grace arrived with his wife in what was an unprecedented visit by both of them they knew something important had happened. She had a bitter lemon and he chose a pint of real ale and with others of the team joining them he made an announcement.

'Next week is the last game of the championship. We play against Stoat Malbury who like us is looking for a win for first place. We would like your support on the day. That's the good news. The bad news is that it appears that two of our village lads have had an accident. The pair are Donald Tomms, which explains why Davey is not here, and Terry Smith. Davey hurried off to hospital to see his boy as soon as he heard. Smithy has gone with him. Both men played a cracking game,' Thomas said.

'I believe that Graham Cook and his team were there and gave them first aid,' Melanie Grace said. 'It seemed that the two lads fell over a cliff edge but I could not make out what Graham was trying to tell us; you know how he describes things.'

There was a ripple of laughter.

Graham Cook's use of English was precise but hardly concise and it was often difficult to understand him although his school teachers seemed to think otherwise.

'He can be a bit long-winded,' said Forest.

Everybody laughed.

And Mutley, just wanting to be part of the crew, farted. The effect was enough to get their attention and, overjoyed that they were calling his name, bounced around wagging his tail. He licked Miles's face when that worthy commented loudly.

'Christ! Mutley what the bloody hell have you been eating? Yuk.' which was followed by muffled protests and a cry for a towel.

'Down Mutley,' said Forest and gave the dog a treat.

'Don't do that, he will only do it again,' protested Swanson.

Sunday dawned cool and cloudy but by mid morning the sun was shining in a blue sky dotted with white clouds wandering slowly above. The vicar of St Seraph's, resigned now to his sole charge, made his way to the church clutching his prayer book and bible was surprised to note the car park was full and there were more cars lining the lane. Already dressed in his clean surplice he strolled into the church and marched along the aisle. The choir was already singing. Bonny Mason was playing a keyboard and the young people were playing softly. He nodded benevolently to the congregation as he passed, made the sign of the cross in front of the altar and turned to face the worshippers.

Seconds later blinking in the subdued light of the Nave his eyes slowly adjusted from the electronic assault of a wall of cell phone cameras.

The noise that followed was of many feet making an exit, an exodus with the west door playing the part of the Red Sea as with assertions that "they had got the Vicar" his congregation diminished to leave a much smaller group of villagers.

'What in God's Holy name was that all about?' Jones said.

Evans the Choir, looking equally stunned, replied.

'It's the Childen Lovers video. I checked. Over four million hits this morning and rising. It seems the town has got to hear of it.'

His voice was almost drowned out by the sound of engines and honking horns, the shouted abuse as drivers blocked each other, trying to hurry away before driving off at speed.

'Let us get on with the service shall we?' Jones said.

'First let us lock the ruddy doors,' suggested Evans and with no delay Thomas Grace hurried to lock the congregation in.

Despite the battering on the doors and windows and the flashing of camera lights through the stained glass windows the reverend Jones conducted the service. He noticed the absence of Stanley White and Mathew Grace from the choir having heard of the accident he had not expected the others. He did not notice that Cheryl was missing.

He delivered his sermon avoiding the morality issues and concentrated on the lesson of the harvest. As he spoke he realised that none of it made sense to him and he was certain that his flock would have no idea either. Soon it would be the harvest festival and he hoped the village would want to take part.

Something else he was aware of.

The alleluias and the babbling had stopped and when he called people to bathe in the joy of the Lord nobody came.

It was Old man Scroggins who explained in no uncertain terms what was going on. He filled the silence with his wisdom.

'We ain't gonna do that automatic stuff no more. Waving yer arms about like Triffids at a pop concert, babbling like idiots and falling on yer arse is gotta go. We likes the singing of the choir and we thinks our poofy choir master's doin' alright, but it ain't church, is it?' Scroggins looked around at the former Triffids and beamed. 'S'right ennit?'

There was a chorus of assent.

'We still wants you to be our vicar even if you is a porno star, but you can stuff that shenanigans right up your holy arsehole,' Scroggins said, eliciting a general ripple of subdued laughter.

'In that case, let us pray,' Jones said and led them through the prayer and responses. Scroggins' colourful language had said it all. He followed the last hymn with the blessing and a prayer and soon they were clearing up with the congregation helping to put the musical gear away. One of the community worshippers approached him during the refreshment break.

'Er, Vicar, our leader, Morris Davis sort of lost the battle of wills last week. We hope that those of us who lost our trust in him will be welcome?'

The man was one who normally acted as a catcher for the swooners and was wont to wave his arms around a lot calling on the Lord. It was a practice Jones didn't mind but was glad that this week it was less prominent. He smiled warmly.

'Who will take the services when you are away?'

'We have decided that Melanie Grace will stand in for me. You realise that you are all welcome. We are all God's children after all,' he replied. It was a comfort to see the man relay his message to the others.

The break over and the dishes and cups washed up, the gowns stowed away Jones called out.

'Open the doors Thomas.'

Thomas unlocked the doors and cautiously opened them.

Other than the local cars and a lot of discarded paper and plastic the place was empty.

'Right, you lot, gets some bags out of store and let's clear up this fucking rubbish for his holiness,' said Scroggins and with a few exceptions the congregation joined in and collected everything.

Scroggins stayed behind with his wife clinging affectionately to his arm and with conviction he spoke to the vicar, Evans and Bonny Mason who had all three thanked him for his initiative.

'Listen vicar. I knows you is a shagger and according to the rest of the vicaring community, them whats Bishops and such, you ain't no longer holy but you oughter tell 'em to piss off. You oughter start the kids events again until the little fuckers go back to school. My missus and some of the other wimmin will help. If I can stop fucking swearing I can help out too,' Scroggins said.

The reverend Jones sighed and, for a moment or two, decided against it but there was only one more week left and it might just work. He gave in.

'I will accept your generous offer,' he said.

Scroggins turned to his wife.

'What's he saying?'

'He says yes,' she said.

The vicar watched old man Scroggins and his good lady totter off and sighed. Salt of the Earth. Yet he needed answers and turned to Evans and Bonny to explain.

'What is happening?'

'I think the vlogger's video has gone viral,' Evans explained. 'The punters want some pictures of their pornographic heroes and you are one of them as you can see. They are collecting pictures of us like ornithologists collect pictures of birds.'

From their position outside the church they could see the activity around the pub. At this time the traffic was light and soon as other more interesting events took over so the crowd disappeared and Sunday wound down to its inevitable soporific close.

Evans the Choir went home and spent the rest of the day doing road work running the tracks around the village and eventually retiring to enjoy his normal Sunday evening perversions. The vicar and Bonny Mason returned to the vicarage and after recovering from a roast dinner took to his bed and fornicated.

Lily Williams took great delight in playing with her two feline friends and had to agree with Sylvester that since she had bullied him into buying the creatures she was content. Happy too about the arrangement the vicar was making with Bonny but a little disturbed by the influx of nosy sightseers whose presence had persuaded her to forgo her Sunday lunch at the Dog and Duck. The village was quiet now and that suited her. For the time being she had forgotten about work and when the kittens tired and settled to sleep she wandered into her work room to check her messages. Grateful that her husband had taken pains to arrange the room with useful shelves and a good desk once used for his model making she slipped into the comfortable swivel seat. After the poor sod had passed away she had had to deep clean the place to get rid of the glue and then re-decorate.

'He was a good bloke,' she said and reflected on why a nice man had to die so young of such a nasty disease. Leukaemia was a foul cancer to die of and it was unfair, she thought, wiping away a little tear.

She switched on the Apple and waited for it to load, logged in and scanned her messages. She downloaded the messages and the address to her phone not trusting the Cloud and left replies. She had until working hours tomorrow to wait for appointments and with a sigh of pleasure she switched off and returned to the living room. Her gardener was due in the morning which meant arranging tea and lunch and making sure the kittens didn't escape.

She reached for the gin, poured a generous amount adding some orange to it and raised her glass. 'To Bertie.' Her husband's estate was enough to keep her in gin and whatever she wanted to put in it for the rest of her life, but she still liked to work. 'And another to Sylvester, may he slip the leash now and then.' She said and giggled.

Although Lily Williams and others in Childen had settled down the parents of those belonging to Graham Cook's Amateur Ornithologists were in turmoil. Graham had been persuaded to explain in words most people could understand what had happened and why. What they learned from him was shocking and explained much of what had been going on in the village during the last three years.

The adults, given the vlog link watched the video with horror, disgust, and in some instances, amusement but all agreed that what they saw was shocking. When questioned, Graham eventually revealed the name of the enterprising vlogger but he could not explain how the boy had come by the data.

'I er, excuse me, have no idea,' he said struggling with the brevity.

Mr Cook arranged a meeting in the village hall for the next Wednesday evening and with a flurry of messages and posts on the village site he managed to raise the funds to pay for the hire and refreshments. Somebody volunteered to arrange the agenda and take the minutes and somebody else suggested they call on the CPO's to listen in. Thomas and Melanie Grace were invited to explain what their son was up to and the parents of the other three lads were asked to attend.

The Cook's intention was to answer the questions but also to arrange some form of security for their enterprising youngsters. In her home, Lyla, she of the cunning plan, was busy designing a fresh achievement badge for all those involved in the Saturday afternoon event. She checked with Graham that there was enough funds to pay for them; was told to go ahead and placed the order. The badge was round, white with a dark grey edge inside of which was written Battle of the Pit in an arc, and underneath was the date. In the centre was a line drawing of a green promontory against a blue sky and, silhouetted, two falling figures. On the green sward running figures converging on a point. For cheapness it could be either safety pinned to a garment or stuck in a member's bird diary.

The subjects of her design lay in their hospital beds in the town hospital. Each boy complained like buggery about the rotten little gits who had chucked them off a cliff. The nursing staff soon tired of their moaning and with a mild spitefulness denied them painkillers in order to give them something more tangible to complain about.

The blokes in the beds either side of them told them to shut up or get their fucking heads kicked in. They eventually settled down to a quiet, if somewhat fearful, evening.

In his great uncle's living room Joshua Scroggins and the four elders, as they were called, planned the "chucking out of the aliens" as Maisie Scroggins described it.

'Them townies is walking around our village taking selfish pictures and sneaking around where theys not wanted,' she said. 'We need to chuck 'em out.'

'I oughter pummel that Grace kid and his mate,' Joshua offered eagerly.

'Joshua Scroggins! If there's any thumping to be done me old man will tell you when, alright?' Maisie said sharply.

'Yes Auntie, I understand,' Joshua said wilting as the old man glowered at him. His great aunt ruled and his great uncle made certain that her orders were carried out.

It was on Monday morning that Sylvester found out about the vlog. He walked into his office, strolled past the staff in his section and at first failed to notice how each one, men and women alike looked embarrassed, gave him a weak 'good morning' and looked away. Arriving at his desk he saw the post-it notes stuck on his screen and read each one before realising they were virtually the same. Except, that was, the one from his boss. That one read simply: "See me as soon as you get in". The others were variations of "Have you seen the link?"

He hung his coat up and sat in his seat, tapped into the screen to begin the day. He was about to dive into his mail when the phone rang and picking it up he heard the boss call him in to the office.

'On my way.'

Sitting in front of the boss's desk with the screen now turned away from him he was stunned. He had hoped the pictures were only local but this was dreadful and now he had to explain.

'Well, what have you got to say? The office knows all about your pornographic stardom; the chief is furious and if it wasn't for the fact we do not give out staff details to anybody we could have been inundated with nosy buggers. As it is we have had to issue a general staff bollocking for spreading it around.'

Sylvester gazed at his boss's tie pin and spoke to that.

'What I do at home is my business and as long as it doesn't affect my work it has nothing to do with the company, but the little shits who took these pictures thought it a good idea to go public. I can do nothing about that, sir.'

'It has if somebody blabs and you are recognised,' the boss said.

'That's hardly likely is it? Nobody outside the company knows I work here or even who I am,' Sylvester said, looking smug. The boss turned the screen again and clicked through the social media until he found what he wanted. Sylvester watched as the pictures changed in sequence.

'If I can see these with your name added then so can everybody else. His nibs is not happy. We are going to let you go but with references and a redundancy package as long as you bugger off now. Sorry Sylvester, and all the best for the future.'

For a few moments Sylvester sat in his chair stunned and until the news sunk in he was unable to move. At last, fuming and angry he rose from his seat, fists balled ready to do some damage but his boss was ahead of him and moments before he announced Sylvester's sacking two security officers walked in.

'Mister Simon will be clearing his desk.'

And with no choice Sylvester went with the two men. A half hour later was out the building bereft of his swipe cards and carrying his personal knick-knacks in a donated plastic carrier bag. He drove out of the car park noticing the smirk on the face of the attendant as he operated the barrier and made his way home.

'That little shitface bastard Mathew fucking Grace is to blame for this,' he said as he drove away. 'The little shit is ruining our village.'

Jenny White, member of the reduced Coven pursed her lips. She and her husband had received the invitation to attend the Wednesday meeting. The discussion was likely to involve Stanley and his friends. Donald Tomms and that Terry Smith were in hospital hurt; accused of trying to hurt Graham Cook. She knew her son was not really bird watching and had turned a blind eye to his activities. Now things were getting serious. He was at work now and so, with a niggling feeling of guilt, she climbed up to his room and looked inside. Luckily the younger kids were on one of the silly schemes the vicar was supposed to be running and for an hour or so the house was empty.

Nevertheless when she went upstairs she crept quietly into her son's room.

She opened his laptop, tapped the enter key and watched as the screen activated, went through the process and displayed the screen. She was surprised when within moments she was actually in to his domain. What he had on the screen seemed normal but for one folder marked "Birds". She clicked on it and was astonished to see the sub-folders open up. Nervously she opened one up and gasped.

'Oh my gosh! What has he done?'

The array of pictures were of girls mostly in a state of undress, as she would later explain to the Coven, and as she explored the other folders she recognised local girls and eventually, feeling sickened, she decided to close down. As the pointer hovered over the icon she saw a document within the main folder and opened it.

There was a list of names and with each one there was a link.

She clicked on one and was faced with a site that she would have rated double X and immediately signed off. With trembling hands she shut down closing the lid and turned away to go out. That was when she saw the brown envelope and cautiously retrieved it from its place on Stanley's shelf. It was not sealed and with no hesitation she emptied the contents on to the desk.

'Oh my gosh,' she said again.

The pictures were wrapped in paper in small batches. Each batch had a name written on its cover; names she didn't know and hastily she put them back and returned the envelope to its shelf.

'What on Earth is he doing?'

But there was nobody to give her an answer and she knew that this was something she and her husband was going to need to deal with.

'My son is a pervert, a peeping tom,' she said, and closing the door behind her walked slowly down the stairs. Even with the other children returning the afternoon seemed to drag on and the chores failed to distract her. The dinner was an almost automatic task which when it was prepared and finally ready for cooking she couldn't recall what it was.

She fed Ian and Molly their meal and put David's and hers ready for the micro-wave when he came home and put a plate aside for Stanley.

Across the village in the Grace household Thomas and Melanie asked Sara to sit with them during lunch to discuss the situation.

'The thing is Dad, is will Mathew own up?'

'He's got to face up to Sylvester and Sylvia Simon, and as long as he has done nothing to break the law then we can see him through it but he has to answer for his actions.'

'What do you know about his activities Sara?'

The question from her mother was given in such a voice that left her in no doubt that untruths or evasions would be found out. Sara decided to tell the truth.

'We, that is Jemima, Marion, Melissa and Terri and Salina knew what the boys were up to. I am sure that the Coven, Amanda and her mob, knew of it and I thought you did too Dad, and so we persuaded Melissa's father to start the scheme. We could then keep a watch on the boys, and the girls who wanted to be with them. We hoped we would sort of be able to sort of, well, you know, like Cheryl and Mathew,' she said and smiled weakly. 'If you get my meaning.'

She kept up the smile during the thoughtful silence that followed and waited for the information to be absorbed. Eventually her mother spoke.

'And what about your relationship with the village boys?'

'That's easy, I don't have any. They're a bunch of morons who could take turns at being the village idiot. For now, until I meet some chap that I like, I will stick with my horse and horse riding. I will opt for virginity until such time as I find somebody I like enough to leap into bed with,' she said and grinned.

'Sara! What a shocking thing to say,' her mother said.

'Oh am I too explicit?'

'No, its not that, I am sure the boys are not all morons.'

'Mathew is,' said her father.

And both women had to agree.

'So what are we to do with him?'

'Talk to him this evening and make him tell us the truth,' Sara suggested.

'I can help with that if he doesn't own up.' Sara said and seeing her mother's suspicious look she hastily added. 'I hacked into his computer.'

'I think young lady you had better go see to your horse and be back here in time for tea. We will sort Mathew out between us.

And obeying her father's command she left them to it.

It was something of a council of war held early that evening between Bonny Mason, the Reverend Jones and Evans the Choir.

The hit count was up over the six million and from what Evans had told them was likely to rise even higher. 'Sylvester has been fired. I have heard much about it in the office in town, and there is this meeting for residents on Wednesday. As an aside I have heard also that Sally Wise's visitor has come to stay.'

Reverend Jones blushed but said nothing.

'That just leaves me then,' said Bonny.

'What are we going to do about these pictures and this, this dreadful situation with the boys and the meeting on Wednesday. Above all what are we going to do about the awful intrusion at church yesterday?'

'I have a few ideas,' said Evans the Choir resisting the urge to tell them he had a cunning plan. With a drink each they set to discussing what the plan was and this time it was Evans who cooked the meal.

At the same time as the trio were indulging in Evans the Choir's comestibles Stanley White was facing his mother and losing the conflict. He had wriggled, lied, and tried to blame all but himself knowing that since he had grown larger his father had not attempted to physically control him. His father's words had no force if they were not backed up by the threat of violence of which

The Birdwatchers of Childen Under Blean

lack Stanley was quick to take advantage. His mother however was of a different mettle. When roused she was formidable.

'Tell the truth,' she demanded and looked at her husband. 'David, we will go and see what I saw earlier and he can explain. I was hoping he would tell the truth without that.'

In his room Stanley watched his mother tap into his laptop and wished he had logged off the night before. He saw the folders opened one by one and then the links opened up. He remained sullenly silent when his mother removed the envelope from the shelf and showed it to his father.

'Now, tell us what you are up to,' she said.

He sat dejectedly on the bed and began to tell the story; trying to explain how he had been sucked in by Mathew Grace and how he was being forced to go along with the scheme.

'It's not all my fault, I was being…'

'Blackmailed into it?' asked his father.

Clutching at straws he nodded and muttered a reply.'

'Yeah, the bloke should be locked up.'

'You know something son, I don't believe you. I see what you have there and it looks to me as if you are making money on the side selling pictures to your workmates. How do I know this?' His father said and with a gesture silenced his wife. 'Remember that I am head of department in the main store, which is why you have your job in the first place. Now, I have had an employee in my office this last week who was found passing pictures around. Being an observant person and annoyed about what was happening I also recognised the face of one of the girls in the pictures. I see the same picture here on your desk. You sold those pictures to that employee didn't you?'

'It wasn't me. I never sold nothing to nobody!'

'I think the CCTV cameras will show otherwise. I also warn you that the Supervisor has correctly made a complaint to the police. Son, you are deep in the cactus,' David White said and shook his head.

Stanley jumped up from the bed where he was sitting and flailing his fists he made to thump his father.

'You rotten old fart! You grassed on me…' and cried out in pain as instead of the soft target he expected something hard and knuckled hit him a few times, he lost count as the pain hit him, and he crashed back on his bed. He lay groaning not knowing which bit to clutch first and listened as his parents removed his laptop, searched his desk and shelving and removed his stock.

'You will likely get a call from the police tomorrow. We will look after this. You may as well stay here until they lock you up although I would rather you didn't,' his father said. Taking the laptop and the envelope with him David White ushered his wife out of his son's bedroom.

'We will look after this.'

The door closed behind them and Stanley was left nursing his hurts and hating his parents.

Slowly recovering he found his mobile and called Mathew but got no answer.

The reason for the lack of response was that Mathew was confessing his misdemeanours to his father and trying not to swear at Sara who he said had betrayed him. What he told Thomas was too much for that worthy to bear and in clipped tones Thomas explained.

'You have a choice. You can go to your room and stay there or you can go out. I do not mind which as long as you are out of my sight for long enough for me to calm down. I suggest you go to the Dog and Duck and mix with some of the villagers. You will find that I am much kinder than they will be,' Thomas said and glared at him.

''I'll go out.'

A few moments after Mathew had hurried out with his coat on against the drizzle and some cash for the pub Thomas slumped in his chair.

'Was I too harsh with him?'

'No love, he deserves more but he may come right with a little kindness. I hope he understood.' Melanie shook her head. 'I'm sorry for him.'

Sara wanted to say that she was not but refrained and just thought it.

Mathew entered the Dog and Duck and made his way to the bar in a manner that could only be described as sidling. His progress enabled him to see where he was going and who was in the bar. He was lucky; the drinkers had not yet arrived and with their possible presence in mind he found a quiet corner and sat drinking his cider. He saw Sally Wise and her companion arrive and was glad he was out of their way. He was feeling lonely and by the time he had purchased his third drink he was sinking in to a dark misery that was about to overwhelm him. He was startled when Stanley slid into a chair beside him.

'What the fuck?'

'Listen mate we're utterly quackered,' Stanley said and proceeded to tell him what had happened that evening. 'And for all we know Terry and Don will quack as well.'

Mathew told his story and afterwards for a time they sat in the dark corner growing more and more depressed. As they sat despondently discussing their situation the bar began to fill up and much to their surprise the Vicar with Bonny Mason beside him and that poofy choir master came in and settled down with drinks. They were joined by Forest Maloney and his dog, Sylvester Simon and the others of the little group. What horrified them was that Terry's dad followed by Don's father arrived and with drinks in hand joined the group. The pair watched them in animated discussion that despite its activity was too quiet for them to hear over the ambient noise.

'What we gonna do. That scheme we had ain't gonna work no more is it?' Stanley said.

'We ain't got no scheme now, and I bet the other blokes are crapping theirselves,' Mathew said looking extremely gloomy.

'I 'll get us some more cider,' Stanley said.

He carried their glasses across the room heading for the bar when an angry voice called out.

'Oy, there's one of the arseholes!'

Stanley, startled, dropped the glasses, stared momentarily at the source of the voice and saw menace. Self preservation kicked in and, with a yelp of terror, he made a run for it.

Mathew, alarmed by the cry and the crashing glasses, looked up from his corner and saw a mob rise from their table to chase after Stanley.

He panicked and, leaping up, he dodged around the tables and followed Stanley.

The drinkers, in full cry, including the vicar, Bonny Mason and Sally Wise and her companion gave chase. Mutley the dog with his master hanging on to his lead, the dog barking excitedly, gave chase. Mathew whimpered and gasped slowing down but somehow managing to dodge into the alleyways with the mob arguing behind him.

'We lost the buggers,' gasped Sylvester.

The group came to a ragged halt.

'Looks like it.'

Mutley whined and howled and with his nose to the ground strained on the leash pulling hard in the direction of the alleyway that the vicar thought the lads had taken.

'That way perhaps?'

'Sounds like Mutley's got his scent,' said Forest.

Mathew, gasping for air and resting for a moment in the darkening shelter of a fence heard the dog howling. The footsteps began again and, whimpering with fear Mathew started off again. Putting some more energy into his fading legs he stumbled on, banging against a fence he was startled when a dog growled from behind it and barked.

'Shut up you stupid mutt,' he snarled, and with the pursuit closing in he put on a spurt and ran gasping for breath just wanting to get away. It was no good running for home until his parents were in bed.

And now the bloody smelly dog was after him.

Mutley put his nose to the ground sniffing as he did when he and master went out but suddenly he was alerted by a scent more compelling than any other.

The smell of a female in season was one that Mutley could not resist. He strained at the leash dragging master along as he eagerly answered the call.

'He's got the scent!' Forest cried out and the crowd, eager to capture their quarry, urged the dog on. They came to a confused halt outside a back gate which Mutley was frantically trying to climb to be repeatedly hauled down by Forest.

On the other side of the gate could be heard the eager noise of a fecund Dachshund bitch.

'Bloody dog. It's led us on a wild goose chase,' Forest said.

The trail was lost and it was with great difficulty that Forest dragged Mutley away. Inside the back yard the German dog howled in excited anticipation. The others drifted away. In the confusion Stanley managed to sneak back into his room and trembling with fear got into bed,

Mathew just kept running until at last he flopped against a tree along the back track and sat gasping for air, his head thumping, chest heaving and legs wobbling. It was many minutes before he got his breath back. The run and the night air had triggered off the effects of the alcohol. His head was spinning, or the world around him was, he couldn't be sure which and it was drizzling again. He staggered to his feet and staggered along the pathway looking for some shelter. He was scared to go home drunk; he knew his father for all his Christian kindness could scrap and was likely to give him a thumping. He would wait until late and use his key to get in when the family had gone to bed. As long as he could evade the vigilantes he was fine with that.

'It's supposed to be bloody Summer but I'm bleeding cold out here,' he said, and wandered on to where the trees covered the pathway looking for cover. Eventually he found a resting place and wrapping his coat around him he curled up and shivered in the cold. He dozed for a while and was woken by the sound of stealthy footsteps on the pathway. He eased himself further back in the bushes as silently as he could. He trembled when he heard a voice whispering close by.

'I'm sure he went this way,' muttered the figure as it passed his refuge.

He lay, terrified in the dark hanging on to what was left of his sanity and his bladder until at last he heard the figure moving back down the path and faint footsteps disappearing in the direction of the houses.

He waited for a long time and with thumping heart he sneaked out of his hiding place and headed for the quarry. He would be safe there until the morning when he could sneak back home. He stumbled along the dark pathway trying not to make noise but his progress was slow and by the time he neared the rough track leading to the gates he was beginning to feel the effects of the evening, especially the cider. He emerged from the path and too late a dark figure was upon him.

'Oh Christ!' was all he could manage before the figure slugged him with a hard fist. He heard grunts and expirations of breath as his assailant battered him senseless. He was dragged unconscious across the rough ground, heaved up onto strong shoulders and dumped on the floor of a shed.

His attacker kicked him hard before abandoning him to his fate.

It would have been better for Mathew if Mutley had not been distracted by an eager bitch.

Tuesday morning revealed a village washed by the first of the September rain and a rush of parents making last minute sorties into to town for the needs of their offspring prior to starting back at school. The primary school was buzzing with last minute cleaning and putting right those niggling problems that occur on any start up. Teaching staff arrived to spend a day training and the equipment set up for the summer activities was stored away. The groundsman made his final touches to the gardens and checked the school allotment, arranged the gardening tools for the children to use and oiled the axles on the wheelbarrows.

Commuters left for work and on the small holdings the work was already well underway in anticipation of the harvest festival. The stables were cleaned and much of the outer wall was whitewashed and the woodwork treated. The piles of manure continued to rot down and as the local growers felt fit they arrived with trailers to collect the bounty. It was the last fun activity of the summer holidays for the children and relief to the stables.

Thomas Grace and Sara had collected their load that morning early and left the trailer at the end of the driveway ready to be unloaded that evening. As they went inside to wash up and get ready for work Melanie met them looking anxious.

'Mathew's not here. I don't think he came home last night,' she said.

'Perhaps he spent the night at a friend's place,' Thomas said.

'The only friend he has left unless he went into town is that Stanley White and if his folks did what we did last night then I don't think Mathew would be welcome. I'll call Jenny,' she said.

Thomas and Sara took turns to shower and when they were done Melanie had news for them. She looked grim.

'As far as I can gather the boys had to run from the Dog and Duck last night chased by Sylvester Simon and his friends. It seems Stanley had sneaked out and managed to sneak back in again. He has already gone on the early bus. Mathew didn't stay there last night,' She said.

Thomas looked grim.

Mathew was missing.

He didn't like what the boy had done but he was his own flesh and blood and that counted much in his mind. Mathew rarely strayed from home. He hadn't got the imagination to arrange an escape route to a safe place other than his own smelly bed. Sara was right; the boy was a moron and would act instinctively. He would run for home.

Sara was due to work at the tea rooms so it was up to him to start looking for the boy.

'Right, breakfast first and then we must start looking for him. Mel, if you can call around I will talk to Horace and ask Forest to help out.'

Whilst Melanie was on the telephone calling the neighbours Thomas walked down to the Dog and Duck, Sara walked with him on the way to work, and on the way he called in on the Maloney house.

'He's already out with the dog. A bit late getting back but he normally walks out above the quarry. Why, what's up?'

'Mathew's missing. He wasn't in his room this morning. Mel normally has to call him a few times but this morning she had to go into his room.'

'Ooh nasty.'

'Yes but these things have to be done. And now I'm looking for him.'

'I have to get off now but you might find Forest up near the quarry on his way back,' she said. He walked steadily trying to think which path Forest would normally take and chose the one that eventually climbed above the quarry. He was about to pass the quarry entrance when he spotted Forest wandering around and heard him calling out for his dog.

'What's up lad. Mutley gone missing?'

'He's buggered off. I thought he'd given up on that of late. I can't find the little sod. He shot off as usual and I waited for him to reappear but so far he's not come back. He often spends time snuffling around and I usually see him and call him. He comes when I call now but today he hasn't. What are you doing up here?'

'Mathew is missing. Did you see him last night?'

Forest blushed and looked a bit sheepish.

'Well actually I did,' and told Thomas the story of Mathew's run and how they lost track of him. 'We gave up I am glad to say and I expect he got away to one of his friends if he didn't go home. Bloody hell here's Mutley and he's got something in his mouth. Come here boy!'

Mutley trotted up to Forest wagging his tail and dropped the object on the ground at his feet. It was a shoe and as soon as Thomas saw it he recognised it as one of Matthew's. 'That's my boy's shoe.'

Forest picked up the shoe and held it out. 'You had better take it then. I er have no idea how Mutley...' Forest tailed off looking embarrassed as Thomas stared at the object. 'I suppose we better look.'

'Perhaps the dog can find him for us?'

Forest had no illusions about Mutley's ability as a search and rescue dog and reached for his mobile intending to call the emergency services. Thomas gripped his wrist and shook his head.

'Come on, give the dog a chance, He might be all right.'

Forest shrugged and realised that Mutley had disappeared. He groaned. The quarry was a mess of dumped items, scrub and artificial strata created by the digging machines. It was a place that at some time the parish council wanted to develop. The plan was to tidy the area up and turn it into a mixture of wild and cultivated gardens. It would mean clearing the rubbish and getting rid of the old sheds.

'Sheds! That's it! Perhaps the little ratbag is in one of the... oh shit wrong thing to say,' Forest said as he saw Thomas's face darken. 'We should look in one of the sheds?'

'Right, and yes I know he is a ratbag but he is my son,' Thomas said.

Thomas being a Christian was against him, Forest thought, because he was obviously getting his fair share of trials and tribulations. The suffering church penitent needs to be reminded of his humility before his God and Thomas was experiencing a little bit more than he wanted. Forest would probably feel the same if Mathew was his.

'Nah, never, don't kid yourself,' he muttered and was glad that Thomas wasn't listening. Instead his neighbour was wandering toward the collection of small buildings left behind when the operators moved out. Together they tried the doors and those that didn't open easily Thomas kicked in with the expertise of a military skirmisher. It was pretty to watch.

The dog was nowhere to be seen.

They tried all four buildings in the immediate area but there was nothing and with a bit of an insight Forest clambered on to a higher tier and saw another, slightly larger shed the other side of a patch of scrub. Mutley's barking came fro that direction.

'I think he might be over there. Mutley's barking and when he does that it usually means he's on to something. Follow me.'

But instead Thomas led the way and instinctively found a pathway around the scrub.

'There's broken ends here at about shoulder height and footprints in the mud,' Thomas said.

As they reached the shed Mutley came bounding out carrying the other shoe and excitedly dropped it at Forest's feet.

'Good boy, good boy,' Forest said and giving Mutley a treat quickly clipped the lead to his collar. Thomas hurried into the building and when Forest followed he saw Mathew lying on his side, bereft of his shoes his face glistening where Mutley had licked him clean. The boy was breathing and snorting and already Thomas was trying to wake him up.

'I'll call emergency services Thomas.'

Forest went outside and called 999.

Whatever it was Mutley had licked up Forest didn't want to know about.

He waited at the entrance with Mutley fretting to move on and now and then farting a stench that Forest tried to avoid by getting upwind. The technique was to make the dog sit and then pay out the lead until he was four or five metres away and make the dog sit but it didn't work all that well as Mutley, thinking this was game, suddenly got up and bounded happily to his master's side. Between them the man and animal patrolled the gate waiting for the services to arrive. Eventually the blue lights battered up the rough track from the road and paramedics arrived to park their car inside the flat gate area. Thomas came out of the scrub to lead them to the shed. Moments later an ambulance arrived followed by a police car with two officers sitting inside. The two officers decamped from their vehicle and wandered over to Forest.

'You call the police?'

He nodded and added a quiet yes.

'What have you found. Tell us before we go and see for ourselves. Christ! What's that smell?'

'It's my dog. He's just farted,' Forest said apologetically.

'Smell's bloody awful. How can you put up with that?'

'He's not normally as bad as that.'

'Right, tell us what happened and do it quickly before the bloody animal farts again.'

Forest explained, and when he offered to lead them to the shed they declined and suggested he leave his address, and for God's sake and theirs he take the bloody four legged vulture home and wash it's belly out with some strong detergent.

'He's eaten something rotten that's for sure,' said the officer.

Mutley looked up at the officer and wagged his tail happily. He was very pleased with all the attention he was getting.

Forest took the hint and walked on home.

Thomas called him much later to tell him that Mathew was in the hospital and would survive what was a vicious beating. Forest immediately thought of how angry Sylvester was last night and how they had all chased the two boys like vigilantes. More police arrived and as they began to sweep through the village asking questions it was apparent that somebody had given Mathew Grace a hiding and dumped him in the shed.

The officers who called on him were the same ones he had met at the quarry. They eyed the dog suspiciously.

'First things first. Can you put the dog somewhere. With an arse like that the creature should be certified,' the officer said. Both men gave him their names but Forest forgot them immediately, but he did put Mutley out in the conservatory.

With tea and biscuits supplied the two officers listened to his story and the events leading up to Mathew running away from a middle-aged mob.

'And you say your dog was distracted by a bitch in heat?'

'Yes, or otherwise we may have caught up with him and stopped anybody doing any more than perhaps dunking him in the village pond after a little duffing up. He's a coward and will run away if he can. I expect that the sight of a group of angry men in full flight gave him an incentive.'

'And what were you doing this morning?'

'Walking the dog as is my wont.'

'And mister Grace met you near the quarry. Did he explain what he was doing?'

'Of course; he was looking for his boy. Mathew had not slept in his bed last night and he was worried. As you do when your children go missing,' Forest said.

'Very well. I expect you will have a visit from a detective officer at some time. A crime has been committed and we need to find the er, the...'

'Perpetrator or perpetrators,' Forest filled in for him.

'Yes and arrest them. Has he any enemies?'

Forest grinned and faced the officer directly.

'That boy may have more enemies you can care to pop into an Agatha Christie crime novel. There are lots of people in the village who would like a pop at him. Not me; I am only a watcher with a smelly dog, a wife who is now an ex-nagger, and a conniving daughter. I also have to get on with a contract in my den, so if you have finished with me I would appreciate it.'

'Sure we have but...'

'Don't leave town?'

The officer looked annoyed.

'I was going to say we may need to speak with you again.'

The officers left and a few moments later he let Mutley back into the house and wisely ventilated the conservatory, opened a few windows and patted the dog's head affectionately. Mutley sat beside him in the den curled up on the floor. Forest concentrated on the task in hand and although at intervals Mutley sent one out he carried on. It seemed the effect was lessening which was a bonus. However the policeman's suggestion of an emetic seemed to be good advice.

In the meantime the officers who arrived to investigate the assault on Mathew Grace learned about the Bird Watcher's Club. He could not help explaining when questioned.

'So all this started because you gave your lad a pair of binoculars and a "what bird is that?" book?' Asked detective Dawson.

'If you put it like that, yes it did. I think that all else followed. You realise my son is an idiot, a moron and his friends are a few feathers short of a dead parrot as far as intelligence is concerned. I know he is my boy, but I cannot condone his actions, although I would want his attacker caught,' Thomas said.

'I can understand that,' the detective said, sympathetically. He was aware that the investigation into the assault on Mathew Grace had opened up a whole can of worms. He was certain that his part in the case was interesting, in particular the vlog which was steadily going viral.

'This vlog thing is going barmy,' the detective said to his companion.

It was a not long after his remark that he and officer Crane was ordered to find the vlogger and do something about it.

'The local press has got hold of the story, and so have some of the nationals. If it gets on to the telly we will have no hope of stopping it,' explained their Inspector. 'Go find the bugger.'

The trail led them a nondescript semi-detached in a quiet suburb on the outskirts of town. Inside was a family consisting of one doting father, a bright eyed mother, a daughter and their geeky thirteen year old son, Simon.

Simon was a vlogger who made short, entertaining movies, made his opinions known and was, as Dawson put it afterwards, a thoroughly nice kid. His surprise at being visited by two police officers was as much of a surprise to him as it was to his father.

'Well, I'll be jiggered, he was making a lot of money from that new one,' his father said.

'Didn't you look at it?'

'No, I didn't. I don't always look at his vlogs; he goes on a bit too technical for me. I'm more hands on with my motorcycles,' he said.

The man had emerged from a garage come workshop where he was working on a classic motorcycle that Dawson thought looked like a nineteen sixties Norton. The man led them into the house to meet the boy.

'My wife is out otherwise she would have taken you to see him. What has he done wrong?'

'We don't know yet, sir,' said Crane.

Inside the house they met the boy who looked puzzled until his father introduced them. He nodded and waited expectantly for them to speak.

'What on Earth have you been up to Simon?' Asked his father.

Simon found it difficult to explain.

'You had better tell these officers all about it son, and be truthful. 'His father said. 'I'll leave you to it.' And Simon was left to talk to to the two police officers.

'We understand you posted a vlog that has become popular,' said Officer Crane. 'Can you tell us about it please?'

'Er, do you mean the rude one?'

'I expect so,' said Dawson.

'Oh, nothing to it really. Somebody sent me a folder. I sorted it out and set it up and that was it,' Simon said and blinked. 'I shouldn't of done it should I?'

'No, it was not a good idea Simon. It has caused a lot of trouble,' Dawson said. 'Can you explain to officer Crane in detail. Run her through it whilst I take notes?'

Ten minutes later the two officers stared at the boy and shook their heads. This nice boy had no idea what the impact of his action was, or he didn't care. It was hard to understand. The kid was a computer nerd, geeky and was utterly indifferent to the content.

'So I understand that all you wanted to do was put together an interesting collage of still pictures. Is that right?'

'Yes miss. It was nice to have some different pictures to use,' he said and grinned. 'They are rather naughty.'

'Can you delete the vlog?'

'Better still, let us take a copy now as evidence and then he can delete it,' said Dawson.

'Oh that's easy, but I can't stop it completely. We have to get the provider to do that. You might find the sponsors will block it. You see, I'm locked in to a contract. You will have to ask them too,' Simon said.

'We could arrest you?'

Simon looked thoughtful and nodded but eventually replied.

'You could do that but this is on an Adult Content stream and although I am only a minor It is my father who owns the account. My father just wanted to help. We set up the contract before I was sent this,' Simon said and smiled.

His smile was a genuine expression which before either officer could speak was changed to a frown.

'I know who sent it. I have it on my log. Would you like to see it?'

'Please, show us,' said Crane.

With lightning movements and flashing of changing windows Simon navigated to a page, scrolled down and highlighted a folder. The name attached was Stanley White.

Dawson wrote the information down, insisted that he open the folder to confirm that the contents were genuine and handed him a USB stick.

'It's a clean one, 32GB,' Crane said. Can you record the vlog and the folder on to it please.'

'Yes miss,' Simon said and again the fingers flashed. He showed them the data on the stick and removed it handing it to them.

As they stood up to leave him both thanking him for his cooperation Dawson noticed some excellent bird pictures on his desktop.

'Did you take those? They are very good,' said Dawson pointing at the pictures.

'Oh no, that's Graham Cook, he's a bit of a bird watching freak. I see him sometimes at school. He does some very nice pictures.

The Birdwatchers of Childen Under Blean

He's a bit hard to understand sometimes,' Simon said, cheerfully.

'Only sometimes?'

'Well, most of the time.'

'Is that the only pictures he sent you?'

'He sends me some of the village with birds in them. I can show you if they are any use?'

And before either of them could demur Simon had pulled up a series of pictures taken in the village of Childen Under Blean of ducks taking off, small birds, a murmuration and a magnificent one of a Little Owl taking off apparently in front of a couple of middle-aged lovers.

Dawson started at the picture.

'Simon, can you close in on the faces of the people please?'

As the boy zoomed in so Dawson slipped his small pocket book out of an inside pocket and thumbed through the pages and holding the small picture close to the screen he said: 'Tanya, look at this.'

She did as she was asked and whistled softly though her teeth.

'That's gotta be him, surely?'

'Thank you Simon. I will talk to your dad now,' Dawson said.

It turned out that Denis Pearce had no idea what his son was doing until the police had called on him. Mister Pearce was a nice bloke, innocent and almost as geeky as his son with his chosen obsession. He restored and ran a small collection of classic motorcycles. Before the officers left he explained that his wife and daughter made knitted animals for sale at fairs.

'What with Simon into his computers and the girls into their toys I have plenty of time for my bikes. You wouldn't like to see them would you?'

'Some other time, mister Pearce, we have some more calls to make,' said Crane virtually dragging Dawson away.

'Pity, I've got a fully restored Velocette Thruxton in there,' he said pointing to the massive shed.

Officer Clark had to move Dawson on.

'My grand dad had one of those,' Dawson said wistfully.

That afternoon Stanley White was called into his supervisor's office. The two police officers standing beside the desk waited until the supervisor had gone before they spoke to him.

'Stanley Johnson White?'

'Yeah, you're police; what do you want?'

'You were with Mathew Grace last night drinking in the Dog and Duck in Childen Under Blean?'

'Yeah, he's my mate, what of it,' he said, and had that sinking feeling he had been dreading since he had stuffed the posting up. This had to do with the old gits chasing them out of the pub and what his father was so uptight about. Had his old man complained or was it somebody else? The old man had said he couldn't do nothing to stop people complaining and said the geezer in charge had to call the police. Sum total. He was in the shit.

'We would like to ask you some questions about last night. We have an idea what is going on but we think you can help us with our enquiries. It would be best if you come with us to the station where we can have a chat. You are not under arrest.'

Yet, he thought.

He had no choice but to go with them and although they were polite and at times quite nice to him the next few hours were very unpleasant. He told them about the evening; how they had met up to talk and have a drink and how the old gits had chased them.

'I suppose I was not as pissed as Mathew, and run faster than him and got away. Anyways, they seemed to want to get him and that Maloney bloke and his stinking dog went after him. I dunno what happened after that except what he didn't answer his phone. I give up on him in the end and went home.'

'Anybody see you going home? Did your parents or anybody in the house see you. We would want to know the time.'

'Shit no. My old man told me to stay in my room. I snuck out the winder and got back in that way. It wasn't late like. Just after ten. They'd be watching the telly. News at ten or some old git program,' he said and looked at them worried now. They hadn't mentioned the pictures.

'So you didn't see your mate after that, or speak to him or any other means of communication?'

'What?'

'Did you text him or send him a post, message him or email?'

'Oh yeah I done that but there was nothing.'

'Have you tried to contact him today?'

'I give him a call but he don't answer.'

The officer sighed and looked at his mate.

'What would you say if I told you that Mathew Grace was assaulted last night and was found badly injured lying on the floor of a shed in the old Lindeman's quarry this morning?'

'Fuck me, bloody hell! He ain't dead is he?'

One of the officers smiled briefly.

'No, he's not dead, but he is badly hurt and in hospital receiving treatment. I am glad to inform you that your friend is alive and likely to survive but there is another aspect of this case we have to take into consideration,' the officer said.

'What? Why don't you speak plain English. You're nearly as bad as that little shitfaced kid Graham Cook. You can't hardly understand that little bugger when he starts talking. Like he swallowed a dickshunry.'

'Selling and distributing explicit pictures which we believe include pictures of underage children, to whit pictures of naked girls, some possibly as young as thirteen. Also we will want to question you on the contents of some envelopes distributed to various members of the Childen Under Blean community and of those leaked to the media and made public,' the officer said and grinned.

'In other words, sonny you are nicked.'

It was a little while later that the two officers formally charged him with distributing pornographic material.

'Now that we have done this we can officially collect your electronic devices which means your mobile and any device such as a computer you have at home. To be fair, because we don't want to stuff around too much, we will take you with us to the village and collect the items and bring you back for an overnight stay in our less than luxurious accommodation, and ask the nice kind magistrate to set bail in the morning,' the officer said, and added: 'You will be much safer tonight in here than at home.'

Stanley whimpered.

At home he identified his laptop, handed over his phone, his cameras and his binoculars and with his father looking on he unearthed the hard copies and his notes and sat on the bed whilst they boxed it all up. The trip back was a relief. He had seen angry villagers gathering outside the house.

His father and mother faced the delegation and between them they persuaded the angry men and women that until the night before they had no idea what Stanley was up to.

'You must have known he was sneaking around spying on the girls?'

'We had an idea but we didn't want to believe it of him,' Jenny said. 'We were a bit slow in sussing out what they were up to and until the Friends of the church proposed their scheme we didn't think about it.'

And like the Whites, Thomas Grace and Melanie had to field similar questions. But instead of apologising for his son's actions Thomas showed how angry he was and eventually managed to persuade his listeners to attend the public meeting.

'I am sure that we can sort this problem out then. In the meantime let the police do their job and maybe they can help sort this whole mess out.' He said, and would argue no further.

That evening when the members of the choir arrived for practice the group was so small that Evans the Choir declared they should all go home again. Evans was smarting a little from the jibes of his work colleagues some of whom had seen the video and were busy passing the link around. Fortunately the activity took place only during the last working hour of the day and he survived until going home time without flattening anybody.

The vicar was in the vicarage and Bonny had popped in but disappeared muttering about police and bothersome people asking questions. He noticed that Cheryl Simon was missing and wondered where she was. She was in her room sobbing where she was hiding from the horrid things her father said about Mathew. The least of all was hurtful enough.

'Serves the perverted little bastard right,' he said.

There was much more after that but she didn't want to listen to any more.

To say that the village settled down for the night would be wrong. It seethed underneath the closed doors and the darkness as evening fell; the night hid the sins of its residents and cosseted the righteous as they went about their business or enjoyed their families.

That was except for the drinkers eager for local news and the few police officers still stationed in the village, and those poor sods on duty at the quarry. The police officers, although they were off duty and relaxing with a pint or two and a meal, were eyed with suspicion by the locals and treated with respect by Horace and Molly. Vernon and Maddy arrived for their weekly treat of a meal out and in contrast to the rest of the locals were quite friendly to the police officers. Vernon always liked to be nice to his customers. The officers and the team had spent a lot on tea and sandwiches during the day and he hoped there would be more to come. He had helped their inquiries by telling them little snippets about the old Bird Watchers Club. He didn't care if they believed him or not as long as it kept the investigation going. Policemen and women ate a lot of toasted sandwiches and drank a lot of tea and coffee.

The drinkers sat at their usual table and eyeing the policemen occasionally they discussed the events of the last twenty-four hours. Sly led off and made a statement.

'We should of let the buggers just wander off. I dunno about you but I've had flatfoots asking me questions what I don't want to answer. It ain't bloody right. Me girl is pregnant with that bloody rat arse kid's child and I lost me job. I am not happy,' Sly said and stared at the police officers and snarled.

'My boy's in clink.'

'My lad is in hospital.'

'The village is seething and rumours are flying around.'

'And the Friends of St Seraph's is falling apart. Choir practice was cancelled and if the public meeting gets underway we will have to do it in shifts,' said Swanson.

It was at that moment when Forest arrived with Mutley and trailing behind him was the vicar and Evans the Choir. Slipping in behind them was Bonny Mason. That they came into the Dog and Duck was unusual; coming in together was a first but what surprised the drinkers was that two of them were wearing dresses.

Forest just smiled and whilst the others sat staring at them he stood up.

'An ale for you Vicar and I take it the ladies would like pink gins?'

And indicating to the others that they make room for the newcomers he went to the bar and ordered the drinks carrying them back and put them on the table.

'And to what do we owe the pleasure?' He asked.

'Coren is upset,' replied the reverend Jones.

Evans snarled.

'It appears that the rugby club had seen the vlog that is circulating at this moment and decided that a cross-dressing rugby player is not what they want in their team. They think that the morale of the side will deteriorate.'

'In other words they don't want poofs in their dressing room?'

Sly said, cutting to the chase.

'Correct. He is somewhat upset and when we asked him to come for a drink with us he refused to change his clothes,' Jones said.

'I had to sort out his make up first but at least we are here,' said Bonny.

'I'm livid, I am, and even people at work are being nasty to me. Makes me sick it does, and me a person who would never harm anybody,' Evans said, and turned to face Sly. 'I am a cross dresser but I am not what you call a poof. I don't like sex. I just like the feel of male bodies. From a young age I took a vow of chastity.'

'Don't you mean celibacy,' said Sly not to be put off.

'Celibacy is for Monks and Catholic Priests, not that the buggers always stick to it,' Evans said. 'My family were chapel and much more strict. I like singing. I once taught music and singing you know. I would like to go back to it someday.'

Sly looked at him and he felt guilty. The poor pathetic figure looked so sad that even with the dress on and the dark shadow on his chin he still looked like a chunky Welshman, and as Sly had always liked him he was moved to apologise.

'Sorry mate, I stepped over the line there a bit but other than the obvious what brings you here?'

'We need to talk about the situation. The village community is falling apart and we have to do something,' said Bonny. 'We need a plan of action. I have an idea and I think you should listen.'

Surprisingly it was Sly who suggested they shut their fat gobs and listen. Mutley seemed to approve and gave his opinion with a large satisfied yawn, stretched his legs and unfortunately spoiled the effect by emitting a fart that no amount of fanning with beer mats could disperse. However when the air had cleared the men listened to what Bonny had to say.

'It will never work,' remarked Davey.

'Oh I think it will,' said Bonny and stared him down.

'Run that by me again,' said Swanson.

'Simple, I will talk to the Old Man Scroggins and ask for his help. He is a rogue but a man of wisdom and not only that he is rich, or the family is, and we could do with some help. The scheme we started will fail else. We could have a meeting to decide. We need to choose where,' Bonny said.

'I will make the church open for the event,' reverend Jones said and bought a round of drinks.

'Cripes, I thought you vicars didn't earn much,' remarked Swanson.

'People can be generous with the collection boxes,' Jones said and laughed. 'I earn enough to buy a drink or two.'

'Yeah we know,' muttered Sly thinking of the vicar's recent extreme inebriation.

The vicar just grinned and raised his glass.

'To us and an end to adversity,' he said.

The others seemed to agree with murmurs of assertion. Mutley wagged his tail.

The public meeting that Wednesday was a shambles. The church committee, the Friends and the parish councillors talked at cross purposes. The villagers were angry and one man even suggested tarring and feathering the only one of the four still standing. Stanley White, back home on bail, hid in his room. His father stayed away from the meeting.

The parish council, facing the angry crowd with had no answers, and when the crowd inside began to demand answers, others outside unable to get in began to demand a hearing, they panicked. Those in favour of storming the White household and grabbing Stanley were held back by those in favour of a proper and peaceful discussion.

Tempers rose and when the first fist was flung a fight broke out.

What few police officers arrived were unable to hold the battlers back, and so, with small clubs and batons, fists and boots, the Scroggins Clan dived in.

At one point during the riot when it was obvious that his small force was ineffective and he was deciding on what best to do a sergeant asked a silly question.

'The old bugger in charge of that mob is a lunatic. Shall we arrest him?' Asked the sergeant.

'Go for it lad if you dare,' the Inspector replied and grinned when Old Man Scroggins clobbered an irate villager with a well aimed blow from what was a strong blackthorn stick.

'Ouch, sod that,' said the sergeant, common sense kicking in.

However, the clan solved the problem and soon the Inspector was more or less in control. He spoke to Old Man Scroggins who had supervised the actions of his lads.

'I don't approve of your methods, but er, thank you. My sergeant suggested arresting you,' the Inspector said.

'Huh, if we hadn't of mucked in this lot would of got properly duffed up.' Old Man Scroggins explained, indicating the cowering councillors.

The Inspector sighed.

Old Man Scroggins, having lived a life filled with danger, scrapping, misogyny, and poaching that had done him all right in his long life it was not going to stop him and his lads from clobbering a few people he had wanted to clobber for years. He had carried out the operation with delighted enthusiasm.

The Inspector recognised a tainted blithe spirit when he saw one and urged his troops to just clear up the mess. From his point of view it was a satisfactory conclusion.

The village woke the next day; some to go to work and others nursing sore heads. Others went back to their tasks and the village settled down into a nervous truce. The truce lasted until Saturday when the Stoat Malbury match; the last of the season was due. Thomas Grace was fired with enthusiasm and the riot of Wednesday had somehow given young Scroggins an equal flame.

Thomas Grace published his team selection for the vital match on Thursday and on Friday he was surprised when Evans the Choir arrived at his house on Friday afternoon looking ragged and upset.

'I have something important to tell you Thomas.'

'And what is that Coren?'

'I will not be wanting to play on Saturday.'

'Why not Coren?"

'I'm sorry, but it is for emotional reasons.'

'What do you mean, emotional reasons?'

'I'm having problems with coming to terms with my identity,' Evans said.

'We know who you are.'

'It's the inner me that is having a conflict with the essential me,' Evans said.

'But you are one of our best players.'

'Maybe so but I cannot decide if I want to play in a dress or trousers, he said.

'I would plump for the trousers. Your legs are far too hairy for wearing a dress,' Thomas said.

'Look you, Thomas, I'm emotionally in turmoil. Play somebody else please,' Evans said looking washed out and limp.

Thomas sighed.

'Not even wearing stockings?'

'It's not that. I don't think I can concentrate,' Evans pleaded.

'You are our best number three, Coren,' Thomas said, and took his friend by the hand. 'Listen Coren, Sly is not up to his best, and without you we could lose this match. Don't let us down Coren. I don't care how you are dressed on the day as long as you play for us. I'm relying on you, and so is the village. Play for the team, for the village and for me,' Thomas said.

Evans the Choir looked at Thomas, his face showing his emotional agony and Thomas, taking both his hands and gently squeezing, said: 'For Childen Eleven, please.'

Evans the Choir hung his head and suddenly looking up, tearful and shaking he croaked.

'All right, I will.'

Thomas gave him a warm hug and held the trembling choirmaster close to him, comforting the Welshman, feeling like a pastor in his church comforting a grieving husband. As Evans the Choir relaxed and stopped sobbing so Thomas let him go and looked at his tear stained face.

'You will play number three for us?'

'Yes, but on my terms,' Evans the Choir said, giving Thomas a lop-sided smile. He left the Grace house feeling much better, determined that, because of Thomas's obvious need for him on side, and the man's sincerity, he would play and do his best on the day.

'Play up! Play the game! Play for England and saint George, even if I am a Welshman.' He came to a sudden halt. 'Sod that for a lark, I will play for Wales and saint David and carry the leek, as the bard would have it.' He walked on thinking of the drama and how Shakespeare had depicted the English King Henry as a Welshman. 'A traitor to Wales, he was,' Evans said, and trotted on home.

He didn't see Thomas bow his head and pray for help from the almighty on his behalf, and his turn Thomas did not see Evans the Choir selecting his cricketing attire for the next day. If he had, Thomas might have had second thoughts about his choice of third bat.

However, the day, when it dawned, promised to be warm. The

forecast was for sunshine punctuated with high clouds. It was with much devotion that the groundsmen prepared the pitch, and locals, not directly involved with the cricket club, helped to ensure the pitch was pristine. If there was one thing that united the Childen community it was the matches between their eleven and the Stoat Maybury team.

With the absence of Peter Mann the Childen Eleven was confident and determined to win. A home match was an important affair and so it was that many of the villagers gathered to watch the play. The police were still in evidence but fewer now despite clearing up complaints generated by Wednesday's riot. The Greens were gearing up for the early trade and Horace was getting ready for the tea break. Outwardly all was well in Childen Under Blean. The cricket green and the ornamental pond with its netted fence saving any ball from a dunking waited for the action to begin.

The groundsmen re-painted the boundary lines describing as best they could the near oval boundary adapted to suit the shape of the green. They rolled the pitch and marked the creases and prior to the match did a check to make sure that nobody had allowed their dogs to poo on the play area. There was nothing they could do about the ducks fowling the playing area near the pond. It was the hope of the fielders that the ball went somewhere else.

As Sylvester remarked.

'The duck shit gives the ball a good polish.' But few players liked the idea and a towel and a bucket of water was kept handy to wash the ball if it got too dirty.

The Stoat Maybury eleven arrived in their cars and settled down in the small pavilion. The two umpires arrived and made themselves known to the captains. Sylvester sidled up to Thomas and whispered.

'Here, one of them's a woman.'

'Yes, what of it?'

'Crikey mate they'll be playing the game next!'

'They already do Sly. We might have a couple of women in our squad next season. You remember earlier in the season we played two teams that had women playing, or didn't you notice?'

Sly grunted and nodded his head.

'That was the hefty wicket keeper and the other one was a fielder what got me out, right?'

'And the Stoat Maybury team are playing a woman today. She's a bowler and from what I have heard she is almost as good as Peter Mann. You and I are opening the batting, Coren is third and I am putting Young Scroggins in at fifth,' Thomas said as they were getting ready for the match.

'Where is that bloody Welshman?'

'He'll be here.'

'He had better be.'

'Count on it. Now, listen to me. I don't want any nobbling. We win this match fair and square. Do you understand?' Thomas said.

'Yes captain, sir.'

Thomas went out onto the field to meet the Stoat Maybury captain and the umpires to take the toss. As he crossed to the pitch he thought he saw Evans the Choir arrive and drop his bag in the pavilion but could not be sure. The brief glimpse he had of the man confused him, and during the short ceremony, at which the Stoat Maybury captain won the toss and chose to bat, he heard the mumble of a minor commotion from the direction of the pavilion.

It was not until his team took the field he saw what the fuss was about.

Evans the Choir was wearing whites.

That was perfectly correct.

His whites were in effect more suited to tennis whites than the noble game of cricket, although Evans had chosen to wear cricketing socks, white shoes and a hat as he usually did; he was wearing a fetching short dress, with pleated skirt and low cut top, complete with white underwear designed for netball players.

Thankfully he was not wearing make up.

'Jesus H Christ!' said Sly as Evans took his normal place at square leg. 'What the bloody hell?'

'Just ignore it and play. You'll get used to it,' Thomas said.

Sly walked to his place behind the wicket shaking his head.

The sight of a hairy Welshman in a dress fielding for the opposition seemed to unnerve the Stoat Maybury openers who called on their captain to protest.

The Stoat Maybury captain listened to his players, spoke quietly to the umpires, huddling around the wicket like conspirators. At intervals one of the small party glanced at Evans who, like the rest of the Childen Eleven, stood by politely waiting for a decision.

Eventually the small group broke up and the umpires called on Thomas to explain.

'What is your square leg playing at?'

'Cricket; he's my number three bat,' Thomas said, his expression blank.

'But his dress is, well, not er, conventional.'

'Looks all right to me.'

'But he's dressed liked a woman on a tennis court?'

'He's having problems with his gender orientation,' Thomas said.

'With that hairy chest and legs, and the five o'clock shadow, nobody can mistake him for anything else but a man dressed up in women's clothes. Most peculiar,' said the woman umpire.

Thomas gave her a smile.

'Er, excuse me, but you are a woman dressed up like a man, and there is no way, I can see you as anything else but an umpire,' Thomas said.

'Play on,' she said, and gave both Thomas and the Stoat Maybury captain a furious glower.

From the beginning it was the Stoat Maybury openers that called the tune and Thomas called on Young Scroggins to bowl.

What happened shook the Stoat Maybury players.

Scroggins first ball was a humdinger and appeared to pass through batsman and bat to splatter the stumps across the wicket. The new batsman faced Scroggins and survived two balls before snicking a high one to leg straight into the hands of Evans the Choir.

A cry of "caught you ducky" wafted across the pitch and Sly called out 'How the fuck was that?'.

The umpire raised her finger and glared at Sly.

'Just Howzat will do,' she said.

The new batsman lasted two balls, prodding the ball out to the infield with no runs. On the third ball he missed completely, his bat swinging up connected with nothing and as he remarked afterwards he felt the wind of its passing as it took the bails and the middle stump with it.

'Howzat?' called Sly and gave the umpire a smile.

She raised her finger and said: 'That's better.'

At the change of overs it was Miles' turn to bowl. Miles was a good, steady bowler who could sometimes spin the ball. The new batsman was a Mavis Baker who faced Miles with her bat resting easy in her hands. She whacked his first ball for a four and punished his bowling with two more and a single.

On his last ball Miles gave it some spin and she lobbed it high to leg where Evans was waiting. She ran one run and called her partner to stop.

Evans ran for the ball, but it was just out of his reach, and with a certain amount of grace he dived to grasp it one handed. The ball hit his hand but spilled out and another fielder quickly lobbed it back.

The impact of Evans hitting the ground at speed ripped the top of his dress revealing his chest and a white sports bra.

'Oh bugger,' he said.

Mavis Baker called out.

'Serves you right you daft cow!'

Evans rose from the devastation and shook his fist at her.

Sean, the twelfth man took his place whilst Bonny Mason made running repairs.

Thomas changed the bowlers without success and eventually, wanting to save Young Scroggins for a push later on, bowled an over. Mavis Baker was piling on the runs and although the Stoat Maybury side had lost two more wickets it looked as if they would put on even more.

First he softened her up with an over by Young Scroggins.

She managed one single and then it was his turn.

He warmed up quickly and waited a moment or two for Evans to resume his place on the field looking nicely strapped up and bowled his first ball.

He did his usual run up, bowled left handed and somehow gave it that twist in mid air that could fool most of his opponents. Mavis Baker was baffled, and when he bowled a slightly different ball next she scored a single putting her off strike. This batsman had faced Thomas before and managed to defend and made two before getting flummoxed on the fifth and tapping it away for a single.

Thomas bowled his last ball at Mavis Baker and although she wanted to play a good clean stroke the ball came off the bat and looped up.

'Catch it!' cried Thomas.

Evans the Choir ran forward and caught the ball neatly, threw it in the air, and to the Howzat! by Sly behind the wicket, he called out.

'No need to shout, sweetie, it's mine!'

The umpire raised her finger.

After that dismissal it was a steady slaughter, but Mavis Baker had added a lot to the score and it was going to be tough going to win, even when Young Scroggins bowled the last batsman for duck.

As they walked off to the pavilion before going to the pub for lunch Thomas caught up with young Scroggins.

'They made a good score. How do you feel about it?'

'We can do it. We need steady opening I think and then go for it. We need 133 to win. That woman was a monster player,' he said and added. 'We should talk to mister Simon.'

'Very well but no nobbling, right?'

'No nobbling.'

During lunch Thomas found out that the woman was Peter Mann's sister.

'Mavis Baker, my husband plays football but I have always played cricket,' she said, and despite her reputation due to her association with the demon bowler Thomas liked her. He noticed later that she and young Scroggins were swapping stories and getting on quite well during lunch. The teams were served sandwiches and ale and many of the local supporters were sitting in and around the bar having watched the first session. The Vicar was there to cheer on the team accompanied by Bonny Mason who was sitting beside him at one of the tables on the terrace. Beside them Evans the Choir sat eating sandwiches and drinking a pink gin. He had changed his top for a new one that Bonny had found for him. The new one had little frills and tassels on it edged with pink, and didn't show so much of his chest.

Thomas thought that the village was growing more strange.

Sylvester Simon was 'chatting up' Mavis Baker, politely serving her sandwiches, and talking about her ability.

'I don't often have the chance to talk with a woman player in our teams. It seems we may be having two on our books for the first time next year as players in our first eleven. We have a women's team but they play in their own league,' he said offering another sandwich. She took it and smiled at him.

'I played for the county. I'm actually rated better than my brother but they don't allow us to play at that level. I've been playing cricket since I was a little girl,' she said.

Sly couldn't imagine her as being little. She was not much shorter than her brother, chunkier, and from the way she whacked the ball she was much stronger.

'And it shows. You are a natural,' he said.

Young Scroggins came back from the bar with beer for him and a soft drink for their guest and more sandwiches. He started straight in to talking about bowling and listened to her advice as she munched on the food. He and Sly let her eat and when the plate was empty Sly replenished it with another leaving them to talk of their art. This time both he and young Scroggins ate from the plate. When time was called the group split up and the two teams took to the field again.

Young Scroggins and Thomas opened the batting and for the first few overs managed a reasonable score between them until Thomas pitched one into the hands of the wicket keeper.

Evans the Choir marched onto the field, his bat under his arm, helmet in one hand and padded up, his skirt flapping in the breeze. He ignored the catcalls and rude comments, put his helmet on, took up position and got ready to face the bowling. Whether it was a malicious bent with Mavis Baker, or that for the moment she was simply annoyed nobody could say, but her first ball at Evans the Choir seemed to whistle down the pitch intent on taking out the middle stump, and Evans with it.

He met it with this bat and deftly punted it away along the ground for four.

The umpire signalled the runs.

'Well done missy,' Sly called out from pavilion.

Taking heart from Evans, Young Scroggins, when he was on strike relaxed and whacked a ball for four on the last ball of the over.

The pair met in the middle at the change over and touched gloves.

'The skirt suits you, Coren, and annoys the hell out of the lady bowler,' he said and chuckled.

Watching Evans running between wickets was an eye opener for his team as well as the opposition. When his team mates cheered instead of clapping and made ribald comments Evans responded with a clumsy curtsey.

'Not so much dying swan as bloody ruptured duck,' said the Stoat Maybury captain.

The ruptured duck proceeded to knock the ball around the field and between him and Young Scroggins they made forty-five before Young Scroggins got cocky and tried a sweep shot. He watched his stumps tumble over and over and walked.

Joining his team mates on the bench he nudged Miles.

'Listen mate, we have a cunning plan. When you go in to bat I suggest you follow it,' Young Scroggins said, and quietly told him what to do.

Thomas Grace sitting nearby caught the words "anytime now she should" but the rest was lost when suddenly Mavis Baker called on her captain to give her a break. Thomas watched her hurry across the field to the pavilion, rush into the end where they had the chemical toilets, heard the door shut which was followed by heart wrenching groans.

'Oy, what's going on?' he said, glowering at Young Scroggins.

'Nothing skip, not that I know of anyway,' he replied.

Then it hit them. The smell didn't exactly waft but tumbled out of the toilet area.

'Bloody hell! That's worse than anything Mutley can do!' said Sly, gasping and spluttering.

With one accord the team moved upwind of the toilets taking the bench and the chairs with them to sit in the free air. A few overs later Mavis Baker emerged looking pale and angry.

'Right, now I mean business,' she said, glowering angrily at the Childen players.

The twelfth man came off and as she took her place her captain had a word or two with her and gave her the ball.

'The Childen lot could win this unless we get the buggers out. Go for it. We will both bowl to the end.' He said.

Between them they bowled the home team wickets until there was only Evans and two wickets left. Sly, for the first time that season was out for a duck, clean bowled by Mavis Baker. With twenty-one runs needed and three overs to go victory seemed a long way off.

The on strike batsman was Miles.

'Listen mate, I got a plan.

Miles muttered to Evans and added. 'Joe said it should work, but it's up to you to get the runs.'

'Whatever you say Miles.'

Miles was a good tail-ender and could score runs when needed but he had a job to do and he was going to do it. The first ball he sent straight back along the pitch. The next one he did the same but angled it past the bowler to score two runs. He watched as Mavis Baker, sweating and looking shaky, but still powerful, took her run up. He watched her carefully as she ran in hoping she would bowl a fast one in the same spot. She obliged, and with his full concentration he hit it just right sending it back fast, rising at an angle that would tempt a bowler to catch it.

She did.

There was a thump. A gasp, and a groan.

The appeal went up and so did the umpire's finger but Mavis Baker didn't.

She lay on the ground writhing in agony clutching her belly where the ball had whacked straight through her hands. Miles was caught and bowled but, so was Mavis Baker.

'Get up you silly cow!' exclaimed Evans, and echoed the laughter of his team mates.

Miles walked. The match was held up for a few minutes whilst Mavis Baker was stretchered off.

The umpires consulted and decreed that the over should be bowled again.

Rory Clarke, the new batsman took a single putting Evans on strike.

The Stoat Maybury captain had to call on another bowler to attack Evans. The man re-set his field and prepared to take a short run up.

He was about to bowl when Evans called a halt.

'One of my pads has slipped. Please wait whilst I adjust my dress,' he said and giggled. As he strapped it back tight again he gave a backward glance over his shoulder at his legs and, smiling, he said: 'Are my seams straight.'

The umpire blushed angrily and snarled.

'As straight as they'll ever will be, get on with it.'

'Oh dear, pardon me, we are grumpy,' Evans said, and got ready to face the bowler.

He whacked the first ball and they took two.

Sixteen runs to go.

Two dot balls later he hit two close to the duck pond.

Fourteen left.

He finished the over with two and hoped Rory would let him get back on strike.

Twelve to go.

Rory managed to defend three balls before accidentally hitting a boundary.

Eight left.

Rory took a single on the next ball and all Evans could manage was another single.

Six left.

The next ball was a lob that Rory should have left but instead he lobbed it to the out field where a fielder ran desperately to make the catch. He was under the ball for a certain catch when with a yell and string of oaths he slipped on the patina of duck poo and skidded along the grass. The ball bounced off his body to run back along the field where it was returned to limit the runs to three.

Three to go and a wicket saved.

Evans watched as Rory faced the next ball.

Rory hit it along the ground and Evans called, racing along the pitch, his skirt flapping as he pumped his legs, passing Rory who was thundering in the opposite direction. Now he was on strike.

He defended a tricky ball and then, the captain who was bowling, sent down a full toss. Evans hit it on the full and sent it soaring over the heads of the fielders and watched the ball make a splash in the duckpond.

Evans the Choir did a pirouette, waving his bat above his head and cried out: 'Beaten the buggers!' and curtsied to his team mates who were jumping up and down cheering.

Evans the Choir, with Rory walking beside him, took off his helmet and gloves and as they passed the Stoat Maybury captain Evans smiled at him.

'My friend, dress has nothing to do with it, as long as you can play,' he said.

As they reached the pavilion Sly met them.

'Er, might be a good idea if you kept up this end, away from the chemical bogs mate. The demon bowler has, er sort of had an accident,' he said.

Evans caught the stench as he walked past and like the rest of the players he quickly grabbed his bag and hurried to the Dog and Duck. Most of the players opted to change in the corner of the quiet bar leaving the Stoat Maybury team to their own devices.

Thomas, gathering the last of the gear from the pavilion, wrapped a cloth around his face as he packed the odds and ends in the spare bag and hurried on out.

'We will have to get a flush toilet for this place,' he said, but in spite of the smell and the poor woman's distress he was pleased. He had never picked young Scroggins as a nobbler although, on reflection he should have guessed it; the young man's family were into that sort of thing.

However, he preferred to believe that it was duck poop on the outfield had saved the day.

It was, as Sly said, not the first time that a duck had saved the game.

On the way back to the pub when the gear was safely stored, the enemy cars were loaded, young Scroggins hove alongside Sly and said quietly. 'Well it worked.'

'Did you slip Horace a fiver?'

'He didn't know.'

'You sneaky bugger.'

'My Granddad taught me a lot,' young Scroggins said.

To celebrate their win the team dug into their pockets and treated some of their most ardent supporters to a drink. On the terrace an impromptu band had started playing. Evans the Choir had changed into his red dress and was singing jazz numbers to the music of a trumpet, a trombone, a clarinet, a banjo, a guitar and a person who had found a snare drum from somewhere. Evans, they all agreed was pretty good.

It was late that night when Sly, drunk and about to be collected by his wife looked at Evans and muttered: 'If the bugger would only shave his chin I could almost fancy him.' Luckily Sylvia managed to drag him home before he embarrassed himself.

Winning the last match of the season, and as long as the results from other matches were favourable, they might even win the championship. The excitement had drawn many villagers to the Dog and Duck that evening including Old Man Scroggins who had watched the game that afternoon and approved of the method used to ensure victory.

Mavis Baker had consumed a strong emetic used to scour dog's bellies of unhealthy nasties. Having smelled Mutley's flatulence the old man had suggested Forest dose the animal with it. Forest declined, stating that he didn't mind the smell.

'There's something wrong with that bugger,' remarked the old man when he heard. He also agreed that given the right circumstances, especially if Evans shaved off his beard, a bloke could do all right with the choirmaster.

That Sunday Mathew Grace was declared to be out of danger and his condition was described as stable. However he was still unable to speak. His parents had visited but there was nothing they could do and so they went back home. The detectives calling on them had asked the inevitable question.

'Does he have any enemies?'

'Lots,' said Thomas.

'Nearly everybody,' agreed Melanie.

The detective sighed and settled down for a long session.

'Tell me,' he said and accepted the tea and biscuits with good grace and the knowledge that to refuse would mean constant reminders of their presence. He recorded the story and also made notes making sure he dated and timed the interview. The session was better than he expected. The Grace parents were articulate and accurate and worked together naturally. What he learned made sense and with the phone and computer data they could build a case against him and maybe have a suspect. When the pair had finished he thanked them.

'Why do you need his computer?'

'Because his name came up during the investigation we are carrying out on Stanley White. I am sorry but your son is possibly involved with a pornographic ring,' he said.

'We know that because we caught him at it and we were going to report him but by then he was clobbered,' said Thomas. 'You are welcome to search his room.'

The detective and a constable as witness searched the room taking his laptop and filled a box with material evidence. They handed Thomas a receipt and went out. That was Sunday morning before church and when Thomas realised that Sara was lunching at the Greens and going on to the stables enthusing about riding with Robert Massingham they rang the Dog and Duck and booked a table.

'You know dear, it may be unfair on him but I am glad Mathew is not here today. I know I should feel anxious for him, and I do, but it is a relief to have him out of our hair for a while,' Thomas said.

Melanie looked at him and smiled softly.

'I know what you are trying to say. Yes, I feel that way too. I think that when he is recovered enough he should find a flat or a room in town. We could afford to help him get started. After all he is going to be a father and I am sure that Sylvia wouldn't want a slob around the house.'

'Yes, let's get rid of him.'

'As soon as he is better.'

'And out of jail,' added Thomas.

With that thought in mind they more or less watched Sara rush in, gallop up the stairs and come down a few minutes later dressed ready for riding.

'Have a nice afternoon dear,' Melanie said as Sara rushed out.

'I bloody well intend to,' Sara cried out and mounted her bicycle and rode off.

'Keen she is,' said Thomas.

And soon they were strolling hand in hand to the Dog and Duck anticipating a dinner they had not had to cook and a drink or two.

'Sexy,' said Thomas and gave her that look which always made her spine tingle. it did now and she realised what was driving her daughter.

'Yes, sexy,' she said meaning their own relationship and what might be happening to Sara. Sara and Robert steaming with lust. It was a disturbing thought.

Sunday was a day of church as usual and with the victory over the Stoat Maybury eleven and the good news that the Childen team had indeed won the championship the village rejoiced. The reverend Jones strutted his stuff in the church and cared little whether or not the Triffids of the charismatic section of his congregation did their bit. The reduced choir sang sweetly; the musicians played as well as they could and he even ignored the fact that Evans the Choir was, underneath his cassock, dressed in a gold Lamé dress that was off the shoulder and his make up, now managed by Bonny, was not as garish as it was the night before. He had also shaved his beard.

The sermon revolved around the meaning of winning and encouraged the listeners to remember that at times a sacrifice will result in a win and equated that with Jesus dying on the cross.

'Because Christ was crucified our sins were purged and we are winners. Christ sacrificed his own life in order for us to win everlasting life in His house,' he finished, and gave the blessing.

He was beyond caring for what happened in the parish; as long as the community wanted him as their vicar he would stay with it. He knew that the church was strapped for cash, short of incumbents and as long as he was wanted he would stay. He wound the service down and after the choir was gone he disrobed and waited for Bonny. Evans the Choir was standing by the door with his back against the stone pillar looking despondent.

'What's the matter my friend?'

'They chucked me out of the rugby club. They said it was inappropriate to have an openly gay person in the team and that some of the players would feel uncomfortable. I explained that I like to dress up in women's clothing and that was all but they told me in polite terms to bog off.' Evans said, and shook his head. 'All right I liked feeling the blokes around me in the rucks and mauls and love it when I'm tackling a player but I don't want to shag any of them. Not my type.'

'Is that why you er, dress like this?'

'It helps me feel myself.'

And hopefully that's all you're feeling, thought the vicar.

'You just need understanding right?'

'Well yes. Thing is I have to go to work and there they take the mickey. I will go of course but I'm not happy.'

'Can you not work from home?'

'Not with this company,' Evans said.

Bonny Mason was close by and had listened to the last exchange, and with a gentleness that almost made Evans cry, she took his hand and squeezed it.

'Go talk to Forest Maloney. He's working from home and I believe you two work in similar areas. Go see him now.'

'What dressed like this?'

'What's wrong with it? Just adjust your bra a bit and straighten your hose and you will look stunning,' she said. 'We will walk down with you and meet you in the Dog and Duck for a gin.'

Forest was startled when Amanda admitted Evans the Choir to the living room, and was even more startled when Evans sat on the settee and crossed one leg over the other for all intents like a woman.

'I need help,' began Evans.

'I can see that,' replied Forest.

'Oh you mean the clobber? No, not that, Bonny tidied that up for me,' he said.

Forest wanted to say that was not what he meant but already Evans had launched into his explanation and ended with: 'So Bonny suggested I ask you how to get started. I believe we work in similar areas and I am quite happy to use my computer at home instead and get paid for it. Can you advise me?'

And despite Evans' bizarre appearance Forest agreed to help him as if he was simply another client. Amanda seemed unfazed. When they had finished it was time for Amanda to go to work and she left them to tidy up. When the Vicar and Bonny knocked on his door Forest let them in and soon all five were walking through the village to share lunch at the Dog and Duck.

Sara Grace finished her shift at the tea rooms and pedalling her bicycle hurried on past them to change her clothes for the stables.

'Good afternoon folks,' she called out and giggling happily she waved her hands. She seemed extremely happy.

This afternoon was to be a momentous one for her.

It was also a turning point for the Reverend Jones. Arriving at the Dog and Duck the group negotiated a table and lunch and during the pre-lunch snifters Lord Massingham suddenly appeared in the bar with his good lady and with warm handshakes invited them to sit with them for a while.

'We have guests due in a half hour or so and if you can spare the time I have the bones of a proposition for you reverend.'

Seated with their lunch postponed the group listened to what he had to say and as he outlined his ideas they heard a plan for their village.

'I will purchase the quarry and ask for help from the village under the old proposal to develop it and I will also purchase the vicarage. From a source within the village I understand the congregation would like to keep their vicar.'

'It may not be as easy as that but it sounds good to me,' said Jones.

'All we need now is a rugby team,' said Evans who was impressed by their acceptance of his attire. That was the gentry for you, being mad as hatters anything was normal, even gold lamé dresses on a Sunday.

'Now that is a jolly good idea. We have room on the sports field for a rugger pitch. All we need is some lads ready to play.'

'I could organise that with Coren here,' said the reverend.

'You play?'

'Hence my interest and my present circumstances,' said Evans but he had no time to explain because his lordship's guests had arrived. However, during lunch the conversation focussed on the quarry and the rugby.

Mutley simply farted his approval.

Amanda who was serving caught a whiff of his flatulent effort and gasped.

'My God! That dog is foul.' She said screwing up her face.

'Our dog has always been foul,' Forest said and laughed.

To their surprise Thomas and Melanie Grace arrived and were shown to a table giving their party a smile and a wave as they passed.

'They seem happy. Perhaps it is not having Mathew mooning around that helps,' Forest said. 'Perhaps that was why Sara was so cheerful when she flew past us on her bike.'

But that was not the reason why Sara was happy. Arriving at the stables she leaned her bike against the wall and walked to the stable to deal with Figaro. She put a halter on him and led him out to the grazing yard. She cleaned the stable piling the manure on the ever growing heap and washed the stable down. She strewed more straw on the floor and plonked hay in his trough. She carried his saddle out into the yard and soon she had him saddled up ready to ride. It was at that moment she saw Robert leading his horse from the back yard ready saddled and her heart skipped a beat. He saw her and he and the horse came across the yard.

'Hi, ready for a ride?' he said.

'Oh yes,' she said and allowed him to help her mount the horse although she needed no assistance.

They rode the trails and whenever they could cantered and galloped the animals through the Trust area and eventually rode back to the stables where they let the horses graze after grooming them. As she had expected the stables were more or less deserted and although the caretakers would be overseeing the complex they were on their own.

Robert looked at her and smiled.

'Shall we?' he said.

'Oh yes,' she said and when he reached out his hand she took it and let him lead her to the feed store. Inside was dim but not completely dark and eventually they found a secluded space.

He kissed her and when she responded he lifted her top out of her riding pants and explored her body. She had left her bra and panties behind glad that her riding pants had side zips.

'We should take our boots off,' she said in between kisses.

The boots came off so did her riding breeches. She felt his

fingers exploring between her legs and gasped flopping over on her back, nipples erect and waited for his member to go where it was wanted. It was hard and hot and she felt it slide into her and as he gasped and grunted with the effort she groaned in pleasure.

At last she was an ex-virgin.

She understood now why Cheryl Simon was so enthusiastic even if it was with her grotty brother. She clung to Robert and explored his muscular body feeling his wet penis still hard and stroked it.

Without thinking about it she masturbated him and felt his warm fluid fall on her belly and groaned when he used his fingers to make her reach a climax.

'Fuck me again Robert,' she said and this time she pushed against him.

'We had better feed the horses,' he said afterwards, and as they dressed neither of them could keep their hands off one another. When they were dressed and out in the yard she looked up at him.

'I like being an ex-virgin,' she said.

He blushed and looked at her adoringly.

'So do I,' he said.

She stopped and stared at him mouth open and shook her head.

'I thought you had...'

'No I didn't. It was just to impress you. Honestly you are my first and be sure I don't want anybody else. I er, fell in love with you when you first came to the stables and I know we have been friends but it took me a long time,' he said.

'I was eleven when I first came here.'

'I was twelve.'

'And why didn't you ask me out?'

'I was afraid you would say no.'

'So I had to throw myself at you.'

'But we are friends and love the horses and doing horse things. I mean all those events and parties afterwards we had I struggled to go further and there was many times I wanted to kiss you and blab out my feelings but I'm no great shakes at wooing. Too shy.'

She laughed and kissed him.

'So it was up to me to make suggestions, embarrass you by getting you to brag about the lovers you never had and make you an offer you couldn't refuse,' she said and moved close to him.

'Tell me lover, did you ever, you know, play with yourself thinking of me?'

He gasped and gulped and said quietly. 'Quite a lot.'

'Now you have me,' she said and closed with him and kissed his waiting lips feeling the hardness between his legs. 'In the stable up against the wall.'

And before they brought the horses in despite the awkwardness of the riding breeches they managed to satisfy their urges.

Sara rode home more slowly than she had ridden to the stables. Robert joined his parents at the Dog and Duck to ride home with them which now their guests were gone it was time to leave. His father told him about the prospect of forming a rugby club in the village.

'Jolly good, about time we had a local rugger club,' Robert said.

Old Man Scroggins, Maisie and the more trusted of the elders of his clan sat in his lounge discussing plans for the Rugby club and the future of the village. Lord Massingham had surprised the old man by suddenly appearing on his doorstep on Thursday evening. They had a long chat, a short but useful argument, and made a deal.

'I wants to fit in,' the old man said.

'And I would want you to, especially if you and yours stop poaching so much of my game.'

'We catches it, we sells it, you grows it and we share the profits?'

'Providing I get my share, I can agree,' Massingham said. 'Do right by me on that issue and I will meet you fairly on the future of the village.'

The old man spat on the palm of his hand and offered it to Massingham who took it, shook hands. He did not wipe his hand until he was well away from the house.

The three other members of the original Bird Watchers Club knowing that their mates were being investigated panicked.

'We are right in the shit,' said one.

'What we gonna do?'

'We ain't go no choice. We gotta fess up. My old man will be bloody furious.' Their elected leader declared.

'Mine too.'

'And me.'

The boys had arrived home on Thursday to be greeted by police officers who demanded they hand over their phones, and laptops. The boys were so frightened by what might happen to them they remained stunned and completely unable and unwilling to go anywhere that weekend. They watched the cricket match but took little pleasure in it and vowed vengeance on Mathew and his mates. For them that following Sunday was gloomy, but for others with freedom in sight, lost virginity accomplished and a new plan for Childen Under Blean in the offing the general feeling was one of optimism.

Evans the Choir turned up at work on Monday dressed in a smart top and matching skirt, a frilly blouse, bewigged as a brunette, legs encased in fashionable bronze hose and sensible shoes. He was not surprised when he was invited to explain his attire to his head of department. The nervous glances from his colleagues as he went about his work were obvious even when they pretended it wasn't happening. When the call from the office came he glanced in the nearest mirror, adjusted his dress and his wig and sauntered along the corridor to meet his supervisor.

"What is the meaning of this; this attire?' His Supervisor, Piers Chapman, said.

'I like dressing up,' he said, inspecting his nails.

'You are causing some disruption Coren and we cannot have that now can we?' The tone was definitely patronising and a little nervous; the sort of nervousness of the convinced sane that they were dealing with a madman.

'Other people are dressed in similar fashion,' he said.

'Yes I know but they are, er women.' Chapman said looking decidedly uncomfortable. 'You are a man and we expect you to be dressed like one. Look, Coren, do you need a holiday to er, sort of get over whatever it is that's troubling you? We can arrange that you know.'

'I've already had my holidays. No, I would like to get back to work,' Evans the Choir said and smiled sweetly, a grotesque gesture for, despite shaving carefully his naturally dark hair shadowed his chin.

His boss sighed and shrugged his shoulders.

'I'm sorry but the MD saw you this morning and freaked out

when I told him that the new girl was in fact a salaried long term employee, namely yourself. He wasn't happy. I have to ask you to take off the women's clothing ...' he paused and watched in horror as Evans started to strip off. If he wasn't caught in a difficult position the poor man would have cracked up laughing at Evans' clumsy parody of the stripper. Open mouthed and astonished he watched as Evans, now completely naked except for the wig, earrings, bangles and handbag headed for the door. 'Come back you idiot!'

But it was too late.

Evans the Choir was already on his way through the offices.

'If I'm not allowed to wear the clothes I want in the office then I will wear nothing!' he explained as he strolled back to his workstation. As he passed his colleagues he left behind him a stir of shocked indignation, amused bemusement, gasps of surprise followed by ribald comments, catcalls and others calling his name adding a few cheers.

He sat at his desk and nodded happily to his colleagues either side of him and, finding the place in the document he was working on, he nonchalantly carried on with the task. He had worked for fifteen minutes when the security team arrived along with, Smithers, his head of department. Chapman followed in his wake looking apologetic and handed the bundle of clothes to him.

'Thank you Piers,' Smithers said, and turning to Evans, he pointed at them. 'These are your clothes. Put them on and these chaps will escort you from the premises. You are suspended until further notice. If you have any personal belongings you may want to take with you please do so now.' He said and snarled. 'Get on with it.'

Evans smiled at him and slowly donned his clothing, filled the proffered bag with his meagre belongings including his pot plants and patted Smithers on his cheek, puckered his lips and said. 'Tatty bye my lovely.'

The man staggered back gasping.

Piers Chapman covered his face with his hands.

Evans the Choir blew kisses using his hands to his now ex-colleagues amid cheers and more ribald comments, hoots and hand clapping as the two security men, one in front of him and one behind, led him out to the car park. They made sure he was in his car and belted up watching him as he reversed the vehicle, and pointed it toward the barrier.

He was asked to roll the window down which he did and one of the men spoke.

'Drive slowly and the barrier will open. Drive fast and it will stay shut. All the best mister and keep your seams straight,' he said, which Evans thought was nice of him.

'Thank you,' he replied and drove slowly as requested moving out past the barrier and driving off home whistling some favourite tunes. Mission accomplished. And once back in the village still dressed in his suit, he chatted with Forest. Amanda supplied them with tea and biscuits having returned from town after dropping Salina off at college.

'You should shave before you go out if you want to impress people,' Amanda said and sniffed. 'Or you could put proper clothes on and dress like a man. I hope you are not going dressed like that when we meet his lordship on Wednesday.'

'Oh no, I won't be wearing these clothes then,' he said. And meant it.

Wednesday evening's meeting took place at the Vicarage. Thomas Grace was there, Old Man Scroggins and his good lady arrived with young Scroggins and some of the clan. The Vicar was host and Bonny, now an accepted ecclesiastical floosie, Evans the Choir, Forest Maloney and Amanda looking daggers at Evans who was dressed in an evening gown and looked ridiculous. He was definitely the wrong shape to wear evening dress. His hairy chest and arms adorned with tattoos under a mass of dark hair and late five o'clock shadow that made even the make-up look shoddy. She thought he looked more suited to bullying other men on the rugby field than as a woman. Horace was there with Maddy Green; her husband was helping Molly look after the Dog and Duck. The local parish councillors were there and of course his lordship. Robert, who was learning the business of being landed gentry, had brought Sara with him.

Amanda noticed that Sara and Robert clung together like the north and south poles of two magnets and more than likely would have to be prised apart.

The meeting began formally, plodded along dismally until Old Man Scroggins banged his stick on the polished table causing the vicar to wince.

'This is a load of old bollocks, we won't get far with all this fuckiin' about. We need to get on with it for fuck's sake. My mob have some dosh to spend and wanna put it into this place and the quarry same as what his nibs here wants. We reckons we can give a lend of some to the village for their share in the quarry so theys can do things with it. We reckons that if we buys the quarry and his nibs buys the vicarage, and we all pays the vicar his salary, we got a deal,' he said, and plonked a sheaf of documents on the table. 'It's all in there. A copy each. Now get the fuckin' drinks out and them sarnies what you got covered up and we can have a read.'

Sara and Robert shared a copy and with a drink each, a shared plate of sandwiches they read the copy and in the shadow of their corner quietly groped.

'It's a good plan,' said Robert.

'Yes of course,' Sara said and snuggled up to him. They kissed and she tasted the remains of his fish paste sandwiches. Who serves fish paste sandwiches? Answer: vicars and posh people.

Reverend Jones was voted to the chair by Old Man Scroggins. 'You council buggers are too long winded. I reckon his reverence is capable of chairing the meeting as you like to call it. If it was up to me I would call a vote now and have done with it.'

His faith in the vicar was touching but intimidating.

Michael Jones took heart from the old man's support and whenever anybody began to stray from the task he called them back to order. Eventually with a few modifications the proposal was ready for the vote.

'I suggest a show of hands,' Jones said and before anybody could object he called out: 'Those in favour.'

Many hands went up and for the record he counted them.

'Those against?'

There were only a few.

He counted them anyway.

'Abstainers?'

The abstainers decided not to cast their votes.

With modifications added and amendments completed, Old Man Scroggins' proposal was accepted, and subject to negotiations with the owners and the church a plan of action was proposed. His nibs promised to release the story to the local newspaper and the meeting ended with friendly handshakes all round.

Robert and Sara emerged from their continuous clinches to join the general chat looking ruffled but happy, and although they were aware only of each other they made an effort to be part of the group. Robert attempted to play the part of the squire's son and, gracefully, Sara followed his lead. She felt like a princess with her prince.

However, their insular awareness made little impact as a piece was prepared for the local paper. It was agreed that is should come under the parish news section and duly a small announcement was added in the local paper as a last minute filler for the "Round the Parishes" feature and was welcomed by the villagers.

Under Siege

The week slid by with nothing more than the continuing investigation into the attack on Mathew Grace, the enquiries regarding the so-called Bird Watcher's Club and the return of Terry Smith and Donald Tomms who hobbled around on crutches. There was a mixed reaction to the news that Mathew Grace had regained consciousness.

Evans the Choir was now openly and permanently, so it appeared, wearing women's clothes. His progress around the village as he did his local shopping was steadily regarded as part of normal village life. Many observers remarked that he would be more convincing if he shaved his legs, tidied up his beard and learned to walk properly in heels.

Even the drinkers accepted Evans in his new role and it seemed that now he was working from home as well as able to be open about his feelings he joined the drinkers at their table. His insights into the affairs of the village made for some lively conversation.

Graham Cook was pleased to discover that his plans for expansion were working. He was conscious of Lyla's adoration and although he was a practical and considered a non-romantic boy he was aware of their mutual attraction and the strange feelings he had when she was close. They sat together on the school bus and met as often as possible at school which isolated them somewhat from what was happening in and around the village.

The adults of the village looked upon Graham's followers benevolently, and remarked on them as they passed by. The group organised birdwatching trips with Vernon Green and that worthy returned good reports of their behaviour.

'They settle down to the task, swap notes, chat to other birdwatchers and share knowledge. That young Graham is a whizz at organisation,' Vernon told parents.

Thomas Grace, who was running the birdwatcher's account, declared that the group was making a steady profit and pointed out that Graham had organised a committee to run the group, adopted a constitution and even had a treasurer.

'They keep minutes and set agendas,' he said.

The Birdwatchers of Childen Under Blean

The parents of the birdwatchers felt comfortable and proud of their offspring. The also bought bird feeders and bird seed from the Greens,' store, and as they also became aware of the need to provide a better environment for the birds and animals so they added more plants and trees to their gardens. Graham's group campaigned for increasing the pollinator count which meant that the Greens also sold seeds and small plants.

Graham and his group shared in the profits.

Sylvester Simon was pleased with their activities and remarked to his friends. 'If that Grace tosser had done what young Cook is doing I would have more time for the stupid fucker.' Which, as far as Graham Cook was concerned, if he had heard it, was praise indeed.

The only drawback as far as they could see was that the group seemed to isolate their children from rest of the kids in the village and the town. In fact their isolation was not all that peculiar; there were many in Childen Under Blean who had very little idea of what was bubbling up to upset their idyllic way of life.

The nearest large town to Childen Under Blean was one of those market towns that had grown larger by swallowing up the smaller villages on the outskirts. It grew to include a number of secondary schools, now turned into Academies and two Colleges handling the vocational subjects needed for industry and one pretending to be a University. It was not but it was working toward the status seeking accreditation for teaching the Arts. At some time in its early formation Evans the Choir had taught music, at beginners' level including Choral arrangement for aspiring conductors. He had left when the College had to cut its costs. Settling for a position with Timmins publishing which was a step down even if it paid almost twice as much. He moved to Childen Under Blean because he heard that St. Seraph's needed a choir master. He presented his credentials to the reverend Michael Jones. and that worthy welcomed him with open arms. As far as Evans was concerned it was the best move he had ever made.

The move also saved him answering some pointed questions about his sexuality.

However, the town was home to two local newspapers and two rival FM radio stations all of which had loyal and parochial supporters. In addition, the local television stations carried local news that linked in to the London networks. People commuted to London but also people from out of town commuted for work and school from the outlying villages. These groups tapped into the printed matter and the broadcasts as well as the social media sites.

Apart from that, the rumours and urban myths, fake news and even more blatant fibs fuelled the more juicy stories and spread faster than the plague, except that unlike the plague it wasn't exactly lethal.

Tales of perversion and blackmail had drifted in from Childen Under Blean and until the vlogger's movie went viral people were only mildly interested. The news of Mathew Grace's beating was linked with that of the two lads "falling" off the cliff and police investigating a pornography ring. It was all very exciting and when a group of youngsters had gone out to grab a bunch of selfies with the actual fornicators things got a little more interesting.

Rumours of opposition to the gawkers by the villagers grew in strength and in the bars and public places discussion began to bubble up.

Sylvester's sacking was only of interest to those who knew him and it passed with hardly a comment but when Evans the Choir was sent home the news passed around rapidly. That following week after Lord Massingham had announced the purchase of the quarry, the headline news on both local papers was about the Childen Bird Watchers Club. Both items told of the lads and the Peeping Tom activities, telling of "spying on young girls".

All that was bad enough, or interesting according to your taste, but when it was learned that the sexual exploits of the Childen residents had been photographed and sold on the internet the townspeople took interest.

What started the intense curiosity off like a rocket was the pictures of Evans the Choir posted on social media. Twittering increased the exposure and local dignitaries uttered their condemnation.

Remarks by the Mayor, designed to express the township's moral disgust only raised interest even higher.

'This sort of behaviour in our outlying communities is not welcome. The sooner the matter is cleared up and the instigators brought to justice the better off our town will be,' he pontificated.

A spokesperson for the Anglican Church body blamed the events on the lack of moral control the Reverend Jones had

The Birdwatchers of Childen Under Blean

exercised over his flock.

'It is understood that he allows strange, unacceptable practices, in his church and we understand that Bishop Mathews has attempted to control the situation. It is appalling that a servant of the church should be involved in such disgusting practices.'

Good meaningful and righteous stuff but in general the announcement was treated as sour grapes by newspaper readers who seemed to believe that the people of Childen under Blean were have more fun than they were.

The pictures of Evans the Choir walking naked through his office on the day he was fired filled the social media sites despite efforts to take them down. The buzz was that Childen under Blean was the place for a fun visit and many townsfolk, mostly the young and curious, with a fair contingent of perverts began planning a visit to the village under the hills.

As expected the rumour of a mob reached the authorities too late to prevent it happening and on Saturday morning the road leading out to Childen Under Blean was dotted with moving vehicles heading for the village.

By opening time the village was at a standstill.

Somehow Old Man Scroggins knew of the impending invasion and alerted his clan who alerted the rest of the village. The Street, was blocked. But the villagers had, with the aid of the roughest old bangers they could lay hands on, helped by the Scroggins Clan, created road blocks on all of the small side streets. It was obvious that the villagers were not going anywhere and neither were the visitors.

The Clan organised the villagers into squads according to the section of the village to patrol the alleys and footpaths. They all reported back to Old Man Scroggins.

The newcomers had come to find the men and women shown on the vlog, especially the vicar and the naked, cross dressing choir master. The road blocks and the defenders behind them stopped vehicles clogging the lanes and closes. The bottom of Church Lane was blocked off to vehicles with a small group of residents on guard and Evans, the Vicar and Bonny Mason were hiding in the Vicarage. with a few residents and Clan members to protect them.

The nature of mobs is that, whatever the original intention, by the time the crowd has reduced to the status of mob rather than demonstrators is that any leadership has disappeared. The townspeople had taken up an idea and nobody really knew what it was. Naturally with a lack of direction and restricted by physical barriers the crowd became frustrated followed by annoyance and then anger. Once there, they had no way out and nobody wanted to leave without first seeing something worth creating a selfie.

Somebody said that the Cross Dresser was holed up in the church and with the anger of the mob frustrated by denial of their objectives the crowd attacked the barriers. The old bangers that blocked the road were pushed over and the guard had to beat a hasty retreat as the mob advanced steadily up the hill chanting.

'We want the naked choir boy!
Bring on the naked choir boy!
- and -
Give us no moans
We want Jones!'

The cry deteriorated to calling out for the naked vicar and the queer boy mixed with arguments as men and women shoved and pushed their way up the hill.

The words tumbled into each other as each small faction tried to outdo the others growing louder as fights broke out.

The delays due to the fighting and bickering gave Old Man Scroggins a chance to organise.

The crowd swamped the village with faces peering into windows and gardens and in spite of the patrols during the first few hours of the invasion managed to take pictures of virtually everything in the village. The most annoying aspect of the intrusion was the flock of drones filling the airspace with their irritating buzzing. Somehow the addresses of the vlogger's subjects was known and soon the crowds trying to get pictures of their heroes blocked the streets.

The flocks of drones hovered outside the known addresses vying with each other to catch a glimpse of the occupants. The result was a series of buzzing dog fights as each operator tried to gain the advantage. Drones clashed smashing into each other to crash to the ground, into each other in mid air and smash into walls or fences.

Fights broke out between angry owners who were pelted with missiles by locals aiming at the buzzing machines. One such defence was carried by Sally Wise and her brother, who sallied out from her front door with a garden hoe and knocked several out of the air before the owners could shift them. He smashed those that fell when tangled and when the mob attempted to stop him he attacked them with the hoe using it like a spear.

He went back inside when the mob grew angry.

Bricks and stones flew at the house breaking windows but was suddenly stopped when Scroggins clan people and locals arrived to beat them back with clubs and sticks.

Thomas Grace, accompanying the clan lads called on Sally and her brother. She came to the door with Colin behind her.

'You two alright?' he asked, and suddenly gasped. He gazed at Colin and for a moment or two he was unable to speak. But, recovering, he pointed at Colin.

'Corporal Lawrence, what the hell are you doing here?'

Colin Lawrence stood still, balanced, tense as he gazed at Thomas and gripped Sally.

'Christ, sergeant major Grace. Shit, you've not seen me, right?'

'I repeat, what the hell are you doing back here? Risking yourself and your, your sister?'

And with a shock Thomas remembered what else Lawrence was capable of. Apart from being a vicious soldier, a mercenary and a violent felon, he was also accused of incest. A very non-Christian attitude.

The problem was that once Lawrence had been a good soldier; a good man in a combat situation.

'You are planning to leave I hope?'

'Yes sir, as soon as.'

'Make sure you do,' Thomas said, and turned on his heel and left.

Graham Cook and his group of fanatical bird watchers had wandered off in the morning before the crowds arrived leaving behind a plan of their route, and by mid day they were cut off from the village. In touch with their parents on their mobiles the group settled a camp near the quarry.

The birds, upset by the chaos developing below, retreated to the woodlands to feed giving the birdwatchers an afternoon of ornithological paradise.

From their position above the quarry Graham and his followers could see the crowds milling around and hear the horns beeping but had no real idea of what was happening. Wisely they had conserved their packed lunches and sat in the sunshine sometime around two to eat their food.

They would find a way of getting home eventually.

'We should build shelters,' suggested Lyla.

Forever practical the group cut bracken, found leafy branches and soon they were busy fashioning low sleeping shelters under the trees in a place sheltered from the north by thick bushes and prepared to retire there when it got dark.

And thus organised they forgot about the village and concentrated on their hobby.

In the village the group's parents' anxieties were assuaged a little by Graham and Lyla's efforts. The youngsters were safe and that was what mattered. The folks could get on with coping with the ever growing crowds taking pictures of everything and laughing whenever they saw a local resident.

From his large, rambling house Old Man Scroggins directed operations. The squads were working and although there was only a few groups of enthusiastic villagers, with his own clan he had enough people to do the job.

When the visitors grew to a mob Old Man Scroggins marched down the road with his escort of young thugs to meet with the less active members of the community who nevertheless were willing to offer support.

'Right folks, the invaders are a pain in the arse as far as I am concerned. You lot should get ready to look after the kids and the wounded if things should get nasty. You can also get on with making tea, cleaning wounds and drying tears. We want you to keep on the phones and together we can send the aliens back where they came from.'

Old Man Scroggins was proud his village and was a strong advocate of keeping Childen under Blean for the Childenites. The occasional intrusion of the police, social workers, and other officials was, as far as he was concerned, tiresome but he was willing to accept them. The village needed the postal vans, deliveries of beer and groceries and of course the tourists who spent money in the village.

Old Man Scroggins had investments in the pub, and the Green's tearooms, interests in some of the local market gardens. His local business enterprises were a good cover for the clan's less legitimate activities. As a new convert to Anglican Christianity he saw it as his duty to protect the weak and vulnerable.

The invasion of the village by townies he equated with the invasion of Rome by the barbarians but unlike Rome he was not going to allow his empire to be destroyed. The stream, the river Eden, known locally as the *Jimmy Riddle,* was his *Tiber* and he had always seen his house as a forum, a place to be protected with other people's lives.

'We will put the plan in action,' he declared and was satisfied when his audience cheered.

He sent Young Scroggins and his group up to the church armed with clubs and sticks, "working" boots and "sensible" jackets and pants. Young Scroggins expeditionary force used the back alleys and tracks to arrive at the vicarage back gate without being spotted. Young Scroggins rang the vicar and told him that there was a party close by ready to rescue them.

'We're all right here thank you.'

'Sod that Vicar, we need you down below for moral support. My Grand da says to brung you and that bloody pansy if he's there,' Young Scroggins said.

He explained to Jones what Old Man Scroggins had said.

'We want you down below for your safety, and to sort of let the villagers know that you are with us. You know, a sort of focus, so we can wade in without having to worry about you and have you the to help encourage the troops. If you get my meaning?'

'We are safe here.'

'Have you seen the crowd?'

'I'll have a look.'

Jones was gone for a few minutes and then when Young Scroggins called again he sounded quite shocked.

'All right, you had better come and get us.'

'It's going to be mob rule,' Old Man Scroggins had said. Quickly the squads gathered to repel the intruders, organised by clan lads who steadily led them to the edge of the crowd. 'The cutting out operation by Young Scroggins he deemed as a wise move in the general strategy.

Moped riders dashed in and out of gaps and cyclists stacked their bikes anywhere they could to wander off looking for the faces they had seen in the vlog.

As often happens when crowds gather without organisation

tempers are short. The tea rooms and the pub were barely able to cope and as Horace remarked.

'The extra trade is good but by cracky I'm knackered.'

'If things don't ease up soon something's got to give,' Molly said. She was right.

Things gave way at the Vicarage.

Young Scroggins and his gang sneaked into the garden and led the Vicar, Bonny and Evans out to the field intending to lead them along the tracks down to the village. They made it to the footpath and across the field but as they crossed the exposed patch past the church they were spotted.

'Look there they are, sneaking off,' cried a voice and like a tidal wave the crowd rushed into the churchyard bent on catching them.

'The one with the red dress - that's the gay boy!'

Evans stopped and turning bunched his fists.

'That's all I bloody need boyo.'

'Come on we gotta run,' young Scroggins said.

'What, in these shoes?' asked Evans. 'You gotta be kidding!'

'You can't fight them all'

'Why not? The bastards deserve a walloping. Give me one of those sticks and I'll show you,' he said, and one of young Scroggins men handed him a spare club.

'And one for me,' said the Vicar.

'And if there's a spare I could do with one too,' said Bonny.

Young Scroggins sighed and from somewhere in the group another two spare clubs appeared. At that moment he felt like Ratty from the Wind in the Willows with a touch of the anxious Mole and hopefully a lot of Badger. He hoped he wasn't really Toad.

'Okay troops, ready?'

Behind him there was a chorus of grunted assent and feeling really stupid and not brave at all he yelled out one word.

'Charge!'

And ran at the crowd with his club raised.

They vaulted over the stone wall surrounding the yard and like marauding Vikings laid into the unsuspecting crowd with vicious vigour. Beside him young Scroggins noted the action of the vicar and thought the man was wasted cracking heads. He could be playing for the Childen Eleven.

It was a rout and with cries of fear and yells of pain the mob ran from the onslaught back down the lane. Evans stopped to pick up a pair of discarded flatties to replace his heels and charged down after some stragglers.

Thwack! went his stick on exposed heads and backs driving the stragglers on faster to escape the terrifying demon in a dress who yelled at them in a Welsh accent.

'I am not a gay boy!'

Followed by another thwack as he struck again.

The fleeing crowd met those coming up the lane and unable to stop crashed into them at speed and with young Scroggins' mob of maniacs behind them tried to fight their way through.

Like an officer on the battlefield young Scroggins called his headquarters and told Old Man Scroggins what was happening. And like such an officer he withdrew his troops and reorganised them.

'Right let's have Evans the Choir with me, the Vicar and his lady behind with the rest of the lads marching forward across the lane bashing people as we move forward. As soon as they look like getting organised our demon cross dresser and me will scream "charge" and we will go in with all clubs thumping, Got that?'

The lads and a couple of girls in the gang cheered and raised their clubs. This action terrified the already battered church lane mob who hurried further down the lane to come up against resistance. The gang walked steadily onward and with looks of sheer pleasure on their faces including that of the Vicar and Bonny they clobbered whoever was in front of them.

A large man tried to grab Evans the Choir by the hair but that worthy, shaking his head flipped free leaving his wig dangling from one ham like fist.

Thwack! Thwack went Evans the Choir's club and the would be assailant fell to the ground to be stomped on by the boots of those coming behind.

'Take that ducky,' Evans said.

'Ducky?'

'Why not? He's the one with the poofy wig,' said Evans and giggled.

The crowd in front were now being pushed into the narrow street leading down to the green and the press coming up or just milling around made it difficult for the fugitives to pass.

At that moment the mob facing the fugitives spotted Evans the

Choir and the Vicar

A voice cried out louder than the rest.

'There's the poofy choir master!'

The mob stopped milling and with some larger men leading made a charge at the small group. Some took pictures and were knocked over slowing the mob enough to allow the group, now no longer with the advantage of surprise, to make a hasty retreat.

As they dashed back up the lane Young Scroggins's group was aware of the clattering helicopters, flashing blue and red lights and the bellow of a megaphone.

At that point Old Man Scroggins's people fell upon the mob in organised columns and sent a column of heavies to rescue the Vicar and his party.

The cavalry had arrived.

The mob in the lane wavered.

Below, close to the village green, the police had arrived in force with fire engines ready to hose the crowd down and police helicopters overhead directing the action.

A drone floated up to home in on Evans and with a neat action he swatted it with his stick and cheered when it shattered sending components flying in all directions.

The Scroggins clan below cut into the soft targets with a viciousness the police could not use. Cries of pain, yells of indignation, attempts to fight back and groans of agony were music to the ears of the locals as they followed the lead of the Clan.

With cheers and Karate yells the locals bashed, kicked and thumped until hundreds of men and women were boxed into the area surrounding the green.

It was at that point Young Scroggins made a fundamental mistake. 'Charge! Charge!' he yelled above Evans' banshee wail and at the head of the gang he ran at the crowd and met with the heavies spoiling for a fight. It was a vicious clash and although the Scroggins gang were much better and more organised the angry mob outnumbered them.

However, the Scroggins gang cut into the crowd downing many of the less able battlers. But the opposition was too many and as one fell so another took his place. Soon Scroggins was forced back into the more open area.

It was then the mob surged forward and at the gates of the church yard Scroggins's group was forced to defend itself. The mob's target seemed to be Evans the Choir and with a cry Young Scroggins ordered one man to call his granddad and leapt at the men who were about to overwhelm Evans.

He didn't make it.

A thug faced him wielding an iron bar wrenched from a garden fence and took a swipe at him. It missed and he had to dodge another blow before he could whack the bugger with his stick. His enemy dispatched, he turned to see Evans standing over the recumbent form of the vicar trying to hold off three men determined to put the boot in. Bonny Mason was screaming obscenities as she raked the face of another with her nails forcing him away from Evans.

Scroggins hacked at one of Evans' assailants who staggered and turned to face him. He heard a horrible crunching sound as with a swift blow he clobbered the man and downed him.

He turned to see a man with a blood stained iron bar standing staring horrified at Evans who lay at his feet bleeding from an ugly looking skull wound.

Scroggins raised his stick.

'You fucking bastard!' he yelled, and whacked the man's kidneys with two smart blows and smashed his collar bone with another. He was about to go for the killing blow when his cousin stopped his arm.

'The old man's troops are here, stay your arm cousin. There is nothing we can do for him.'

Young Scroggins contented himself with knocking the man unconscious.

And as he stood appalled at what had happened he was aware that the noise of the mob had stopped. Men and women stood gazing at the carnage, stunned by the sight, and with cries of horror backed away leaving the defenders on their own.

At that moment there was a yell from below and it was apparent that the villagers were on the move.

Whilst the battle in front of the church was going on, in the centre of the village the locals began to contain the visitors into a mass of panicking nosy parkers. Eventually the nosy parkers broke and surrendered allowing the local lads through to deal with the people in Church Lane.

Old Man Scroggins rubbed his hands together with glee and with his squad of thugs made for the front line.

'Right lads, into 'em!' he cried out and laid into the enemy with his stick.

With a roar of approval the villagers followed him and it was a treat to see how the locals got stuck in. The intruders gave way and soon they were running before the avenging crowd to be bottled up in and around the village green.

Trapped between the Scroggins army and the Police the visitors milled around trying to escape.

The police numbers were nowhere near enough to control the riot but at least they tried. Officers attempted to create a chain to contain the battlers prior to pushing between them but it was no use. The crowd wasn't having it.

Eventually Superintendent Masefield, the senior officer in charge, managed to mount the back of a police Defender with a megaphone.

"Police! Police! Police! We urrrggge youuu tooo stop …' the rest was lost in an electronic feedback that allowed a few odd noises to emerge and the message was lost. Masefield wished he could call on armed officers to fire a few rounds in the air to grab the mob's attention. He was restricted by the politically correct rules regarding controlling of mobs, devised by the people who did not approve of that sort of thing. What annoyed him, apart from the battling mob below, was the little group of drinkers sitting on the terrace cheering their side on.

In the centre of the village and on the roads around trying to make sense of what was happening his forces were struggling to form up. It was no use, he had to admit defeat. With a sigh of resignation he dismounted the vehicle and standing beside the pond he used his radio to call on the riot squad.

No sooner had he done so than the mob surged toward him and he and his small squad were pushed backwards. He slipped on something smelly and wet.

'Oh crikey what next!' He cried out and with his arms flailing he fell through the tangling net into cold, muddy water. Ducks quacked with alarm as he struggled to keep above water, slipping and sliding unable to get to his feet.

A voice above him said: 'If we don't get the bugger out he will drown. It ain't deep but we don't drown coppers do we?'

He was lifted out of the water and came face to face with Old Man Scroggins.

'Cripes, bloody old Masefield. Come to save us have you?'

'I came to stop a riot you old fool,' the Superintendent said.

Mistake. He was was dropped straight back in the water and left to climb out on his own.

He emerged from the pond helped by a couple of constables as the first of the squads appeared. It seemed that they were already on their way. With their arrival, like a miracle the Scroggins clan and many of the villagers disappeared.

The trio sitting on the terrace below the Dog and Duck watched as the police herded the hordes of non residents out of the village. Some were able to drive away but many were forced to walk into town. Arrests were made and vans were used to carry the transgressors away. The wounded and hurt were treated, statements taken and those unable to walk or drive were carried away in buses. By the time the operation was over and the police had erected barriers and road checks the drinkers were somewhat tiddly.

But by now it was apparent that the day had ended in tragedy. In spite of Old Man Scroggins' plans things had not gone as he had expected. The mob had taken its toll.

In the lane in front of the vicarage the air ambulance had taken off with two men lying on stretchers and medics in attention trying desperately to save their lives. It was touch and go for Reverend Jones but it was too late for Evans the Choir who was declared dead on arrival.

The rest of the casualties were treated by the land based services and Bonny Mason opened up the church and the vicarage as a base for treatment. She was hurt but not the only one to suffer that day and with her wounds dressed she joined the villagers in helping out the hard pressed medical teams.

Superintendent Masefield was not a happy bunny. He sat in a police van wrapped in blankets trying to stop shivering waiting for somebody to find him some dry clothes.

'The WI women are giving them a wash and you will soon have them back,' said a WPC. He groaned and sunk lower in the seat.

Thomas Grace sat in his office and eventually picked up the telephone. He had seen the look in Lawrence's eyes. He knew that look. It was the calculating soldier look that should have been the hallmark of the good soldier but that was deceptive. Colin Lawrence was a hard man, a man who had taken up with

The Birdwatchers of Childen Under Blean

mercenaries. That was after he had committed some nasty assaults disappeared. Thomas had heard of his activities in Africa and rumours of action against ISIS as an advisor. From all accounts his activities in the middle east were suspect and again he had disappeared.

Now he was back here.

With a shock Thomas realised that Colin and his sister Sally had featured in the pictures Mathew and his friends had taken. With another shock he knew who it was who had beaten his son so badly. Only a man who knew what he was doing could have hurt the boy like that without actually killing him.

Thomas sighed and picked up the telephone. The number he dialled rang for a while and clicked, buzzed and changed to another, more subdued tone, to be answered by a mellow voice.

'Roger? It's Thomas Grace.'

The enthusiastic reply amused him. Roger, always the Public Schoolboy, with his silly chatter.

Thomas explained about the village riot and finding Colin Lawrence.

'Cannot the local blue chaps corral him?'

'Well yes, I suppose so, but he will be armed, and dangerous.'

'You think our chaps could do better?'

'Certainly sir, his sister is with him.'

Roger Wise gasped and answered.

'Ah, rum do, don't you know. Well, toodle-oo old chap, I'll see what I can do. Address old fruit and the local plod's monica will help.'

Thomas gave him the information and promising to catch up at some time he hung up.

He didn't like what he had had to do but... the but was a trail off to needs must. He sighed; Colin Lawrence was at one time a good soldier.

The officer in charge of the riot police organised a sweep through the village to flush out the last of the rioters was surprised to see a troop of youngsters marching down from the hills who, ignoring the police officers, lined up in front of the tea rooms. He marched to where the group stood under the shelter of the verandah and called out.

'What the blue blazes do you lot think you're up to?'

The young leader came forward and blinked at him.

'It may not be obvious to you sir, but we are waiting for our parents to collect us. With a view to reassuring them that we are all safe and well we thought it a wise move to remain in the area of the woodlands until the incident here was over. If we are in error please accept our apologies. We were out bird watching when the invasion of our domiciles began. When we saw your people had resolved the situation satisfactorily enough to deem it safe to return we abandoned our temporary shelters and marched down the track in an orderly fashion. We will need sustenance and it will be certain that our parents will be worried although we have communicated...' Graham said and was cut off when the officer interrupted his speech.

'Does this kid always talk like this?'

'Yes sir,' Lyla said and looked up with a smile. 'All he means is that we have come home safe and sound.'

'Well why didn't he say so?'

'He did sir, you have to have patience,' she said.

And within a few minutes men and women came to claim their offspring thanking the policemen for looking after their kids and soon even Graham was gone.

For the officer in charge it was an unnerving experience.

Aftermath

Evans the Choir's funeral procession consisted of one horse drawn hearse, one dark car and a long column of villagers on foot. Those from outside the village parked their vehicles in the village and walked to Evans house to join the slow march. The choir was already dressed and waiting in the church, his rugby club team mates had swallowed their pride and turned up to show their respects. The press arrived, if not en-masse, at least in numbers enough to splash the event on their front pages.

The men of the Scroggins clan lined the route and on both roads in to Childen Under Blean nervous police officers controlled the traffic. The Oswalds and the Greens stood by to serve the mourners food and drink and more Scroggins clan people made certain that outsiders were turned away. Scroggins clan women and villagers of other families helped serve the food, tea and coffee on the village green under tents using the Greens' tearooms as their base. It was said that the Women's Institute spent the day before the funeral making cakes and scones and for the first time in living memory offered them for free.

Mathew's friends were escorted to the church and put under the charge of Joshua Scroggins who was instructed to treat them kindly.

'You watch and listen and shut your bleedin' gobs except to sing and pray or I'll shut 'em for you,' he said as they were settled into places in the small chapel. 'Uncle told me to remember the words of Jesus, from Mathew, chapter six, verse fourteen; summink about forgiving people what done wrong, and it goes on in verse fifteen what if you don't, then rotten things will happen to yer. Now, if you don't behave I will be the one what does rotten things. Got it?'

'Yes Joshua, we got it.'

Joshua Scroggins' grin was wide and terrible.

The funeral went off well even if it was somewhat awkward because of the reverend Jones having to use a wheelchair. Melanie Grace was to attend at the grave-side if Jones couldn't manage; the reverend himself still suffering from his hurts. Old Man Scroggins had scraped around the records and found a vacant plot, collected money for it and paid the dues and presented it to Evans' estate.

Evans' family managed to send his sister Blodwen who was pleased to discover that her brother had surprisingly chosen her as the main beneficiary. The executor was Forest Maloney.

Evan's successor regarding the choir turned out to be Bonny Mason who didn't mind that Barry Smythe preferred playing the old organ.

'I liked that silly Welsh bugger,' Barry said wiping a tear from his eye. 'He always had time for me. This is the last time I will play the organ in church. It's up to you now Bonny. Now he's gone it's not the same.'

Bonny filled in the gaps and although the organ was wheezing and groaning Barry was getting music out of it. She listened for the sound of horses trotting up the hill and the shuffle of many feet and began to conduct the choir and the music. The church filled and soon Evans coffin, carried by some of his rugby club mates, progressed slowly to rest before the altar.

The service went well with none of that triffid stuff. A few people said some nice things about Evans. Forest Maloney stood up to speak and as he moved to the front Mutley followed him. He stood beside the coffin with Mutley lying underneath it as he spoke. It was an entertaining speech setting out what he and the other drinkers thought about Coren Evans.

'... and in the end, as we all know he gave his life like any soldier to defend his comrades. Although I was in virtual hiding that day, being trapped as it was at the pub,' he paused to acknowledge the ripple of laughter; 'I could see him in the forefront of the action wearing his favourite dress and giving his all for his friends.'

Forest bowed his head and in the silence that followed there was a slight sound and Mutley suddenly sat up looking surprised.

The stench hit Forest's nostrils moments before it wafted across to the front rows.

'Jesus Christ Mutley! Did you bloody well have to?' Forest exclaimed and glowered at the dog who sat up looking pleased. When the front rows of the congregation began calling his name loudly and holding their noses Mutley wagged his tail and bounced around happily.

Master was pleased.
People were pleased.
Mutley was pleased.

Mutley bounced a little too far and being a strong dog shifted Evans the Choir sideways in his enthusiasm to jump up and lick his nice master's face.

The coffin teetered, slid a little, gathered momentum and with a screech of polished wood against polished wood toppled sideways and crashed to the floor.

Mutley yelped and barked. The coffin knocked him across the stone floor into master's legs. Smelly dog and master fell together to slide and roll past the pulpit coming to a halt against a pillar.

Reacting to the unusual situation Mutley, startled and frightened, bit his master's leg. Forest cried out in pain.

'Fucking dog! The fucking dog's bitten me! For Christ sake!'

The congregation, having chuckled during Forest's eulogy, laughed out loud.

Evans the Choir's funeral service was held up for a further half hour as Forest's bite was cleaned and dressed and the coffin replaced on the stands.

Forest finished his speech with Amanda holding the dog on his leash, and eventually the procession continued to the graveside.

With Mutley walking beside him Forest swore and cursed as he followed the mourners to the graveside. Amanda and Sara walking with him suggested he put Mutley on the lead.

'He's alright,' he said.

Despite of, or because of the unfortunate incident of the bitten leg, Evans the Choir's funeral was one that went down in village history to be remembered and embellished as the years went by.

Before the funeral took place, and after it was over the police were busy in the village trying to clear up Evans the Choir's murder, dealing with the complaints from those who were hurt in the riot and a desire to arrest offenders. At the same time the investigation into Mathew Grace's beating continued.

As a result Sylvester Simon was asked to "help with enquiries" and questioned on his activities the evening the two boys were chased out of the Dog and Duck.

'Yes, I chased after the bugger but I didn't do nothing to him. None of us could run as fast as he was legging it through the village. We lost the bugger when Forest's stupid dog tried to climb over the fence to get at the bitch. I was knackered and went back to the pub,' he told the detective.

'Anybody see you?'

'Me mates and the landlord.'

'You had a good reason to assault mister Grace.'

'What thump Thomas? No way! He's captain of the cricket team.'

The detective looked weary.

'No, I meant Mathew Grace.'

'Oh, sorry, I never thought of the little shithead as a mister.'

'You didn't go out later that night and find him?'

'No. I was too pissed to go out. Besides, the landlord likes to lock up and he didn't give me an outside key.'

'But you threatened to give him a going over as you put it.'

'I would like to but when it comes to the act mate I got to live in the village and his father, poor sod, is a friend.'

The detective sighed.

It seemed to him that there were so many people angry with the group of boys that it was hard to find anybody who didn't want to give them a good beating. The team were slowly eliminating the suspects and hopefully getting closer to the perpetrator. Even the local vicar was a suspect.

The reverend Jones understood that he too was a suspect and although he stretched his memory for his activities on that evening he failed to convince the detective that he was not roaming abroad in the village.

'I know that being man of the cloth you should be telling us the truth but I would dearly love to know if you have any proof that you were in bed asleep and dreaming of heaven,' the detective said exasperated by now with the vicar's assurance that he should take his word for it.

'Reverend, I know that you are hurt and tired but I need to know. I would like to eliminate you as a suspect. I know you are not telling me the truth, so come on mister, open up. Tell me what you were doing that evening.'

Reverend Jones sighed. He was tired and aware that whatever happened the questions would not stop. He gave in.

'I was in bed with Bonny Mason experiencing a little Heaven between us. She will corroborate that, if you ask her,' he said and slumped in the bed.

'Right, now we are talking. Give me some times and we can take it from there,' the detective said.

Jones told him what he wanted to know and looked at the man pleadingly. 'You will try and be discreet, I er, have just reconciled with my wife and family,' he said.

'I will do my best, sir.'

Worried about him Elizabeth and the girls arrived to visit him not long after the riot and fussed around him. He enjoyed their attention and lay propped up listening happily to what they had to say.

'Of course, I will expect certain conditions to be met,' she said and had to agree, having little choice.

Throughout the session he found it difficult to take his eyes off his eldest daughter's cleavage.

'Damn,' said Sara when she looked at the slip. The test was positive. She had missed two periods and despite the message her brain was receiving she had a test anyway. 'Bugger, I should have remembered.'

She sent Robert a text and within minutes he sent one back. She grinned. It was plan for a marriage or put up with a scandal. Either way they had to put up with the scandal. 'Oh well, I was going to Uni. My career is fixed now. Wife and mother. Bang out the heir to the Massingham fortune and some little Massinghams and learn to be a toff,' she said and giggled.

< C U Sat. LOL >

She answered knowing that right then he was with his father somewhere on the estate and as Saturday was tomorrow she was eager for it to arrive.

She sat in her room for a while and thought about life with Robert and with a strange feeling of release she went downstairs for the evening meal.

The dinner over, Sara was tempted to tell her parents that she was pregnant but decided to wait until she had spoken properly with Robert.

Even if she had wanted to speak up she had no opportunity because at that moment two police cars went hurtling past. All three hurried outside to see what had happened to see the lights flashing not far from their house.

'Where are they going?' asked her mother.

'I don't know,' said her father.

Sara counted slowly to five and was about to start on six when the telephone rang. As her father hurried inside to answer it she grinned.

'That was bloody quick,' she said.

A few moments later her father returned and announced: 'The police have turned up at the Wise house.'

Sara didn't stay to hear the rest.

In the Dog and Duck the drinkers had heard more news and although speculation was rife at least they had some idea of what had gone on. Horace had told them, having delved into his village history; the gossip he was so good at remembering.

'Put it this way. What Horace told me was that this Colin Lawrence what arrived at widow Wise's doorstep was recognised by one of the coppers when they checked up on him. It seems he was wanted for something nasty a long way back. He should of stayed away but what Sally Wise had to offer was too much for him,' Sylvester said, and before he could continue he had to endure their ribald comments.

'You ought to know about that all right, mate,' said Martin.

'Yeah and if you wanted to deal with women and pussies we all know what that means for you,' Davey said and flinched when Sylvester glowered at him.

'Don't be so fucking crude,' Sylvester said.

'Come on, what else Sly?'

'Thanks Miles. At least we have one sensible person at this table. I heard that they were getting ready to bugger off when the cops called. Somebody was hurt.'

'Who was it?'

'Dunno, nobody could see because of the coppers.'

Swanson said: 'This place is getting a reputation.

And as it was his turn to buy the beer Swanson got up from the table and went to the bar. Things were getting exciting but he didn't really want that. He liked the plodding laziness of his village as it used to be.

As it was the beer took over for a while and the discussion focussed on how many men had been questioned about Mathew's beating.

'Even his old man was questioned when it came out he used to be in the army,' said Miles.

'What was he, the bloody Chaplain?' Sly said, laughing at his own joke.

'No, he was an instructor, you ought to know, he instructed you all right,' said Swanson. 'He used to teach unarmed combat and other things to some tough soldiers. We know that because of his badges. I looked him up. He's one tough cookie but it's hardly likely he would clobber his own kid like that.'

'I would if he was mine,' Sly said.

'Perhaps you would but most of us would not. Not to our own anyway,' Martin said.

Sylvester had to agree.

He also had to go home reasonably sober.

For once Forest had left Mutley at home which the drinkers agreed was a good idea.

'Except that we usually go home when the smelly dog farts,' Davey said and groaned when Sylvester obliged with a trumpet sound from a sideways shift and a slightly raised leg.

Detectives Clive Dawson and Tanya Crane alighted from their car and walked slowly to the Wise house. The blue lights flashed making pretty patterns on the surrounding homes. As usual the uniformed officers had parked where they had stopped and already were thundering around the building.

'All we need is a squad to plod along the road hup-hupping with riot shields and sticks and we have it all,' said Crane.

'So much for the elephant of surprise,' remarked Dawson.

'Oh well, let's do it. Weapons ready?'

'Loose and to hand,' he said.

With uniformed officers creating a cordon the pair walked up the path and knocked on the door.

From within came a male voice.

'Fuck off copper!'

'Oh dear,' said Dawson.

Tanya Crane moved to one side and drew her pistol cursing a little as her hand scraped across the flak jacket she wore underneath her coat.

'Colin Lawrence, we have you surrounded. I would rather you give up than have to come in and get you,' Dawson said.

'Like I said, copper, fuck off!'

'Now come on Colin, you don't really mean that do you?'

From behind the door came a louder shout.

'What part of fuck off don't you understand? Go away, fuck off!'

By instinct Dawson moved quickly as the wavy shadow behind the marbled glass raised an arm. The bullet went past carrying glass with it. The shot was answered by two from Crane's weapon and from within there came an agonized scream.

Dawson was about to fire his gun but the idiots with the door rammers smashed the back door down and ran inside.

'You idiots, the perp is armed!' Dawson cried out but his words were lost as coppers banged into the hallway. One opened the front door and grinned.

'We've secured the house,' he said.

'Idiot,' said Dawson, holstering his weapon.

Lawrence was already being attended to watched by a tearful Sally Wise who was restrained by two policewomen.

Dawson leaned down close to Lawrence.

'I think you're nicked mate.'

He ignored Crane's sharp, disapproving intake of breath. He liked the phrase and wanted to use it as often as he could.

Afterwards in the car they sat exchanging notes. The operation as Crane succinctly described it, was a cock-up, but at least they had made the arrest.

'Nice bit of leaping Clive, almost a Strictly movement there. You don't dance do you?'

'As a matter of interest I do, why?'

'We should go together sometime,' she said.

'Are you chatting me up,' he said, grinning.

'More or less, I like a dancing man with a gun,' she said.

'We ought to sort out Lawrence, he said. 'Oh Tanya, you're on, for the dancing I mean. And nice shooting.'

'Thank you. I take a pride in it,' she said.

'I suppose we had better get on with, it' he said.

'What, formally charge the bugger?'

'No, have a look at the scene and all that, until the chief arrives anyway.

They began the initial examination but it was the chief who arrived and took over. When the forensic team arrived and donned their blobby suits the Chief chucked them out.

'Write your report on the shooting. I'll talk to you later,' the Chief said. 'This place is not like it used to be. I don't know what's got into 'em lately.'

They left him muttering to himself.

'You really fancy dancing then?'

'Yes, my Mum and Dad used to dance. I watch Strictly and love it. Like South American do you?'

'Love it. You know, I think coppers ought to take up ball room dancing and martial arts,' Dawson said.

'What, to help with their well being?'

'Not just that but being a good dancer helps when you're dodging some mad bugger's bullets,' Dawson said. 'He nearly got me. Went right through my jacket. That's why I panicked.'

'You mean the movement was instinctive?'

'I'm not a hero.'

Crane laughed and squeezed his hand.

The reverend Jones, having missed out on conducting the Harvest festival service, was preparing for Christmas and now that he was feeling better he had agreed to a small party at the vicarage.

The WI had made a cake, Bonny Mason had organised some of the choir to sing a little welcome and a few selected parishioners gathered in what seemed to him an impromptu garden party. The weather was cool and sunny with clouds scudding overhead driven by a wind that blew the fallen leaves into animated piles.

He didn't have to circulate as most people came to him. He noted that his daughters were busy serving drinks and sandwiches. He approved of that but he wished they would wear something less provocative.

'Have you heard the news Vicar?'

The speaker was Millie Small who looked up at him with her round, beady eyes and round face. He shook his head not trusting himself to speak; she was wearing a low cut dress revealing her bosom and despite his vow to Elizabeth he couldn't keep his eyes off the view. Once a lush always a lush, he admitted. Sinner, pray for thy salvation and lead me not into temptation.

'They is charging Sally Wise and her so-called brother. They been doing some nasty things from way back. He's in clink for bashing up that Grace boy so they say. They shot him but he and that tart were on that film thing starkers in her window,' she said, her eyes sparkling. 'You never know what goes on in the village do you?'

'Much of late Millie, much,' he said and listened to her confusing version of the details until, eventually he was rescued by the call to a speech from Thomas Grace.

'... and in conclusion to the welcome back to our revered reverend I would like to announce that the cause of all this recent upset in our village, namely my idiot son Mathew, has promised to come to church, and make a formal apology for his actions. I insisted that he face up to his responsibilities,' he said, and grinned broadly. 'I told him that I would beat the holy crap out of him if he didn't.'

His announcement was greeted by a cheer.

'Saves my lad Joshua doing it,' remarked Old Man Scroggins.

That same afternoon Sara Grace was taking tea with Lord and lady Massingham.

'I know we should have waited until after the marriage Mummy but, well, we sort of...' Robert looked embarrassed.

'You rogered her on the hay bales, right?' Lady Massingham said and looking down her nose at Sara she raised an eyebrow.

'That is correct ma'am,' Sara said feeling like a servant.

'Who seduced whom?'

'I did him,' Sara said barely a second or so after Robert declared it was his doing.

Lady Massingham sighed and looked to her husband for support. He in turn took a sip at his brandy and lazily replied.

'It was cornfields for us, our own of course; we just couldn't keep our hands off each other. We barely made it to the church before our Maggie was born. I suppose you want to make a go of it?'

'Marry you mean sir?'

'Er yes, of course, can't have you living in sin or taking feudal rights in this modern world. You will marry I hope.'

'Yes father we do. We agreed,' Robert said.

'Good ho, then get on with it. Buy a couple of rings, make arrangements with the reverend and let's have a party. What do you say dear?'

'Yes, go for it, happy cornfields is what I say,' she said cheerfully. And after that the discussion was of their coming wedding which was, to Sara's surprise, ended with her being asked to call them both by their first names.

She thought that her five 'A' levels made a difference.

The pair rode to her house on their bicycles later in the afternoon and locking the bikes together walked into her house hand in hand. She led him through the doors and the narrow hallway and stood in the living room feeling guilty.

Her parents were fussing around Mathew who sat slumped in an armchair looking gloomy.

'You know Robert,' she said, as they stood clasping each other closely. 'We are getting married.'

'What? Married? When?' exclaimed her father.

'As soon as the reverend can manage it,' said Robert.

'Why so soon?' Melanie asked looking askance at her daughter.

It was Mathew who said the obvious.

'She's up the fucking gut,' he said.

'Yes Mathew, I am as you say, up the fucking gut, pregnant and we would like it not that I should waddle down the aisle like the bride who is all fat and wide,' Sara said, feeling somewhat archaic.

'I got me own problems,' Mathew said.

'Ah yes old chap, you have charges to answer, need to heal the old body and you have a child on the way,' said Robert affably. 'As your future brother-in-law I would suggest you make an effort to stop being such a bloody moron and try to become a useful citizen and take responsibility for your actions. Show us you can do that and we may be able to help you. Otherwise, as far as I am concerned you can get lost.'

'I ain't done nothing,' Mathew said.

'Tiresome oaf. You and your friends have caused us all a lot of trouble. One fine man is dead because of you; another is badly hurt and others have been slandered and made objects of derision or lost their jobs, and you say "I ain't done nothing". You idiot. I am glad your parents and your dear sister do not share your stupidity,' Robert said, and turned to face Thomas and Melanie with a smile. 'I came to ask for your daughter's hand in marriage not to berate this geezer.' He pointed at Mathew.

Both Thomas and Melanie laughed and with smiles and nods shook Robert's hand warmly and hugged their daughter.

'Of course, we would be happy to welcome you to our family,' said Thomas.

'Stuck up prick,' said Mathew quietly.

Sara glared at him.

What surprised Mathew was that evening despite his grumpiness his father insisted on him going with the party to the Dog and Duck for a meal.

'What about mister Simon?'

'I haven't invited him,' Thomas said.

The Sunday service was a subdued affair. The presence of Old Man Scroggins and some of his family and, to the surprise of the rest of the parishioners Sylvester and Sylvia Simon were there too. Mathew Grace walked in with his parents, his sister and Robert Massingham. When Sylvester came in Mathew whimpered and tried to hide up but he was spotted. Cheryl was already singing with the choir and had glanced at him a few times. He was not sure of her reaction.

'Ah right laddie, you and me need to talk,' said Sly sliding along the pew to sit with Mathew.

'What are you going to do?' squeaked Mathew.

'You going to make an honest woman of my daughter or do I finish what some other bugger started?'

'Jesus Christ, why is everybody so horrible to me?'

'Because you is a nasty piece of shit, a pervert and a shifty little backslider. Nothing like your folks who are fine upright citizens. Got it?'

Mathew nodded.

'You going to marry my daughter?'

'Do I have to?'

'Yes because, sonny, I think you will.'

'Er will she have me?' he asked hoping desperately for a "no".

'Like a shot, for some unfathomable reason she says she loves you.'

Mathew groaned.

'Er, can't we just live together?'

Sylvester, snarling, answered, as they say, in the negative: 'I want you where I can find you. You marry her as she asks and if, hopefully you last long enough, you might turn into a human being. Just remember that somebody got to you before I did.'

Mathew felt his skin turn pale and tried to back away out of range but he was trapped. Sylvester's fist clenched and unclenched and Mathew knew that even here in the church he was not safe from this hooligan's anger.

He gulped.

'It looks like I have no choice.'

'You don't and we will fix up the details this afternoon,' Sylvester said. 'Don't run away.'

The service ran its course; the newly formed core of the rugby club with Joshua Scroggins sitting amongst the members sang their hearts out and even Nobby Clarke edited his prayers of their usual profanities.

When called upon Mathew stood up in front of the congregation and made his apology.

'I come to say sorry for what me and my mates done. It started off as a bit of fun – we didn't mean no harm – but we got, like, too sort of, like involved. I dunno what to say really but I'm sorry if I caused any trouble, like, I mean like, for all the trouble what I did cause,' he said, all the time keeping a wary eye on Joshua Scroggins.

The congregation was silent for a moment or two until the reverend Jones called for prayers of forgiveness. Mathew was aware that everybody joined in and relaxed. It was with mixed feelings when after the whole thing was over Cheryl came to him and kissed him.

'You done all right there Matty,' she said.

He embraced her, resigned to his fate.

That evening the drinkers had much to talk about and as usual Sylvester held the floor.

'As I see it, I've got a son-in-law coming whether the bugger likes it or not. We got a society wedding coming up and all sorts of things happening in the village and we keeps our vicar. I reckons we ought to honour our poofy choir master somehow.' he said.

'I've got that in hand. I approached the Friends and they said they wanted to put up a stone for him. First we got to sort out his house but his sister says she wants to wait until the Spring. I thinks we can have a stone erected for him then,' Forest said.

'What you doing about your Cheryl?' asked Swanson.

'We settled on a registry affair, hopefully before Christmas. With me carrying the shotgun. My missus is making the Grace girl's wedding and bridesmaid's dresses for a fee.

'Just think, if Evans the Choir was alive she could be making one for him,' observed Martin, and for that remark he was ordered to buy the beer.

'He would look pretty in pink,' said Davey.

Mutley, feeling the joy of their laughter farted and wagged his tail when they called his name.

'You know what,' said Sly, 'I think I'm getting used to the bloody smell.'

Forest looked pleased.

The Birdwatchers of Childen Under Blean

It was a cold and sunny day when Mathew Grace and his Birdwatchers went to court and by all accounts the group expected to be, as Mathew put it, banged up. He was surprised when Joe Scroggins called on his parents to explain that his Great Uncle was going to help out.

'Great Uncle Ebenezer wants to help. He's getting our legal beagles on the case and maybe, just maybe, we can get the silly buggers an easier sentence. As long as Mathew and the other lads do as they are told we can swing it,' Joe said.

'Right, what did you have in mind?' Asked Thomas.

'The boys go around the village and apologise. If they get Community Service then we want them to do extra in the village. He wants to meet the boys at his place.'

Mathew listened to what Joe had said and his face paled.

'I apologised in the church. What more does the … Old Man want?'

'If you turn up you'll find out.'

And when they arrived at Old Man Scroggins house they learned what was to happen to them.

'Me and my nephew will make sure you gets to court on time. You four will make proper apologies to al them girls what you perved on, or I'l personally beat the fuckin' shit outta ya. You work for us from now on until we thinks you done enough to make up for your stupidity. You give your birdwatching gear to young Graham Cook, and if you reneges on anything we asks yer to do, we gets Joshua to have a word with yer. Got that?'

In court Mathew was a little miffed when he and his friends were described as moronic, and his school records as a boy with learning difficulties was offered as proof of diminished responsibility. He could believe that of the others but like them he suppressed his indignation and looked properly contrite.

The sentencing was put off for two weeks and as they rode back to the village Joe explained that the legal beagles would press for community sentences.

'They might want psychiatric reports,' Joe said.

'What, we is supposed to be nutters?' Donny asked desperately.

Joe chuckled. 'Nah, just feeble minded.'

There was nothing they could say about that. There was also nothing they could do that day when Joe told them to get changed and report for two hours work helping to clear some of the weeds from the duck pond.

They didn't complain.

They didn't undergo psychiatric reports either. The Judge gave them all two hundred hours community service and, because of their, albeit enforced, penitence within the village, declined to put them on the sexual offences register.

'It is in the interest of your community that you learn by your mistakes, and that I understand you are already committed to working within the village, your commitment to community service will be slotted in with that. I am certain that the work will give you all ample opportunity to reflect on your misdemeanours,' the Judge said, summing up.

'What the fuck's he on about?' asked Terry quietly.

'Fucked if I know,' said Mathew.

Joe Scroggins explained to them afterwards in simple terms after they had dealt with the clerk's office.

'What about the other gits?'

'Fined and frightened,' Joe said.

Community service was better than being put inside.

Mathew and his friends, during their duty around the village, although at first they grumbled and tried to skive off soon gave up on that when the Scroggins lads came to fetch them.

'Christ, we may as well be in clink,' said Donny.

'Nah, don't even think about it,' said Terry.

'Hard bloody work, it is,' Stanley said.

'But we gotta do it,' Mathew said, gloomily.

But that was at the beginning.

Eventually the villagers came to expect them around the place working, and some even remarked that they were becoming almost likeable. Donny had even taken up with Amber Scroggins, one of Old Man Scroggins' numerous grandchildren.

Lucky for Mathew, at a time when his father in law was getting fed up with him, Cheryl gave birth to her baby boy. Mathew wanted to call him Bump Sylvester Grace but had to settle for Coren instead.

'After the pouffy choirmaster?' he asked.

'He was a nice man,' she said, and so Bump became Coren on his birth certificate but Mathew always called him Coren B.

It seemed he was acquiring a sense of humour.

The miscreants did their service, worked for the village and surprisingly found that despite their misgivings developed into more or less useful citizens. Donny and Amber moved in together renting one the Scroggins Clan flats. They were also the first couple to take advantage of the Friends' holiday scheme and booked a week at Centre Parcs and such was the discount that others in the village followed suit.

Mathew and Cheryl were married quietly in town and ensconced in the Simon home which arrangement was fine for Cheryl but terrifying for Mathew.

Terry Smith dropped out of Mathew's circle and joined the army. His parents agreed that it was the best thing he could do. When his father mentioned his son's aspirations to Sylvester that worthy was cynical.

'Maybe somebody will knock some sense into him, or failing that some foreign bastard will shoot his fucking lights out,' Sylvester said and wondered why Smithy didn't talk to him for a few weeks.

Stanley White lost his job but was taken on by the Scroggins clan part time and when his duty was finished he stood like a penitent in front of Old Man Scroggins and begged for a job.

'Me dad is making noises about me moving out. I don't want to leave the village,' he said.

'Scared are you?'

'Yes sir.'

'Good, then we can find some work for you. Start next Monday at the yard. You gets yer wages and if yer does it right we might even make a man of yer. All right cully, don't wet yourself, just bugger off home and have a few days off,' the old man said, and when he had gone he said to Maisie: 'I'm too bloody soft hearted.'

'I think he'll be alright,' she said.

On the day after Sara and Robert's wedding Graham Cook and his troop of birdwatchers disappeared into the woodlands camouflaged with twigs and wearing earth coloured clothing to watch the birds around the streams and small lake that fed the river in the valley below the hills.

It was in the makeshift hide that Graham and Lyla discovered there was more to the birdwatching lark than just watching the birds.

The experience took both of them by surprise.

In Memoriam

On the day the memorial was raised the whole village was there. Bonny and the musicians had managed a PA system, and the Scroggins Clan had paid for the refreshments supplied by Greens Tea Rooms and the Dog and Duck. Evans the Choir was to be commemorated with an open air thanksgiving service.

The day chosen was the anniversary of the battle before the church and now that the troubles were over the village was once more the quiet place it had always been.

Reverend Michael Jones, had long ago abandoned the triffid style of worship in favour of a more orthodox and less lively Anglican fashion which, he said, saved his gammy leg. The former lively worshippers made do with the occasional noisy expression, and with the organ finally failing supplied the musicians.

As a concession to their tastes Bonny allowed them to sing Gospel style at times often regretting it when the clapping failed to keep proper time.

Bishop Mathews was invited to conduct the service but declined, "on religious grounds". It seemed that despite his recommendation that Reverend Jones be removed from his living, the influence wielded by Lord Massingham on the relevant selection body prevailed, and Jones was confirmed as the vicar.

Old Man Scroggins' timely interference in the village plan had paid off. For his part, the reverend Jones, was willing to do much to keep the peace in Childen Under Blean, and to do so had allowed the villagers to elect him to the parish council.

At least his duties helped him maintain his fragile fidelity; a thing Elizabeth was grateful for. He was in training to become an inactive and secret lecher. He had joined the drinkers at the Dog and Duck, and this move had kept him honest.

But now he had to concentrate on giving his best to what was, for him in particular, an emotional event.

This day was to be a celebration and as the music played and the choir and congregation sang in the late Summer sunshine it seemed appropriate to allow free expression.

The sunshine was most welcome.

The stone for the monument and its surround came from the local quarry. The stone was block I.2 m high by 0.6 m wide and

0.6 m depth, polished on the face and dressed on the sides and rear and polished for cleaning. It was anchored deep to deter theft. The inscription was picked out in black. On the right hand side of the polished face was scribed the outline of a pair of red, high heeled shoes.

It was covered in a cloth ready to be unveiled although most people knew what it would look like, but convention needed to be followed, and Lady Massingham was asked to pull the cord.

The worthy Lady stood beside the vicar as he made the dedication.

'We are gathered here to remember our friend Coren Major Evans, the man we knew as Evans the Choir; the man who dedicated himself to our church music. We know now that he loved his music but was attracted to the role of Choir Master because it was a way of wearing a dress in public. We all knew he was different, odd and probably a quiet pervert but we respected him, and when he finally came out and wore his best red dress and red shoes that evening in the Dog and Duck having been rejected by the Rugby Club, we knew he had come into his own.'

The Vicar paused at that moment as if to gather his thoughts and around him there was silence.

'We accepted that he was different and let him live as he wished, although his choice was somewhat disturbing; many of us being homophobic, nevertheless we subdued our revulsion. When the day came that he was called upon he made his stand, fought alongside us and in doing so gave up his life. It is my privilege to be here and dedicate this monument to a man who stood over a fallen comrade in battle until he too was struck down. I cannot say any more than to give thanks to him for saving my life and protecting others. I commit his soul once more to God. We will never forget this day, which we will remember as the Battle of Childen Under Blean.

The vicar paused for a moment or two to wipe away some rebellious tears, blew his nose on a large handkerchief handed to him by his daughter Terri, and continued.

'I dedicate this stone to the memory of our departed friend and to the honour of our village with the blessing of our Lord and Saviour. May the blessings of God be with you. In the name of the Holy Spirit may Peace be with you. Amen.

There was a mutter of "Amens" and a few Alleluias.

Lady Massingham stepped forward and, posing for the

cameras, took the tasseled end of the cord in one hand and announced to the watching crowd.

'It is with reverence and great humility that I reveal this monument for all to see and remember our brave queer master,' she said, unaware of her mistake.

There was a ripple of laughter as the curtains drew aside to show the markings. The watching crowd cheered and clapped, hooted and made all kinds of noises which eventually died down enough for the reverend Jones to speak.

'Thank you Lady Massingham. Now I have a small duty to perform on behalf of his friends,' he said, and watched by the villagers and the hovering television cameras he laid a pair of women's red shoes at the foot of the memorial and took two wobbly steps back bowing his head in silent prayer.

The choir sang *Amazing Grace* and as the tears rolled down his cheeks he made the sign of the cross. The song ended and Lord Massingham stepped forward.

'It is with great humility that I speak to you all today on this solemn occasion as we remember our friend and celebrate his legacy. Let it be known that other than this monument we dedicate today there will be other monuments to his memory in the village. As a member of this community, and rather more endowed with the wherewithal than many,' he paused for the laughter, rude remarks and cat-calls to die down before continuing, 'it is incumbent on me to make some useful and timely donations to assist the village. I am proud of Childen Under Blean and the people who live in it, and I am proud to be part of the community. So, bless you all and let us go and devour the refreshments.'

That was the cue for a cheer and a general drift down to the village green where the refreshments were awaiting their fate.

Some of the villagers placed flowers around the stone and Bonny retrieved the red shoes and placed them reverently in a plastic "bag for life" to be stored for next year.

Lord Massingham's short address was added on to the report as an afterthought but he didn't mind that; he had only agreed to speak because it was expected.

The part of the ceremony that was made the most of was Lady Massingham's unfortunate verbal error. The objections to her short speech kept the letters columns of the local papers alive for a few issues. The electronic media was alive with tweets and posts, but with all that went on, the residents of Childen Under Blean simply got on with their lives.

Lady Massingham remarked to her husband and to her new friend Colleen Wyvern and her husband: 'I don't know what the fuss is all about; he was queer, wasn't he?'

- And in Conclusion

On the day of the dedication, some months after the battle, the drinkers sat at their usual table and drank a toast to Evans the Choir.

'To my favourite poof,' said Sylvester and drank a little from his glass. 'My ratbag son-in-law and his mates are doing their duty and all is well in the Simon household.'

Miles fished in his pockets and took out a folded newspaper article which he flipped open, turned around twice and then looked up at them.

'This might be interesting.'

'Read it then,' said Forest.

'Right. It says here; "Colin Lawrence was convicted of theft by fraud, failure to appear in court and assault on a police officer." And it goes on to say that his sister Sarah Lawrence, also known as Sally Wise, was accused of harbouring a criminal and of living on the proceeds of criminal activities.'

'And according to the pictures taken by Mathew Grace and his mates they was also carrying on an incestuous relationship,' said Swanson.

'And that thought makes me bloody sick,' said Sylvester.

'I can understand that,' said Davey grinning broadly and making a rude gesture with his arm and fist.

Beneath his chair Mutley farted.

The group apart from Forest and the dog got out of their seats and fanning the air with their hands waited until the stench dissipated

'That bloody dog ought to be banned from here,' complained Martin.

The drinkers laughed.

As promised by Lord Massingham, the Childen Under Blean Rugby Club was formed. The reverend Michael Jones was elected to take charge, and soon, supported by a stick, he could be seen barracking the players during training. He was manager and coach until, to his surprise, David White came to a training session and offered his services.

The Birdwatchers of Childen Under Blean

'I used to play League, regular, and when I moved down here I played Union. I ain't much good but I can help out with training,' he said.

Jones grinned.

'Do your best, David. Just remember we have fifteen men in the playing team.'

'I know, and they are allowed to scrum down and maul, and they don't have to kick the ball back, and all that. I used to play prop. I got mashed most weekends,' David said.

'Thank you David. I will be glad of the help.'

'Well, you know, after what happened to Coren..."

'Thanks, yes. As long as you don't encourage the lads to dress like him...'

David White grinned.

'Hetereo through and through, me,' he said, and shook hands to seal the deal.

'We will have a committee meeting in the Dog and Duck to choose the names for the first fifteen and the reserves for the first match of the season. You will be there?'

It was at the meeting the name of the club was chosen. The reverend Jones gave them all a copy of the match schedule for the season, a list of players; juniors and seniors, and announced that the kit was ready.

'We have shirts and shorts, green and white with the logo on it. That is, CBRC in an arc with the red shoes on a white field in a red circle. All we need is a catchy name for the teams. Anybody got an idea?'

There was a hum of discussion and, in a lull in the chatter, a hand shot up.

'Yes Sylvester?'

'What about calling them the Childen Queer Boys?'

When the laughter and ribald remarks died down, the reverend Jones called for another suggestion. The problem was that everybody liked Sylvester's suggestion.

'We could call them "The Childen Choir Boys", and when we have a girls' team we can swap,' suggested Bonny.

The name was adopted but the team was always known as "the queer boys" by the locals.

The Childen Under Blean Cricketing Eleven requested that their cricket shoes be coloured red and the lads playing football were encouraged to buy red football boots. And when finally the entrance to the quarry was gated and the quarry fenced the Scroggins Clan insisted on incorporating red shoes in the logo.

Fitting in with the general theme Graham Cook's Birdwatchers adopted the red shoes logo for his burgeoning organisation. The village parents looked upon the birdwatchers fondly; remarking on the wholesomeness of Graham's enterprise, and encouraged their offspring to take up the fascinating hobby.

When Graham and Lyla explained some of the more advanced aims and objectives to them, the youngsters became even more enthusiastic.

As Graham was heard to say: 'The pursuit of a healthy pastime, leading perhaps to a lifelong interest, is most appealing to the young, enquiring mind, and should be encouraged to develop by all right thinking, and supportive parents. The benefits are a better understanding of nature, and all things the natural world has to offer. As you can imagine, such study leads also to a better understanding of our own complex nature.'

His comments had much to do with his and Lyla's intense relationship and the symbolic burning of their vows of purity.

On the day Blodwen Evans formally took possession of her brother's bungalow Old Man Scroggins' arrived in his van to help clear the furniture. He and some of his lads piled out ready to work.

She was waiting with the Vicar who had arranged the clear out prior to her return from Wales.

'Morning Vicar, Mistress Evans, you all ready?'

'We are. We have packed and labelled boxes and Blodwen has marked the boxes she wants to take with her.' Michael said and led them into the house.

The Scroggins boys lowered the back and soon with care and a little reverence they carried the Welshman's belongings out and stacked them neatly. The marked boxes were loaded on to smaller vans to be delivered to their new owners. The vicar 's task was to help supervise the cleaning and make sure that the items were properly dealt with. Women from the Friends and the WI came to help out and soon the house was abuzz with voices as the women cleaned and polished.

'Pity you're not moving in here love, it's a lovely house, 'said Millie Small.

'I have a house and a family back home but I will keep this one and rent it out. It would be nice to rent it out to a family,' Blodwen said brightly.

Millie looked at her and smiled.

'I think we might have somebody who needs a place if the rent is not too high. We can train him and his wife to fit in, whether he likes it or not,' she said.

'That would be nice,' Blodwen said, and being a practical woman she made a note of the name and who to talk to. Mathew and Cheryl Grace and their baby boy Coren seemed to be a nice couple.

'It was nice of that Bonny Mason to take on his pussycat. She wants to know if she can keep her. She says it reminds her of Evans the Choir but if you want her she will give her up,' Millie said.

'Oh no, we don't want another cat in the house. She can keep her,' Blodwen said and smiled weakly.

'I'll tell her when I see her,' Millie said.

Meanwhile the vicar prowled the house checking on the drawers and cupboards. Most things were packed and all they had to do was empty the built in wardrobe. The heavy furniture was carried out to the truck and stacked. Scroggins House Clearing was in progress.

Michael still needed a stick for support and evading the men carrying things he headed for the spare bedroom where Evans had kept his clothes.

There was a built-in wardrobe cupboard and it was this the vicar was going to clear. He opened the doors to reveal a row of dresses and outfits, wigs and a neat row of shoes; all of them women's wear in good condition. He shook his head feeling sad for the man and began to remove the clothes and fold them up on the bed.

One dress, a full length, waisted number with a flared skirt was definitely quality. He lifted it and swung it around aware of the swish it made as the skirts flew out. He placed it against his body and pushing the door to he looked at himself in the mirror.

'Not bad, blue, just my colour,' he said and swished around a little, smiling thinking of Evans. 'Suits me. I could fancy myself in this.'

And hearing the sound of footsteps approaching he quickly put the dress on the pile and turned to remove another. As he placed that one over the blue dress he felt a pang of regret. The newcomers were some women from the church who had come to collect the garments. With cheerful helloes they pounced on the pile and arranged the garments in smaller piles ready to be taken away.

'We can deal with these,' Millie said. 'Blodwen agrees they should go.'

'I'll put the shoes in the boxes,' he said.

'Please do your reverence. Some will be glad of these,' she said indicating the dresses.

'I daresay, good quality and mister Evans had good taste,' he replied, beaming ecclesiastically. 'You know I could almost wear some of them myself.'

'I should hope not your reverence,' said the other woman pursing her lips. 'I certainly hope not.'

'No, no of course not,' he said blushing deeply and turned away to fill the first of the shoe boxes. He was glad when the women had left with the dresses and to help them he carried the shoe boxes outside. Back in the room he carefully put the half dozen wigs into boxes. He was tempted to try them on but he heard the men coming in to clear the room and turned to the chest of drawers. He expected it to be empty but the drawers were full of small garments. The top two were filled with women's underwear and the bottom, deeper two, were filled with bedding. The bedding he fitted directly into the cardboard boxes. The underwear he took time to separate into smaller cartons. It was a strange experience fondling silks and cotton as he placed them in boxes; previous to this he would normally be removing such items from warm bodies anticipating carnal activities. This was different, he felt the thrill of touching the material suddenly understanding why Evans liked wearing it.

Whilst the room was still empty he took two pairs of panties, one cotton and the other silk, and slipped them under his shirt.

'God, that feels wonderful,' he said and when the footsteps came nearer he carried on packing.

The boys carried the boxes and the chest out to the vehicle and two more came in to remove the bed. He walked out behind them and seeing that the removal was done he said goodbye and drove home.

On the way he stopped opposite the memorial and crossed the road to stand gazing at the stone. He stood for a while, tears rolling down his cheeks and without saying a prayer he eventually turned away and drove the last hundred metres back to the vicarage.

When Elizabeth asked him why he was so sad he answered quite honestly. 'It is sad having to take away all those memories. I hadn't realised how much I liked our heroic choirmaster.

She hugged him and murmured.

'He was an odd man but harmless and we all liked him.'

He had to agree with her but as they embraced he couldn't help thinking about how nice he would have looked in Evans' blue dress.

Printed in Poland
by Amazon Fulfillment
Poland Sp. z o.o., Wrocław